Shibboleth

Shibboleth

A perfect murder?

Shibboleth

(n), Judges 12:6, *From the Hebrew* **sibbolet**, 'Ear of Corn', Mid 17th Cent.

A long standing belief or principal that is, in fact, false.

Source :—Pocket Oxford English dictitonary, Fourth Edition, 1952.

P.P.K. Walther

authorHOUSE®

AuthorHouse™
1663 Liberty Drive
Bloomington, IN 47403
www.authorhouse.com
Phone: 1-800-839-8640

First published by AuthorHouse   06/09/2011

ISBN: 978-1-4567-8433-1 (sc)
ISBN: 978-1-4567-8434-8 (ebk)

Printed in the United States of America

All characters named this book are fictional and bear no resemblance to any real person, living or dead. On the other hand, some of the situations described were real and are reported as such, but solely from the authors' point of view, some others are fictional & yet others are hypothetical or pure conjecture. There is no 'order of priority' in that previous list, the whole story line is an unequal melange of those possibilities.

Throughout this book the author has striven to maintain technical accuracy, without compromising the story line. It is, however, for the reader to sift the real/ possible/plausible/ true from the chaff of fiction (remember 'The Lady in the Lake' case ?) . . . .

Notice

I, Robert Fenn, hereby assert and give notice of my rights under section 77 of the Copyrights, Designs and Patent Act 1988 to be identified as the author of 'Shibboleth', although written under the pen name of P.P.K. Walther.

Robert Fenn

Dedication

This book is dedicated to the memory of Manana Tshomashvili, a friend who I didn't realise meant as much to me as she did, until she died as a result of a car accident in Georgia. She knew the bare bones of this story, but didn't live long enough to read even the first draft. I hope that, somehow, somewhere she knows and approves of the final document.

A Momentary Meditation

Ask why a man did what he did, rather than why he did not do what was expected. At every action, no matter by whom performed, make it a practice to ask yourself, 'What is his *object* in doing this ?'

Marcus Aurelius, Roman Emperor & Philosopher A.D. 168

Prelude

Monday, July 11th. 1983, on board flight AC 051,

outbound from London Heathrow.

He was dog tired, but he had been lucky to get a centre row of five seats to himself. It wasn't too much luck, he reflected later, the 747 was only about one third full in Economy, so almost everyone had sufficient room to stretch out and sleep. THAT, he thought, was the real stroke of luck, everyone was concerned with sleeping, even the flight attendants wouldn't see anything different in his behaviour. Immediately the 'fasten seat belts' sign went out, he folded up the central arm rests and stretched out along the seats to sleep, he had not slept for about thirty six hours and need for sleep gnawed at him.

As he tried to sleep, thoughts about the previous two days kept flooding back to him, so his mind swirled continually and sleep stayed remote and intangible. He found himself replaying vital scenes from the last two days in his memory and analysing his role in them. Had he kept sufficiently in the background, would anyone remember him, could anyone identify him ? Of course, that first little bag snatching drama in the airport before he had really got started had moved him temporarily out of anonymity into centre stage with the group of holiday makers and, don't forget, a policeman. Reviewing the holiday makers, he was sure that he had been forgotten by now, if not almost immediately. Once they had landed and hit the beer and the beaches, they wouldn't remember him, even the couple of photographs that were taken would only prompt imperfect memories. However, the policeman was a different matter, he had seen him close to, but hadn't seemed able to remember his name, especially when the rest of the holiday group had crowded around, trying to give their versions of the events. On balance, he felt quietly confident that the policeman couldn't really separate him from any other member of that group and besides, there had been no 'hue and cry' when he had slipped quietly away into the departure lounge. So, on balance, he felt that he was probably safe there !

Sleep still wouldn't come. He knew his exit from Heathrow had been unremarkable, he had just followed the arrows out until he was at his little van, but some-one might just remember him, but that was a risk and had to be accepted. They had all been tired, part way through 'the grave-yard shift', when boredom and fatigue were both high, but he couldn't totally exclude the chance of someone remembering him. To cover that eventually, he just had to rely on his disguise to sow confusion and doubt, should anything be remembered in the future.

Driving through the village had been risky, even more risky had been going to the cottage, but THAT was the whole point of this exercise. He had heard people, not seen any and had deliberately tried to be heard at the door, but after that he had been quiet and had operated without lights as much as possible. 'Country eyes', he knew, were sharp, but even if they could remember the van and its' registration number, in a few hours' time how could he be linked to it ? Probably that was the safest cut-off point in the whole exercise, he smiled internally to himself. If the van was missed, all the evidence it contained would be lost, never to be used against him; it would be seen to be just another dirty van and what van isn't dirty ? "O.K.," he thought to himself "don't get too cocky, you nearly pranged the van on that grass verge and gave the whole game away AND you were seen by people in the filling station and at the building site". That part of the proceedings had both been necessary risks that had to be taken, one judged earlier, in cold blood, to be necessary, the other forced on him by circumstances. All he could hope was that neither had been so significant as to produce an untimely memory. Only time would tell, however; but the longer the time before those memories were disturbed, the less distinct any memory would be, he hoped. That, perforce, would have to be his protection, IF ever they could relate last nights' events to him !

He had been moving about enough for one of the flight attendants to ask him if he wanted a drink. He sat up and heard a grumpy male voice ask for 'a large Scotch, to make me sleep !', so he asked for the same and was given a small whisky bottle, a plastic tumbler and a radiant smile. As sleep began to overtake him, he found himself thinking about the flight attendant, but if he couldn't remember her face, how could she remember his ?

He was shaken gently from his slumbers and, as consciousness returned, he felt panic knot his stomach. "We're getting ready to land at Halifax, you have to sit-up and put your seat belt on", he glanced up at the attendants' face to seek recognition, but already the man had moved on to waken other sleepers. Nothing too unusual there, he thought and as he tightened his seat belt, the knot of panic relaxed. He felt refreshed, but emotionally drained. One more flight, from Halifax to Windsor and then he would be back in Detroit within minutes, if needs be. Landing at Windsor was unremarkable, although he wasn't able to sleep on the smaller plane. Tired or not, he knew that the period of maximum danger had passed when he sauntered out of the arrivals terminal.

Chapter 1

1998.

"Mrs. Bradley, I have here a Coroners order to disinter your late husbands' body. It is our intention to subject Mr. James Bradleys' body to forensic tests to determine if he was fed with substances that contravene the Dangerous Drugs act of 1971".

Detect Chief Inspector Radcliffe of the Suffolk Constabulary said quite formally and unemotionally to Anne Bradley on the front door step of her 'olde English cottage' in Claydon. Unbeknown to Anne, her natural herbal remedy business had been under investigation for some time, initially by the Trading Standards officers in Ipswich. Anne grew all her own herb and plants in her own field under the most stringent of 'organic' conditions using no chemicals. It was her proud boast that all her products were completely natural and of the highest quality, as indeed they were. Most of her customers were not interested in the herbs or plants, only the products she made from them.

Over the years, Anne' remedies had helped many people and her reputation similarly. Abuse of her restorative tea had occurred and had had very different effects on some people. Many older patients had slipped away to a soft but gentle death, after drinking cups of strongly brewed 'Restorative' tea. Little would have been noted had not one of her customers in Ipswich confused two cups of tea and given the restorative tea to her doctor, whilst she drank Rose-hip tea.

Anne Bradley had been manufacturing and selling herbal products for most of her life. She was a simple country girl, but learned in the ways of plants and herbs. As a child, she had been interested in flowers, not just as pretty things, but for their other values, too. Throughout her childhood and adolescence, she had courted the old folk learned in the arts of healing with flowers and herbs, with tinctures of root and berry. By her mid twenties, she was a repository of herbal lore that had few equals. After her marriage, she treated her husband, children and herself with herbal remedies, occasionally, she would treat a neighbour or a child, should the local doctor did not seem able to effect a cure.

Her reputation as a local 'wise woman' had grown and spread. By her thirties, she had a stall in Stowmarket open-air market and was something of a local celebrity. Then, as the late seventies and early eighties dawned, Annes business boomed, with the beginning of the 'New Wave', when 'natural' remedies became favoured. In London, both princesses were interested in alternative remedies and their interest ignited fashionable interest in natural remedies.

Anne Bradley became a minor national celebrity, making a few appearances on television, becoming known for her cures. Demand grew so large that herbalism became her full time job, needed as she sought out suppliers of herbs and flowers from which she could make her herbal cures.

To supply the growing market, Anne and her husband Jim, opened a shop in Ipswich, at the back of which Anne and a few paid helpers produced her medications. In the midst of all this, Jim fell ill, with what Anne diagnosed as 'heart strain', but was termed an aortic aneurism by a cardiac consultant. Both Anne and the cardiac consultant prescribed rest, reduction in stress and calm. An operation was not needed, said Anne, the body would cure itself, given rest and the correct herbal remedies, so Anne took it upon herself to cure her husband. From the old books, heart strain simply required the tincture of St. John Wort. Anne duly prepared the tinctures herself and fed them to her husband, who thrived on them, he was happier and regaining both strength and activity again. She did not know for how long to treat her husband Jim, so she relied on his reactions and he certainly was better than before. Over a few months, he regained much of his previous form, although he was at pains never to strain himself.

Once he seemed to be recovered, Anne prescribed a herbal tea, rather than the stronger tincture. During the change to tea, Anne prescribed something to give him a little more 'get up and go'. Ginseng was tried, but, to Anne critical eyes, it seemed ineffective, so, just for her man, she made him a special Foxglove tea. That drink seemed to work wonderfully, Jim had plenty of energy and was involved in everything, so Anne took to selling her brand of Foxglove tea as an improved restorative. Foxglove Tea proved to be an instant hit, sales soon had to be limited to only 2 boxes per customer. Jim, almost seemed back to normal, but in the heat wave of early July 1983, he suddenly worsened and died.

Throughout this final desperate battle for life, Jim Bradley was nursed by his wife and Anne tried her best, preparing extra strong infusions of her remedy and feeding it to him herself.

James Bradley was buried on a Monday morning in July in the church yard of the "Holy Trinity" church in Higham Green, his home village, in Suffolk, but close also to the boundary of Cambridgeshire. A few close friends attended, the village of Higham Green being almost deserted as people went to the nearby towns when the rundown of agriculture reached their rural backwater. Old Josh, the sexton, had known Jim as a lad and commiserated with Anne,

"Forty nine don't seem like any age at all for a man like him. I used to run him off my apple trees when he were a nipper, but then his dad ups and took him to the big town an' I never see him again, until today. Don't you worry about your Jim, he'll be all right now, I went an' dried the grave out this morning, so's he'll not be laying in the damp".

By mid-afternoon, the grave was closed and all the rain—soddened earth piled on the coffin. Darren, the job creation apprentice sexton, commented that there seemed to be an unusually high mound on the grave, but Josh, phlegmatic as ever, just said that mound would sink down as the earth dried out. It would be Darrens' job to keep an eye on the grave mound and flatten it down. That said, Josh walked into the church, gave the Vicar the plot number and location of the Bradley grave and left to get a drink, whilst the vicar filled in all the necessary forms to complete the legal internment of James Bradley.

Now, fifteen years afterwards, D.C. I. Radcliffe stood at her front door with a warrant to exhume her husband. Why, in Gods' name? What on earth for? Couldn't they let the dead rest? Anne Bradley, tears filling her eyes, stumbled back from her front door and ran into the lounge where she fell on to the settee, face down, crying inconsolably. D.C.I. Radcliffe followed her indoors as did the female P.C., whilst the young male P.C. stayed outside, standing on the left hand side of the door to prevent interuptions whilst Radcliffe was indoors. In his career, D.C.I. Radcliffe had seen almost all reactions, Anne Bradleys' distress looked real and natural enough for a widow suddenly confronted with the Coroners' Order, but she might just have been a good actress. Nevertheless, he waited until Anne had calmed down, helped by the policewoman who had gone into the kitchen and carefully selected the tea, before making Anne a cup. She returned with the tea, which Anne carefully sipped out of the steaming cup. Once Anne had thoroughly calmed down, he began again, but this time less formally than before and in an almost conversational tone.

"Mrs. Bradley, I have here an Order to exhume your late husbands' body, because we now wish to investigate his death."

"Why, he been dead and gone these fifteen years" said Anne, with great restraint in her voice, "You said something about dangerous drugs, a minute ago, he didn't have anything that wasn't natural !".

"Yes, I'm sorry about that, me being too formal, I'm afraid. We think your husband died due to unnatural causes and we would like to find out if it is true, that's all" said D.C.I. Radcliffe. "Well, it said heart failure on the Death certificate, do you think the doctor didn't know what he was doing ?" asked Anne.

"There have been a string of a odd deaths over the last few years and our doctors think they know what it is and they think that your husband might well have been one of the first, so they need to examine him to see if they can find what they are looking for. You know how unemotional these scientists are, it's all one big experiment to them!"

"I teld 'im not to get mixed up with all that crop spraying, but would he listen to me? No! Said it was all for the best and everything would be alright, but now you're telling me it KILLED him?" "Yes, Mrs. Bradley, something like that. Do we have your permission to exhume him, or must I serve this 'ere warrant ?" asked D.C.I. Radcliffe, sounding as if he had given Anne a choice, "you don't have to be anywhere near. On the other hand, I do, and it's not a job I look forward too, I can tell you that !"

This appeal to reason seemed to work, Anne sat up, dried her eyes and said that she supposed that everything must be O.K., but would he ask 'the scientists' to disturb Jim's body as little as possible, please ? Radcliffe said that he'd do that for her and thank you very much, they'd be off now.

As he walked away, D.C.I. Radcliffe had reason to feel happy, he had just been given the right to exhume the body of a suspected murder victim, by the suspected murderess and no requirement for a lawyer to be poking their nose in! Back in his office, Radcliffe set the wheels in motion for the exhumation. At this stage, there was little for him to do, some beat constable would have to call into the church and verify the grave site and mark it so that it could be found, correctly, by the Sexton and the Pathologist, screened off and then opened. He would have to be there, he was responsible for identifying the correct grave (so the constable had better be right. Couldn't afford any cock-ups with that, all too sensitive, he thought), but he didn't want physically to BE there. ('Why do those ghouls, the Pathologists, insist on opening graves at dawn?' his thoughts ran on. 'Are they still superstitious? '). Someone had to be there to represent the legal authorities when the coffin came out of the ground and he had drawn the short straw. At the best, it would just mean a boring sit in the cold dawn air waiting whilst others did the work. He was sorry to have given up smoking, because he felt that when they were digging down to the coffin, a cigarette would keep him good company.

With the warrant being served and accepted, he knew it would only be about two days before the early morning call, best to get it over with and out of the way and move back to real police business. 'Best just to let things take their natural course and time. Go with the flow and don't rock the boat', thought D.C.I. Radcliffe as he sat down to enjoy the days remaining before his scheduled dawn visit to the grave yard.

Blind insistence that 'natural' was best had killed a few people over the years, but, generally, on neither a frequent nor regular basis. Anne Bradleys' products generally fell into this class, some people swearing by their health restorative properties. Anne Bradley herself had made many bold statements on behalf of health products, most of them being printed on the product wrapping. Jim Bradleys restorative tea wasn't one of her much hyped range, however, and sold almost by word of mouth. Anne's use of foxgloves as a source of tea was fully in line with the old remedies from which she worked. As the forensic pathologist was to say at her trial, the active ingredient extracted from foxglove is digitalis, and digitalis is a potent heart stimulant. Digitalis has a strong effect, for it reduces the pulse rate whilst increasing blood pressure. Hightened blood pressure increased the strain on the body's blood vessels, which in people with aneurism it can make the arteries inflate like balloons. For that reason, calm living in a cool climate is the recommendation for sufferers, hot weather being the major climatic factor in blood pressure increase. Should the aneurism bursts away from the aorta, the victim dies suddenly, dropping like a deflating balloon as the heart pumps the bodys' life blood into the thoracic cavity; exactly what happened to James Bradley on that hot summers' day.

At first light, on a cool and damp September morning, three figures pulled and pushed mobile screens around the grave about to be opened, one was the pathologist, pulling, using both hands to get the screen to move. D.C.I. Radcliffe was more circumspect, using one hand on the top of the screen and one hand to hold his overcoat closed. Charlie, the Sexton, pulled and pushed with the best of them and manoeuvered his screen to where he had been told. When everyone was happy that the screens hid the grave from any morbid on-lookers, Charlie lit a cigarette, took a long satisfying drag, then walked between two screens. Soon he was contentedly piling earth from the grave to one side, taking the correct professional pride to make a smooth, regular heap. As the dawn grew lighter, the sound of falling soil seemed to dominate the church yard as Charlie's regular digging rhythm grew to seem mechanical. At last, there was a wooden sound and Charlie said,

"That's the coffin lid, I'll have to dig round and free it, otherwise the suction'll hold it down and we'll never get it up".

"Take your time, we don't know if we want to bring it all up, just clear us a walking space around, so's we can lift the lid and take samples" said the pathologist, interrupting her observations of hedge-hogs feeding before hibernation.

At the comment of "don't know if we want to bring it up", D.C.I. Radcliffe knew only too well that he did and he had to fight to prevent loosing his breakfast. Shoveling continued, this time not the leisurely affair of the previous time, but uneven short bursts as Charlie cut away the soil to the right hand side of the coffin to create a standing space down the whole length of the coffin. He came across a thin layer of sand, removed a further small amount, then he felt his foot begin to sink down, into a hole. Charlie leaned on the coffin lid to pull his foot clear of the hole and, as he did so, he caught a glimpse of white bone under his boot.

"I think that you'd better come down here and have a look at this" Charlie said and the Pathologist casually slid through the screen and peered down.

"I don't remember seeing in the records that this was an old boneyard" said the Pathologist.

"No, it isn't" replied Charlie "this is all new ground here, there aren't any old graves registered here".

"Curious" said the Pathologist "I'll get the policeman. He'll have to see it".

Radcliffe had heard this interchange and was really not too keen to peer down into a grave, but he stood up and walked into the screened-off area and peered down. He saw what Charlie had discovered, looked at the Pathologist, who saw the green sheen on Radcliffes' face and his clenched teeth.

"O.K., we'll have to bring the box up, just to get a look at this new one. D.C.I. Radcliffe'll O.K. that, I'm sure, when he's finished ejecting his breakfast".

Just why are the police so sensitive, when it comes to things like this ?, thought the Pathologist.

With the help of the local 'beat' policeman, they had the coffin containing James Bradleys mortal remains lifted onto the left hand side of the excavation. Radcliffe was still around, but hiding out of sight when the Pathologist asked the 'local' to fetch in the 'Scene of Crime' forensics team from Ipswich to record this new corpse, before she examined it.

In the meantime, the Pathologist decided not to waste time and had Charlie lift the lid of the coffin.

"You should be here to witness this" shouted the Pathologist to Radcliffe, only to be greeted with more retching. "Oh, carry on", she told Charlie, "you can witness this instead".

After a brief visual examination of the corpse of James Bradley, the pathologist moved the remains of Jims' best suit around, looking for stomach or liver remains, but only saw a leathery piece that could have been anything. Immediately, she put it into a sample bag and wrote on label "stomach, J. Bradley" and the date with more conviction than she felt. She needed more tissue for analysis, but little else identifiable remained, so she pulled a pair of scissors out of her bag and took hair and nail clippings for analysis, adding them to another marked bag. She stepped away from the coffin, stored the samples neatly in her bag and then indicated for Charlie to replace the lid and secure it. She then stepped outside the screens, peeling off her latex gloves as she did so and walked towards Radcliffe.

"That one'll be straight forward," she said nodding towards where the coffin lay "we'll either find the stuff, or we won't, but it'll be the other one that'll be more interesting" she said. Radcliffe could only nod miserably in agreement.

When the Crime scene forensic team arrived, they approached the excavation and removal of the skeleton much as archeologists would have done. As earth was removed from the grave, it was sieved to locate any extraneous matter, all that was found was one cigarette end. Once the skeleton was fully exposed, photographs were taken of it and then the pathologist climbed back into the grave and looked the complete skeleton carefully over.

She said "Female, age at first estimate, between 25 and 40, no obvious signs of violence. Take care, I think I see sign of hair remains. Recover them." After this, the removal proceeded bone by bone. All the large bones were removed and bagged and then passed out to the pathologist, who gave each one a swift cursory glance and said "Femur, left" or whatever was appropriate to the technician who labeled the bags accordingly. Radcliffe was beginning to recover his composure once more and was becoming interested, he forgot his earlier revulsion and actually leaned against the coffin to gain a better sight of what was happening. Before the skull could be removed, the Pathologist went back into the grave and gently rocked the skull forwards, so that the atlas vertebra was released. Her gloved hand was under the neck vertebrae to support them so that they did not become detached and fall. Her assistant remove them one by one from her hand and then she peered onto the earth under where the neck had been. She cheered in triumph, and asked for a pair of forceps and removed a very small, frail bone laying on top of the earth, looked at it and said "She wasn't strangled", before bagging the item herself. As the skull was removed, the Pathologist reminded the forensic people to recover any head hair strands and a few fine, wispy light colored hairs were bagged. Before the pelvic girdle was removed, the Pathologist said the same thing, then reminded the forensic team that pubic hairs were shorter, darker and generally more curly than head hair and that they would have to look harder to find them. Find some they did, so these were bagged and labeled and joined the head hairs in the 'soft tissues' box. At last, the whole skeleton had been recovered and the pathologist and her technician drove away to the Pathology laboratory in Ipswich General hospital, where the investigations would begin in earnest.

As the Pathologist drove away, the forensic team began a painstaking search of the earth from the grave that had just given up it's remains, simultaneously, D.C.I. Radcliffe began to question Charlie, the Sexton, about the grave.

"Only been 'ere 'bout 12 years, it warn't me who planted James Bradley, but old Josh, sexton afore me" said Charlie.

"Where can I find Old Josh ?" asked Radcliffe.

Charlie pointed a short distance away, to the middle of the grave yard "'Bout there he is" he said "Got 'is favourite spot when he got 'is self planted in '85. You can ask 'im all yer likes, but he baint sayin' nothin'".

"Where you the deputy Sexton, or whatever they're called, in '83 ?" asked Radcliffe.

"No, I baint under-sexton, 'til early '84, so I don't know 'bout this one. This one 'ere is my fust one. You all 'as remembers your fust", said Charlie laying his arm lovingly over a grave-stone. "Who was the under-sexton then, is he still alive ?" demanded Radcliffe.

"Ole Josh told me it was some 'job creation' trainee, from local unemployment office. Name of Darrel or Daffy or some such modern name", replied Charlie "'baint never met 'im, he left afore I came".

"So there is no one here who could remember this internment and if there was anything unusual about it, like that sand" asked the detective.

"Only the parson, he's been here since '79 or so, he might remember. That sand was one of Josh's little touches, he used it to dry out the grave if it was wet. Said the family always liked to see their dear departed in a dry 'ole. Means it must have rained since the grave was dug. Ol' Josh was very proud of the comfort of his graves, he was" said Charlie.

"How long before the funeral would Josh dig a grave, do you know ?" asked Radcliffe.

"Once the funeral details were announced and we knew it was comin' 'ere, Josh'd dig the 'ole when it was convenient, p'raps two to three days afore the funeral, but it might just be the day afore." answered Charlie. "Go an' look in the Sextons' record in the church, it'll tell you when the grave wus dug and when it was filled in. Josh sometimes put some notes down as well, so there might be something for you there." he said as an afterthought.

Looking in the Sextons' record, Radcliffe could see that Josh had excavated the grave on a Friday and that the internment had taken place on a Monday and that Josh had noted that there had been rain over that time, but quite when was not stated. A detective constable had been given the task of trying to track down the under Sexton, name unknown, but who had worked in one of the job creation schemes. It took four fruitless days of searching to find the appropriate unemployment office, but only a couple of hours to get all the details of the scheme that had produced an under Sexton. At last, the police had a route to finding a living witness to the digging of the grave. Friends in the Inland Revenue finally tracked down the whereabouts of the holder of the National Insurance number obtained from the unemployment office to Cambridge University. Phoning the number that they had been given, soon showed that the man concerned was employed by one of the colleges as a gardener and that the Police could visit him anytime during the working day. Darren was tending to a flower bed when, on the Monday afternoon, the head Gardener approached him with a dark coated man at his side. Quickly, uncomfortably, the head Gardener introduced the detective to Darren and then edged away, to give them privacy, yet still be close enough to hear their conversation. As briefly as possible, the detective sketched out what they had found and asked Darren about his memories of that time.

Darren had only stayed for the one summer, Josh had scared him with stories from the crypts and had expected Darren to do the bulk of the work. When his 'training' period expired, Darren happily re-joined the dole queue. Darren, as he remembered it, had probably dug the grave, whilst Josh took care of the formalities of paper work which helped Darren vaguely to remember the internment. It had rained in the evening two days before the internment and heavily overnight the day before the internment. Old Josh had climbed into the grave and dried the floor as much as possible, climbed out and then thrown sand in to dry up the last small pools, they then had waited for the funeral to arrive.

"Did Josh say that there was anything unusual about the grave ?" asked the detective.

"No, but he scared me to death with creepy stories while we waited" remembered Darren. "That earth was so water-logged that when we filled the grave, the heap was much too high. Josh said it was all the water and that I had to tamp it down everyday until it was flat enough to roll down. After a week, I'd had enough, so I dug a couple of barrow loads off, to lower the pile, dumped them near another grave and then rolled the grave down".

Aware that his head gardener could still hear, Darren was respectful and told the truth without the embellishments of Josh's character that he would have liked to, Darren had not always liked working with Josh, who he remembered as a grumpy old man. There was nothing else to tell, the detective had heard everything that he wanted to hear, so he thanked Darren, commented favourably on the flowers, got a cutting and left.

After the detective walked away, Darren bent back to work & the head Gardener came up and said "You did nothing wrong, giving him that cutting will only go in your favour. I'll forget his visit today."

Radcliffe made the Pathologists' life a misery, wanting to know everything that could be found out and couldn't be diverted by being told that 'It will all be in the report'. By the end of a week, the Pathologist was expecting the results of the lab. tests that had been commissioned on the contents of Mr. Bradleys stomach (as the leathery object had turned out to be), trace tests from Bradley's hair and trace tests from the hair found on the skeleton. As expected, James Bradleys stomach contained traces of digitalis, of such a strength that even an old, but sound, heart might fail. Nothing was found in the hair samples, showing that the long term doses had not been too strong, so the supposition was that as the 'restorative' tea was brewed stronger and stronger to try to help Jim Bradley, only became fatally strong immediately before his death. Not that that would keep Anne Bradley out of court, although it would later contribute towards her acquittal.

Chapter 2

(1998)
One body too many

Every result from the unknown female skeleton became more interesting because of their very lack of answers, as nothing could be found to indicate the cause of the womans' death. During the painstaking re-construction of her skeleton, the Pathologist examined each bone closely and found no obvious life ending injury. As far as could be ascertained, a young, uninjured completely naked woman had been buried face down in a grave readied for James Bradley.

No cause of the womans' death could be established, for none could be found. Tests on the hair remains had shown only that her head hair had been dyed with a commercial hair colourant and that certainly wouldn't kill her! No traces of any poison residues could be found either in the head hair or the pubic hair recovered. Only one interesting point found by the analyst was that the woman's hair had been found to contain the genetic fault which showed that she would have been at risk of contracting breast cancer had she lived longer. That that test was conducted at all was only due to the laboratory being involved in the on-going breast cancer research programme. So nothing, no clues, nothing suspicious at all, except the body!

Even the ultra fragile hyoid bone had been recovered intact and unbroken; had she been a victim of domestic violence and an attempted throttling, the hyoid would certainly have broken, but no-one had strangled her. To try to get more information on this mystery woman, the Pathologist had examined her teeth and found only high quality dental work there. Should her dental details be widely circulated there were hopes that a dentist could identify the body from her dental records. She held out little hope, for the police circulate only the dentists in the locality and ask that dental records be examined, but the pathologist knew her dental work had been expensive and that, almost certainly, placed her from London or some other big town. People from big towns move around much more, and much further, than do country folk, so she could have been, quite literally, from almost anywhere.

When he read the report sitting in the pathologists' office, D.C.I. Radcliffe said "So, we have no established cause of death and a Coroners court is due to be held. You know what the verdict will be don't you ?"

"Open verdict", replied the Pathologist. "Until we have a verified cause of death, all we've got is an illegal burial in consecrated ground and you don't have your murder enquiry".

"Speculate for me and tell me what you think !" Radcliffe said to the pathologist. "Well, it *could*, have been poison" said the Pathologist, "We found nothing in the hair samples, so that rules out stuff like arsenic, cadmium or lead, so we're left with a short term, swift acting poison. Could have been cyanide, but I doubt it, unless she breathed it in. I can't help thinking about those nerve gasses that occasionally turn up, from those hidden military stocks nearby. One of them would have killed without skeletal traces, but that's a long shot. That she was buried, face down, suggests that she was deliberately killed and disposed of. She could have been drowned, gassed, suffocated or poisoned from all the information that we have. Around here, the use of agricultural poisons is common. My best guess is that it was one of them, you would need a poison that was effective in small quantity (then it wouldn't be missed) and swift acting and commonly in use. To me, this all points to liquid nicotine, a few drops would have killed her, if it had been put on her skin and this stuff is more available around here than most places, people use it for fumigating commercial greenhouses. Yes, nicotine would do the trick & she wouldn't even know, had she have been a smoker"

"So, you are saying that she was killed deliberately, with malice or forethought, that would make it murder" said Radcliffe.

"Yes, had she been accidentally killed with nicotine, why bury the body ? A simple accident, call in the police and bury her legally" said the pathologist. "It's this thing about burying her face down that I keep coming back to and now it makes me certain" she said "Adulteresses were always buried face down, alive, but with their hands and feet tied so that they couldn't climb out. She was dead when she was buried face down".

"So, what are you saying ?" asked Radcliffe "Did her husband bump her off after her affair and bury her face down because she cuckolded him ?"

"No, I don't think so" replied the pathologist "those women were always buried alive, so that they could regret their sins before they suffocated. She was dead, not bound at all, let alone hand and foot, but he certainly knew the old country traditions to bury her like that".

"So, you're saying a countryman, but a sophisticated countryman?" asked Radcliffe.

"Yes, and maybe even compassionate at that. Her killed her first to stop her suffering" was the reply.

As he spoke to the head of the regional C.I.D., Radcliffe kept the post-mortem report close by and quoted from it frequently. "All we have to go on is a supposition, produced by the Pathologist and me. Oh, and there is that fag end we found in the grave. That's all".

"I know it's a far out theory, but we can't construct anything better, because we've got nothing more to go on!" he said.

"I have had the dental records circulated and I have widened the area of circulation, because of what was said about the quality of the dental work, but we've heard nothing yet."

Radcliffe listened for a while and then said "I've initiated a review of the missing persons' list for the time that that grave was opened, but I've heard nothing yet. It would be helpful, Sir, if you ask your pals in other forces if they would search their mid-year 1983 missing peoples lists for women that have not yet been accounted for and who fit the description. That might give us a lead that we can use to unravel this case".

With the assurance from his boss that all would be done to circulate the description of the corpse nationwide, Radcliffe rang off and sat wondering about the mystery woman and the reasons for her being buried in a grave on his patch.

Chapter 3

Identity Crisis

It took a number of months to get the information fully circulated throughout the U.K. and another few months until it really caught the notice of the detectives working on missing people lists. Requiring information many years old, the initial impressions made were not very great. When all the various police forces began to search their records, it was generally seen as mediocre, low priority work, undertaken only by junior officers, fresh out of training, with the result that old files were seen by inexperienced eyes. Unsurprisingly, only negative results were forthcoming. In September 1998, the Chief Constable of Suffolk, tired of being nagged by his detectives, casually mentioned the problem to his friend, the Chief Constable of Merseyside police, at the Chief Constables' annual dinner in London. Being assured that his request would be reviewed by the Merseyside C.I.D. officers who worked on 'Missing Persons' at that time, he at first relaxed, then suddenly realised that he had been given the key to the problem. In his next request, he specifically requested that officers who had been involved in 'Missing Persons' in mid 1983, be appraised of the description of the skeleton in the hopes that some-one may remember something. Many irritable older officers throughout the U.K. police forces were displeased when asked to review old case notes, but a request from on high was tantamount to an order. Many old notes were thus dusted off and read. Detectives in the Thames Valley force were no different to their colleagues throughout the country, they moaned and griped like everyone else. D.C.I. Rigby kept the old 'missing persons' paperwork as far from him as he could, so that it did not distract him from the investigation of a car ringing group based in Oxfordshire. When the car ringing investigations entered an unexpected hiatus in November, Rigby found himself with more spare time on his hands than he could usefully employ, so he reviewed the missing persons lists again. Something had caused a bell to ring somewhere deep within his memory, but it was only when he got hold of the old files with his hand written margin notes that he felt his flesh begin to crawl. He turned swiftly to the reported disappearance of Caroline Meadowcroft nee Ellis, who had vanished, on an unknown date, whilst her husband was working in America. He looked at the photograph, not too clear after all these years, and his heart gave a lurch, he had a better photograph of her than this one and she still looked like the twin of Sylvia, his dead elder sister

As he sat there, his mind opened his dusty mental files of the case. He had been sure, convinced, that her husband, Dr. James Meadowcroft, had killed her back in '83. He had investigated, even used the good offices of a friend in the S.I.S. to ascertain the possibilities of James Meadowcrofts involvement, but to no avail. Without a body, without forensic evidence, without a witness, any case against Meadowcroft would remain purely circumstantial. During his earlier investigations, using a route suggested by S.I.S., he had arrested a number of illegal immigrants and a drug pusher, but had had not the slightest 'sniff' of Meadowcroft. After that operation, he had been told to leave it alone and wait for Meadowcroft to make a mistake, but had continued for a year or so collecting snippets of evidence where he could find them and adding them to the file. None of them was the slip he had been waiting for Meadowcroft to make and, over time, he had let this hobby investigation slide until it was stowed away in some dark, forgotten corner of his memory. Not now ! Now it was right back to the forefront of his memory and he felt again his passionate belief that Meadowcroft was a murderer and remembered his silent promise that he would see the man behind bars for the crime. His emotional response to the seeing the case file again surprised him, as did his enthusiasm for the case, he remained seated and called down to records and had them bring up all the case files that were relevant for him to review. It was whilst waiting for the case notes to arrive that he drafted out a note to D.C.I. Radcliffe, the officer in charge of the case in the Suffolk constabulary, saying that he was sure that he had an identity for the victim. Rigby did not want to appear too enthusiastic, he had to check the case notes, but there was this inner certainty that his memory was not playing him false.

When the case notes finally arrived on his desk, he sent the secretary away to get a road atlas, so that he could check the locations accurately and then locate them one to another. Pouring over the maps of South-East England, he saw that his suspicions were confirmed. Higham Green was not far from Chilham St. Margaret, where the last definite sighting of Caroline Meadowcroft had occurred and was well within quick driving range of Higham Green, although the maps showed only country roads in that area. With more enthusiasm than he had felt for a long time, Rigby tore up the note to Radcliffe and decided that he was so convinced that the skeleton was the remains of Caroline Meadowcroft, that he would phone D.C.I. Radcliffe and pass on the message himself. When Radcliffe eventually came on the phone, he heard a bored voice ask who he was. "D.C.I. Rigby, Thames Valley, I've got a likely identity for your female skeleton" was his reply. Immediately, he heard the tone of the other voice change, something like enthusiasm breaking through, "You have ? Who was she and why was she on my patch ?" was asked in something of a gabble.

"I think she is, was, Mrs. Caroline Meadowcroft, who was reported missing, from her cottage in Chilham St. Margarets by her sister, in July 1983" said Rigby, now feeling the excitement of the chase coming on him.

When the two D.C.I.'s met, over in Ipswich's new police headquarters, D.C.I. Radcliffe began to sense D.C.I. Rigby's excitement. "I've been waiting for this moment for fifteen years" was how Rigby opened their discussions. He laid all the years of files down on Radcliffes' desk and began from the beginning. "It was the mid summer of 1983 when Caroline Meadowcroft was reported missing by her sister, Shirley, who still lives here in Ipswich. In late summer, her husband returned from a working trip to the 'States and reported her missing to his local nick, that's where I work. He was very fluent, hadn't seen her since he went to Florida, had tried to 'phone her both at home in High Wycombe and at her cottage in Chilham, got no reply from either message. Not as though he was expecting one ! We started all the usual checks and follow-ups, but found nothing, she'd vanished from the face of the earth, with, we assumed, a lover, who was noted over in Chilham by the locals one night. Nothing ever turned up, no jewellery, no credit cards, no bank withdrawals, she could have lived on her cash for a while, but then she would have had to get some money from somewhere, but she never did. In the meantime, he lived like a hermit for a couple of years, then started a long legal divorce process, where her side wasn't represented. After the divorce, he lets her sister use the cottage indefinitely and a year after the divorce, marries an American that he met during his working visits over there. After that, he has lived a normal, quiet life, still working at the same place as 15 years ago and creating no waves. A couple of parking tickets, that's all !"

"Well, at the moment, we haven't got a cause of death, I can tell you it wasn't violence, but nothing else. Our pathologist can make a good case of murder to me, but can't find anything to show that she didn't just die naturally in her sleep one night and the boy-friend or husband or gardener or somebody just buried her to get her out of the way !. So, unless you have something solid, we are looking at an open verdict from a Coroner, nothing stronger and no chance of a murder investigation. All we could get your boy on would be an 'illegal burial in consecrated ground' charge an' all that means is a wrist slap, even IF we could make it stick !" said Radcliffe. "Oh, but I KNOW that her husband did her in, you've been a plod long enough to know that sense that you get when you just KNOW that somebody is guilty. Well, I've known it about him since I first saw him. This skeleton just proves to me that I'm right !" "O.K., so I accept your feeling, we all have 'em about some cases, but what are we going to do ? At the moment, we've got nothing, we need a break. Our Pathologist can give us nothing, not even probable cause of death." was Radcliffes' reply.

"So, it's up to us to untie the knots! Let's start at the beginning and look carefully for the loose-ends in this case. We have all the time in the world and we've certainly got more experience of crime than the husband had" mused Rigby.

"What do you know about the husband ? What was his alibi at the time ? Why couldn't you crack it then ?" Radcliffe began to interrogate Rigby.

"Hey! Hold on, I need to re-read all this" he said, waving a thick file "My memory's good, but not perfect. And there is something, can't quite place it yet, that seems to say why I wasn't surprised that you

found her in a grave. It'll be in here, no doubt, but I've got to read all
the notes. What I can tell you is this, I've met the husband a couple of
times or so, when he's been acting for us in some cases. He's a biologist,
specialises in the environmental side and he's one of these guys who
knows the answers to odd little questions that crop up in investigation.
You know the type, looks at the same evidence that you and I do and
comes up with a completely different angle. Been very useful at times,
he has." muttered Rigby.

"Well then, that's how we've got to look at this case. We're not
seeing the wood for the trees, so to speak, so we've got to look in a
different way" suggested D.C.I. Radcliffe, "Let's try to plan the job
ourselves, to try to fit into his shoes"

Trying to plan their version of the job soon ran onto the rocks,
neither detective could produce an alibi as unshakeable as the one
that Jim Meadowcroft apparently had. His alibi seemed unshakable,
the airlines had confirmed his presence on the flights to and from the
U.S., whilst the local police in America had confirmed his presence
that he was where he had said he had been. As evening drew on, the
two detectives sat back in their chairs, rubbed their eyes and stretched.
D.C.I. Radcliffe lit a cigarette, smoked it down to a stub, then ground
it out in an ash-tray and idly said "Do you know, that all we found near
the skeleton was one of these ?" brandishing the cigarette stub. "That
exhumation was as clean as a whistle otherwise".

"What ? Only a fag end ? Is that all ? Nothing else ?" commented
Rigby, uninterestedly.

"Yea, only a Marlboro stub right at the bottom" confirmed Radcliffe
"Name was on the filter tip".

They decided to go to the police local for 'a pint and a think' as
D.C.I. Radcliffe suggested and sitting in the bar waiting for his beer
D.C.I. Rigby looked around. Like almost all pubs.' in the U.K., tied
houses were full of advertising for the brewery's other drinks and
cigarettes. A Marlboro advert caught Rigby's eye, it showed a mounted
cowboy standing in front of imposing cliffs and bore the legend "Smoke
the great American cigarette". Rigby closed his eyes and began to lay
back in his chair and stretch, when all of a sudden he stopped dead
"That is IT!" he cried and turning to Radcliffe said "That's it, that's the
clue we've been looking for, don't you see ?" D.C.I. Radcliffe looked at
his opposite number perplexed and said "What is ?"

"Oh, don't you see it ? You've got an American cigarette stub, Marlboro weren't a common brand here then and Meadowcroft was supposed to be in the 'States when his wife went missing. He got careless and left a cigarette stub in the grave, probably forgetting that he'd bought American cigarettes and that those cigs. weren't common over here ! Oh, my good lord, I do believe that we've made the first crack in the case. Cheers" he said and quaffed half a pint in one swallow.

As soon as Rigby's insight had been explained to him, Radcliffe saw the same logic and accepted it with the comment "Of course ! We never thought to check on anything like that"

"No reason why you should, you had no reason to suspect an American link. So, we're almost able to establish a link between him and the scene of the burial."

Although Rigby was excited, he suppressed his feeling apart from allowing himself a smug little grin. "I'll phone my gaffer in the morning and tell him that we've found an important link, that'll probably be enough to get his blessing for me to stay here a while longer" opined Rigby "I'll tell him that we can probably break the back of the case in not too long". After two more drinks, Rigby left the 'pub to go to his hotel, to be ready for an early start the next day.

For bed-time reading Rigby had the case file, so, propped up in bed, he began to read the notes of the case that he had made fifteen years previously and hoped that he would be able to continue to see them in the new light that he had just perceived. It was whilst reading some statements that he, as a young detective, had obtained from people at Windsor University, that the next piece began to unravel from Meadowcrofts' alibi. Simon Ingram, a tall, athletic student at the University in 1983 had known Jim Meadowcroft well, having been a regular squash partner at the time. In Simons' statement, Rigby found the seemingly trivial piece of information that Jim Meadowcroft had won the charity flower bed digging contest a few months before going to the 'States in 1983. Rigby himself had had a look at those flower beds, at the old folks home, 15 years ago. Even now he remembered how much they reminded him of graves, being about the same dimensions and dug to depth of six feet to put in all the compost to ensure excellent flower growth with minimal maintenance by the old folk. "So, our man was fit enough and fast enough to dig a flower bed in under 2 hours, so he could have dug a full grave in about one" he mused to himself "better and better".

It was when he began re-reading the police report from the Winter Park, Orlando county police that he began to see another flaw revealed in what had appeared to be Jim Meadowcrofts' cast-iron alibi. Meadowcroft had hurt his knee, had seen a doctor and stayed in his motel room. Or so he had said. In the report in front of him, Rigby read that Meadowcroft hadn't been definitely sighted for two or three days, witnesses had just said that they had assumed that he was there. So, thought Rigby, I've probably got the time when he left the 'States and came back to England. Making a note to check the airline timetables of that year, he decided to go to sleep as happy as he had ever been since he joined the police force. He decided to contact the Winter Park police again to ask if any thing further had come up.

For his first job in the morning, Rigby scanned the report made out by Ipswich police and there, staring at him was the supporting evidence in the estimated date of burial. Caroline Meadowcrofts' body could only have been buried after the grave had been excavated to inter James Bradleys' body and before his body was interred. That gave a two day window of opportunity and James Meadowcroft had hurt his knee on the day that the grave was excavated, so he had had two days to get from London and back to Orlando, assuming that he had left Orlando on the day that the grave was dug. Looking at the airline timetables, he assured himself that the flights allowed for a stay of about one days' duration in the U.K. in which Caroline could have been killed. He went so far as to identify two prospective inbound flights to the U.K. from Orlando that Meadowcroft could have used for his nefarious purposes. He began to re-consider the Florida police report and decided to do so when he got to Radcliffes' office. Rushing to get to the 'station for an early start, he missed his breakfast, intending to make it up with large mugs of canteen tea. He pulled the flight timetables with him and roughly bundled them into one of the pockets in his black police issue trench coat. Almost running, so great was his enthusiasm to get started, he charged down the pavements seeing no-one and consequently barged a number of people out of his way, he was deaf to their comments and curses. He ran up the stairs into D.C.I. Radcliffes' office, to find Radcliffe sitting at his desk, a large mug of steaming, sweet, brown tea by his right hand. "We've got the bastard" were his opening words, only to be greeted with a blank look from Radcliffe and a comment of "Good Morning to you, too". At this, Rigby emptied his pockets, strewing maps, note-books and flight time-tables over Radicliffes' desk and launched into his discovery of last night. In the enthusiasm, the mug of tea ceased steaming and grew steadily colder whilst both detectives suggested alternatives and possibilities to get from Orlando to Heathrow and, a day later, to return to Orlando. By lunch time, they had produced a couple of weeks work for themselves, having so many possibilities to check, including flights from and to Jamaica, this possibility had been suggested to Rigby some fifteen years previously by a Special Branch/M.I. 5 contact of Rigby's. His checking on this route had netted both drug runners and illegal immigrants, but not James Meadowcroft, and had been the first positive good mark in his record, one that put him to the front of his peer group and ensured that he got the higher profile cases and consequently better regarded.

As they broke for lunch, Rigby realised how hungry he was, although this did not stop him speculating on the possibilities that had been on offer to Meadowcroft. Overcome by the thrill of the chase, both detectives went on head long into the problem. It was during lunch that Radcliffe asked the question that had slowly formulated in his head and become uppermost in his mind "Just what name are we looking for ? If your bloke was as clever as you say, he wouldn't have traveled under his own name, so what name did he travel under ?" This caused more than a momentary pause in the transfer of sandwich from the plate to Rigbys' mouth. "We never did figure that one out. He certainly used another passport, his own only had his immigration and exit stamps for the days that we know he was there, so he used somebody elses'. Must have done, no other way" was all that Rigby would allow himself to say between mouthfuls. "Yes, but whose name, if we don't know that, then we are not even looking for a needle in a haystack !" and as he said that, D.C.I. Radcliffe got a brief flash of the tenacity, better still the obsession, that haunted his opposite number. "We can get a handle on this thing by a process of lateral thinking" said Rigby, as if he were reciting a lecture, which he was. "We are looking for a trace with this profile" he continued, "a U.K. male passport holder, who went from America to the U.K., probably Heathrow and then returned to the U.S. within three days of his arrival. All the U.S. flight details will be available through the 'freedom of information' act and the others, we can get because of inter-force police co-operation. If we get all the guff on computer, then our search will be that much faster AND be done by your IT people, NOT us ! That'll get us a short list that we can do something easy with. Ever since Forsythe told everybody how to do it in 'The Day of the Jackal', all we've got to do is cross check the passport details with death certificates details. Where they show that a dead man got a passport, then Whammo, we've got the name he travelled under. Compare that photograph with his passport photo and we'll have him dead to rights ! We must thank Forsythe, he told 'em how to get that other passport and all the bloody would be Jackals do it and we snaffle 'em right up. Too easy ! Come on, let's get back, we've got work to do".

Arriving back in Radcliffes' office, they found an internal memo awaiting them. Radcliffe read it and said "Damn, damn, damn & damn again !" To Rigby, he said "The bloody Coroner has decided to hold an inquest in a weeks' time, so we've got to find something to stop him giving an open verdict, or at least get him to give a temporary open verdict pending ongoing investigations". "Best way to do that is to get results, so let's get stuck in" was Rigby's counter. At that, both men went for the 'phone, Radcliffe won and got their I.T. people ready for the job and then he got hold of his secretary and told her what he wanted & from whom and ushered her out to get on with it. "So now we wait" he said "What else useful can we do ?" Rigby remembered his intention to contact the Winter Park police force again, so he telephoned his enquiry to the author of the 1983 report, only to find that that particular man had left the force about 10 years previously. In desperation, he spoke to the Sheriff, who hadn't been there in 1983, but promised to review the report and any follow up information and fax copies over to Ipswich. When eventually they arrived, they consisted of the original report and the policemans' notes, which added nothing to the contents of the report. Reading the report with Radcliffe, Rigby was undeterred, Meadowcroft had not been definately seen during the crucial two days, but he could have been seen, the witnesses were themselves confused. "What use is that ?" asked Radcliffe "We can't prove that he wasn't there". "No, but the reverse applies to him. He can't prove that he WAS there, either" said Rigby "it now becomes a balance of probabilities and as to who can convince a jury one way or the other ! It's something I think that's in our favour."

Within a day, the first files were down loaded in Ipswich and, if no-one else, the police I.T. boys were busy teasing out the potential fits to the profile defined by D.C.I. Rigby. Both Radcliffe and Rigby had kept themselves busy writing the police case for the Coroner to consider. Neither of them truly had their heart in the job, for they knew that with out something more tangible than 'police intuition', they were not on very solid ground. At every possible distraction, one or other of them would leave the word processor and talk to the I.T. boys to find out what was happening. In a mood, compounded of enforced inactivity and 'gung-ho do something to make things happen', Rigby decided that Dr. Jim Meadowcroft should know that his ex-wifes' remains had been found and invited to attend the inquest at the Coroners Court in Ipswich. To that end, he drove away after lunch on the Wednesday and arrived at the University at about 4.00 p.m., walking to uninvited into Jim Meadowcrofts' room some ten minutes later. He announced himself with the words "We've found your wifes' body in a grave in Suffolk". Startled, Jim Meadowcroft said "that's impossible, I just spoke to her half an hour ago". "No, no, not that American woman, Caroline Meadowcroft nee Ellis, who went missing fifteen years ago". "She hasn't been my wife for over twelve years, so she isn't my wife now !" retorted Jim Meadowcroft, angry at the interruption to his work. "She was when she was buried, wasn't she ?" asked Rigby ingratiatingly. "Was she ?" asked Meadowcroft. "When was she buried ?" "As far as we can tell," began Rigby, "it was about the time that she was declared missing". "What, when I was in the 'States, back then ? What happened ?" asked Meadowcroft, his interest stirred despite his affected dis-interest. "We were hoping that you might be able to help us with that point" said Rigby smoothly. "Oh, so that's what this is, another forensic consultancy for the Thames Valley Force ? Sorry, but the first rule of forensic work is not to work on something that you have a personal interest in, it clouds the judgement" replied Meadowcroft. "No, it's not that" said Rigby "She was your wife at the time and you are, sorry, were, her closest relative and we need you at the inquest". Although Meadowcroft had made a number of court appearances in his role as forensic biologist, he had never attended an inquest before and did not know the formal requirements, so he took D.C.I. Rigby's word at face value and asked where and when the inquest would be heard. "Monday next, at the Ipswich Coroners' Court," he was told "First case on in the morning, so be there well before 10.00 a.m. to see the Sergeant of the Court to find out where your seat is". Meadowcroft agreed, thinking that an inquest was an unpleasant way to start a new week, but picked up the internal phone and asked one of the department secretaries to book him out for the whole of Monday and cited "Police business' as the reason.

Back at Ipswich, the computer trawl through the files had produced a number of suspects, which Radcliffe noted and asked for further details from the computer of the Public Records Office at Kew. When Rigby returned, he wanted to be able to show that he had continued pushing to find evidence. On Thursday morning, Rigby looked at the list produced and personally demanded that the I.T. boys get the information from Kew, double quick, then back to the writing of the Police case for the Coroners' consumption. Rigby actually could not start the document the way he wanted to; over the years a photograph of Caroline Meadowcroft that he had never returned to Dr. Meadowcroft had burned its' way into his psyche. At first, he had seen a resemblance between Caroline and Sylvia, his elder sister, then so recently killed, but over the years Carolines face had replaced Sylvias' totally until Caroline and Sylvia had become indissolubly one and the same in his affections. He started the report with a brief, uncontroversial description of the grave, how it had been found, where it was, the state of the body and the establishment of its' identity. Then, he began to make an issue of the way that the body had been interred, face downwards, the traditional punishment for an unfaithful wife. That Caroline Meadowcroft had been unfaithful to Jim Meadowcroft was not a point at issue, it was too well known by too many people to be in doubt. Without mentioning Jim Meadowcroft directly, Rigby inferred that only a cuckolded husband was likely to bury his wife that way. It was not directly stated at that point, but strongly inferred, that Caroline had been buried by her husband. It became necessary to bring in his investigation of Jim Meadowcroft, dating from 1983, and to review his 1983 alibi in the light of the findings that were emerging in this on-going investigation. Finally, he requested that no final 'open' verdict be given as such, as this would hinder a police investigation in progress that was very likely to become a murder investigation; where the combined Suffolk and Thames Valley police forces, given sufficient time, could almost certainly produce a prosecution. In support of this proposition, Rigby began to list the salient findings of this new investigation and the openings that were there to be exploited by the police in their forthcoming investigations. He was fairly confident that the Coroner would take his request, and the reasons for it, quite seriously, but, he thought ruefully to himself, you never knew with Coroners !

Chapter 4

Inquest enquiries
(1998)

Ipswichs' Coroners court had recently moved into new premises in the recently re-developed city centre. So recent was this move, and so unknown was the new street name, that it took Jim Meadowcroft sometime to find the court and the correct entry doors. Fortunately, it was Sunday evening and Jim thanked his lucky stars for their decision to drive over to Ipswich on Saturday and spend the weekend there. It was Beckys' first time in Suffolk and she was entranced by the scenery along the Orwell. Taking her to the Pinmill, the old smugglers pub on the Orwell, was a history lesson to her, she still considered herself an American at heart and to sit in a pub older than her country amazed her. She heard other American voices in the bar, too, airmen from Lakenheath and other nearby U.S. air bases, equally amazed that such an old building still existed, never mind that it was still in use for it's original purpose ! Sitting in the front bar, she heard the sound of water close by and said something to Jim, who told her the history of how the smugglers came in, right under the bar floor at high tide and how they entered the bar by a trap door in the floor. 'Direct deliveries' was how he jokingly put it.

Jim and his wife were staying in a city centre hotel over Sunday night, so that Jim could get to the Inquest early. They had organised to leave the car in the hotel car park over Monday and pick it up when they left to drive home. By a fortunate accident, their hotel was within easy walking distance of the new court, so when they loaded up their car in the morning they had but a short distance to walk. Becky couldn't take enough photographs either in the old part of town or in the countryside, the Suffolk Pink houses delighted her and the general character of the town intrigued her. Jim foresaw that she would dally on route to the court, so he 'accidentally' locked her camera in one of their suit-cases as they packed. After settling the bill and loading the car, a quick walk through the streets in the fresh morning brought them to the court in plenty of time. Jim immediately found the Sergeant of the court, was told that he was named as a possible witness and was to sit in the front row of seats. Becky had to take a seat in the body of the spectator seating. Various people came into the court and sat near Jim at the front, he recognized none of them until, just before 10 o'clock Rigby entered with another man, both of whom sat on the same row of seats as he. Rigby was deep in conversation with the other man, but paused briefly to acknowledge Jim with a brief lift of his hand. That caused the other man to look sharply at Meadowcroft, who noticed his dead fish eyes and unsmiling face. Then Shirley and Dick Hallewell, Carolines' sister and brother-in-law, rushed in, just beating the ten a.m. dead line. Meadowcroft, who had not seen Shirley and Dick for over ten years, waved to them, but his friendly overtures were not returned.

Precisely at ten o'clock, the secretary to the court walked in and announced that the Coroners court for the district of Ipswich was in session and the coroner, sitting behind the desk asked him to read the details of the business of the day and to present the first case. This he did in a sombre voice.

During a legal dis-interment, a unknown skeleton had been discovered and had been examined on site by the local pathologist, before the remains were removed. At this stage, the pathologist was called to give evidence, which she did in a strong voice and with very little reference to notes. When it came to the point where the police had been called, the man siting alongside Rigby looked up and began to take interest in the Pathologists' evidence. As required by law, the Pathologist had examined the remains and tried to identify the cause of death, but had been unable to do so. Forensic tests, performed by highly competent, recognised laboratories, had found no traces of toxins, although the test were conducted on only a few hairs & the skeletal remains, as no soft tissues remained. Here, the Pathologist detailed all the other tests and examinations carried out and the general lack of evidence of the mode of death. As there was no hint of identity at that time, the only information that could be passed on to the police was a general description, a dental history and the odd-way that the internment had taken place. Only a few questions were asked of the Pathologist, there were precious few facts to be verified.

D.C.I. Radcliffe, as the investigating officer, was then called to give his evidence and confirmed that he had received the Pathologists report and discussed it with her. He then confirmed that he had issued a request to all other U.K. police forces to examine their 'missing persons' records to find a potential candidate, but nothing had happened for some time until the Chief Constable of the Suffolk Constabulary had mentioned it in, passing, to his opposite number of the Thames Valley force at a social function. Only then was a likely candidate identified as Caroline Meadowcroft.

At this point a loud sob broke the train of Radcliffes' recital as Shirley Hallewell held a handkerchief to her eyes. D.C.I. Rigby, of the Thames Valley force had suggested a possible dentity as Caroline Meadowcroft. Checking Mrs. Meadowcrofts' dental record against that of the skeletons showed them to be identical and thus a tentative identity had been established. That Caroline Meadowcroft had been reported missing within the local area and at the time that the Bradley grave had been open were significant extra confirmatory details that the skeleton actually was that of Caroline Meadowcroft. After some further questions of fact were asked of D.C.I. Radcliffe, he was dismissed. Caroline Meadowcroft had initially been reported missing, in July 1983, by her sister. On his return from America, in August 1983, her husband had informed the police that she was missing from home.

With all the established evidence now presented, the Cororner sent the jury out to consider their verdict. Before they left the court, he informed them that investigations were continuing and new evidence was likely in the near future. In this particular case there was, as yet, no direct evidence of the method of death, but there could well be some produced in the near future. Their safest option was to deliver a verdict of an adjournment, to allow continuing police investigations. With that direction, the jury was sent to consider its' verdict. It did not take too long. They then returned saying their deliberations had led them to the choice of the adjournment. Thanking the jury, the Coroner said, that in his opinion, they had reached the correct verdict. He, himself, had been convinced by the results of on-going police investigations that an open verdict would be wrong, so the issuing of an adjournment, subject to continuing police investigations, was a just and sound one.

At this point Rigby glanced at Radcliffe, unable to hide his grin of success, but was brought back to earth by the Coroner telling the court secretary to issue that order with a six month review clause. With that, the jury filed out and the court began a twenty minute recess before the next case was due to be heard, people began to leave their seats and make for the exit. Both Shirley and Dick studious avoided contact with Meadowcroft as he walked towards them, so he changed his direction marginally and went up to his wife, who was looking a little baffled.

"Is that all there is to it ?" asked Becky "Why did we have to come all this way, eh ?"

Jim Meadowcroft, himself puzzled, could only shrug his shoulders and say "I suppose so, but as to why we were asked to attend, I don't know".

Before they could get out of the building, they were confronted by Rigby and the man they now knew as D.C.I. Radcliffe, of the Suffolk Constabulary.

"We're getting the evidence on your wife's murder, so be ready to answer some questions" Rigby said to Jim Meadowcroft.

"She ISN'T his wife, I am !!" replied Becky "Even I know she left Jim to go whoring around with all the yuppies that she could leech off".

"With all respects, you only know what you have been told by him" answered Rigby smoothly "You assume that he told you the truth and that's what you choose to believe. He knows a damn sight more than he has ever told anyone and I intend to be the FIRST person to hear all he knows. You'll hear the truth from me in due time". Rigby was warming to his theme and was only stopped when Radcliffe put a restraining hand on his arm and muttered "Not yet".

"I assume that you are going to pursue these dreams of yours in a legal way and not like this. Say or infer anymore and I'll have you up for slander or whatever it is & even if your pal here" retorted Meadowcroft angrily indicating Radcliffe "lies in the best Police tradition, there are plenty of people here who are listening and WILL tell the truth ! Either charge me or stop harassing me. If you can't charge me, then you've got no evidence and you are just blowing hot air!"

Shirley and Dick Hallewell were hanging around at the edge of the group, observing the happenings, but holding their own counsel, although their body language indicated their belief that Jim Meadowcroft was a mass murderer. Jim put his arm around Becky and pushed his way out into the open air. After taking a good, deep breath, still holding Becky tightly, he began walking back towards the hotel and their car.

"You've told me before just how he's harassing you (here her American accent was pronounced when she said 'HARASS-ing'), what's his beef? Was he one of your wifes' lovers?"

"Nice idea, but no, he's not her type, he was too poor and too dumb back then, 'tho' he would have been within her exploited age group. Anything from 15 to 50 was O.K., if they had money and would spend it on her!" Jim told her with a touch of humour.

"He's been dropping in to the University, unannounced, every so often for the past 15 years and saying the same sort of things. He really is fixated on getting me for something, I don't know why".

"Why don't you do something about him? Report him, or something?" she asked.

"Oh, I've done THAT, but he's really is the Teflon man, nothing you throw at him sticks. And, besides, it has almost become an annual tradition. I almost miss him when he doesn't come. One thing that he DOES do, though, when he comes is to make me realise how much I love you and how I glad I am to have found you" Meadowcroft said kissing Becky as they walked on.

"Well, he is a cool character, THAT much I'll give him" commented Radcliffe as Jim and Becky pushed away through the crowds and out of the court doors.

"I can see why he's been so difficult to pin down for so long. Don't look so bad, we're tugging at his alibi and it's beginning to come unraveled, soon we'll be able to tie him up with threads of his own making!"

"God! Whenever I see him I just want to able to arrest the bastard and frog march him into the cells. For the past fifteen years, he's been thumbing his nose at us stupid coppers, walking away from killing his wife and thinks we can't prove it. But not now, all his talk about 'arrest me or shut up' will get him nowhere; the next time he says it, I'll make sure that I've got enough to arrest him on and throw the bloody key away !"

"We'll do it ! We've got the result we wanted from the Coroner. Now it's up to us an' we'll get there" Radcliffe mused "let's get back to work to do the job".

Chapter 5

Investigations

Soon after their return to the office after the inquest, both the detectives got to work to try to prize loose more threads from Jim Meadowcrofts' alibi. By this time, the results were beginning to come in from the Ipswich I.T. team. All together, the U.K. had received over 100 flights from Florida in the two day time window that their investigations covered. By dint of excluding the flights that arrived at distant airports, like Manchester and Glasgow, which were too far away to get to Chilham with enough time to do 'the job' (as they so euphemistically called it). This reduced the total, but not by much, especially as 'intermediate' airports such as Birmingham and Luton couldn't so easily be ruled out and had to be considered. Rigby had a surprise, one which caused him almost to throw his hand in there and then. Stanstead Airport appeared as a destination for charter flights and charter flights were one possibility that he had never previously considered. This problem was compounded by July being the peak period for charter flights to and from Florida.

"Jesus Christ, look at all those flights to Stanstead" he cried "No wonder that we never got a sniff last time".

At that time of the year, in 1983, Stanstead was handling nearly as many Florida flights as Heathrow, all of them charters, for various holiday companies and almost all the travelers were U.K. passport holders. Rigby and Radcliffes' task had just doubled.

"God in Heaven" said Radcliffe when he saw the metres long computer list of flights, few of which could be crossed off and safely ignored.

"Thank the Lord Harry for computers" remarked Radcliffe, "them I.T. boys got us into this shit, let 'em get us out of it ! Just tell 'em how you want the stuff cross checking and let 'em run it through their toy again and then we'll review their findings".

Rigby phoned the chief of the I.T. section and had her report to them as soon as she could. In the meantime, he ordered a large pot of tea for the pair of them from the canteen and five minutes later a civilian canteen lady arrived carrying a tin tray with a large, multi-chipped brown enameled tea pot and two large mugs on it. She handed it over and left, nearly bundling the I.T. chief down the stairs. Rigby poured two mugs of the steaming brew, passed one to Radcliffe and pulled the other into his work area before addressing the I.T. lady. He described to her, in detail, what he wanted and how the information ought to be cross collated. Part way through his dissertation, she held up a hand and said "Just tell me what you want, I'll decide how we cross check every data stream. Do you want to include any other foreign streams?"

Rigby was dumbfounded and couldn't understand what was meant, Radcliffe saved his bacon by interrupting and telling Rigby that, in plain English, she would organise the cross checking and was there any other information that he wanted to include in the cross-checking ? Trying to appear completely at ease, Rigby took a long draught of tea and thought, he then asked about the possibility of cross checking all the passengers' names with data from the Public Records office. After explaining that he was trying to identify U.K. passengers flying from Florida to U.K., then returning to Florida and then wanting to check the validity of the passports of those identified with the Public Records Office data.

"That", he said emphatically "should identify our man".

"O.K." said the I.T. lady, "we'll set that up for you. It'll be about two days before we can finish all the programmes to begin your the cross referencing for you and it'll take about a day to stream all the tapes, that's if all the incoming streams are clean, without any glitches or bugs. If it is, we could have something ready for you by next Monday".

"Next Monday ?" exploded Radcliffe "I thought computers were supposed to be fast ? This is a murder investigation and I want top priority !".

"You haven't got murder status yet, to my knowledge" she replied calmly. "What you want will take some time to write the programmes for, but we'll do our best and push through as fast as we can. There's not much load at the moment, so we want something to do".

Defeated by the assurance that she showed, Rigby sat down, saying simply 'O.K.'. Jo. turned and walked out of the office.

"You have now met Jo., our I.T. Supervisor" commented Radcliffe to Rigby "A very self assured young lady, who really does know her job, so you'd best keep on the right side of her".

"Where did you get her from ?" asked Rigby.

"She was recruited direct from University, somewhere near your manor, I think" Radcliffe replied. "See that big Harley down there ?, that's hers. Lives with her boy-friend out Martelsham way, where they spend their spare time restoring old motorbikes. Come to think of it, she came from Windsor Uni., isn't that where your guy teaches? ".

"Yes, wonder if she knew him?" muttered Rigby "Must ask her next time I see her".

Monday came and, wonder of wonders, after lunch Jo. arrived at the office door with a few folded sheets of computer output. As she came in, she said "You were lucky, we got no other priority stuff, the sifting programmes worked first time and the Public Records's tape was clean, so everything worked like a dream".

She handed the sheets to Rigby, saying, "I've divided it up, integration by integration, so the bottom page shows you the names that fit every one of your defined characteristics. There aren't many!".

Rigby took the sheets and thanked her, to which she just turned round to leave the office. Rigby suddenly became active and spoke to her before she left, asking her where she had come from and on being told 'direct from Windsor University' asked if she had ever known a Dr. Meadowcroft there.

"Everybody knows Jim Meadowcroft" she replied "He's a character there, more of a student than most of the students, must be over forty now and still into sport and motor-bikes. He's never grown up, but a nice guy to know, always willing to help if you're in trouble".

"Was he chasing the female students, then?" enquired Rigby, seemingly almost solicitously. "No, funnily enough I always felt safe when I was in his office, not like some of the others. He likes women, tho', always has some photos of beautiful women on his wall. He doesn't have to worry, have you seen his wife? Must be in her early forties now and still looks as gorgeous as a model. She's nice, too."

At that, Jo. turned and left the office to go down into 'her lair' as Radcliffe called it.

"An unsolicited recommendation for your man" commented Radcliffe, "if I didn't trust your judgement, I'd say that we were chasing the wrong guy".

"If this guff is all that that Hells' Angel of a computer operator of yours says it is, we'll soon know" was Rigbys' reply as he sat down to read the computer output.

There were only three names on the final sheet, one, that of a woman could be dismissed immediately. Both of the two men remaining had used Heathrow as their entry point (at this point, Rigby gave a silent sigh of relief) and both had left again from Heathrow within 48 hours and both had passports that were definitely not completely 'kosher'. In a quick phone call to the Passport Office, Rigby requested that the highest definition photographs possible be transmitted to him at Ipswich. All he had to do now, he thought, was to look at the photographs and he would know the alias that Jim Meadowcroft had traveled under, then he could arrest him and break his alibi within the 48 hours arrest period that the law allowed. All he had to do was sit and wait.

To pass the time until the photographs arrived, Rigby and Radcliffe talked, of course they talked shop, of course they talked about the Meadowcroft case. During the talk, Radcliffe was surprised as to how far Rigby unwound, especially when he told about Sylvia, his elder sister, who had been murdered during a bungled rape attempt and how much Caroline Meadowcroft looked like her and reminded him of her.

"I wonder what drove him to murder her ?" asked Radcliffe.

"We have a psychologist around here that we use at times for psychological profiling of criminals. Could be worth a word with him to see if he can give you a way to approach Meadowcroft to crack him early".

"What? You mean you've got a 'Cracker' type guy who tells you to look for men wearing ladies knickers, that sort of thing?" asked Rigby astonished.

"Yes, he was more or less forced on us by the U.S. air bases we used to have near by, they wouldn't believe anything unless it came from the shrink" replied Radcliffe casually "He proved so good that we kept up the contact. We've used him a few times ourselves an' he seems to be a bit good. Why? Do you want to talk to him?"

After agreeing that it might be useful, Rigby suggested the morning of Tuesday, so as not to let the hunt get too cold.

Promptly at nine o'clock on Tuesday morning, a mediocre looking man presented himself at the front desk of the police station and asked for D.C.I. Radcliffe, the desk sergeant recognising the psychologist, called the crime office to say that the psychologist had arrived. He was taken upstairs by Radcliffe and introduced to Rigby, who began to chat to the expert. That conversation was sustained for five minutes before the psychologist broke his flow by saying that he was sure that his life and back-ground was not under investigation here, so could he be told what the case was so he could contribute. Rigby took up the challenge, but on his first mention of Meadowcroft was stopped by the Psychologist who told him that he wanted information about the crime, not about suspects. After analysis, the attribution of a suspect would be covered once he had reviewed the crime against the psychological profile. Within ten minutes, Radcliffe finished his monologue and then the psychologist began to ask questions. A further half hour passed, after which the psychologist said that he had formed the image of a very angry man, cold & calculating and a danger to any near relative or friend who crossed him. He would be highly intelligent and a deep thinker, quite controlled, even retiring, until a threshold was passed and then something was bound to happen. Not an angry reflex, but a calculated and coldly effective response. Then, having said that, the psychologist asked to be told about the suspect. Rigby was only too pleased to provide the information sought. Over the next twenty minutes Rigby reported all the details he knew about Meadowcroft and finished by asking if there were any more questions.

"I am a University academic, myself" said the Psychologist "from Essex University, in Colchester, so I have some personal knowledge of their psychology". He went on "Some of the points of your criminals' profile are certainly general in University academics, others not so. What you describe is a lone wolf, angry and affronted, such a psyche would be so obvious in the relatively closed University group that he would be ostracized by all around him. It is possible, of course, that his wifes' behaviour drove him over the edge and into a mini-breakdown, when he demonstrated these unappealing tendencies and then, almost spontaneously, recovered. I don't think that's possible myself, he will have been scarred by his history and his character would have been recessive for some time. What I find very symbolic, as you do, is the face down burial, consciously or not, he was punishing her for her adultery. Of course, it might have been a particularly devoted lover, who accepted her infidelity from her husband, that's how he's there, but could not accept her infidelity from him, as he saw it. Your crime profile has a lot that could fit an academic at any time, we're all arrogant and infallible, but check for odd behaviour for about a year before the crime and for some time afterwards".

Whilst Radcliffe showed the psychologist out, Rigby tried to come to terms with the criminal profile that they had just been given, about half of it confirmed his suspicions of Meadowcroft, whilst others facets plainly did not accord with Meadowcrofts' known record. When Radcliffe returned, they sat and talked over the information from the psychologist. It was only when Radcliffe said "Of course, what old Tanner just told us will be the perfect profile, he'd be the first to acknowledge that differences can exist between reality and his predictions".

"So we've still got a case, do you think ?" asked Rigby quietly.

"I think, Yes! Phone Tanner tomorrow and tell him where you think the profiles' match and get his opinion and work from that" was Radcliffes response.

Wednesday morning came and Tanner was told of the subjects' partial fit to some areas of his psychological profile and promised to phone back after further consideration.

In the meantime, the passport photographs were received from the Passport Office. They were not originals, or even real photographs, but digital prints of the duplicate photographs lodged with the Office at the time of application.

"Look at these useless things !" cried Rigby, "they aren't clear and they're just paper !"

Radcliffe looked at the print-outs and suggested that they get their favourite I.T. 'Hells' Angel' to take a look and see if she could tidy them up, by digital enhancement, whatever that was. When shown the print-outs, Jo. agreed that they were useless and that she could probably enhance them. In truth, using a computer and the right software, Jo. could make them look like anyone they wanted by blending two images & they used just such software at the station. Taking the base digital file sent from the Passport Office, Jo. brought both up and attempted to clarify the images with the software, but the results weren't particularly successful. Apparently, what had happened was that the original photographs had been automatically scanned by an early low resolution digital scanner, so there were very obvious limits to what she could do. When she printed up her best results, she was not at all pleased, they were very little better than the first output. Jo. decided that she would try a little image matching to try to introduce some high lights and contrasts, which she could manipulate to enhance the pictures.

First, she needed two base faces onto which she could build the detail of the desired photographs, so to explain this to Radcliffe and Rigby, she went to their office, only to find it empty and unlocked. Jo. walked in and saw a random pile of other photographs on Radcliffes desk. Thinking that photographs so randomly scattered around would only be general photographs for witnesses to look at when they tried to identify suspects, she ruffled through looking for average faces to use. Both photographs that she chose were in colour, whilst the ones she wanted to enhance were monochrome. Small black and white photographs were all that was allowed by the passport office in the early 80's, a decision that had kept many small photographic studios open beyond their natural life span. By the mid 80's automatic colour photo-booths had become common and their output had been classified as suitable for passport applications. With that decision, many small photography shop closed.

Taking both photographs, she returned to her room and scanned both images in to a file, returned the photographs to the office and began to work on the images. Starting with the thin, long faced man, she marked the location of his eyes and mouth and then faded away almost all of the detail. Importing one of the Passport office files, she merged it on her screen with the faded face from her scanner. A few more minor changes and a much clearer image stood out on her V.D.U., Jo. printed the image and filed it for delivery to Radcliffe, not noticing that it still carried the mans' name. She then did likewise with the second image. As she had scanned the second photograph into her computer, she thought that it looked vaguely familiar, but couldn't identify it, so consequently thought no more of it. Her memory was not playing her false, indeed it was acute. The familiar face that she couldn't quite remember was that of younger Jim Meadowcroft, more than 15 years before she had ever met him, without his moustache and with the then fashionably long hair. Once more, the resulting image was clearer and looked much more like a cleaned up version of the image transmitted by the Passport Office than the base face from which it had been constructed, although, inevitably, it contained some features of the base face. Once again, pleased with her task, Jo. printed the image, complete with the passport holders name and filed it with the first to be sent to D.C.I. Radcliffe the following morning. It was late, Jo. had worked until nearly seven p.m. to generate the images for Radcliffe and she was keen to get home and have a drink.

Whilst the images were being 'electronically cleaned up', Dr. Tanner had called Rigby to discuss the psychological profile and how fully his suspect fitted it. During the talk that followed, Rigby learned that some of the characteristics could be hidden by being sublimated into some other, socially acceptable behaviour. "For instance", he was told "much of the aggression can be sublimated into competitive sport. In the modern world, sport replaces war, but without the bullets. Psychologically speaking, highly involved sportsmen are close to combat soldiers and share many characteristics. Both live in world where violence exists openly and revenge is always contemplated. Was, is, your suspect a keen sportsman ?"

"We know that he played sports, but mainly individual sports and he would always play squash against the students and would always try to win. We were told that fifteen years ago and it was repeated last year, as well" answered Rigby.

"Ah well, there you have a long time experience of this mans' latent aggressive tendencies. Yes, yes, that could easily explain the apparent lack of anger and it would also explain some of the apparent self control." commented Tanner "Sport is a well known for its' aggressive personalities. Just look at the number of times on television you see one footballer deliberately fouling another in a way that could cripple the other man for life and then shows no remorse for his actions. Indeed, frequently they try to justify the level of violence expressed against fellow players, when a normally moral, educated, less aggressive personality would have clearly defined limits, usually below the pain threshold, that they would use. Yes, I am more and more convinced that sport fulfils the missing aggressive element in your suspect, especially as he is an individualist, too".

So, Suffolk Polices's 'Cracker' seemed to be saying that Meadowcrofts' psychology matched that of a calculating wife murderer, but could be missed by an outsider because of his interest in sport. 'Good !' thought Rigby, one more brick in the wall towards putting his man away !

Discussing his telephone call over an after work drink with Radcliffe, who had heard only Rigbys' comments in the office, Rigby found himself getting excited that the chase appeared to be coming to a conclusion. Radcliffe, whose habits some times made him appear to be a simple, slow witted country copper shocked Rigby by making two remarks about the case. Firstly, Tanner was, in his experience, frequently close to the mark about peoples' character, so he (Rigby) had better begin to act more cautiously around Meadowcroft.

"What he could do, if provoked, might be very nasty for you. Don't approach him alone anymore, is my advice".

His second remark was to shake the whole basis of Rigby's faith in the approach he had taken to the investigation for 15 years.

"What if he stole and used a foreign passport for his travel back here ?" asked Radcliffe quite shrewdly. Rigbys' world shook and teetered on the brink of collapse for a moment.

'Gawd' thought Rigby, 'if he did we're up shit creek without a paddle'. Slowly drawing his thoughts together, he answered "He doesn't have enough criminal contacts to do anything with a foreign passport. I know he works next door to Heathrow and could easily have got in there, but about the only other usable passport for him would have been American, with any other, he would have to get a visa to go into the U.S.A. At that time the Yanks didn't need a visa to enter the U.K. and the Brits could easily get a multiple re-entry visa from the American Embassy. That facility didn't extend to other nationalities entering America. He's too British to pass as an American even to a Brit, the Yank immigration service would have saved us all a load of trouble and locked him away if he'd tried it. He didn't, so they didn't, so we've got to shake a thread loose. With a British passport, he would have had all the documentation and he would have used it to get the U.S. visa in other passport".

"O.K." replied Radcliffe, "just as long as you've covered it. It'd bring the case down round our ear 'oles if some smart Q.C. had've asked that in court and stumped you like I just did".

Smiling weakly at his partner, Rigby pick up his beer glass, indicated to Radcliffe, who nodded and passed his over glass, so he walked to the bar to buy new drinks with a new respect for the 'country copper' and his keen mind.

As he walked into the station on Thursday morning, Rigby was passed the envelope that Jo. had left for him the night before. Written next to his name was the message 'Best I can do' and the initials J. D., as he went into the office he pulled out the two print-outs. On top was the face of McMahon, the thin faced man. Rigby looked at it and immediately rejected it, then he unfolded the photograph of Stone and stopped walking. He stared at the print-out for a long while and then gave a whoop of pleasure. He was still grinning idiotically when Radcliffe entered and was greeted with the words "We've got the bastard !".

"Well, Good-Morning is more usual, but I suspect that you're talking about Meadowcroft" replied Radcliffe raising an eye-brow.

"Too bloody right, old son, your I.T. Hells' Angel is pretty bloody good, look at that ! You can recognize him from it now !" Rigby was agitated now "Can I get some of your technicians to do a facial measurements comparison, to formalize the identification ?"

"'Course, that's what they're there for. Shall I ring 'em or will you", but as Rigby already had the phone in his hand, Radcliffes' question was totally superfluous.

On demand, the technicians came and took away the print out and a number of mens' photographs, all of which would have to be blown up to the same size as the print-out, so that direct measurement could be taken and, where necessary, quoted without any multiplying factors in court. All day Thursday, Rigby was like a cat on hot bricks, he couldn't sit still and neither could he concentrate on anything for more than a minute. Every minute, he looked at his watch and muttered 'Come on, come on !', eventually Radcliffe banned him from the office and sent him away to the canteen to sit and smoke and not distract him from his work. At the end of the days work on Thursday, the technicians still had not reported back and Rigby was becoming a nervous wreck. Nervous or not, it did not prevent him from dragging Radcliffe off to the pub at the earliest opportunity and even buying the first round of drinks.

Mid-morning Friday, the senior Identification technician announced that they had a definite fit with one of the photographs, number nine, and he would begin to write the report to the detectives. Neither Radcliffe, nor especially Rigby needed to consult their note-books to know that photo number 9 was a modern photograph of one Dr. James Meadowcroft and that an identification by facial dimensions was almost as good as a finger print. Despite the jubilation that he felt, Rigby had to damp down the pleasure and begin to take a cold, calculating look at the evidence and as to what it told them.

"Well," mused Rigby more to himself than Radcliffe, "we can now prove that he came back to the U.K. from his trip to Florida during the time he was supposed to be laid up with the injury. We can place him in the cemetery, even the grave, at the time of his wifes' burial by the fag end, an American cig, no less ! He fits the psychological profile pretty tightly, he knew of his wifes' adulterous behaviour and resented it, as he also resented her earning more than he did and towards the end felt nothing for her."

"So, you've got opportunity, you've got motive, but you don't have provable means" argued Radcliffe. "You can't go and pick him up just yet until you know how he did her in".

"Your Pathologist gave plenty of possible means, so I suggest that we give the evidence to the Crown Prosecution Service for them to make the big D. If they say Yes, we charge him, if they say No, we dig round some more. Pity we can't pick him up and ask him a few more questions" commented Rigby.

"Why not, in Gods' name ?" Radcliffe asked "We are pursuing on-going investigations and he is the prime suspect, so we must continue to investigate, if only to keep the Coroner happy ! If we get anything out of him, it'll add to the case, if we don't and CPS tell us to drop it, then he walks. If CPS tell us YES and we've got him in custody, then we don't have to apply to re-new the arrest warrant. Get everything off to the CPS before lunch, tell 'em its top priority and ask for Murdoch to look at it, he's worked with us before and makes quick decisions. He had to, if the suspect was with the U.S.A.F., otherwise, they'd whip 'em out of the country double fast, so as not to stain their record on friendly territory. Just make sure that it goes out on a Suffolk Constabulary header, then they'll believe the urgency."

"You're getting excited about this, aren't you, you crafty country boy?" asked Rigby.

"Seems silly to waste the opportunity of getting him in over the week-end. It's always a good ploy, makes 'em feel lonely and then they cough it all up much the sooner ".

Radcliffes experience seemed sound, so Rigby sent the information off to the C.P.S. and then phoned ahead to High Wycombe to arrange a Thames Valley police car for himself and Radcliffe to go and arrest their suspect. That done, they had time to have some food before being driven to High Wycombe police station in a Suffolk Constabulary squad car.

Chapter 6

Ipswich Interrogations

With a great display of noise and speed, the Thames valley police car swept into the central courtyard of Windsor University and stopped at the bottom of the steps leading to the Huxley building, the home of the Natural Science departments. Three men climbed out of the car, Radcliffe, Rigby and a uniformed constable, and hurried up the steps. Rigby knew the way and lead the others directly to Meadowcrofts' office. Without waiting, he burst straight into Meadowcrofts' office, quickly followed by the other two,

"Get out of here" he said to the tutorial student sitting in front of Meadowcrofts' desk and as she scrabbled to pick up her books, he said again "get moving, I've not got time to waste".

She was up and out before she could really think, her books cradled in her arms.

"What's happening there ?", the question came from a curious cleaner.

"I don't know" replied the student "that rude man just burst into Jim's room and told me to get out quickly" replied the student as tears began to run down her cheeks and all her books fell to the floor.

She dabbed ineffectually at her eyes with a grubby tissue before asking "What does it all mean?" to an empty corridor.

"Well done, that's your most macho display so far" remarked Jim Meadowcroft to Rigby "Now get out of my room and apologise to Louise for the interruption".

"I am arresting you for the murder of Caroline Meadowcroft, nee Ellis, on or around July 10 th. 1983. You do not have to say anything, anything that you do say will be taken down and may be used against you. You've just been formally cautioned, do you have anything to say ?" demanded Rigby.

"I presume that I get the statutory one phone call so that I can call my lawyer ?" said Meadowcroft.

"At the station" rapped Rigby "get moving".

"My wife, then?" asked Meadowcroft.

"You murdered your wife, or did you forget ?" sneered Rigby "Constable, get him outside and into the car".

Faithful to orders, the constable pulled Meadowcroft towards him and then pinioned his right arm behind his back and marched him at some speed down the corridor, through the doors, down the steps and into the back seat of the police car. Rigby and Radcliffe followed close behind, seemingly walking at a sedate pace and brusquely pushed their way through the rapidly forming crowd and got into the car. Both sat on the back seat, one either side of Meadowcroft and as Rigby said "away, constable", the lights and sirens began as the car pulled away.

Despite his anxiety, Meadowcroft kept his own council and said nothing, although both Radcliffe and Rigby tried to provoke him to make unwise comments. He assumed that, within minutes, he would be speaking to his lawyer from High Wycombe police station, but that was not to be. As the police car drove up to the front door with a practiced flourish, D.C.I. Radcliffe climbed out of the back seat and looked across the short, narrow road to the civic library which seemed to be set at the back of a row of shops and offices. It reminded him of his old station in Ipswich, cozy and local, unlike that soulless glass and concrete artifact that they had recently moved into. Rigby pulled Meadowcroft out from his side of the car and asked Radcliffe if he were ever coming into the building. That broke his revery.

At the front desk, Meadowcroft was, once more, formally charged and stripped of his valuables, belt, shoe laces and tie and then taken to the holding cell, his requests to be allowed to talk to his solicitor were met with a practiced comment, "When you get to your destination". With that, he was put into a cream painted cell, which had only a little graffiti on the walls and was illuminated by a bare low wattage bulb. He couldn't see well enough to read, had he have had anything to read, so he just sat, dispiritedly on the ledge bed, leaned back against the wall and closed his eyes.

Whilst the desk sergeant was labeling and bagging Meadowcrofts' possessions, the Suffolk Constabulary car came back, its' driver having just finished a mug of tea at the railway station a couple of hundred yards up the hill from the police station.

"Nice area you've got here, but these hills ! Scare my wife half to death they would. It's as flat as your hat in Ipswich and that's how the wife likes it".

"Yes, High Wycombe earns its' name ! Best get off and find your D.C.I., he'll be wanting to take the villain to your nick, no doubt".

Rigby had just given Radcliffe the tour of the premises when the driver appeared.

"Go to the canteen and get yourself a cup of tea, we'll be ready to move as soon as we've had ours" said Radcliffe from behind a large, steaming mug of tea.

At the University, witnesses to the occurrence were entertaining anyone who would listen to their version of the police visit and the arrest of Dr. Meadowcroft, as it was assumed to be. Louise was bravely dealing with her temporary celebrity status, having been the nearest thing to an actual witness to the event. She dried her eyes and told everyone, with only a little hyperbole, what she had 'been part off'. Rumours ran wildly around the whole place, the Huxley building was agog with fanciful details of the police raid, people still looked out of windows to see if all the 'SWAT' team members had left as silently as they had come. In the Natural Sciences department, work had stopped completely, no-one was even attempting to appear to work any more when Louise was summoned into the Heads' presence and questioned all over again about the police intrusion.

Louise had just begun sniffing again, having just declared herself traumatized by the whole incident, when the red phone on the Heads' desk rang its' one shrill note. This was important, the red phone was the management phone, the one on which God himself, in the shape of the Vice-Chancellor, spoke to his minions. Louise had never seen the Head react so swiftly to anything before, the note still hung in the air as the receiver left the rest.

"Yes Vice-Chancellor".

"No Vice-Chancellor".

"I'm currently interviewing the only witness, Vice-Chancellor, one of our students".

"Yes, Vice-Chancellor, I'll personally escort her to your office" (here a grave look appeared on the Heads face and Louise sniffed still harder).

"Yes, Vice-Chancellor, as far as I know, the policeman burst into Dr. Meadowcrofts' office without invitation and told our student to 'Get lost', or some such thing. Yes, Vice-Chancellor, we'll be over as fast as we can get to your office, Vice-Chancellor".

All levels within the University responded in their own way, the secretaries phoned their friends to ensure that their version of what happened was the authorised version, academics got hot under the collar about police brutality, the cleaners and porters sat together in their little cubby-holes and explored the worst possibilities. Only the cleaning lady on Jim Meadowcrofts' floor did anything useful, when she locked his office door. No-one, in their debates, thought of the simple humane act of phoning Becky Meadowcroft and telling her. She was left to sit alone and wait.

After listening to Louise's story, the Vice-Chancellor asked a few questions, he was really a nice old guy thought Louise, he asked his secretary to take Louise into the outer office and give her a cup of coffee. As the door closed, the Vice-Chancellor picked up his private phone and instructed the University solicitor to begin proceeding against Thames Valley police for trespass and material damage. He was, and always had been, proud of the independence of Universities and, whilst subject to the law of the land, they were private institutions that could not be violated at will by the police. They had not been invited onto the site, they had no warrant, thus they trespassed on private property; the police must learn that they, especially, are not above the law, but subject to it. A trespass prosecution should rattle their confidence enough to make them think twice before any other incursion.

Becky was at home and began looking at the clock when Jim wasn't home by 6.30. 'This is not like him at all', she thought, 'he would always ring me if he were going to be late'. By nine o'clock Becky was frantic with worry, she had heard nothing at all, knew nothing out of the ordinary and was almost unable to think. In a state of numbness, she began phoning around the local hospitals to enquire about road accident victims, but got no information on Jim. Next were the local police, who had had a shift change since Jim was taken to the station and, since Becky only talked about road accidents, could confirm that her husband had not been involved in any accident on their patch. She was advised to try the hospitals, when she said she had, the only other advice that could be suggested was to phone his company and see if he had been unavoidably delayed. That she did and was connected directly to the security department, as the switch-board had long since closed for the night. It was there that she heard the story from one of the 'campus coppers' (as Jim called them) who was about to go home at the end of his shift, after spending most of his shift listening to other peoples version of what had happened in the Huxley building. It rapidly became obvious to the security man that Becky knew absolutely nothing of the events of the day and that she had absolutely no idea of any reason for such an obviously strong arm arrest. She knew Jim was not a physically violent man, although he was fit and strong and that he might verbally assault someone in his own defence or of a third party, but that it would go no further. All she could learn was that he was taken away in a Thames Valley police car and not even which station he had been taken to.

"I shouldn't interfere like this" said the security man, who was ex-police himself, "but do you, or your husband, have a solicitor?".

"Only the one we used when we bought the house" said Becky.

"He'll do, phone his office up. With luck you'll get an answer-phone message with an out of hours number. If you don't get it, then phone all the solicitors in your phone book until you get an out of hours number. Phone it, tell 'em what you know and get them on to the job. Only a brief can get the police to give out information and your husband will need all the help he can get. I know of one of the D.C.I.'s there today and he's an expert at provoking people into making damaging replies. Wish I could help you more, love" he finished.

She phoned the first solicitors' name in the book that she thought that she recognised. As expected, she got a pre-recorded message giving a mobile number and the terms of usage of that number ('only in the direst emergency'), got through and felt reassured when the man recognised her voice and remembered both her and Jim. She tried hard not to gabble out the story, but probably did, however she presented the story, the solicitor on the other end was galvanised into action.

Within an hour, he phoned Becky back with the bare bones of the story, assured her that Jim was alright, but that he had been transferred to Suffolk Constabularys' care. At that, Becky could add a little to the story and told the solicitor what she could construe from the facts. At the mention of D.C.I. Rigby's name, she was interrupted by the solicitor who said that he'd contact a friend in Ipswich and get him to get over there immediately and hold the fort until he himself could get there. With a quick 'I'll update you when I can tell you something', he rang off, consulted his electronic diary, then phoned an Ipswich number.

It was around midnight when the lawyer finally arrived at Ipswich police station and asked to see Dr. Meadowcroft, who he understood was under arrest at this station. Although the desk sergeant tried to delay the inevitable as much as possible, he couldn't withstand the threats of retaliation issued by the lawyer and soon lead the lawyer to Jims' bare cell occupied, another cell in which a weak bulb glowed, illuminating the space sufficiently to prevent restful sleep. Of course, the police claimed that the light was required to prevent prisoner suicide or self-harm, but it was also well known that this cell, after only a few days, produced the highest confession rate in the whole cell block. Although the police swore ignorance of this effect, the cell was nicknamed the 'singing cell' because of the alacrity with which the confined prisoners 'sang' confessions from its' bare walls. It was also known as 'hard mens' cell, the feelings of isolation and solitude that it produced were as effective as solitary confinement on the prisoners's psyche.

Jim Meadowcroft had been acquainted with that particular cell for about eight hours, having left it only for two short visits to the interrogation room. Both visits were brief, he was kept in handcuffs and sat on a bare wooden chair, opposite the chair of the investigating officer, who sat behind a simple wooden desk. Once the investigating officer had been Rigby, the other time Radcliffe. Both had tried the 'bad cop' approach, simultaneously trying to frighten Meadowcroft and produce indefensible comments from him. To their utter frustration, Jim Meadowcroft just sat quiet both times, although biting his lip at times to prevent himself talking. It was only when he was absolutely certain that he had himself under total control that he spoke and then that was only to say "You have my statement. I have nothing further to add", he was very careful to say exactly the same words each time so that the detective concerned could gain nothing from variation, nor exploit any variation in his speech.

Mentally, Jim Meadowcroft was not in the interrogation room at Ipswich, he was back in time about 20 years to one of the Officer Training Corps weekend that he had attended as a student. They had been subjected to 'enemy' interrogation by the Regular N.C.O.'s of their platoon, to teach them how best to withstand it. Jim withstood that particular trial very well, even though he had had his nose broken during the course of one particularly physical bout of interrogation. No big deal, he had broken his nose three times before on the Rugby field and twice afterwards, so he had no aquiline profile to lose. What disturbed him was the lack of food and drink. He had been provided with no food and only one drink since being taken from his office at the University.

45 watts of weak lighting did not disturb him, nor stop him sleeping fitfully for short spells. He was awake as the cell door was opened to admit the solicitor, who introduced himself to Jim and then, very curtly, told the officer to leave them alone as he wished to talk to his client.

"Be sure you go back to your desk and don't hang around within ear-shot, or I'll have you before the disciplinary board so fast that your feet won't touch the ground!" said the lawyer sharply. Believing the warning, the desk sergeant departed at high speed.

"I'm actually acting as a locum for John Hartley, your solicitor. He's coming over himself, but won't be here for a couple of hours, so, in the meantime, he asked me to hold the fort for him" was how the lawyer introduced himself.

Jim couldn't remember hearing him give his name. When Jim responded to the question of 'why are you here', he told the full story, beginning fifteen years ago with his first wifes' disappearance and (the then D.C.) Rigby hounding him. Some remains, identified as his wifes', had been found a few months ago, then his visit (at D.C.I. Rigbys' request) to the Coroners court and then about his arrest, soon after lunch that day, at the University.

"O.K. what have you told them ?" was the next question and he repeated the standard answer was "You have my statement. I have nothing further to add". At this the lawyer smiled and said "You've watched too many films. You ought to know that the Thatcher government passed into law that refusal to answer police questions would be taken as a sign of guilt, however don't change your lines until your legal representative sits along side you during interrogation. What have you been charged with, by the way ".

"Haven't yet been told, I've only been read my rights and told that I've been arrested" said Meadowcroft. "Am I entitled to food and drink here ? Because if I am, they've given me nothing. I haven't eaten for over 12 hours and 1 drink in 9 hours is torture".

This startled the Lawyer, who muttered something about depravation then assured Meadowcroft that he, himself, would organise food if the police didn't within a few minutes. It was obvious that the lawyer was getting angry on Jims' behalf at the treatment meted out to him. Both Jim and the lawyer had begun to relax in each others presence when the desk sergeant arrived saying that Mr. Hartley had arrived and would come to talk with Jim once he had de-briefed the Lawyer. That effectively broke up the meeting, but before he left Jims' cell, the Lawyer said to the sergeant "This man has not been charged with any offence, he has not been fed and is being treated worse than a convicted criminal. Before I leave here this morning, I want to see this man fed hot food and given hot drinks, otherwise your police complaints people will be round here like bees around a honey-pot !".

"Before you go, can you phone my wife, to tell her the score, please ? She must be out of her mind with worry" asked Jim.

John Hartley first words to Jim Meadowcroft were "They've classified you as a category five prisoner, which means that they perceive you as a threat to interviewing officers ! Why, I don't know. Your treatment has been indefensible, so far, but it will improve substantially now that my friend has got the bit between his teeth. He's actually a human rights lawyer for one of the big charities, so he'll happily tie the local police up in so many legal issues that they will grind to a halt ! Now, tell me why are you here?"

For the second time that night, Jim Meadowcroft repeated the story, beginning with why he supposed he was there, emphasizing that he had not been told, but simply just read his rights. "It seems that Rigby now thinks he can pin something on me. I was verbally abused, insulted and provoked all the time I was in the car by both Rigby and his pal, Radcliffe. Then they started again when I got here."

"What did you say?" asked Hartley anxiously.

"Nothing other than what you told me the time Rigby was harassing me in the University a few years ago. You know, "You have my statement. I have nothing further to add"".

"You have said nothing more, have you ? Doesn't really matter, I'll see the statements and, with all the furor that's been stirred up by **an independent lawyer** (hem !), if they are hostile to you, we'll get them withdrawn".

John Hartley had settled into his stride now, a cool professional detachment took him over and Jim Meadowcroft simply sat and listened to the instructions that he was given.

When the next 'interview' was held, John Hartley sat alongside Jim Meadowcroft, ready to advise him, it was obvious from Radcliffes' demeanor that some one on high had had a word with him. Jim wondered if that had been the human-rights lawyer, talking in his seemingly casual way, to the Chief Constable. Whoever it was, Radcliffe was subdued and the questioning was questioning and not the baiting of the previous day. At the end of the interview, when between them, Jim and John had totally frustrated Rigby, John asked Rigby when and what Jim was going to be charged with, only to be told that 'the file is with the C.P.S. and they'll decide the nature of the offence and the charge'. John assured Jim that he would be in Ipswich all week-end and would be present at all interviews and, unless he was charged by mid-day Monday, they would have to release him.

"If they do charge you, watch what you say, silence will then be detrimental to your case as the law now reads that silence as an admission of guilt. It is really that obnoxious Michael Howards' new law that has fundamentally changed the 'innocent until proven guilty' concept into 'guilty until you prove your self innocent', just like it was in the Soviet Union" said John. "When you say anything, preface it with 'As I remember, the facts are . . . . ', then we can dispute everything that they say. No-one has a flawless memory and without a copy of your statement of fifteen years ago, you will make mistakes. You've just got to cover yourself if a comment you make now disagrees with the facts you stated fifteen years ago."

Saturday passed, then Sunday passed and it was mid-morning Monday when the cell door swung open and Rigby walked in followed by Radcliffe. Jim Meadowcroft knew something was afoot from the smirk on Rigbys' face. "James Meadowcroft, I arrest you in the name of the law for the premeditated murder of Caroline Meadowcroft, nee Ellis, on or about the tenth of July 1983. You do not have to say anything, but anything you say, can and will be used against you in court".

He was then told that his solicitor would be informed and would be present at every interview and with that Rigby turned on his heel and left, followed by a grinning Radcliffe.

"You were right about your contact at the C.P.S., he moved unbelievably quickly for a bureaucrat" said Rigby across the office desk to Radcliffe.

"He isn't a paper pusher, he's actually a silk, pushing for a knighthood" Rigby was told "He's made his pile and wants a title, so public service seems the best way. Or, at least, he thinks so !" "Let's begin to organise our next interview with our good doctor and his brief, so that we can pin him down so tightly that he'll cough and tell us all we don't know" spoken by Rigby over the shuffling of paper as he re-organised their notes.

"If we start at the beginning of the evidence, with the American cigarette butt, then we can go onto his feigned injury and demand proof of his being in the 'States and then that will lead onto his false passport and the photographic evidence".

"Hold on there" said Radcliffe, "Let's be a wee bit canny about this. If we lay EVERYTHING down at once, then we will give him chance to begin undermining everything at the same time. Instead, let's start by asking him about that time and see if we can fool him with the witness statements. I know this Max Webber, a bit of a villain he is, always on the edge of something or other. If we go and talk to him, we can jog his memory !".

For the process of re-checking witness statements, both Rigby and Radcliffe decided that it was imperative that they talk with Max Webber about his statement of fifteen years ago. They did it in full style, knowing that a police car driving and stopping in Chilham St. Margarets would soon be known to everyone in the village. Whoever the police were looking for, however innocently, would become the talk of the village. Radcliffe was relying on just that embarrassment effect to allow him to manipulate Max Webber as he wanted to.

When the police car arrived in the village, it was near 1 p.m., so Radcliffe told the driver to stop at the Maypole, while he and Rigby went in. Lunch time had always been the village meeting time in the pub and so Radcliffe was confident of finding Webber there and maybe, as a bonus, even with something 'dodgy' going on. Radcliffe, followed by Rigby, strode into the lounge bar and as they entered the conversation stopped, as if a switch had been turned off. Webber was quickly seen and identified by Radcliffe, who walked towards him, barely breaking stride as he did so. "Well, hello Maxwell, and what deals are you up to today ?" was how Radcliffe greeted him.

Rigby held station behind Radcliffe and subjected the rest of the lounge bar residents to his implacable gaze.

"Oh, hello Mr. Radcliffe, who are you looking for ?" asked Max Webber in a guilty tone of voice.

"You actually" said Radcliffe "what illegal operations are you involved with right now, eh ? False M.O.T. certificates, is it ?" he said turning over the cover of the book that Webber had hurriedly closed.

"No, Mr. Radcliffe, I was just re-issuing a lost certificate and needed to check my records" answered Webber, but Radcliffe cut him short, picking up the M.O.T. book, just saying "Get outside to the car, we'll talk to you there".

Pushing the book into his pocket, Radcliffe glared at everyone in the lounge and walked towards the door. As he passed the bar man, he said loud enough for everyone to hear "I'm disappointed in you Pete," and continued on out of the pub.

Max Webber was standing by the rear of the car, Radcliffe walked around to the boot and indicated to Webber to join him there, so Webber walked mildly to him. Holding the M.O.T. book in his hand, he used it to wave at Webber as he emphasised this points.

"First" he said "I'm keeping this book and you'll be able to count yourself lucky if I don't give it to 'Traffic' and let them loose on your customers. Secondly, you made a statement, years ago, soon after that Meadowcroft woman went missing. Remember ? It would be extremely useful to us if you remembered the car and the drivers face you saw when you were walking Jilly Abbot home. Jillys your wife now, isn't she ?" Radcliffe asked with mock sincerity

"Does she know about your little scheme, here ?".

"'Er, well, Mr. Radcliffe, 'er knows nothing about this, so don't be going to tell 'er, will ye ? I'll tell ye all yer wants to know, leastways, all I can remember about it" said a defensive Webber. "You did know Mrs. Meadowcrofts' husband, didn't you ?" more of a statement than a question from Rigby.

"Yes, yes, everybody knew Dr. Meadowcroft, Dr. Jim most people called him" responded Webber.

Seizing the initiative, Rigby continued "Are you sure that the driver of the car you saw wasn't Dr. Jim ? You also heard someone or something at the cottage later that night didn't you ? Was that Dr. Jim ?"

"I can't remember what I said to the p'lice back then, I suppose it COULD have been Dr. Jim" blurted out Webber.

"Not only could it have been Dr. Jim, it WAS Dr. Jim you saw, wasn't it ?" said Radcliffe quietly, but menacingly.

"Yes, yes, now I remember ! I wasn't sure when the car passed us, but I heard him, I recognised his voice, when he was tellin' 'er to open the door as he wanted in. Yes, it WAS Dr. Jim, wasn't it Mr. Radcliffe?" confirmed Max Webber, angling for favour.

"If you say so, lad, it was. Just remember, the next time that anyone asks you that question, I've still got this" Radcliffe said, waving the fake M.O.T. book in Webbers' face. "Get back inside and help them all to improve their memories" Radcliffe said dismissing Max Webber with a wave of the M.O.T. book.

Back at Ipswich police station, the two D.C.I.'s sorted through the fifteen year old statements until they found the ones that they wanted. Armed with their documentation, they began to read and organise the old information, Radcliffe phoned a duty sergeant and told him that Meadowcroft was to be interviewed and to contact his solicitor, so that he could be there at the time and arranged the interview for three p.m. As it was to be an important interview, where new evidence would be presented, Meadowcrofts' solicitor should definitely be present. John Hartley was waiting for Jim Meadowcroft when he walked into the interview room, John stood up as Jim entered, they shook hands and talked quietly for a couple of minutes.

"Well, I'll be interested to see what this new evidence is !" said Jim grimly "Rigby's been chasing this for fifteen years and this is the first new evidence that he has admitted to".

Just then, the door opened and in walked both Radcliffe and Rigby, accompanied by a uniformed sergeant, who lounged against the wall near the door.

"Good afternoon" said Rigby brightly, "I see that we're all here, so let's begin !"

"Why did you murder your wife in July 1983 ?" Rigby asked Meadowcroft, looking directly at him.

"I didn't, you know I wasn't even in the country at the time of her disappearance" said Meadowcroft warily.

"Oh yes you were, we have the name that you used, we have a copy of the passport application and a copy of the photograph, Mr Stone. That WAS the name you used wasn't it ? I mean to get into and out of this country when you were supposed to be injured in the U.S.A., wasn't it ?" "No, I don't know anyone called Stone and I certainly did not use the name Stone" replied Meadowcroft defensively.

"Ah, but you see, we have the application photograph and we've had it dimensionally checked against one of yours and they match ! Do you know what that means, Dr. So Sodding Smart Meadowcroft, do you ? It's as good as a fingerprint ! We've not just got near matches, we have a perfect bloody match and you know what that means ? It's you, without any shadow of a doubt!" Rigby was triumphant now, almost shouting in his confidence.

"You can't have such a good fit, I didn't have a passport in the name Stone. This is a set-up" Meadowcroft was sounding hunted now.

John Hartley had hold of Meadowcrofts' arm and began urgently whispering in his ear.

"It's not true, they've done something !" said Meadowcroft in answer to Hartley whispers.

"I need some time alone with my client" said John Hartley, trying to cool the situation down. "O.K., five minutes" said Radcliffe ungraciously, then stood up, indicated to the uniformed sergeant towards the door with his head and then walked out himself. As he closed the door behind him, he said to Radcliffe "Did you see the bastards' face drop when I called him Stone ?".

"Yes, but he didn't look stunned, only surprised. You had him off balance then, why didn't you ask him the big question, 'Why did he kill his wife ?', you might have cracked it open then and there !"

Radcliffe sounded concerned, but looked quite cool and calm. "No, I want to make him squirm and wriggle, I want to enjoy this, I've waited a long time for this moment" was Rigby's reply "Just wait 'til we tell him about the witness and then the cigarette stub, tell him we know about his wifes' affairs, THEN I'll ask him the big question. He'll crack then and there, I promise you!"

In the interview room, Hartley was asking Meadowcroft about the passport photograph and the name Stone urgently.

"As God is my witness, I know nothing about this passport photograph or the name Stone" replied Meadowcroft "have you seen the photograph ? Does it look like me ? How can it, it's not me !".

"Well, he right in saying what he has, a good fit of photo dimensions is almost as good as a finger print. If they have got an exact match, as he says, then they've either got a photograph of you or your twin brother. And as you don't have twin brother . . ." the rest was left unsaid.

"This is unbelievable, somehow they've frigged the thing, I never applied for a passport in the name Stone. That is just not true !" replied Meadowcroft, he had himself under control now and was thinking rationally once again.

At that moment the door re-opened and all three of the policemen walked in again, the uniformed sergeant was the last in, closed the door behind him and re-commenced leaning on the wall. Rigby began by asking a seemingly innocuous question, "Do you know anyone nicknamed Dr. Jim ?" he asked mildly.

"Yes, it's a nickname frequently used by students at the University for me, but I'm not supposed to know" replied Meadowcroft warily.

"Did any one else use to call it you ?" Rigby was deceptively quiet.

"It's a name that I had on and off since I left University at the end of my student days", Meadowcroft was attempting to fence with Rigby now, by answering the questions and giving nothing away.

"Did anyone in Chilham use that nickname ?" quietly asked by a seemingly uninterested Rigby. "Most of the village, as I remember" came the vague reply.

"Would it surprise you to know that someone referring to you as 'Dr. Jim" told me this very morning that he recognized you in the car you drove through Chilham and he heard your voice later pleading with your wife at the door ?" Rigby asked, questioning smoothly and calmly, just waiting like a patient fisherman to strike and drive the hook home.

"Yes, it would! He would have to have bloody good eyes and ears. I wasn't there", an equally calm reply from Meadowcroft. "We, that's me and D.C.I. Radcliffe here, were both told this morning that our witness could positively remember you there. It was him who referred to you as Dr. Jim, not a name that I knew you by until then" jubilantly spoken by Rigby.

"He's wrong" a categorical statement from Meadowcroft.

"How do you know ?" Radcliffe, this time, asking quietly.

"Because I wasn't there !" this time Meadowcroft shouted the answer. Hartley got hold of his arm again and once more whispered urgently into Meadowcrofts' ear.

"Gentlemen, I need another five minutes alone with my client" spoken by Hartley over Meadowcrofts' shoulder whilst he still held, restrainingly, onto his arm. Once more, the departure scenario was re-enacted. Last out was the Uniformed sergeant who closed the door behind himself.

"Just what the bloody hell is going on here ?" asked Meadowcroft of Hartley.

"Beware, they're trying to get you make an outburst that can be used against you. Keep calm". "Yes, I can see that, but I was wondering about this sudden return of somebody's memory after fifteen years. That was never said to me in '83, or at any other time since then. Now today somebody says that they remember, after 15 years ? I don't believe it, they're leaning on someone !" Meadowcroft thumped the table to emphasize his point.

"I agree with you, there is something funny here, perhaps a witness has been encouraged to say he saw you" agreed Hartley, "but if he repeats it in court, it'll look to be very strong".

"I never thought that you were as cruel as I've just witnessed in there" Radcliffe hardly sounded concerned by the sight.

"I'll bet they're shitting bricks in there now" commented Rigby unconcernedly "just a bit more line, then I'll pull it and he'll be on my line with nowhere to go".

Rigby smiled his wolfish smile, exposing his stained teeth to view. Why should he bother ? In his mind, he had the case as good as closed out, although it would be nice to get a confession he thought.

"Give 'em another couple of minutes to wriggle a bit more, then we'll go in and blow their little ship clean out of the water with the Marlboro' stub and the wifes' men friends !" Rigby was actually smiling in expectation as he spoke to Radcliffe.

Rigby was already seeing the news-paper headlines, he being described as the tenacious up-holder of the law, who finally closed a fifteen year old mystery. He was flying on the wings of euphoria and so was not seriously listening to any-one else. Radcliffe looked at his watch, then tapped it and motioned for Rigby to follow him back into the interview room. Both officers entered the interview room, followed by the ever present uniformed officer and both sat facing Meadowcroft and John Hartley

"We have direct evidence that can link you to the grave site. It looks unimportant, but it links America, you and the grave" Rigby was closing in for the kill. "We have a cigarette stub, more correctly an American made Marlboro' cigarette stub, which we recovered from the grave at about the depth that your wife was buried. Explain that !" Rigby felt like a matador about to try and find the bulls heart with his sword.

Meadowcroft looked him direct in the eyes, he looked tired, defeated ? Rigbys' pulse raced, then Meadowcroft spoke "You could well have found the killers' cigarette stub, well done. As for me, I have never smoked cigarettes, one cigar at Christmas time, maybe, but never cigarettes ! So it can't be mine".

Hartley jumped in here "My client can prove that he has never smoked cigarettes, so this evidence is rubbish".

"Don't either of you forget" and here Rigby was pointing his finger at both Meadowcroft and Hartley, "I've been in his office when it stank of cigs and the ash-trays were overflowing with cig. ends, don't try and tell me that they were modern art and that he used 'odour de fags' as an air freshener ! So I KNOW he smokes".

Hartley looked at Meadowcroft, who raised an eye-brow questioningly, but neither man spoke. "We also know, and have known for years, that your wife was having a number of adulterous affairs" triumphantly spoken by Radcliffe.

"Tell me something new" was the only reply to come from Meadowcroft.

"So, you admit to having known about her affairs?" asked Rigby interrogatively.

"If I remember correctly, it was ME that told YOU about them when you first interviewed me !" responded Meadowcroft.

John Hartley urgently leaned towards his client and whispered something in his ear, Meadowcroft glanced towards John Hartley and then looked at the table top.

"Most men would be angry at their wifes' affairs, angry enough to do something about it." shouted Rigby "But you, you cold blooded bastard, let her carry on, then you killed her and buried her body in an open grave, when you were supposed to be six thousand miles away ! But you gave yourself away because you couldn't refrain from the final gruesome touch, a warning to future wives. Burying her face down was the traditional way to deal with an unfaithful wife and that you couldn't resist ! Hoping, I suppose, that when her body was found a few hundred years hence, someone would say 'behold, the body of an adulteress !' but it wasn't hundreds of years later, it was only fifteen years later and I was still on the case. You got that wrong ! It's going to be a pleasure getting you convicted for premeditated murder. I only regret that we've done away with hanging, you deserve to swing".

"I must protest, on my clients behalf, to these aggressive and hostile approaches to questioning my client. You've asked almost no questions, but spent the time throwing vague and incorrect assertions at him. I have told him to cease co-operation with you until you ask questions in a professional manner", John Hartley was trying to be both diplomatic and conciliatory simultaneously.

Turning towards Hartley, Rigby snarled at him "Your client will make an appearance in court on Monday to be charged with premeditated murder. We expect a trial in Crown Court, at a date to be determined. Don't expect to get him bailed !"

Chapter 7

Trial by jury

As Rigby had predicted, Meadowcroft was soon in court and arraigned for trial at the next session at Suffolk Crown Court. John Hartley tried to arrange bail. Rigby was once more proved correct, bail was refused, so Jim Meadowcroft was incarcerated in Ipswich jail as a temporary remand prisoner. Becky visited Jim every week and tried to keep his spirits up by talking about the affairs of the University and the neighbours, to make him feel still a part of his home community. It did not work, all Jim ever looked forward to was seeing Becky come through the visitors room door and then that radiant, sunbeam smile of hers turn on as she saw him. That sunbeam smile had been the thing that had truly captivated him on their first meeting. Ever afterwards, he always believed himself so lucky that he could marry and spend time with her. Jim Meadowcroft was not the only one who looked forward to Beckys' visits, almost all the other inmates did, too. Her presence in the visiting room seemed to lighten the atmosphere for everyone and her silky walk to, and from, Jims' table, was watched as avidly by all the other men as it was by Jim himself.

Being used to the intellectually stimulating environment of a University, the mindless repetition of prison life and the stultifying effect, even more so as a remand prisoner, of petty detail lay heavily upon Jim. His physical condition deteriorated, partly due to the diet, partly due to the lack of exercise and lack of fresh air, but his intellectual condition suffered most. Life in jail was so boring, so repetitive, so SAME, no day differing from the previous or the next. As a remand prisoner, his times for 'socializing' were spent with the 'B' category convicts in the prison proper. With only 1 television between about 200 prisoners, the daily stimulation consisted only of a diet of the various soap operas' with which each T.V. channel seemed to fill their daily schedules. He had little in common with the men around him, his contacts were limited and the ever present threat of violence if one broke the unspoken 'code' appalled him. 'Lock-up' time in the cells, was 8.30 p.m. each evening until 8 a.m. the next morning, forcing him to spend twelve hours of each day with people whose company he would not have sought. It was not that they were not 'nice' people, but their interests were not his and never seemed to raise above the navel of any woman that they had known. By an unspoken agreement, no-one spoke salaciously of Becky (in his presence, at least), although he knew that she was the prisoners favourite visitor. Her walk through the visitors room, from the door to his table, always quietened the room. Even the 'screws' looked, that he knew.

John Hartley had briefed a young defence counsel for the case, young and vigorous, John had said and so, at first, he appeared. His initial visits had stimulated Jim to think about and to try to contribute some analytical thoughts to his own defence, but as the period between counsels' visits grew longer, Jims' depression grew deeper. Jim, himself, would not have thought of himself as depressed, but his acceptance of the deadly dull, daily routine as a remand prisoner ground away at his resolve and, however enlivening were Beckys' visits, the routine rapidly recaptured his brain and exerted its' leaden influence on his mind.

As the young counsel began to examine the evidence that the police had said that they would use, at first he accepted that a *prima fascia* case existed against Jim and various points of potential conflict were highlighted. Most of these, Jim could answer with answers that had been verified fifteen years ago, what he could offer no explanation for was the likeness of the passport photograph of Stone to his face.

"Accidental likenesses cut no ice with juries, we must have a much more definitive explanation than that, otherwise that piece of evidence will become overwhelming" was the counsels' studied reply. Simply to still Jims' comments, the counsel requested a copy of the Stone passport photograph, but as it showed little detail, he only filed it for further action, meaning to get one of his Chambers' clerks to compare it with the police evidence. There was plenty of anecdotal evidence to

Meadowcrofts' non smoking habits, much of which would no doubt be revealed by witnesses during the trial, but the Marlborough butt still could not be explained satisfactorily. As the butt was from an American made cigarette, not a U.K. made one, the link with Carolines' burial place and America was proving very resilient and not easy to disprove. Jim could offer no insights, neither could the counsel. At one of their meetings, when Becky was present, this connection with the grave and America was discussed. When she asked how extra evidence was obtained, she was astonished to learn that much was gained via family members and by the delving of the Chambers' clerks.

"Why don't you get a P.I. onto the job ? He'll at least know how to dig facts out and check them" was her reaction, to which the Counsel bridled a little and very nearly said 'that this is Britain, not America'. He said nothing, but his thoughts were plainly visible on his face.

"Well, if you won't, I will. This is my husband that we are defending here and I don't think this is a time to get all prissy and anally retentive. We've got to do the best job here that we can !" Becky's American 'can-do' spirit had never left her, she had never become a recessive British University academics' wife, one more reason why Jim loved her and many academics' wives disliked her. It gave them a reason for their jealousy of her, they could never admit that her looks intimidated them.

Becky went looking for a private detective and found one, after interviewing many, she was just learning that most private detectives in the Home Counties seemed to specialize in divorce investigations and were more 'peeping Toms' than detectives. With two of them, she had more than the usual trouble getting rid of them, these two obviously looked at Becky as the prize to be won, rather than their (potential) employer. In short order, and in no uncertain terms, she told them that she was unavailable, uninterested and unwilling, so they unhappily ceased their attentions.

Eventually, Becky found a suitable detective, one that sexism had made her hesitant to contact. Having been brought up on an All-American diet of male P.I.'s, she had purposely avoided contacting the female name listed in the 'private investigators' column of her local 'Yellow Pages'. When she met the female investigator, she found an ordinary, mousy woman, a few years younger than herself, totally unprepossessing at first glance, but who, on talking to, proved to have a sharp mind and definite ideas of what to do. Becky rapidly appreciated how good the woman was, more especially as she wouldn't touch divorce work at all and so, after a 30 minute talk, Becky was glad that Jims' case was going to be well supported by a neutral investigator.

First to be checked was the positive sighting of Dr. Jim by Max Webber in Chilham at the fateful time, fifteen years before. Stacey (her working name) didn't barge straight into the village, but somehow contrived to emerge in an unthreatening way in the 'Maypole', apparently known by everyone. In short order, she found out that Max Webber was the local 'wide boy', who seemed to be able to do, or obtain, anything. Talking to someone, she was told that the supply of M.O.T. certificates had dried up in Chilham since Radcliffes' visit to Webber, but that if she wanted an M.O.T. for her car, Max could still get them, but it would be from a 'friend' and would cost more. Sniffing around some more, Stacey unearthed the fact that Radcliffe and Webber were known to each other and had an obvious 'modus vivendum'. Radcliffe did not bother about Webbers' 'business ventures' unless they became too blatant, but the M.O.T. certificate scam had always remained low key, never become blatant, but had attracted Radcliffes' attention. Since the day of that visit, Max Webber had sold no more M.O.T.'s, Radcliffe had been seen taking away the master book, although nothing further had happened and it had never been investigated. Leaving the obvious unsaid, Stacey reported these developments to Becky, who immediately passed them on to the young Counsel, who had become another of her admirers. He was unwilling to use the findings at first, which Becky put down to an English sense of 'fair play', although, as more results appeared, he took notice and built them into Jims' defence.

When the trial opened on Wednesday, the scheduled day, the full majesty of the law was at once apparent. All the court dignitaries were in full ceremonial outfits, be-wigged & be-gowned legal Professionals, the judge, prosecution counsel, defence counsel, clerks of the court and all the various minions hovering around both Counsels. Even the police offers in court looked the part in clean and tidy uniforms. After the jury had been sworn in, they elected a foreman, who made himself known to the clerk of the court. He was a local shop-keeper, respected by all, but on whose shoulders would fall the task of declaring the judgement of his fellow jurors on the accused and that was the role he was not looking forward to. Then, the clerk called the court to order and into his podium chair swept the judge and arranged his papers neatly before him, at that stage the clerk called for the accused to be brought to the dock.

Into this maelstrom of formality was lead the remand prisoner, whose fate would be decided in the next few days, he, in many ways the star of the show, looked both pallid and unkempt. His shirt was now obviously far too large for him, his suit hung on him, sizes too large. His hair was dull and lifeless, yet more grey than ever before, his eyes did not sparkle, rather they looked dully, deep set and devoid of emotion.

Such was the picture that Dr. Jim Meadowcroft presented after four months of remand. He tried to respond to the aura in the court and did so, weakly. That was as much as he could achieve, he was now as totally reliant on the actions and abilities of others as he had been when he was new-born. After the accused and the attending prison officers had established themselves in the dock, the clerk read the charge out to the prisoner and he was asked how he pleaded. "Not guilty", the answer came out surprisingly strongly from the pallid creature in the dock. Here, the judge checked both prosecution and defence counsel were ready and then asked the prosecution counsel to open the case for the crown.

As he stood up, the Q.C. leading the prosecution demonstrated his theatrical ability. A big, distinguished looking man, he accompanied his own oratory with flowing hand movements, simultaneously both theatrical and engrossing. He had obviously worked hard on the speech he delivered, his words and gestures were perfectly timed. According to the prosecution, Meadowcroft had found out that his wife was cuckolding him and had hatched a plot to get even with her. Despite his enfeebled condition, Jim Meadowcroft could not help himself but be drawn into the tale being spun by the performer in front of him & on his right hand side. Various parts of the tale according to the prosecution were highlighted, as were the devices to be employed in demolishing 'this gossamer web of lies and deceit', as it was called, to reveal the truth to the jury.

During these histrionics, Meadowcroft found himself retreating back fifteen years into his memories and thinking, 'it wasn't like THAT'. So realistic were his daydreams that he had to work hard not to nod or shake his head or not to cry out when tale became too unbelievable, even to him. Eventually, the story teller wound his tale to an end, by indicating Meadowcroft and loudly declaiming "There stands the man accused of a cold, deliberate and premeditated murder of the woman he swore to love for better or worse. Look at the wretch, it seems hardly possible that he is capable of performing such an evil deed, but he was and never shown regret for it in the fifteen following years !".

When the prosecution counsel sat, the judge asked for the defence counsel to outline his case and the young counselor began, arguing the case in a very University debating chamber manner, but without the thespian character used by the prosecution in his rendition. To give the young counsel his due, he did not appreciate the impossibility of his task (the young are ever like that), but the very theatricality of the prosecuting counsels' performance had woven a spell of his omnipotence around the jury. He tried his best, but his understated presentation, though scrupulously accurate, was pitched at the wrong level. An Oxbridge debating society would have closely followed the arguments, but the jury of stolid Suffolk folk believed that they were being patronized. So, by the end of the defences' opening speech, more of the jury were in agreement with the prosecution than with the defence.

As the prosecution opened its' detailed case, the jurors were aurally stroked and told that an impregnable case would slowly be built against the defendant. First witness to be called was Charlie, the sexton of the Holy Trinity church in Higham Green, where the skeleton had been discovered. After confirming the most basic details of the discovery and that D.C.I. Radcliffe had been present and had brought in the 'Scene of Crime' technical squad, who took over from him, Charlie's brief appearance in the legal spotlight was over. He was glad that the prosecution counsel asked him only the questions that he had rehearsed with him. When the defence counsel said 'No questions', Charlie could have cheered and he happily quit the witness box to return to his secluded life in the church-yard.

Next witness called was the Forensic Pathologist, who had been there when the 'Scene of Crime' technical squad had fully exposed the skeleton under her gaze and then had removed the skeleton, bone by bone. As the removal had proceeded, the Pathologist had dictated detailed records and these records were referred to as evidence was given. Next, her laboratory investigations were detailed, what had been sought and why and the results of these investigations. When asked what the cause of death was, the answer was given as 'no obvious cause', when asked to speculate on cause, the pathologist repeated the results of the discussion with Radcliffe on the same topic.

"So, here we have a death with no detectable cause ?" said the theatrical counsel.

"Yes" answered the pathologist.

"Most unusual, don't you think, a death without an obvious cause ?" asked the prosecution, "Most unusual" answered the pathologist.

"It could indicate murder by someone with an advanced biological knowledge, could it not ?" prompted the counsel.

"Yes" answered the pathologist "or medical knowledge".

Slowly the defence council came to his feet, he had been caught a little off guard with the last question and the reply. All he could think to ask of the pathologist was "Why would such biological or medical knowledge be required ?".

"Biologists frequently have to kill specimens without either short or long term obvious damage. On the other hand, some medical knowledge was necessary to know how a human body might react to poison, suffocation or whatever was used" replied the pathologist.

Unbeknown to the defence counsel, he had just asked the question and received the answer that the prosecutor had planned!

After the Pathologist was dismissed with the rejoinder that her re-appearance might be needed, D.C.I. Rigby was called to the stand. At this point, the prosecution counsel explained that, in some ways, D.C.I. Radcliffe was logically next, but to prevent Radcliffes' dismal and subsequent recall to the stand, the story would be more logical and easily followed if D.C.I. Rigby gave evidence first. After being sworn in, Rigby was to relate his knowledge of the case, which really began back in 1983. He began with his first involvement, as a fresh D.C., with this case and made a special point of mentioning Meadowcrofts' seeming disinterest in Caroline Meadowcrofts' whereabouts. Meadowcroft had also said that he expected Caroline to leave him at any time and that he (Meadowcroft) wasn't too surprised that she had left him.

"It was as if he knew and had no further interest in her" said Rigby, "this I found very suspicious, she was an attractive woman, then, added to that the fact that most murders are performed by partners, made me feel that Dr. Meadowcroft was hiding something".

With that statement, the judge intervened and said

"There is no evidence of murder here, yet, this is what this court has to decide, the Jury will disregard that statement".

With that, the prosecution counsel brought Rigby back to the latest part of his investigation. Rigby began by describing how the body had come to his knowledge, how his memory had been stirred, how he had searched the 1983 'missing persons' register and suggested a possible identity. Dental records, although taking time, had confirmed his suspicions and from that time he had been seconded to work with D.C.I. Radcliffe in Ipswich. He confirmed that the Coroners court had issued an adjournment to allow investigations continue and that this case was the conclusion of the ongoing investigations.

At that point, the prosecution counsel began to ask Rigby about the results of the investigations, so the court was told of Rigby's fifteen year worry over the two days that Meadowcroft could produce no direct witnesses for, and therefore could not prove.

"Using this as a key", he went on, "I began to speculate as to just how Meadowcroft could have done it. We know that he did not enter the U.K. under his own name, so we speculated he must have acquired a false passport. Thanks to the American "Freedom of Information" act, we have been able to scrutinize all the British passport holding airline passengers who flew from Florida to the U.K. and back again within that time frame".

"Did your investigations reveal anything ?" asked the prosecuting counsel. "Yes, they did. Two male suspects and one female, we felt safe in ignoring the female for this case," continued Rigby "I obtained copies of passport photographs for both male suspects, both of which were computer enhanced. One was identified as the suspect, but using the name of Phillip Stone".

"How, actually, was the suspect identified?" Rigby was asked.

"Initially, by myself, but formally by facial dimensions" replied the detective.

"How accurate a fit were the matching facial dimensions?", again asked of Rigby by the prosecuting counsel.

"Perfect, not one dimensional variable in the standard ten measured."

"How sure are you about your identification?" asked the counsel.

"A fit as good as that is as good as a matching fingerprint and as trustworthy" was Rigbys reply. "So, having established that Meadowcroft returned to the U.K. for the crucial two days, under the name of Stone, how can you place him at the scene? If you can't place him there there may be a perfectly rational explanation for his visit, although, I cannot, for the life of me, think of one" the prosecutor asked, accompanied by wide theatrical gestures.

"We have three further items of evidence, plus a psychological profile. One of which is that a witness has been re-interviewed and remembers both seeing and hearing the accused and seeing his car in the village of Chilham St. Margarets on the evening of one of the two days in question, so we are pretty confident" said Rigby.

Before any further questions could be asked, the judge intervened and suggested a lunch break, to allow the jurors to marshal all the facts in their heads.

Chapter 8

Post Prandial Problems

As soon as the judge left the court, the defence counsel walked to Meadowcroft and asked him about the witness. Jim had been galvanised by the informationabout a witness from Rigby, but said he had no knowledge of any witness, then added quickly, "My car was at Heathrow whilst I was away, perhaps they can confirm that it was there for four unbroken weeks?"

"No chance, after 15 years; N.C.P. records aren't held for five years, never mind fifteen !" was the young Counsels' comment.

"I put it in one of those private company long term parks and had it serviced and cleaned" Jim Meadowcroft rapidly replied.

"That's got a better chance of being found. They might have something, do you remember the name ?" the counsel was excited.

"No, not exactly, it was something like 'Pink Elephant Parking' or some such thing. I had a Y registration beige Austin Ambassador at that time" was all the information that Meadowcroft could give.

Without further hesitation, the counsel open his mobile phone and called Stacey, the private investigator who would be giving evidence for the defence later in the case. He passed on all the information he had got from Jim and asked her to try to find something out.

After the lunch break, the judge called on the Prosecution to resume its' case, which the prosecution counsel did with an extravagant series of flourishes. He spoke of the witness who could positively place Meadowcroft at the scene, who would be called to testify 'in due time' and then returned to D.C.I. Rigby and the further evidence he was to reveal.

"Before lunch, you spoke of three further pieces of evidence and a psychological profile. One we know, is to be the witness, but what are the others ?" asked to lead Rigby back onto track and through his story.

Rigby took the lead and continued "Other than the witness, physical evidence was found in the grave, at the level of the skeleton. As this evidence came to light whilst D.C.I. Radcliffe was alone technically in charge of the investigation, he will talk in detail about it in his evidence, but it is the filter of an American made cigarette. Not, please note, not an American cigarette, but an American MADE cigarette, which is not, and never was, on free sale in this country".

"Next was the burial position of the body. Mrs. Meadowcroft was buried in a face down position, head facing to the west, or the sun-set, as the old wives' tales would have it. It was, in rural areas and in less enlightened times, the classical position to bury an adulterous wife, although back then, the wife was bound hand and foot and buried alive. From the evidence recovered, Caroline Meadowcroft was not bound and also probably dead at the time of her internment. In his statements made to me both this year and fifteen years ago, James Meadowcroft admitted that he knew that his wife was having serial adulterous affairs and that he was 'going to do something about it', if I may paraphrase a little. At that time, fifteen years ago, I thought he meant that a divorce was in the offing and not that murder had already occurred."

Pleased with himself, Rigby paused to draw breath before he continued. "During my earlier investigations, I was told that Dr. Meadowcroft, as he is formally known at his place of work, had won a grave digging competition competing against an experienced, manual land-worker. This competition occurred some six to nine months before the actual internment, but was accomplished in less than one hour and was timed by judges. As I recall, it was an event held at the University at which the accused taught and was ostensibly a charity event organised by the Students Union."

"I well remember my own student days" said the prosecuting counsel "we did silly things, but a timed competition to dig a grave seems too gruesome even by the madcap logic of modern student Unions. It would have been, however, an excellent test for some-one planning a murder to take undertake in order to help with the time planning of the crime. Is that how you saw it D.C.I. Rigby ?"

"No, not initially, I regarded this bit of basic information as just superfluous. It was only later that you can begin to appreciate the logic of taking part in such a competition. We ignored this morsel of information until Caroline Meadowcrofts body was discovered and identified. Up to that time, she was only classified as missing, not dead and buried. When taken with the knowledge that the accused returned to the U.K. for two days, during which time he intended to kill his wife and dispose of her body, does it make sense to know how long the burial would actually take. Every other timing in the plan would revolve around this central action."

"Thank you, Mr. Rigby, I understand your emphasis on this topic now. Until you explained it in detail, I can fully see how anyone not with full knowledge of the overall plan would have regarded that seemingly useless piece of evidence as just that. Useless !"

This was delivered with the counsel nominally looking at Rigby, but, during his histrionic performance, making eye contact with almost every juror.

"All we have left, I think, is the psychological profile evidence that you gleaned." this addressed directly to Rigby.

"Dr. Tanner is a psychology lecturer at Essex University and has been used on numerous occasions by Suffolk Constabulary in this regard. I understand that it was the U.S. airbases stationed around this region that caused the use of psychological profiling in the first place". "What did Dr. Tanner tell you about the psychology of the perpetrator of the deed?" Prosecution counsel had inadvertently taken on an American persona.

"We got a detailed profile of an intelligent and cold, plotting personality, who was probably very sports inclined and highly competitive. Also, the character was liable to be highly aggressive if confronted, angry and somewhat vengeful. All together, a person apparently quite normal, but able to harbour grudges and coldly plot revenge against someone they identified as the cause of their problems or distress."

"And how does that profile compare to that of the accused ?" Counsel now appeared genuinely to be seeking information from the detective.

"From my personal knowledge of the accused, I would say pretty closely, at times his outbursts, when talking to me, have had a frightening quality. He is known to play sports in a very competitive manner at the University, always measuring himself against younger, fitter opponents. As Dr. Tanner himself put it, the cold plotting and high intelligence level are symptomatic of research academics in Universities, their job calls them to build evidence slowly and then act decisively to get research funds or patents. I don't think that I need to add that Dr. Meadowcroft is research active at his University".

Saying that, Rigby concluded his explanation of the accused psychology as had been explained to him by Dr. Tanner. With that, the prosecutions questioning of D.C.I. Rigby was concluded and the judge asked if the defence had any questions for this witness. On hearing an affirmative answer, the judge indicated by a wave of his hand that Defence might begin his questioning, but also said "Please take the floor".

Once more, the University debating stance seemed to occupy the counsel as he stood and clutched a handful of notes. "Detective Chief Inspector Rigby, you are very definite in your answers and your knowledge of my client".

At this Rigby demurred and smiled

"How has this personal knowledge come about? Is it because you have hounded my client remorselessly for fifteen years and think that you know him well?" asked the young counselor. Taken somewhat aback, Rigby was caught off-balance and said "I have not hounded your client at all".

"How many complaints has my client made against your imperious behaviour in the past fifteen years ?" asked the counselor, determined to keep Rigby agitated, "Come now, it is some ten or so is it not ? Almost one per year since this whole sorry thing started. How did you manage to retain this case?"

Rigby could feel himself under attack and desperately wanted to slow things down.

"Do you have a personal grievance against my client that you are trying to expiate by your continuous hounding?" again the young counselor was aware that he was attacking from an unexpected direction and that Rigby was uncomfortable.

"What is it that offends you about the liberty of my client ? Do you have a personal vendetta against him for some personal reason?" How close he was to the true explanation of Rigby's fixation, the defence counsel would never know.

"Is disinterest in your wifes' activities a capital crime in your book, Mr. Rigby ?" Rigby mumbled an answer and the counselor asked him to repeat his answer clearly for the benefit of the jury who might not have heard him clearly.

"He had no interest in his wifes' whereabouts" said Rigby in a stronger voice.

"Not really surprising, when he had expected her to leave him, don't you think? My client did actually tell you that he knew of his wifes' activities and that he expected her to leave home anytime she found someone willing to support her, didn't he ?" defence counsel pursued Rigby relentlessly over the point.

"As my client expected his wife to leave him at almost any time, would you say that his evident lack of surprise was because his expectations had occurred ?" the probing of Rigby continued. "It could have been." began Rigby.

"Yes or no ?" demanded the young defence counsel "We've had your speculations earlier, please answer my question Mr. Rigby !" demanded the young man.

"Yes" answered Rigby.

"So, my client exhibited what you now seem to believe was a perfectly natural reaction, and you suspected him for it ? Mr. Rigby, that is not a very professional police reaction, is it ?" prompted the counsel.

"No" answered Rigby, quite mildly.

"But you still continued to suspect him ?" probed the young counsel.

"Yes, it just seemed so odd" muttered Rigby.

"So", said the defence counsel "you've just told me that you now believe that my client, the accused, presented a normal reaction when you first interviewed him fifteen years ago, but that you suspected him for it and that your suspicion of my client was unprofessional".

"Yes, but . . ." began Rigby.

"Yes or no, Mr. Rigby ?" asked the young counsel quickly.

"Yes", an almost inaudible answer from Rigby.

"Thank you, Mr. Rigby."

"May I now bring you, in your professional capacity, back to the question of the two days in which you believe my client travelled from

America back to Britain, murdered his wife, buried her body and returned, undetected at the time, to Florida ?" asked the young man quite calmly. D.C.I. Rigby was no where near as calm, his solid base had been definitely rocked.

"Did you, or did you not, ask the" here defence counsel referred to his hand held notes "the Winter Park police department, in Florida, to check out at the motel where my client had registered?"

"Yes, I did. It is normal police procedure" answered Rigby.

"And what was their answer ?" asked the young man.

"They confirmed that the accused was there over the days he was registered. They confirmed his meetings with the doctor and that he used the prescription that he was given. They could not find a witness who actually saw the accused over the two days we believe he came to Britain", Rigby was moving onto more certain ground now.

"Did my client ever give you any answer as to why no-one might have seen him on those two days ?" asked the defence counsel, innocently.

"Yes, the accused answered that due to a knee injury he rested in bed for two days, once he got home from the doctors and that it was only after he thought his knee was feeling better that he left the motel room" answered Rigby.

"Once more", said the young counsel "did you find my clients' actions strange or unusual?" "No", a firm reply from Rigby.

"So why did you continue to suspect him, especially as the American police confirmed to you that my client had spoken to Dr. Levy by telephone, to ask when he should get out of bed and start using the leg again ? You did receive that confirmation from the Winter Park police, didn't you?" probed the young counsel maliciously.

"Yes, I received that confirmation, but telephone calls can be made from anywhere and I believed that it was too neat an explanation" answered Rigby, now back on a firm footing. "I believed it to be a planned attempt to bolster an alibi. Such a call could have been planned to re-inforce an alibi should anything have gone wrong".

Rigby was now adamant in his answers. "Without a visual sighting, the accused cannot prove that he WAS there" continued Rigby.

"True" answered the defence counsel, "but, by the same token, you cannot prove that he wasn't!"

"There is a witness, willing to swear that he remembers seeing the accused in Chilham St. Margrets' during those two days" Rigby was sounding triumphant now.

"Be that as it may, that witness statement is new this year and, fifteen years after the event, may be in error ", the young counsel was now sounding defensive.

"Your identification of my client with the passport of Phillip Stone was done entirely by scientific comparison of two photographs, one from the Phillip Stone passport application and a known one of my client, wasn't it ?" a straightforward question asked by the young defence counsel.

"Yes, that is the usual way" Rigby answered formally.

"I'm looking for an explanation", asked the young man quietly "as to why your experts identified the Stone photograph as being of my client, when they said to me that the passport office notarized copy with which I provided them was of too poor a print quality for them to be able to do the job ?".

"We had the print computer enhanced by the I.T. department of Ipswich Police" Rigby was proud of this part of the investigation "and used the enhanced version as the basis of comparison", he concluded.

"So you didn't use the notarized passport office provided image, you used a modified image? Is that correct?" the young counsel had seen a potential flaw.

"Yes, we were assured that the modifications only cleaned up the transmitted image and so were quite valid" Rigby was comfortable, now, answering questions.

"Hmm, quite strange tho' that the significant details must be modified to be useful" commented the defense counsel.

"As I understand it, there is no modification, just lightening of the computer image" Rigby liked sounding authoritative in court.

"Can I take you now to the subject of the filter tip of the American cigarette that was found in the grave ?" asked the young defence counsel patiently.

"It is your assumption that the cigarette was smoked by the person who interred Caroline Meadowcroft and was dropped, accidentally, in the grave, near the body".

"Yes", confidently, from Rigby "there is no other way that it could have been found where it was".

"Further, it is your assumption that it was my client who dropped that filter tip there" asked directly of Rigby.

"Yes, that filter tip was made in America, as was the cigarette from which it came. It must have been brought here from the 'States at the time of the internment. And there is only one person who could obviously have brought it over" responded Rigby looking directly at Meadowcroft.

"I must ask you a few points to clarify aspects of your last answer" smoothly said by the young man.

"You affirm that the cigarette was made in America and must have come from there to the grave?"

Rigby was pleased to agree with that statement.

"Have you heard of R.A.F. Lakenheath ? And do you know what it is ?" a quietly spoken leading question from the young counsel.

"I assume that it is a British Air force base at Lakenheath" Rigby answered glibly. "Quite right TODAY" said the young defence counsel "but in 1983, it was the U.S.A.F. base Lakenheath and, as you may be aware, it had a PB where personnel could buy American goods at American prices with dollars. Not only could the American personnel of the base buy the goods, but the British personnel working there could, too!"

Warming to his theme, the young counsel continued "There was always some 'leakage' of U.S. goods into the local community, but the American & local authorities were never too bothered, so long as the leakage remained at small levels. Cigarettes were always a problem, on the base they cost less than half the price of off-base prices, so there was always a ready market for cigarettes with the locals and always a few U.S. service men willing to make a few more dollars. Do you know where Lakenheath IS, Mr. Rigby?"

Suddenly, Rigby felt unsure of his facts, he stuttered through a few comments, but was cut short by the defence council

"Caroline Meadowcroft certainly had male friends from Lakenheath, remember her sister, Shirley, had left a message on her answering machine about a visit to Lakenheath? Are you proposing that one of Caroline Meadowcrofts' friends provided cigarettes for her non-smoking husband, my client, to mark her grave with? I can think of a thousand explanations for the location of that cigarette filter and none of them involves my client and I am equally sure that the members of the jury can easily explain that cigarette butt without involving my client!"

Rigby looked like a man at bay, a major brick had been pulled out of the impregnable wall that he thought that he had erected to enclose the accused. A low murmur from behind the defence counsel indicated that the prosecuting counsel had readily accepted the circumstantial explanation, but was now modifying his views.

"I can see that the day has weakened you, Mr. Rigby" commented the young man acidly "there are just two quick points that I must clear up before I finish with you".

Continuing smoothly, he asked about the grave digging competition that Meadowcroft had won in 1982,

"Was it a grave digging competition, Mr. Rigby?" he was asked.

"I was under the impression that it was" Rigby muttered.

"You must learn to be precise, Mr. Rigby. Were you not told that it was a charity competition to prepare a flower bed for an old folks' home? And my client participated for his department side, by invitation, and only dug out the flower bed? Indeed, I know you knew, as I spoke to the same man as you did, but I questioned him a little closer than you apparently did".

In his minds' eye, Rigby could see the student getting a charming version of the third degree from the defence counsel and telling him everything. He knew the feeling, except his third degree wasn't that charming.

"Would you answer me, please, Mr. Rigby. You were aware that the contest was not a grave digging one, but a flower bed making one, weren't you ?" remorselessly, the defence counsel exploited the weakness.

"Yes, it's just that the digging part was deep enough to be a grave" a weak reply from Rigby. "You did know that the flower bed dimensions and depth were specified by the organising committee and that they got the dimensions from the head gardener, who provided the compost to be put in by the next competitor ?" a direct thrust at Rigby, which he could only parry with "No".

"One last point needs clearing up, before we finish and that is the psychological profile drawn up by Dr. Tanner" an eager defence counsel attempted to push rapidly on, only to be interrupted by the judge who reminded him that it was he, as judge, who decides when the days action is finished and not an excitable defence counsel.

Chapter 9

Trial by Jury, day 2

Promptly, at ten a.m. on Thursday morning, the trial resumed. This time there was none of the theatrical, sequenced quality of moves of the opening day, no-one appeared at a dramatic moment. Everyone seemed simply to assemble and then the judge appeared from behind his seat and asked the prosecution to present their next witness. This time the prosecution counsel declaimed to the court that his next witness would be D.C.I. Radcliffe. Since the court had adjourned the previous day, the defence counsel, distinctly underwhelmed by Rigbys' performance on the stand, had spent time coaching Radcliffe, to try to teach him how to protect himself from the quick thrusts of the young defence counsel.

On Wednesday evening, at the prosecution cases de-briefing session, the counsel made his displeasure known.

"Today", the prosecuting counsel growled to D.C.I. Radcliffe, "really proved the 6 P rule". Before Radcliffe could ask what the 6 P rule was, the counsel continued and counted the P's off on his fingers, "Poor Preparation Produces Piss Poor Performance".

Thus, much of the Wednesday evening had been spent improving the preparation of Radcliffes' evidence.

"Try to be more definitive in your answers and try not to get pushed into a 'yes/no' situation, or you might find the point being used against us", 'just like today' was left unsaid, but the emphasis was unmistakable and comprehended by Radcliffe. For all of his 'country copper' image, D.C.I. Radcliffe was actually very astute, he had listened to the counsels' account of Rigby's showing and had analysed the shortcomings himself. He was committed to repeat none of Rigbys' mistakes.

"D.C.I. Radcliffe", the prosecution counsel requested and obiediently Radcliffe walked to the witness box. After being sworn in and identifying himself, Radcliffe began by detailing the circumstances surrounding the finding of the skeleton, later identified as that of Caroline Meadowcroft. He reported, in a factual voice, how, as first officer at the crime scene, he had called the 'scene of crime' technical back-up squad and used the forensic pathologist before any further digging was undertaken, to minimise the loss of potential evidence. He detailed the findings of the pathologist as presented at the Coroners Court, finding that were accepted by a simple nod of the judges' head. Radcliffe explained how the skeleton had been reconciled with a missing person report and finally identified by dental and medical record confirmation. D.C.I. Rigby had been sent, by Thames Valley Police, to work with him to bring the case to a conclusion, which this case was expected to be. He and Rigby had worked very closely together for many weeks assembling the details of the evidence that had been, and would be, presented in the prosecution of this case. Throughout this long monologue, the prosecution counsel stood, happily relaxed listening to a confident and competent witness present evidence, little of which was in dispute. Only a few questions were asked of Radcliffe, the main one being the professional relation between himself and Rigby.

"We worked, essentially, as an equal partnership as there was no formalised division of power. Because we operated from my home police station, I suppose that that made me the senior officer, in effect" answered Radcliffe.

At that, the prosecuting counsel smiled to himself, 'with luck" he thought 'that will help to limit the damage of Rigbys' appearance yesterday'. Details of the local investigations were presented by D.C.I. Radcliffe in a thoroughly down to earth manner, with none of Rigbys' attempts at providing a killing blow. THAT, by orders from the counsel, would be provided by the counsel himself in his summing up speech when he reviewed the evidence and could tell the jury what to understand by it. Max Webbers' witness evidence was noted about his recognition of 'Dr. Jim' in Chilham on a night within the crucial time frame set by the recorded time from the grave being excavated to

James Bradley being legally interred there. Mr. Radcliffe's home police force had also provided the I.T. back-up for both the airlines search and the passport picture 'clean-up'. Facial identification had been done by the Ipswich technicians, 'competent, trained & experienced officers, all of them' according to D.C.I. Radcliffe. As for Dr. Tanners' evidence, Mr. Radcliffe did have long term personal experience of the use of psychological profiles, especially when dealing with the U.S. air force authorities, and he usually found it acceptably accurate as a definition of a criminals' character.

Throughout his statement, Radcliffe did not openly criticize D.C.I. Rigby, but just noted that he seemed driven and in a hurry with this case. It was obvious that for much of the later detail of this case, Radcliffe was able to answer, so all the questions he received from the prosecution counsel were these and deliberately presented to look 'matter of fact'. Much of the influence of the questions was as a damage limitation exercise after Rigbys' poor performance on the first day. He was succeeding, Rigby was beginning to be presented as something of a zealot, whilst Radcliffe increasingly appeared as wielding restraining influence as a 'cautious country cop'.

By the end of the prosecutions' examination of D.C.I. Radcliffe, much of the damage caused by Rigby on the previous day had been repaired and was reflected in the prosecution counsels' relaxed and extravagant gestures.

Neither the effect of this studied low-key approach on the jury nor the relief in the prosecution counsel's posture had escaped the young defence counsel. He and his group of people had also spent the Wednesday evening reviewing the case and determining how best to examine the witnesses. Early on in the evening review process, Stacey had joined the group and spent almost an hour alone with the young counsel detailing the findings of her investigations. Thanks to Staceys' unspectacular, but ruthlessly efficient, investigative technique, she had provided much information that the young counsel had faith in and would use in his witness examinations. Before the defence counsel could begin his questioning of D.C.I. Radcliffe, the judge, always aware that regular breaks in the concentrated business of a trial was helpful to the jurys' understanding of the case, called the lunch adjournment until 2.00 p.m., when the defense counsel would begin their interrogation of D.C.I. Radcliffe.

"Good afternoon to you Mr. Radcliffe" began the young counsel, "I hope that you have been fully fortified by your lunch and that you are prepared for my questions".

Such a friendly overture was meant to disarm Radcliffe, but he didn't relax his guard.

"Before I begin my questions, I would like to put on record my total agreement with all your actions at the time of the discovery of the skeleton. No-one should be in any doubt whatsoever that your actions were both legally and morally correct."

Radcliffe inclined his head in this acknowledgment of his professionalism and almost permitted a smile. Prosecution counsel wasn't so grateful for this praise, to him it presaged some bad business afoot, although he couldn't see what it might be.

"Could you confirm that you have previous knowledge of Mr. Max Webber, who is, I believe, your witness who claims, after fifteen years, to have remembered seeing my client when he was supposed to be in Florida".

"Max Webber is known to the Suffolk constabulary" was all that Radcliffe would say.

"Fine." said the defence counsel, continuing "A few weeks ago you, in company with D.C.I. Rigby, had a meeting with Mr. Webber in the "Maypole" public house in Chilham St. Margarets, did you not ? A meeting that began in the "Maypole" and ended some minutes later outside, by your car ?"

"Yes", a monosyllabic answer and nothing else, from Radcliffe.

"May I ask what that meeting was about ? Was it in regards to this case ?" the defence counsel purred.

"No", again a monosyllabic answer from Radcliffe.

"Oh, that's alright, then" replied the young defence counsel, "In that case, you won't mind me asking what this meeting was about, will you ?"

"It was simply some Ipswich business that I decided to do whilst we were in the area. D.C.I. Rigbys' presence was accidental, he just happened to be with me at the time." Radcliffe explained fluidly and with no hesitation.

"Mmmm." commented the young man, looking quizzical. "Funny how D.C.I. Rigby seemed to have come away with the impression that he had found a witness to the events of fifteen years ago. I wonder how that happened ?"

"No idea." still monosyllabic answers from Radcliffe.

"What's happened to the book of fake M.O.T. certificates that you took from Webber ?", a simple question in a simple form presented by the young counsel.

"It is subject to ongoing investigations by Suffolk constabulary", answered Radcliffe formally. "Oh, it's just my suspicious nature, I suppose" replied the defence counsel, "I thought for one moment that you were holding it as a lever to ensure Webbers evidence".

Radcliffe said nothing, but pursed his lips and looked dyspeptic.

"You have served in this area for twenty years, or so, haven't you Mr. Radcliffe ?", a statement more than a question from the defence counsel.

"Yes" answered Radcliffe, stiffly "Nineteen and a half years, almost to the day".

"Your service has a fair overlap time with the presence of the American Air Force in this area, does it not ?"

"Yes", Radcliffe returned to monosyllablism to give as little away as possible.

"You must have been aware of the 'leakage' of American goods, mainly cigarettes, from their base PB's into the surrounding civilian population ?"

Radcliffe could not have admitted not knowing about this, it was the open secret that separated locals from outsiders, so he simply said 'yes'.

"If my information is correct, the authorities, both British and American, were not interested in this trade, so long as the quantity of goods remained relatively small and no illegal goods were involved ?" asked the young man calmly.

As most members of the jury had probably taken advantage of this trade, he could not deny the basis of it.

"You are correct" said Radcliffe more stiffly than he intended.

"So, in your opinion mind, do you think that until the U.S. air force left, it was not uncommon to find locals smoking American made cigarettes ?" silkily, the defence counsel pressed the point in such a way that Radcliffe could not avoid agreeing with him, so he said simply "Yes".

"Now, Mr. Radcliffe, about some of your fellow workers at Ipswich police station," an unexpected change in the direction of questioning temporarily unsettled the D.C.I. "How well do you know the work of the I.T. team ?"

"Not well, I don't think anyone knows their work well, they haven't been with us too long, so we haven't got a great depth of experience", Radcliffe said, unwilling to be caught like Rigby had been by becoming loquacious.

"Your reserve is understandable. In your somewhat limited experience, do you trust their work?" At last, a seemingly reasonable question from the young counsel.

"They have always seemed to do a good and trustworthy job for me" was Radcliffes reply.

"This 'cleaning up' of the digital image sent from the Passport office, do you know what they did ? Do you know how they did it ?" enquired the defence counsel.

"To both questions, No. I don't know what they do and I don't know how they do it." was Radcliffes cautious reply.

"Do you still trust their work, not knowing what they do, or how they do it?" questioned the young man.

"Yes, quite simply, you have to let fellow professionals get on with their job and trust their work. No-one can be expected to know all the ins and outs of every job !" Radcliffe was sounding somewhat aggrieved by the attempted slur on his fellow workers.

"I apologise for any unintended demeaning of your I.T. team. I understand that you hold the abilities of your I.T. superintendent, 'The Hells' Angel', I believe you call her privately, in high esteme? Is that not so?" smooth as whipped cream, the question slid from the defence counsels' mouth.

Taken aback by hearing his private nickname for her used openly, Radcliffe just stuttered out a simple 'yes' to that question.

"So, past experience teaches you to trust the output from your I.T department ?" continued the young counsel.

Believing he had to show faith in his fellow workers at the Ipswich police station, Radcliffe answered "Unquestioned faith !".

At that definite comment, the prosecuting counsel tried to hide his shock of such an opening presented to the defence counsel, who didn't appear to register the approval, or show any desire to follow it up.

"Now, Mr. Radcliffe, about Dr. Tanner, your psychologist. I believe that you were instrumental in bringing his advice into this investigation ?"

"Yes, that is correct", a wary answer from the detective "I suggested that a psychological profile might be a useful aid in weighing the evidence against the accused."

It took only a few more questions to reveal that the Suffolk Constabulary had begun using psychological profiles at the behest of the American authorities, when Suffolk Polices' investigations seemed to concern American service people. According to Radcliffe, the use became so widespread that the Americans would act against their own service people, simply on the psychological evidence.

"How extraordinary !" was the young counsels' comment.

"So having experience of psychological profiling and its' uses, I suggested to D.C.I. Rigby that it might produce some useful information." concluded Radcliffe.

"Ah, but did it ?", once more the young counsel lunged in to the attack with a question.

"I thought the profile too vague, but D.C.I. Rigby readily accepted it" was the uncritical comment made by D.C.I. Radcliffe.

"Something about the character of ardent sportsmen appealed to him, I think" mused Radcliffe as much to himself as to the court, "I know the bit about sport being war without the bullets and the latent violence in sports seemed to be important."

"Does that mean that all sportsmen were suspected by D.C.I. Rigby ?" asked the defence counsel "Because many of the yuppy types in the City, that Caroline Meadowcroft seemed to prefer, were also keen sporting types, too."

"To my knowledge, that aspect of the profile was never tested any further" answered the detective.

"Indeed ? So the profile was read solely as it could apply to my client and no-one else" asked the counsel.

"Yes, I cannot recall anyone else being compared with the profile" Radcliffe was taken aback by having to answer such a direct question, especially when the counsel loudly commented "How unfair".

Radcliffe had little time to ponder the ramifications of that answer, as the young counsel told the judge that, at the present time, he had no more questions for D.C.I. Radcliffe, but would both D.C.I. Rigby and Radcliffe hold themselves ready for a possible return to the stand as defence witnesses.

"So ordered" said the judge and called for a thirty minute recess.

After the recess, the prosecution brought forward its' new witness, the one who would identify Meadowcroft as having been there, in Chilham St. Margarets, on the disputed days. As soon as the judge re-commenced the sitting, theatrically, the defence council told the court that they would present an indisputable witness, who would definitely identify Meadowcroft as having been seen in Britain at the time he was supposed to be in America. At the announcement, a general buzz ran around the court and it was only silenced when the council grandly declaimed the name of Max Webber. At the call of his name, Max Webber stood up and strode arrogantly to the witness box and was sworn in as he entered the box. There he stood, a young man in his early thirties, middle height & thinly built with a small, scraggy moustache. He had tried to dress in his best clothes to look 'the part' as the Prosecution counsel had suggested, but all he had achieved was to emphasize his lank, greasy hair, pale pock-marked skin and 'general street-trader' appearance. As he watched Webber saunter to the witness stand, the prosecution counsel heart sank & he thought that he would have to lead this witness very carefully to get his evidence without him antagonizing the jurors. At first, all seemed well, Webber confirmed his name and identity in a confident manner and answered the early questions really quite competently. It was when Webber had to give his evidence about seeing 'Dr. Jim', as he called him, that he began to lose the aura of belief.

With the basic facts confirmed, Webber began looking around the court to seek out D.C.I. Radcliffe before he would willingly answer any more questions. When he did, his answers were not confident and the details had to be coaxed out of him, so the impression sent to the jury was one of hesitation and not one of a witness confident in his story. Eventually, the prosecution had gleaned all the salient facts from the witness, but as a confused mass of data, which, had the prosecution counsel not known the story, would have made little sense. To ensure that the jury received the Prosecution version correctly, the counsel took Webber through his whole story again, only allowing Webber to answer 'yes' at appropriate times to confirm facts. When he was happy that the jurors had been told the story in a logical manner did the counsel thank Webber for his testimony, which he was sure "was a burden lifted from his heart", and tell the judge that he had no more questions for this witness. To the counsels' dismay, on hearing that said,

Webber tried to leave the stand, looking as if he wanted to leave not only the witness box, but the court too. Webber was prevented from flight by the clerk of the court, who waved him back into the witness box and was heard to say "not yet!' to him in a firm voice.

Knowing that Webbers' discomfort was increasing by the second, the young defence counsel delayed standing as long as he thought prudent, every second being employed to increased Webbers' unease. Eventually, he stood and seemingly sought to relax Webber by talking generally about the case and as Webber relaxed visibly, the counsel told him that a mans' freedom rested on his testimony.

"I don't know anything about that," Webber said "but I did see him, just like I said".

Talking quietly and unthreateningly to Webber, the defence counsel got him to confirm some of the salient details once more.

"You ain't catching me out. I know what I know" confirmed Webber.

"My job is simply to check the details of your story, so with your leave we'll begin" said the counsel.

Webber looked askance at the counsel, as he didn't fully understand what had just been said, but he pulled his shoulders back and attempted to look like a pillar of the community.

"After fifteen years, you remembered seeing and hearing Meadowcroft AND his car on the nights in question ?" said the young counsel incredulously.

"Yes, I've already said that" replied Webber petulantly.

"O.K., as your memory is so good at the moment, tell me about the car that you saw. What colour was it? Give me a general description of the car. Large or small? Noisy or quiet? Anything special about the shape of the car?" asked the young counsel, sounding increasingly interrogative.

"Well, er, it were beige coloured, with a fine, brown line down the side. Sort of big and quiet and looked like a wedge with a big hatch-back door" answered Webber without noticeable hesitation.

"I must say, your powers of observation are first-class, Mr. Webber" complimented the counsel, at which point Webber smirked, looking proud and very pleased with himself.

"Such an observant man as yourself cannot have failed to notice many other details, some of which I'm sure that you, yourself, haven't thought important, but really are", now the defence counsel began to play on Webbers' pride.

"You are sure of the colour of the car and the line upon its' side ?" asked the young counsel. "Yes, I can still remember them clearly after all these years."

Webber was feeling the most important person in the court. Meadowcroft, on the other hand was beginning to feel hunted, he had had a car fitting Webbers' description, a beige Austin Ambassador which he had hated. Frequently he had said that that car 'would be the death of me', a statement that now began to seem prophetic to him.

"I say, your eyes must be very good" commented the defence counsel.

"Country eyes be sharper'n townies' eyes" answered Webber, by now believing himself to be irreproachable.

"Yes, they must be" confirmed the Defence counsel "especially as you identified the colour accurately under sodium lighting !" continued the counsel. "Sodium lighting makes beige look to be a dirty brown colour and the brown stripe look black !" commented the young counsel.

"Er, well I knew the car an' I recognised it, so I know what colour it was" answered Webber. "Are you saying that you saw a car that LOOKED like the defendants' car, or are you saying that you saw the defendants' car?" questioned the defence counsel.

"'Twas the defendants car, right enough !" confirmed Webber, "I'm certain of that !"

"Your honour" said the defence counsel, turning to face the judge, "I would like to introduce, as evidence, information from the 'Pink Elephant Long Term Parking Co.', here given and attested under oath, that their records clearly show that my clients car was continuously parked with them and was serviced and valeted, from my clients' departure to America until his return over a month later. Registration particulars have been checked with the D.V.L.C. in Swansea and they confirm that the parked car was registered to my client at his High Wycombe address and that he held the registration of four motor-cycles simultaneously, but no other cars".

As the judge studied the documents put before him, he nodded in agreement and accepted them into evidence in the case.

At this point, the prosecution asked "May I ?" quite simply and was handed the document by the court clerk. Everyone had suddenly ignored Webber, who was left standing alone in the witness box and who was beginning increasingly to worry over his own future. Quickly, the prosecution counsel read through the document and his concern was plain to see, he checked the details once more, shook his mane of white hair and clasped his right hand to his brow.

"Mr. Webber, do you have anything to say about the evidence that you have just given? Don't forget, you are under oath!" asked the judge quietly, but in the court room it resounded like a clap of thunder. Aware that he was now, truly, the focus of every eye, Webber tried to compose himself and organise a realistic sounding excuse. There was no way that he could tell the truth about Radcliffe and Rigby suggesting the 'memories' to him, he knew that that approach would destroy him quicker than a snow flake vanishes in the flame. He had to think of a plausible excuse and he had to think of it NOW! Neither tactical nor strategic thinking was Webbers' strong suite, what he lacked in them, was overcompensated by instinct.

Automatically, he began to say "Eer, well, I was so sure that I saw Dr. Jim at the cottage just before his missus went missing, but it might have been another time . . . ."

"Are you admitting that you are mistaken ?" thundered the young counsel, most out of character. "Er, yes, I must be" muttered Webber, looking around and catching Radcliffes' eye, he gave a shrug hardly noticeable if you weren't looking for it.

"I order that this witness be discharged. He has shown his memory to be faulty and thus unreliable. I hereby instruct the jury totally to disregard this mans' evidence" as he said this, the judge was looking harshly at Webber and he then transferred his gaze to the prosecution Counsel. "Mr. Henty, you might wish to contemplate the validity of your case. Much of your evidence appears circumstantial and your most important witness has just been shown to be deeply flawed. Your other witnesses had better be sound, otherwise I will order your case confounded and this case be dismissed. Nothing that I have yet heard has convinced me of any degree of guilt on the accused part".

"Yes, you honour", the prosecution counsel was no longer demonstrative, had he been so he would have attacked Webber.

"Mr. Webber" said the judge looking at the witness "You took an oath to tell the truth when you entered the witness box in this court. Only your prompt retraction has saved you from a charge of perjury.

Leave the witness box now, you will give no further evidence in my court. Mr. Henty, I am prepared to call a recess in this case to allow you time to replan your case, before you re-present any more witnesses, do you wish such a recess ?".

"Yes, my Lord".

Chapter 10

Day 3 of the prosecution

Friday morning dawned dull and overcast, a miserable wind swept through the streets of Ipswich blowing yesterdays' wet newspapers along in leaping, circular spirals, which collapsed as quickly as they had arisen. As everyone went to the court, the weather affected them all, a harbinger of winter to come and the unpleasantness of the days ahead. Everyone, that is, bar the defendant. His cell beneath the court house was warm and snug and not for him the cold, dank morning air. He was bodily comfortable, if mentally uncomfortable. That MaxWebber had been apparently so willing to bear false witness against him had profoundly unsettled him and his mind railed at the injustice of it all. He hadn't killed Caroline, although he could have done so and maybe would have done so, had she not already been dead when he got there. He didn't know who had, if anyone, but it certainly wasn't him and now acquaintances, if not friends, were seemingly happy enough to lie in court. Did they all hate him that much? For what?

More than ever, he realised that for the first time since childhood, he was totally reliant upon the ability of someone else. He had no possible role to play in his immediate future, all he was was the target of the lies and hatred, totally exposed in court to everyones' contempt. As he entered the court room, he was as miserable as every-one else, but for them the weather could brighten, for him all that the future promised was extended monotony as the legal mill ground ever onwards. As he took his seat in the accuseds box, all he could concentrate on was endurance, physical and mental, and how long his meagre stock of both would last.

At last, the court assembled, the judge arrived and took his seat, then asked the prosecuting counsel if he were ready to continue the case for the prosecution.

"Yes, My Lord, we will continue" was all Henty said, the legal niceties overwhelming his theatrical presumptions.

"Call your next witness, then" instructed the judge who sat back, mentally to adjudicate on the various statements about to be presented.

Next prosecution witness called was Darren, the ex Under-Sexton from the Holy Trinity church in Higham Green, where Caroline Meadowcrofts skeleton had been found. Mr. Henty wasted no time at all establishing the basic facts as pertained to this case. Once again, the known two day open period of the grave was re-confirmed, as were other details discovered about the grave. All details were clear and concise, even Henty admitted that much. Some details of the grave were down to the Sexton of that time, Josh, who had died some years before. Where he could not definitely tell why something had been done, Darren just said that he acted under Joshs' instructions. Little of any value was gleaned from Darrens' evidence, other than to re-inforce that the burial of Caroline Meadowcroft must have occurred on one of only two possible nights. Seeking to maximize the value of the confirmation of the two day time window, the Prosecuting counsel reminded the members of the jury that near mid-summer (when the grave had been open), dusk came at 9.10 p.m. and dawn at 5.15 a.m. Whoever had interred Caroline Meadowcroft had worked to a meticulous plan. Here he looked directly at the defendant, then continued 'And had probably trained to be able to undertake the task in such a short time'. "However", he continued "that works on the assumption that it was all done over one night. Killing one night and burying the second means that less risk would be taken and the job more easily finished, it would also allow for an appropriate grave to be located."

Darren couldn't add any information to that scenario and so Henty concluded the prosecution questions and passed over to young defence counsel.

"How did you get the job as under Sexton ?", he asked Darren.

"Job creation scheme" answered Darren simply.

"Do you know why you were selected for the under-Sextons' job ?" he asked, in a puzzled manner.

"I wanted to be a gardener and work in open air and that was the nearest job they had to my choice" responded Darren, quite honestly.

"How old were you then ?", another straight forward question from the Defence counsel. "Seventeen", another straight forward reply from Darren.

"Didn't you get bored ?" asked the defence counsel, "Did you smoke on the job ?" he continued. "Old Josh only allowed me to smoke in our shed," was the answer.

"You were seventeen then, surely you didn't do everything that Josh told you to do, did you ?", the young counsel appealed to Darrens' youthful vanity.

"No, I used to smoke were I wanted to, when I wanted to" answered Darren "Old Josh didn't like it much sometimes, all he could do was to scare me when we was in the crypt, which he did frequently !"

"Did Josh smoke at all ?" asked the young counsel.

"Yes, that's what was unfair, he smoked in the crypt, in a new grave, all over, but he wouldn't let me" was the reply.

"Do you know why, were you ever given a reason ?" a serious look now on the defence counsels' face.

"He always smoked roll-ups," at this a questioning look came from the counsel "I mean he always rolled his own cigarettes and evil smelling things they were, too. He always said that his cigarette stubs rotted down, but that filter tips wouldn't and it would be disrespectful to the dead to leave a filter tip in a grave". Darren's memories were in full flow now, he remembered things that he hadn't thought of for years.

"So, Josh rolled his own and you bought filter tipped cigarettes?", the young counsel was looking for a little confirmation.

"Yes" commented Darren.

"What cigarettes did you buy, did you have a favourite or a regular brand ?" conversationally, now, from the young counsel.

"I must have tried all the filter tipped brands, I didn't like the continental brands, too strong. I did like the American cigarettes that we could sometimes get cheap, but I would smoke anything as a rule" Darren was remembering his youth easily now.

"Most smokers give their friend a cigarette from time to time. Did you and Josh do that ?" said the young counsel continuing their conversation.

"Only once. Josh's roll-ups were too strong for me, it nearly choked me. Mind you Josh wasn't backwards at coming forward to have one of mine! He knew that I'd never ask for one of his, so he was on a safe wicket there!" replied the day-dreaming Darren.

"Can you remember if Josh borrowed a cigarette from you that day that he inspected the Bradley grave ?" once more a conversation question from the defence counsel.

"No. Sorry, can't remember" was Darrens reply.

"But it is possible that Josh that would beg a cigarette, isn't it?" continued the young Counsel.

"Yes, Josh was always happy to smoke somebody elses' cigarettes" answered Darren.

Darren was released as a witness and was immediately replaced by Dr. Tanner, the psychologist. All the opening questions to him from the Prosecuting counsel were to establish the extent of his relative experience working with the police service. Briefly, and being lead by the counsel, he outlined the important points of a number of cases where his psychological profiling had been a major factor in identifying the criminal. That all the cases identified concerned the U.S. forces until so recently based near Ipswich, could have been construed as support for American detective methods, was carefully avoided. What was presented by the prosecution was the image of a psychologist who had a particular gift for that work and that that psychologist was Dr. Tanner.

Coming to the present case, Dr. Tanner confessed that the killers' psychological profile probably wouldn't fit the perpetrator, increasing maturity would have markedly affected some aspects, but fifteen years ago the profile would have been a closer fit. As he described the character traits, both he and the prosecution counsel took pains to emphasize the match with that of the defendant. It was only when it came to the stated 'possibility of later break down' did Dr. Tanner comment that he knew of no breakdown event in the defendants past and nothing appeared in his medical records that could be taken as a breakdown.

When asked "What effect would that lack of breakdown have on the criminals' personality", he answered that he would expect the perpetrators' psyche to be twisted up, with the result that the personality would be highly unstable and potentially very violent.

Looking directly at the accused, the prosecution pointed to him and asked if this twisted psyche could result in apparent dis-orientation, depression and apathy.

"Yes" was the answer "That could be one of many possible scenarios, but the dis-orientation would be more real than apparent".

"So, we could be looking at some-one fitting your profile fifteen years ago and the result today?" asked the counsel theatrically throwing his arms around.

"Yes, we could" was Tanners answer.

"My Lud, I have no more questions for this witness" said Henty, looking long and hard at Meadowcroft as he turned to take his seat.

"Good, Mr. Henty, I think that this is an appropriate point at which to recess for lunch" said the judge looking at his watch. "We shall re-convene promptly at two p.m., when the defence will examine this witness. Dr. Tanner, please remember that you are still under oath and I charge you not to speak with anyone about this case during recess".

As the judge signaled for the defence questions to begin, the young defence counsel stood in response and began his questioning of the psychologist.

"Dr. Tanner, some time ago, you made a statement that some, or many, of the psychological details you attributed to the perpetrator could be attached to many of your colleagues. Do you still hold to that opinion?" no-one could ever accuse the young counsel of being indirect in his questions.

"That comment was made in a light-hearted manner but, yes, I still hold to that comment in the same manner" Dr. Tanner refused to be shaken by the direct attack policy.

"In what way would those comments be applicable to your colleagues ?", the defence counsel persisted.

"I have many colleagues who seem permanently to live in the University sports' hall. They are competitive in both sport and in getting research funding. To get research funding, they are secretive and unemotionally plan ahead. In those ways they have similar psychological profiles to the perpetrator, but they are not wife killers!" Dr. Tanner was adamant on that point.

"We have no proof yet that wife killing actually occurred" corrected the young counsel "That comment must be your own supposition, Dr. Tanner, but are you saying that many people in my clients profession share those profile similarities? Does that not make them very general in nature and therefore equally un-specific ?" as always, the young counsel went straight to the point.

"Yes and No" replied Tanner. "Yes, that they are general and No not to the degree needed to kill ones partner."

"Do you mean Yes, we all have them and No not to the extent of planning murder ?" asked the defence counsel wanting clarification.

"Quite" was all Tanner said.

"So, some details in your profile are general in nature, whilst others are specific and the occurrence of both sets together gives the specific, personalized profile of the perpetrator ?" more probing now from the defence counsel.

"Yes, and it is exactly this combination, and no other, that defines the killer" explained Tanner. "Have you psychologically tested my client to see if he measures up to your standards ?" enquired the defence counsel.

"No, but a review of the police records, attested by witnesses over a fifteen year time scale, give the character depth. If you like, it has been the time scale over which these characteristics have been pronounced that demonstrate their strength" explained Tanner.

"You are quite happy that the accused adequately fits your profile" enquired the young counsel. "Yes" answered Dr. Tanner.

At that answer, the young counsel was dumbfounded and had no more questions to ask. He had wanted to take the psychological profile apart piece by piece, but Tanners' assurance and equanimity on the stand had sunk his hope of casting doubts on Tanners' evidence. Instead, all he could do was to turn to the judge and say "No more questions, my lord" and watch as Tanner was thanked for his expert evidence by the judge and released from his role as a witness.

Finally, the prosecution called Carolines' sister and Jims' ex-sister-in-law, Shirley, to the witness stand. Jim Meadowcroft found himself leaning forward and looking intently at Shirley and thinking 'What has she got to say ? She has said nothing good about me all the time I knew her and her husband.'

What, indeed ? As Shirley was sworn in and went through the opening preliminaries, Meadowcroft was concentrating harder and harder to her evidence, leaning further and further forward on his seat. Shirley admitted that she had known that Caroline was having numerous affairs, mainly with men that she had met at, or knew through, her work in the City and that Caroline had used the cottage ('Aunty Gins") in Chilham St. Margarets' as the general rendez-vous with her men friends. It took no hard questioning to be told that Caroline had said on numerous occasions that she expected Jim (her husband) to do something 'about it'. Shirley also said that Jims' frequent and sometimes lengthy stays abroad ('He said he was working, but he never produced anything that he'd done!') had been the cause of Carolines infidelities. Caroline was reported, by Shirley, to have told Jim frequently to 'clear-off for good for all the use he was as a husband'. Jim listened intently and thought to himself, 'I never heard her say any of that to me!'

Jim, according to Shirley, had threatened to 'get rid of Caroline' a few times. At this point, the judge intervened and said that everything that he had heard, so far, was merely hearsay and was not evidence that the jury should be concerned with.

"Did you", asked the judge trying to sound like a kindly old man "ever hear any of these comments yourself from the defendants' mouth?"

"Yes, Sir," answered Shirley," When they came over to us for the weekend, I heard them arguing once or twice and he (at this point, Shirley pointed directly at the defendant) said that 'he would get rid of her' and 'sort her out for good an' all'."

"Thank you" said the judge kindly "that evidence is acceptable".

As the prosecution counsel probed deeper, Shirley's venom got more and more poisonous. For her to have heard all the things she was saying she had heard, Shirley would have had to live with them full time, but she hadn't. Once Jims' character was truly blackened, Shirley seemed to run out of things to say and, simultaneously, the prosecuting counsel seemed to run out of questions.

Before the defence counsel began to ask questions of Shirley, the judge suggested a half hour recess. Publicly, he said it was for the jurors to get their thoughts together, but privately it was for him to relieve himself and have a cup of tea in chambers, where he could appreciate it and relax in private for a few moments. Thirty minutes later, the judge once more signaled the young man to begin asking questions. Initially surprised at Shirleys' uncompromising recollections, the defence counsel had spent all the recess talking with his client. Apart from some general comments, Jim had not been able to give unambiguous answers to Shirleys' observations, but the counsel had said that he wanted to try to destroy Shirleys' validity completely and to give the lie totally to her comments. All Jim could say was that he knew that Shirley and Caroline had spent weekends in each others company both at the cottage and at various functions, but that now, at this remove, he couldn't remember details.

"Don't worry, that's good enough ! If you can't remember detailed dates and times, then it's odds on that she can't either!" commented the young counsel, grinning as he thought of the pleasure of stirring Shirleys' past for every-one else to hear.

When the recess ended, Shirley was still in the witness box and still looked as prim and proper as before, an attractive enough woman from whom moral rectitude seemed to flow. Once more, the young counsel began by seemingly talking to her in a diffident sort of way and asking questions with simple and obvious answers. As soon as Shirley had dropped her guard sufficiently, the defence counsel apologized, saying that his next question may sound a little impertinent, but it wasn't meant to be so. (In fact it was meant to be completely impertinent and to unsettle her). When he asked how many weekends she had spent at the cottage with Caroline, Shirley answered in hazy terms, 'Yes, she had spent some weekends with her sister. They had both used it as a retreat'.

"Other than your sister, were there ever any men there that were neither your, nor your sisters', husband ?"

Shirley gasped as if she had been hit in the stomach and stepped back, then trying to stand on her dignity and fend off the implication of the question. She fluttered her hands and stuttered an answer, but before she had finished, the defence counsel said that if necessary he could prove that there had been a number of such clandestine weekend meetings. Shirley looked around the court, into the spectators area to seek out Dick, her husband, she found him, locked eyes with him, only to find him glaring furiously at her. No comfort there! In desperation, she burst into tears, only to be told by the young counsel that he knew that she and her sister had had numerous liaisons with many men during these so-called week-end 'retreats' to the cottage.

Shirley blurted out through the tears "It was all Carolines idea, I just went to see what she was doing".

"THAT, I would have thought, was quite obvious !" answered the counsel, almost shouting.

In the spectator area at the back of the court, Dick stood up and pushed his way to the exit and left. As the tears subsided, Shirley felt exposed, she looked for Dick, but couldn't find him, then looked pleadingly at the Defence counsel, begging, with her eyes, not to be asked any more questions.

To no avail, after apparently consulting his notes, he continued "In many ways, you acted as your sisters' pimp, did you not?"

This brought a fresh outburst of tears and an admission that she had only tried to help her sister. "Strange how helping your sister to cheat on her husband should seem so trivial a point that you didn't mention it before recess. I can now see how you talked so much with your sister that you knew all about my clients feelings for her. Or were those comments taken completely out of context, just to impress the jury ? They know now the true background to those comments !", thus saying the counsel waved her away and the judge, still trying to be a kindly old man, leaned over to her and told her she could leave the court.

Shirley walked across the open court area, straight up the aisle and out of the rear door followed by her solicitor and reporters from the local newspaper, who scented a juicy sex scandal to investigate and report on, to increase readership.

"It's early, but not too early to suspend this hearing until Monday morning at ten a.m." said the judge and then turning to the jury reminded them not to talk about the case to anyone.

After that, he stood up and entered his chambers by the door behind his seat.

Chapter 11

Beginnings of a defence

Monday morning dawned bright and clear, one of those ideal days that are always talked about and remembered in Britain, but so rarely experienced. Today, the young counsel would begin his defence of Jim Meadowcroft in an attempt, as he saw it, to destroy completely the circumstantial case which was all that the crown could mount against his client. He had worked out his two opening witnesses, the first would be Meadowcrofts' long time G.P., whilst the second would be Rebecca Meadowcroft, Jims' second wife, Becky. After the media coverage of the first day, the crowd was almost non-existent and the young counsel walked into the robing room without attracting attention. He walked into his place in court and sat at the desk whilst all the other, more minor functionaries, of both prosecution and defence teams took their appointed places. Precisely at ten a.m., the Court Usher called the proceedings to order and the judge entered the court and took his seat. As soon as he was comfortable, the judge called upon the defence counsel to begin presenting his case for the defence.

Defence Counsel stood, said "If it please your Lordship" and then began to outline the defence case and how he would show 'Unequivocally' that the prosecution case was totally without foundation. Their case rested on no more than a hypothetical two-day gap in his clients' Florida trip when no witnesses could actually be found to support him. He told the jury that the prosecution case was totally circumstantial, unsupported by any forensic evidence at all, only by the personal

"If I might be allowed to complete my answer ?" at this the prosecution nodded "Even a trained psychiatrist cannot know every type of breakdown as each breakdown is unique to every individual, although every form has some common factors."

"Ah, so you admit that you do not know the symptoms of every type of breakdown? And are you still confident that the accused did not suffer any type of breakdown?" a riposte from the prosecution, who was going in for the kill.

"He showed no symptoms related to any mental unbalance at any time that I met him" replied the doctor, keen to get away from this verbal battle.

"From which you assume that he never had a breakdown ?" calmly asked by the prosecuting counsel.

"Yes", a monosyllabic reply from the G.P.

"You are aware that even short periods of unhappiness, not even as deep as depression, can be indicators of a minor breakdown. And, it all depends on the personality of the individual involved ?" questioned the prosecuting counsel theatrically.

"Yes", another monosyllabic answer from the medic.

"Are you trying to tell this court that you never saw the accused unhappy at any time ?", now the prosecution was turning the knife.

"No" replied the doctor "but I . . ."

"Thank you doctor, that is all" theatrically interrupted the counsel.

After the doctor had been discharged as a witness and left the stand, the defence counsel called their next witness, who was Becky, the defendants' wife. As she walked to the witness stand, the eyes of all the men in court were upon her, but she gave no sign of either knowing or caring. After the oath had been administered, she took her place in the witness box, cool, calm and composed and looked about her. As the young counsel stood up to begin his examination of her evidence, she looked at him and a slight, happy smile spread on her face, which caused the young man to catch his breath. 'I know her', he thought, 'yet that look gives me pleasure!' Immediately afterwards, he caught himself thinking 'What a woman!', he coughed to bring his attention back and thought, once more to himself, how sexist his thoughts were when really he believed in equality.

"Mrs. Meadowcroft" he began, studiously ignoring Beckys' look at him, "Please tell the court the facts, as far as you are aware of them, of the injury the defendant suffered in Florida in 1983".

"I actually spoke Dr. Meadowcroft before I met him" she said evenly "I was the secretary to Dr. Levy in Orlando when he phoned to talk to Dr. Levy about his injury. Dr. Levy talked to him for a while, then came out of his office to book an appointment for Dr. Meadowcroft on the Thursday morning. I then saw Dr. Meadowcroft when he came to the practice for his appointment and we talked. He invited me to go out to his research site on the coast at the week-ends to top-up my tan".

That must have been nice for him thought the young counsel, but asked, in fact "What do you know about any medication that Dr. Levy prescribed for him?"

"I know that he was prescribed a common anti-inflammatory pill when he left the practice that second visit, because he had to ask me where he could get the medicine." was Becky's answer. "Do you know if he persisted I taking the medication?" was the next question asked by the defence counsel.

"I believe so, when I visited his working site, every Friday I took him a weeks' worth of prescribed pills" Becky stated simply.

"So, for some weeks afterwards, he continued to take the prescribed medication ?" asked the defence counsel, just to drive the point home.

"Yes" said Becky.

"No further questions" the young counsel told the judge, who looked at the clock before inviting the prosecution counsel to begin his questioning.

There was no doubt that the prosecution counsel was a little jealous of Becky, just sitting there, looking earnest, she distracted the jurys' attention from him.

"Mrs. Rebecca Meadowcroft", he said with a flourish," I have but one question for you. You say you took the defendant his medication each week when you visited the research site", here Becky gave a slight nod in acknowledgment. "Yes? Good, now the single question. Do you know beyond any shadow of a doubt that he took the medicine as directed and didn't simply throw away the pills to make it appear as if he were taking them?"

"I saw him take some of the pills that I gave him sometimes" answered Becky calmly.

"You can't be absolutely sure that he took all the medicine that he was prescribed, can you?" demanded the prosecution counsel, attempting to dominate Becky by the force of his personality. "He took some, but I can't be sure he took them all" Becky answered sweetly.

"So, for all you know he might have been faking that injury ?", a declamation of fact by the counsel.

Smiling sweetly, Becky said "I had chance to try him out, don't forget, and he wasn't faking any injury that I could see".

Defeated by her obvious charm, the prosecution counsel simply said "No more questions" and the judge released Becky as a witness. Short as it had been, he had enjoyed Becky being nearby his solitary seat, he couldn't re-call her, instead he just called a two hour lunch recess.

After the lunch recess, when the trial re-started, the young defence counsel called his next witness, who was Stacey, the private investigator that Becky had hired. After being sworn-in, Stacey was asked about her investigations on behalf of Becky Meadowcroft. Webber's 'identification' of the car had been shown false by Staceys' investigation of the long-term parking company close to Heathrow. Also, the possible relationship between Radcliffe and Webber concerning the supply of fake M.O.T. certificates had been exposed by her & had lead the young counsel to question the very veracity of Radcliffes' statements. Now, she started on D.C.I. Rigby's attachment to the case, lead by the questioning of the defence counsel.

"Your investigative operations are based in High Wycombe ?" asked the young counsel.

"No, not actually IN Wycombe, but a few miles outside in a small village called Bledlow Ridge, although most of my work is in and around High Wycombe", Stacey replied, being as literally accurate as she could be.

"Even so, you know, or are known to, a number of police officers in the High Wycombe area, are you not?", the young counsel was attempting to lay a trail for the jury to follow.

"Yes" replied Stacey, "I served in the police force with some of them, before I went free-lance". "Using your personal contacts with serving officers, what did you discover about D.C.I. Rigbys' initial handling of the case against my client?" requested the counsel.

"D.C.I. Rigby was assigned initially to this case when he first joined the High Wycombe police as a detective constable straight out of training school. He was convinced that the defendant" and here

Stacey indicated the accused "had murdered his wife and wanted to prove it. His initial investigations came to nought on the murder, although he produced some success in arresting drug offenders. He never ignored any possible clue and assiduously collected anything he could find about the defendant." continued Stacey.

"So, D.C.I. Rigby seemed fixated by the defendant and his missing wife ?" asked the young man. "Yes, so much so that Rigby kept a photograph of Caroline Meadowcroft pinned to his office wall, next to one of his dead sister" answered Stacey.

"Remarkable" said the defence counsel. "Do you mean to tell that court that D.C.I. Rigby has had a photograph of the deceased on his office WALL for fifteen years ?"

"Yes, there are two photographs on his office wall, one of Caroline Meadowcroft alongside one of his dead sister, unless you know which is which, it is possible to confuse them. Both women looked so alike. I have signed witness statements from fellow police officers and even the office cleaners, which will substantiate the identities of both women in the photo's and the length of time that the photographs have been there." said Stacey.

"So, it seems as if D.C.I. Rigby was a fan of Caroline Meadowcroft ?" asked the young counsel questioningly.

"No, probably not, the Meadowcroft photo only appeared after Detective Constable Rigby began investigating her disappearance. That of his sister preceded the Meadowcroft one and appeared soon after she was killed during an attempted rape, the offender was apprehended and convicted. And no, before you ask, it was not the defendant in this case" Stacey completed her statement to answer everyones' unasked question.

"Ah, so we have a photograph of the deceased in this case kept alongside one of the detectives' murdered sister, both women looking alike, kept on the office wall of the initiating detective in this case, for fifteen years. Is that what you are saying?" asked the defence counsel.

"Yes", replied Stacey quite simply.

"Thank you, can I now move onto other evidence that you have uncovered ?" asked the defence counsel. "Can you shed any light on the fact that American Air Force personnel sold cheap American cigarettes in this area, that they had bought from their P.B. ?" asked the defence counsel.

"Yes. For many years, sales of goods from the American P.B's were known to be happening around all U.S. airbases in the U.K. Generally, the goods involved were cigarettes, drink and petrol, all of which found their way onto a sort of 'grey' market in the U.K., close to the airbases. It was one of the worst kept 'secrets' of all time" replied Stacey.

"So, U.S. goods were quite freely available in the vicinity of U.S. airbases for many years ?" commented the young counsel.

"Yes, the practice dates from the war-time years and was so established that it became part of the scene" responded Stacey, wondering what direction this questioning was taking.

"Thank you." said the counsel and then continued "What do you know about Caroline Meadowcrofts' contacts with American service personnel?"

"Once more, that is an open secret, I have not been able to talk to any of her American friends, as they have all returned to the 'States, but locally, around Chilham St. Margarets, that is, she and her sister were widely known to spend weekends with American Service personnel, openly, at her cottage there. I understand that this is not new information to the court." said Stacey.

"No, it is not, but it is evidence that, I think, stands re-stating" commented the defence counsel, then to the judge, "I have no more evidence for this witness".

With an exaggerated flourish, Henty, the prosecution counsel stood up. "You have twice talked of things that are, as you so calmly put it, 'open secrets'. I refer, of course, to the availability of American P.B. stock goods on sale in the U.K. and of the 'interactions, shall we call them ?, between Caroline Meadowcroft and her sister with U.S. service personnel at the Chilham St. Margaret cottage"

Henty was trying to rework old evidence.

"Yes" commented Stacey quite calmly.

"What grounds do you have for making such outrageous accusations ?" asked the prosecution counsel in a tired voice.

"All the locals around U.S. airbases, including Ipswich where we are now, have some experience or knowledge of the situation that existed up to a few years ago, before the U.S. forces left. For them, 'Sergeant Bilko' was not a fictional character, but a real statement of what they saw happening almost daily. As to the mores of Caroline Meadowcroft and her sister, the older locals in Chilham St. Margarets, who can remember back fifteen years, will confirm my evidence" Stacey sounded offended as she answered the question.

"Yes, Yes" replied Henty, then turning to the judge said "M'lud, I have no more questions for this witness".

After Stacey had left the witness stand, the judge quite openly looked at the clock on the wall to his right and declared a thirty minute recess before any more witnesses could be called.

When the court re-convened after the post lunch recess, the young counsel recalled the forensic pathologist, in reality virtually working from a script supplied to him by Stacey, as yet another result of her unofficial investigations. As soon as the pathologist had taken the witness stand, the young counsel began by asking the pathologists' opinion on the original passport photograph that had been supplied by the Passport Office. He had acknowledged that the proof of identity via the passport photograph was the most directly damning evidence against the accused, so he had exercised his right to obtain copies of both the original print-out and the 'cleaned up' version. One of these he gave to the pathologist, it was the unmodified print-out that Rigby had been so dismayed at.

"May I have your comments on the photograph in front of you vis-a-vis positive identification of a suspect ?", the young counsel asked.

"Assuming that this is the best print that can be found . . . ."

"It is", assured the defence counsel.

"Then it is virtually useless for identification purposes" continued the pathologist.

"Are you saying that you could not get sufficient information from that print to prove identification ?" asked the young counsel.

"Personally speaking, I wouldn't trust any measured data from this photograph, it is all too blurred and dark. Because of the darkness of this photograph, the accurate measurement of the relative locations of the eyes, nose and mouth would be impossible. There would be just too much margin for error" opined the pathologist.

Passing the pathologist another print, the defence counsel asked similar questions about its' usefulness for identity purposes as he had for the first one. "Oh, much, much better. All the important measurements could be easily and unambiguously made from this one!" the pathologist answered quickly.

"Would you be happy with a facial match, made by detailed measurements such as you have mentioned, taken from this print?" probed the young counsel.

In answer, he received an unequivocal "Yes" from the pathologist.

"If the dimensions matched, I would not question the identification", answered the pathologist readily.

"How would you get from the first print, which you said was useless for identification purposes, to the second, which you infer is ideal ?" asked the young counsel.

"These are both digital images, computer images, and the lack of clarity of the first exists as random digital 'noise' almost. They could be cleaned up by using a computer programme to 'remove' the digital noise, before being reprinted." Now the pathologist was almost lecturing the young counsel.

"Thank you. Is there any other way to clean up such images?" a question for the sake of a question, more to keep the counsel in the questioning sequence than for information.

"Yes, there are any number of ways, although they all come down to removing the spurious noise by comparison to a 'clean' image. Each I.T. section will have a favourite method that it knows and trusts and has experience with." It was obvious that the pathologist was happy with these bits of knowledge.

"Thank you for your expert evidence" said the young counsel, then as an after thought "Is there anything else that you can say about the two photographs?"

At this, the pathologist picked up a print in each hand and looked from one to the other rapidly at first, then more slowly, peering at various parts of print and holding them close together to cross compare each with the other.

"Yes", finally answered the pathologist, "I doubt that they are the same person, they are very similar, but not the same."

"What did you say ?" demanded the young counsel.

"These two photographs are not of the same person, they are very similar, but not identical. Your second print is not a cleaned up version of the first that you gave me, it has been changed in some subtle way that I am not sure of at the moment, but it has been changed" accurately and deliberately, the pathologist made her point clear.

"Are you saying that anyone identified by dimensional analysis of that second print is NOT the person in the first print?" asked the young counsel excitedly.

"Yes, with a high degree of probability, you see there are some minor details which are different between the two prints. For instance . . . .", before the answer could be completed, the defence counsel asked "How high a degree of probability ?"

"Oh, I would say about 50-60 % at least" replied the pathologist "you see, there are these details . . . ."

"Different faces?" questioned the young counsel once more, "you say that they are different faces in the prints that you have ?"

"Yes, with a high degree of probability, which means probably different people" answered the pathologist didactically.

"How can you be so sure ?", the defence counsel was really gripped now.

"There are small features, which are not too clear on the first face and not there at all, on the second. There's also something to do with the way the corners of the eyes and ears align on one and differently on the other. Marginal differences, minor differences which are easily overlooked. But without spending more time and doing actual measurements, a number of hours actually, it is difficult to prove unambiguously" continued the pathologist.

"Now you are saying that more work is needed to validate your statement ?" asked the defence counsel dismayed.

"Yes, more to prove it to someone else, but for me, I'm quite satisfied" answered the pathologist. "How can that be ?", the defence counsel was becoming desperate now.

"Well, I've had so much experience looking at identity photographs of faces and skulls that as I compare two photographs side by side, I scan rapidly between them, concentrating on various minor features. It's my experience of comparing two faces very closely indeed and doing that for the last twenty odd years that I'm using here. It takes a long time to validate this experience, but it has never yet been proven wrong "concluded the pathologist.

"I accept that your statement is based on personal experience, but how could such an error have been made ?" enquired the young counsel.

"Very few people are as experienced as I am at comparing faces, most experienced pathologists will be, I'm nothing special. We are more experienced at comparing faces than policemen, for I guess that's what you're driving at?" said the pathologist.

A brief nod came from the young counsel.

Continuing, the pathologist said "Policemen are very good at identifying a face from a picture, but poor at critically comparing the face with the picture. We can't be poor, as frequently the identity of the dead rests with us, so it becomes second nature to look for differences, police are trained to look for similarities. So, I say the two faces are almost certainly not the same and then need time to prove my judgment. I hope that explains it sufficiently for you ? Oh, and to answer your subsidiary question, the similarity could be an artifact from the process used to digitally clean-up the first print to make the second!" smilingly, the pathologist concluded the lecture knowing that this one, at least, had been understood and appreciated.

"My lord" cried the young counsel "May I move that these prints be examined by the pathologist in order either to validate or repudiate their similarity. My clients freedom may well stand upon that crucial piece of evidence".

"I so order that these two prints be closely examined for differences by a forensic pathologist in the pay of this court. Until this evidence is finally available, I rule that identification by means of photographic evidence is not yet proven. Why the police did not, as a matter of course, undertake this, I cannot imagine. I bring this court to recess and to re-convene tomorrow morning"

With those words, the judge ended the fourth day of the trial, the first day which had seen a beam of light shine in the defences' case.

Chapter 12

Differences in the latter days

Once the clerk of the court had called the court to order and the judge had taken his seat, the defence counsel submitted new evidence, the result of the pathologists' examination of the two prints. A copy was presented to Mr. Henty, the prosecuting counsel, as soon as the judge allowed the submission and the judge asked if Henty wanted an immediate recess to allow him to study the document. Henty willingly accepted the recess, as his brief review of the reports' conclusions were deeply disturbing. Court was put into recess until after lunch, which was brought forward to mid-day, with the court to reconvene at 1 p.m.

During the two and a half hours available to him, Henty read and re-read the report and tried to contact the C.P.S. Being close to lunch time, the London bound staff of the C.P.S. were taking advantage of a warm, sunny day by leaving early for lunch in one of the parks or sitting in a pavement cafe, basking in the warm sun-shine. Once he had fully digested the contents and implications of the report, Henty had sent a copy of the report by fax to the C.P.S. case officer and scrawled 'Extremely Urgent, for your eyes only'. It was the second part of the message that ensured that the report was put centrally on the case officers desk, for his attention when he returned from lunch. It was the second part of the message that also ensured no-one else read the contents of the report and thus could appreciate the true nature of the emergency Henty faced in Ipswich. As the time for the court to reconvene came closer and Henty had received no direction from

average face image, Jo was quite open and said that she took a number of photographic images off Radcliffes' desk and then selected the one dimensionally most close to the subject photograph.

"Who were these people, whose faces you used ?" asked the young counsel.

"I deliberately didn't ask, nor read the names where available, to prevent bias creeping in," replied Jo truthfully "I just helped myself to a number of photographs from the collection on D.C.I. Radcliffes' desk and used the best."

"Is that the usual procedure ?" asked the young counsel.

"This work, by its' very nature, is unusual. There is no usual procedure to my knowledge. I just did the most obvious thing" answered Jo.

"Why ?" the young defence counsel asked.

"There was a question of speed involved and as most detectives have photographs from a number of cases available, I felt sure that I would get a random face selection" replied Jo.

"But both Radcliffe and Rigby were working on only 1 case at that time, this case !" retorted the young counsel, "Your photographic choice was anything BUT random, all those people had something to do with this case !"

"Oh my God," said Jo, clutching at her mouth, "are you saying I might have used a photograph of Dr. Meadowcroft accidentally?"

"As I see it, there is a very distinct possibility" the young counsel said, in a quite straightforward way. "Do you know the accused ?", now the young defence counsel attacked from a different direction.

"Yes, he taught at the University that I attended, but not in the same department" said Jo, fighting back the tears.

"How long have you known Dr. Meadowcroft ?" boring in for the kill he felt was there, the young counsel now began to sound waspish.

"I was there six years ago and graduated after three, so I would have known him vaguely from '92 to 95" answered Jo quietly.

"Did you see a face that you recognized in your 'random' pile", now the young man was prodding Jo's conscience.

"Yes, one I knew and that WASN'T Dr. Meadowcroft and one other that I haven't been able to place, so it could be anyone. You see so many faces in my job" Jo. replied cautiously.

"Are you sure that you would recognize a photograph of Dr. Meadowcroft taken in 1982 or '83?" asked the defence counsel.

"No, I'm not at all sure" was all that Jo. managed say before dissolving into tears.

When it came to Henty's turn to question Jo., he went to great lengths to get ask her questions that allowed her expertise to be seen.

'Yes, the facial re-construction technique was an old method, but it was a foundation stone of the whole process'.

'Yes, average face form could play some role, but that was if the work was done in a slipshod manner'.

'No, she had not made the identification, she didn't know who had, or what photo's they had used'.

By the end of her stint in the witness box, Jo was certain that she would move jobs as soon as possible. She might not have made a mistake, but there again, she might have and she didn't like the potential consequences that that error may produce. Henty, on the other hand, was sure that he could still employ the pathologists' one in a thousand chance positively against the defendant although he knew he would have to do some quick thinking to do so.

Whilst he was trying to plan his campaign, Henty's thoughts were interrupted by the judge. "Normally, I would call a recess here and proceed onwards after recess, but I believe that as both counsels will be making their closing speeches straight afterwards"-here both counsels nodded-"In the interests of fair play, I intend to close todays proceedings here and re-open tomorrow, to give both counsels an equal opportunity to present their cases to a refreshed jury. This court will re-convene at 10 a.m. tomorrow morning".

Despite all the appearance of fairness, the judge had been shaken by the pathologists' report on the differences and wanted the prosecution to have the best chance possible to win this case. It was his opinion that time would be needed to organise an effective prosecution case after todays' evidence and this was his ploy to give them time. There was also another train of thoughts in the judges' mind, should there be a conviction, there would be ample grounds for an appeal hearing. Were that step to be taken (disastrous, in his opinion), he wanted to be viewed as being pro-defendant in any later case review, which would thus be less injurious to any promotion chances that he might have.

Chapter 13

Day of Decision

When the court resumed on the Wednesday morning at 10 o'clock, it was the sixth day of the trial, a trial which the prosecution had expected to be complete within four days, five at the very outside. This over-run was bringing administrative problems to the court system, as scheduled cases were shuffled back and some cases were postponed with an indeterminate date to begin. Despite the growing chaos in the administrative sections, the judge was concerned that justice must be seen to be done and, although he was appalled at the weaknesses exposed in the prosecutions case, he expected a conviction to result from the jurys' deliberations.

Indeed, as the court re-convened, the judge called upon the Prosecution counsel, Henty, to begin the Prosecutions' closing speech. Mr. Henty, who had gratefully accepted the extra time, so considerately provided by the judge, to re-write and restructure his speech totally, stood and began to declaim, in his best voice, the case for the prosecution.

"Members of the jury," he began "it is for you to make the decision of guilt or innocence in this case. That is the British system. Our case for the prosecution, which you will signify your acceptance of by a guilty verdict, rests principally on circumstantial evidence. We have shown, clearly and unequivocally, that there was a two day time window for which the accused cannot provide an alibi. It was within this two day time window that Caroline Meadowcroft was buried, that we know, for that is the only time that the grave was open. That the two unprovable days of injury and burial are the same MAY be coincidental, we have tried to show it not to be so. Various items of so-called proof have been proffered by the defence, but cannot be proven beyond any shadow of doubt. In our case we have established, and provided examples, errant be they, that that two day time window was adequate to return to this country, undertake the murder, dispose of the body and return to America. In a statement made at the time, two witnesses, one of which was later proved to have a faulty memory for events of fifteen years previously, did see a car in the vicinity of the cottage at Chilham; once more within that fateful two day time window. We have no registration number for the car, so cannot trace the owner and cannot prove that it was in the control of the accused. You have heard the Pathologist state that there is a good chance that the photograph of the illegal passport holder isn't the accused. What was NOT said is that there is still a chance, a chance large enough for many of you to accept to put your money on, that that photograph IS the accused! Don't forget, the holder of that illegal passport WAS in this country for those critical two days!

Unfortunately for the defence, it was impossible to hide the fact that the accused had trained for the task of digging a grave, an operation performed in near record time by the accused, in front of many witnesses. All the defence had to say to that was that it was a student inspired scheme that the accused competed in, but it is our contention that the accused took advantage of the charity work to determine the time over which he could excavate a grave and so limit his disappearance from sight to two days. Once more, the two day period emerges as critical. Plotting for a two day gap in a foreign visit and coldly using that time to best effect is part of his character, part of who he is. We cannot be certain of the method of murder employed in the case of Caroline Meadowcroft, a fit and healthy young woman. That is, unless you can believe that she quite conveniently died within that two day time window, if you can't believe the theory of a convenient death, then she was murdered in cold blood."

At this point Henty took a short drink of water, before he resumed.

"You have heard, from D.C.I. Rigby, how even immediately after his wifes' disappearance, the accused was dis-interested in her fate. Why? Was it because he knew what had befallen her? If you listen to the defence, their contention is that her departure was expected.

How true! Especially when you plot her disappearance! D.C.I. Rigby, even at that point of his career, was immediately suspicious of the defendant's attitude. Nothing he has seen over the following fifteen years ameliorated those initial feelings, they were only reinforced by the defendants attitude at the time of the coroners' investigation."

Once more, Henty took a sip of the water in his glass, using the water drinking routine almost as the end of a paragraph.

"That the accused fits a psychological profile drawn up of the murder is also a telling point. That the accused had no mental breakdown was not proven, his doctor admitted his own lack of knowledge of the potential symptoms of the appropriate type of breakdown, so that he did not breakdown cannot be proven. WE know from his background that the accused is subtle and calculating, two important aspects of his work and his character. Plotting for a two day gap in a foreign visit and coldly using that time to best effect is part of his character, part of who he is".

Once more, the water glass was used to punctuate the speech.

"We must now come to forensic evidence, or lack of it, as in this case. Little was made of the forensic experience of the accused, actual forensic experience paid for by the tax payers of this country and all invested in the accused. I don't know about you, but I would expect a forensic expert to cover their tracks cleverly, but not perfectly, for someone was seen at the cottage within those desperate two days. Whoever it was clearly left their calling card, in the shape of a cigarette filter in the grave. An American made cigarette. On this topic, the defence has sought to project a smoke-screen by suggestions that American made cigarettes were common place around here at that time. That remains totally unproven, they were in common circulation here, in Ipswich, but we are thinking about in a village some thirty-odd miles away, deeper in the countryside. It is our contention that that single cigarette filter was brought from the 'States by the murderer and lost, or forgotten, during the burial of Caroline Meadowcroft. We all know who claims to have been in America at the time, but unfortunately cannot prove his claim for those crucial two days! This whole case revolves around those two days and who you believe as to what happened during those two days."

Another sip of water, theatrically taken.

"Members of the jury, I submit to you that the man you see before you as the accused is, in fact, guilty of the murder of Caroline

Meadowcroft and I urge you to return that verdict at the end of your deliberations."

With that Henty closed the case for the prosecution and sat down, with a flourish of the water glass.

Moments after Henty had seated himself, the defence counsel stood and began to present the case for the defence. Crucially, he left his meticulously written notes to respond to the speech of the prosecution.

"Members of the jury," he began "the counsel for the prosecution has seen fit to build his case, in his last submission to you, on what he calls 'those two critical days'. It is our submission to you that there were no critical two days at all, the defendant was injured and remained in bed until he felt better. Nothing unusual about that, who hasn't done it at some time and, I suspect, fifteen years after the event two critical days can be established for virtually anyone! So, I say, no critical two days at all. Now, to confound the specific allegations high-lighted by the prosecution. It has been alleged, by the prosecution, that the chances of the illegal passport holders' photograph being my client are the type of odds that you, personally, would accept for a wager. I don't believe that to be the case, with the exceptions of the National Lottery and football pools. I submit that no-one would eagerly wager their own money on a ten thousand to one gamble, but that is what the prosecution counsel is asking you to do with my clients freedom."

In his sincerity, the young counsel was trying to project that concern, but was only successful in projecting panic.

"Much has been tried to be made of my clients' apparent disinterest in the whereabouts of his wife fifteen years ago. Very easily explained, they were heading for a divorce and my client actually made the comment that he had been expecting to be left at any time. Yes, he was not interested in his wifes' whereabouts, but that is no crime, at least their marriage had broken down, which is an excuse in its' self. I am amazed, also, how my learned friend" here he indicated Henty "can denigrate and find evil in charitable work undertaken by my client. Had he been plotting the murder and burial of his wife, how better could he have published his intent than to have taken part in a public event that requires that something like a grave be dug? My learned friend called my client 'subtle and calculating', such an open exhibition would be neither subtle nor calculating. So, the very psychological profile upon which they rely so heavily, contradicts their ascertations on this very topic. With that point, my learned friend has been disproven by his own character analysis! This very analysis called the killer subtle and devious and yet the prosecution seeks to prove their case by what, even they admit, was a public competition. This, we contend, just highlights the paucity of their so called evidence.

We must examine the evidence of that American made filter tip. My client has never smoked and has been anti-smoking for the last nearly twenty years. To infer that he smoked on the burial night is too absurd to comment upon, to suggest that he smoked on that night and left the cigarette stub behind compounds both absurdity and illogicality. Don't forget that my client is seen by the prosecution as 'subtle and calculating' on one hand and as a person of some 'forensic experience', to make the suggestion that he smoked a cigarette and the forgot about what happened to the filter tip, defies belief! Were you to believe that statement, then you have to believe that my client acted in a manner at one point totally in agreement with his predicted psychological profile and, moments later, totally in disagreement with this profile. This the prosecution ask you to believe, but this is not possible! There are other explanations, completely unexplored by the prosecution, that more readily fit the available evidence which, unfortunately, do not involve my client and so cannot be used in an attempt to blacken his character.

During the course of this case, you have heard how Caroline Meadowcroft and her sister used to 'entertain' American service men at the Chilham cottage, I now submit to you that those Americans certainly had access to American made cigarettes. That point was proven beyond doubt during the trial, or at least I believe so, and that it is more likely that the cigarette filter was provided by one of them rather than my client, who was three thousand miles away at the time. That scenario is far more believable and likely than the unsupported, unbelievable fabrication that my learned colleague tried to spin to you a few moments ago. Indeed, a scenario involving an American service man and the first Mrs. Meadowcroft will more readily explain all the hard facts of this case far better than the conjecture which you have been forced to listen for the past six days. Members of the jury, I submit to you that the case that you have heard essentially represents the victimization of my client by an obsessive and delusional professional policeman. I further submit to you that the facts, as such, in this case can be far more easily woven into a believable story that doesn't involve my client, rather than one in which he is the criminal."

With that, the young counsel sat down. His throat felt tight and dry and he was still in the throes of an adrenalin rush, which had begun as he stood to deliver this final speech and had only increased more and more as he identified the weaknesses in his opponents' scenario. Such a great adrenalin rush had made him sound nervous and unsure of his case. That was the impression that the jury took away with them as a result of his speech. Technically accurate though his speech had been, all the power in it had been eroded by the edgy appearance and delivery.

It now fell to the judge to direct the jury before they went into their secret conclave in the jury room. In theory, the judge should have directed the jury in a neutral manner, bearing in mind the evidence that had been presented. Where the evidence been all one sided, the judge should have highlight the strengths or weaknesses of the evidence presented, but this he did not do. True, at the times when the prosecution case was so seriously breached that collapse had seemed imminent, such as when Rigbys evidence had been seriously compromised, the judge had almost thrown the case out of court. It was all the more surprising, then that the line that the judge chose to follow was to indicate the strengths of the prosecution case whilst mercilessly questioning the weak points presented in Meadowcrofts' defence. He emphasised the two critical days concept for so long that the jury seemed directed to think of no other. His amplification of the Florida police's comment that they hadn't found anyone that could support the accuseds' story ended without bringing their attention to the statement about the transitory nature of the motel population. That follow-up investigations had even tried to find witnesses, but not succeeded was not mentioned. That important fact just seemed too unimportant to note. All in all, the judges summing up could only be taken as instructing to the jury to believe the prosecution case AND, of course, to find for them.

During these final speeches, Jim Meadowcroft sat in the dock and listened to the three speeches. Had anyone looked closely at him, they would have seen a series of emotions cross his face, at times he seemed to be looking within himself, as if reliving some decisive event from another part of his life. Immediately before these periods of introspection, he would shake is head briefly and mutter quietly 'No, no, it was not like that'.

As his disagreement with the versions presented grew, the emphasis of his words would change. When things were almost correct, there would be no emphasis on any word, the whole phrase sounding like an academic correcting a slightly erring student. As his disagreement grew, the emphasis would start on the first word, 'no', and proceed down the sentence, until, when 'that' was emphasised, there was total disagreement between what he knew and what was being presented. To an independent observer, such as the crime reporter of the 'Ipswich Gazette', Jim Meadowcroft had disagreed with almost every aspect of the case presented by the prosecution. It was these almost unnoticeable actions that caused the reporter to use them to try to assemble a true version of the demise of Caroline Meadowcroft. Mr. Henty might have been surprised, however, at some of the points where Jim showed no obvious disagreement, once more the reporter noted Jims' agreement by his body language. Equally, during the defence questioning and presentation, only rarely had there been any movement from the accused and even then at surprising points.

However, it was during the judges' summing up that it had been possible just to hear Meadowcrofts' whispered words and see his head do the single, quick shake. He appeared hardly ever to cease shaking his head and his muttering "'no, no, it was not like that'. Not only was the reporter aware of this, but it was noticed by a member of the jury, who translated the whole performance as an act of regret for his actions and proof positive that his place really should be in the dock. He swiftly made all the other members of the jury aware of Meadowcrofts' actions and his belief that they were all seeing the effects of a guilty conscience. Throughout the judges' summing up, most members of the jury did not listen to what was said, but concentrated simply on the defendants' reaction to parts of the speech.

Once the judge finished his summing up and the jury were invited to go to the jury room and reach a verdict, the court emptied. Jim Meadowcroft was taken back to the cells under Ipswich Crown Court and there was allowed to meet his counsel, who was certain of victory and Jims' certain release. Jim still seemed in a daze and took nothing in that the counsel told him, he was still reviewing his version of the events in his minds' eye . . . .

Chapter 14

The Jury Returns its' verdict

When Jim Meadowcroft emerged from his reverie, he was surprised for a few moments to find that he was in the court cell in Ipswich. His momentary surprise passed and he began to notice that his counsel was there and was working on some paper work.

"What are you doing?" Jim asked.

"Preparing the appeal" was the short answer from his counsel.

"I know that I've been disconnected recently, but I can't remember being sentenced" was Jims' reply.

"You haven't, the jury is still out, but I feel it's wise to prepare the appeal in advance, just in case. I think the judge mis-directed the jury and I want to remember as many of his comments as possible. So, shush, let me write !" his counsel obviously didn't want any distractions from his client.

"They are wrong, you know, I didn't kill her. I didn't love her any more, but I didn't kill her" Jim said, almost conversationally.

"That's not important if we win, but do let me get on with this appeals paper !" asked his counsel.

Becky was allowed to come into the cell and entered just as the guard said "Might be the last time you see him for some time", typical gallows humour and not appreciated by Becky. Whether it was meant to be humorous or prescient, the comment was not received in the best manner, Becky just hissed "you mean Mother" at the guard and walked directly towards Jim. She had been body searched before being allowed in the cell, a job that the female police guard had enjoyed and would enjoy telling her male companion about at length. Jim stood up to greet her, he already looked years beyond his mid forties, an awful warning of how he could look in his dotage. They kissed and then sat together on the cells' wooden plank bed and talked quietly.

Becky, doing her utmost to encourage Jim began to talk about what they would do when he was free and the nightmare was finally over.

He listened for a while and then said "What if I've no longer got a job? What will we live on?". At least his attitude was positive in that he wasn't talking about jail, but it still wasn't bright. Becky knew that she was looking down a long, dark tunnel should Jim be jailed, but she couldn't imagine the long, dark tunnel that Jim was staring into. Jims' vision was worse, worse from the experience of the short time that he had already spent in jail on remand, worse from the mental stultification inherent in the system. So bad was Jims' vision that he believed that he would never emerge a free man again. He didn't know how long they had together, they had both excluded the counsels' presence from their private world, so they tried to make the best possible use of it. As they chatted and touched each other, both were aware that time was running out for them, This might truly be the last time that they would ever be this private, so that they had to extract maximum pleasure from each second.

A gentle cough caused them to look around and the counsel was on his feet.

"I'll leave now, see you back in court", he said simply.

Almost as he passed through the door, the guard entered and said "The jury have made their minds up and will be ready in a minute. I've got to get you back into the dock".

With that, Jim kissed Becky very hard and then walked around her and out of the cell, followed by the guard. Along the pale green corridor they went, then up four steps at the end and directly into the dock, facing the judge. By the time they arrived, the jury had begun to file back into their seats. Some gave Jim a quick glance, of pity or loathing or sympathy, he couldn't tell, although the whole world would soon know their decision. Once the jury had returned, the clerk of the court asked them if they had reached a decision in this case; the foreman stood up and said, simply "yes".

"Unanimously or by a majority?" he was asked by the clerk of the court and answered "A majority of nine to three".

A gasp ran around the court, to have been out for over six hours and yet only to come to a majority decision, meant that neither side had provided a totally convincing case. Inwardly, the judge groaned, there would be an appeal to the verdict, whichever way it went and that would be more work for him, explaining things at the appeal hearing. He had had reminders sent to the jury every hour saying that he required a unanimous decision, until after the fifth hour, he said that in the interests of Justice a majority decision of at least 9 to three would be acceptable. Still, if the worst came to the worst, he would claim that his summing up had only reflected on the mediocre cases presented by both counsels.

"What is your verdict?" asked the clerk of the court, aware that all eyes were on him and no-one was breathing.

Chapter 15

A reporter seeks for truth & finds . . . .

"Not Guilty", softly spoken by the foreman of the jury, one of the three dissenters on the verdict from the 12 jury members.

A soft murmur ran around the court. Few visitors were in the court to hear this climatic statement from the Jury. Becky and Stacey, sitting together behind the counsels' area, hugged each other and cried aloud with joy. John Demuir, the young defence counsel, looked stunned, almost as if he had not expected victory. Henty, Rigby and Radcliffe looked at each other quizzically, both policemen relaxed as Henty shook his head, his brow deeply furrowed in thought. Jim Meadowcroft remained seated, his face completely impassive, although he still remained tense. Only the judge seemed completely impassive. In the reporters Gallery, the man from the Ipswich Gazette smiled a small smile and gave a brief nod of his head.

Suddenly it appeared as if the sound had been turned back on again. Talk erupted throughout the court. After a few moments, the judge struck his gavel loudly on his bench to restore order to the court.

"Prisoner in the dock, you have been found not guilty by a jury of your peers. You are free to leave this court without any let or hindrance and with no stain on your character".

At that point Jim finally stirred and looked around him like a man newly recovered from a dangerous illness, as though viewing everything anew. Behind him, the escorting police officer opened a side door and pointed the way to floor of the court.

"Go to your wife, she needs you" said the officer somewhat brusquely.

As Jim left the dock he looked around, noticing for the first time that day the locations of the other players in the drama. Rigby and Radcliffe were almost within touching range to his left, still looking surprised and uncomfortable. Henty bent towards them, speaking urgently, but they showed no sign of even hearing or understanding what he was saying.

By the time Jim had walked to the bench behind which Demuir sat, Henty had risen and addressed the Judge.

"Your Honour, I now announce the prosecutions intention to seek leave to appeal this verdict".

Nodding slightly, the Judge acknowledged the intent to appeal. Privately, he thought to himself that any appeal would not help his reputation with the appellate judiciary, whom he wished to join. At Hentys' announcement, Demuir simply looked to the judge and saw him nod in acceptance.

Jim stood alongside the young defence counsel, when Becky, having got herself onto the floor of the court, quite simply assaulted him in her joy at the decision.

"Defence counsel. Do you have any further intentions with regards to this case ?" requested the judge.

"My Lord, at the moment, we intend to undertake a prosecution for wrongful arrest against D.C.I.'s Rigby and Radcliffe" announced Demuir.

"That action may best be undertaken after the prosecution appeal has been heard" said the judge sagely.

Throughout these interchanges, the Gazette reporter remained seated, looking from one principal to the other. His notebook wasn't ignored, but he was trying to decide whether he thought Jim a murder or not. All the signs and symbols that he had scribbled were his thinking map as he tried to make his own mind up. There were very obvious holes in the prosecution case, those he could see for himself without problem. To his mind, the biggest unresolved point was how Carolines murderer had known about the open grave in Higham Green? Who would have had no knowledge of the open grave at the Holy Trinity church in time to plan and execute the murder? Whilst the crowd still milled around the court room floor, the reporter had to make contact with either Jim or Demuir to have any chance of a follow up the story of Caroline Meadowcroft.

Jim revelations of Prison life were the first that he had revealed to her and she wept as she selected Jims' clothes.

Downstairs, Stacey had been as busy as their single bottle of bubbly would allow her to be. Becky came back into their dining room looking so upset that Stacey was forced to ask her why she was unhappy when she should be ecstatic with joy. On being told what Jim had said, all the explanation that Stacey could offer was that her contacts in the jail had told her that Jim had looked out for himself, but as a consequence had become 'tightly buttoned up'. She told Becky that that shower was probably the first button opening up, more would follow in time. As Becky dried her eyes with a crumpled tissue Jim walked in, looking pink and smelling of herbal shampoo. His first action was to give Becky a big hug and to kiss her on her ear, Stacey received a big, saucy wink.

"You look nearly normal again" commented Stacey. "That shower has washed all the dust out of those creases on your face and your hair looks darker, too".

"Yes, Darling, you've gone soft and a bit flabby, so it's back to the gym to get back into shape" noted Becky. "You should have seen him in the shower, Stacey, white and flabby like I've never seen him before. You, my man, are going to get fit and hard, double quick!"

Jim looked at Becky and raised a questioning eyebrow, only to be given a glass of champagne and a full-force radiant smile by Becky. Jim drank his champagne slowly, it was not his favourite drink and he was acutely aware that his time in prison had caused his tolerance to alcohol to fall. Before the party got to the tedious stage, Stacey excused herself, leaving Jim and Becky alone for the first time since he had been arrested. Within minutes, both had emptied their glass.

As the empty glasses touched the tabletop Becky said "You look tired and even if you aren't, I'm tired of missing you".

Jim answered with a rueful smile, but didn't have time to say anything.

Becky got hold of his hand, pulled him towards the stairs and said "Come on, to bed and tonight is a night in the buff for both of us. I've missed you for too long and I hope that you've been missing me!"

Within a week of returning home, Jim was back at his job in Windsor University. By a ruling from the Vice Chancellor, his absence had been treated as though on sabbatical leave, although there had been some opposition to this ruling. Some colleagues had fought for Jim, when the University Council had proposed his dismissal. These friends had successfully argued that dismal could only occur if the University had been brought into disrepute by Jims' actions, their argument was that should Jim be proven innocent, he would not have brought the University into disrepute, although the Police that would have done so. Even so, it was a close run race, won by brave colleagues against the Universitys' administration.

No matter that Jim had been freed by the court, there were still sufficient small-minded people who continued to condemn him and not want to co-operate with him. He slowly worked himself back into his old role and within two months, it was as if he had hardly been away at all. He was back into his sports habits quickly and began to return to his leaner, fitter former self, although the creases remained etched on his face, although, perhaps they were no longer as deep as they had been.

At about the time Jim was almost physically back to his usual standard, the appeal was heard. There had been quite some pressure for the leave to appeal to be refused, but on the balance of probabilities the appeal had been allowed. Just before the case was to be heard, John Demuir arranged to see Jim to brief him about the possibilities. Jim was told that he would not need to attend; three Law Lords would revue the evidence and the written record of the trial. Their decision would be whether their belief was that, on the balance of the evidence presented, the correct verdict had been reached. Should they adjudge that an incorrect verdict was presented, they could order a re-trial when any new evidence could be presented.

It was a tense time for Jim. Demuir was much more relaxed about he process, believing that the court records would show, unemotionally, how weak had been the prosecution case. Within a week, the result of the appeal was released to both counsels and John Demuir went to High Wycombe to tell Jim and Becky the result.

"Well, you're home free now!" said Demuir "The Law Lords came out unanimously against the prosecution and questioned their reasons for sustaining such a weak case".

Jim simply smiled with relief, he couldn't say anything.

"You can sell your story to that reporter chap and even confess to killing your wife and the law can't touch you. There is no such thing as double jeopardy in British Law." Demuir told him "But please don't

Chapter 16

. . . . *stranger than fiction.*

Jim answered all the questions that the journalist asked him. They started from the precept that the journalist had arrived at by the end of the trial. That precept was that Jim was innocent of the charge of murder, but that he knew far more than had ever been suggested during the trial. Jim neither agreed nor disagreed with that idea of the reporters', he simply accepted it as a suitable point from which to start answering questions.

"Where does the story start, for you?" requested the reporter.

"For me? Really when I came home from Florida and my wife wasn't there" replied Jim.

"You said that your marriage was going wrong. When did that start" enquired the reporter.

"Fairly early on in the marriage, actually. Caroline wanted to give up work and become a housewife. She gave up her job, became a housewife and in a month was going up the wall with boredom, so she got another job" replied Jim.

"When did you get to know that Caroline was being unfaithful?" the reporter asked.

"I sort of found out about by accident. She was always telling me about her secretary, who had divorced and how she always had 'male friends' around her and how shocked she was by her morals" commented Jim. "Then Caroline told me that she had been given the role of unofficial company social secretary, arranging all the functions and everything."

"Was her secretary involved in this 'unofficial' social secretary job as well?" enquired the reporter.

"Certainly" replied Jim "Marvellous how, in retrospect, things look so obvious".

"When did things go irreparably wrong?" the reporter asked.

Jim went back to the Brazilian trip in 1982 and how Caroline had reacted when she heard about it.

"Wouldn't it have been easier to have taken her with you?"

"Not really, I took her to Jamaica on my first trip abroad, but she was a disaster! I had never known that Caroline was really as racist as she was. She patronized all the Jamaicans we met and was contemptuous of them and their country. Because of her attitude, I nearly lost that contract and a number of good friends. After that, I dare not take her anywhere." stated Jim.

"And she became her companys' unofficial social secretary?" commented the reporter.

"Yes," Jim said "She could turn the charm on when she wanted to, when she didn't, she could be the complete bitch. That, I didn't know until after we were married"

"Is that why you didn't take her to Florida?" enquired the reporter.

"Well, by that time, she had kicked me out of the communal bed-room and we really communicated by notes. She had established another life for herself which did not include me, so I never considered taking her to Florida, even if I could have afforded it!"

With a look of concern on his face, the reporter asked "Wouldn't she have liked America?"

"Probably not. She formed her opinions of America from American television shows, so she thought them loud, arrogant and uncouth. Definitely not her kind of people" said Jim.

"That's odd, I thought that she had a number of lovers from the American air bases" questioned the reporter.

"Her logic would have said that they were different Americans because they were in Britain and that they would, somehow, have been civilised more by that experience" commented Jim.

Much of this information concerned the reporter, if true, he had to re-evaluate his opinion and change his belief from Jim being pro-active in the domestic problems to being reactive. That change would require a complete re-evaluation of his approach because Jims' reasons for action would have been different from those he had theorised. Further questions about Carolines' attitude followed. When Jim said that he thought that Carolines' mother was much to blame, the journalist swiftly interrupted him for more details on that comment.

"Mrs. Ellis moaned consistently about Shirleys husband, Dick, to Caroline whenever we went to see them. Dick was never good enough for her daughter, or so she thought. I know that she said the same things about me to Shirley whenever Dick and Shirley visited them." was Jims answer. "Apparently, both of her daughters had married beneath them and could have done better, or so Mrs. Ellis thought. I know what she said about Dick to me and I assume that she said similar things about me".

"How do you know?" asked the reporter.

"I liked Dick. When we visited Dick and Shirley, Dick and I would go to the pub together and compare notes" was Jims' ready answer. "It was only the revelations about Shirley in court that caused the break-up of their marriage".

All this was new to the reporter and shook the basis of which he had been certain and he decided to arrange a second meeting after he had had time to rethink his ideas about Caroline. He left Jim to return to Ipswich, where he intended to trace Dick and verify Jims' information.

Working for the local newspaper gave him a number of excellent sources of information, all of which he tapped into to find Dick. Dick proved to be remarkably easy to find and they were talking whilst the information was still fresh in the Reporters memory. Once confidence had been established, Dick seemed happy to re-confirm Jims' comments about Carolines' mother. It appeared that Mrs.Ellis was more disappointed in Carolines' choice of husband than in Shirleys' and that Jim, although he never knew it, had constantly been the target of her comments. Dick was quite open with the reporter when he said that he thought Mrs. Ellis was a major contributing factor to Carolines' behaviour.

"Jim was so happy doing his 'thing' and didn't notice, or ignored, what was being said about him" was Dicks closing comment.

It was a month later that the reporter contacted Jim again. Once more he agreed to rely on written notes and not to use a tape recorder, so another meeting was arranged. This time, the meeting was organised in Jims' office at Windsor University. From the opening, the reporters questions were not as aggressive as they had been at their first meeting. His researches had shown that Jims' comments were slightly biased, but, essentially, true and couldn't be judged by his previous standards. This time, the reporter wanted to talk about Jims' first working time in Florida, when he had hurt his knee and met Becky, who had been doctors' secretary. Although the reporter was still intent of proving that Jim was responsible for Carolines' death, he had been forced into a re-evaluation of the actual circumstances surrounding those times. During his researches, he had re-read the prosecution case and was appalled by the lack of direct evidence against Jim. Dr. Tanners' psychological profile had been so general that the reporter himself had taken to comparing his colleagues with the statements made by Tanner. He was shocked when he realized that almost any modern involved, dedicated worker could be fitted into that profile, so he rejected it, but there was something important that nagged away in the back of his mind that he could neither ignore nor remember.

It was whilst he was reading his notes immediately before going in to talk with Jim that the nagging idea suddenly revealed itself. As soon as he saw the title 'USAF Lakenheath', a light came on in his mind. Lakenheath had been a base where fighter planes had been deployed and with fighter planes came fighter pilots, the elite of any air-force. Demuir had made that comment himself, saying that Dr. Tanners psychological profile would fit a fighter pilot better than Jim Meadowcroft. Had he known, or did he just suspect, something thought the reporter? Or was he the first to make this particular connection? Exploring the possibilities in his mind, the reporter almost seemed breathless. Having an American fighter pilot as his accomplice certainly was a key, a magic key that opened locks not visible to the average person. Thinking rapidly, the reporter tried to remember what was happening in the summer of 1983 and could only remember the deployment of cruise missiles in the U.K. Thatcher and Regan remembering that Churchill once referred to Britain as 'an unsinkable aircraft carrier' agreed that Britain should become the most easterly base from which to threaten the U.S.S.R. Certain bases came under very tight scrutiny at that time, whilst the others, less high profile, apparently continued on as usual. It was through these less high profile bases that the constant flux of American service and civilian personnel needed for cruise missile deployment passed unnoticed. 'What easier?' thought the reporter, an entry and exit point into and out of Britain and close to the scene of the action, too!

With that thought a number of clues fell into place and made startling sense. So that was why the Holy Trinity church at Higham Green was chosen. He made a bet with himself that the burial of James Bradley had been reported in the local newspaper. That, he knew, would tell the conspirators that an open grave was available for a few days and he was certain that that report had triggered Carolines' demise. Of course, for this scenario to have operated Jim would have had to have had a co-conspirator at Lakenheath, but that would not have been impossible, after all they would have had something in common, Caroline! With the realisation of that possibility, the reporter sat almost stunned.

Jim had to shake the reporter by the shoulder to bring him back to himself again. After shaking his head and making a few excuses about 'day dreaming', the reporter spent only a short time with Jim and asked him only a few trivial questions. Once the reporter had left his office, Jim sat and began to wonder why the reporter should have spent so little time there and asked such trivial questions, when he had arranged this meeting 'as a matter of urgency'. Within minutes, Jim had forgotten about the reporter and settled back down to his work. Looking for a thinking space, the reporter walked to the coffee bar at the University, bought a mug of coffee and sat at a table where the ash-trays were piled high with cigarette stubs. He lit himself a cigarette and pushed a crushed Marlboro packet towards the ash-tray. 'Marlboro', why is that name significant? he wondered, then he remembered. After a Marlboro cigarette stub had been found in Carolines grave, the prosecution had tried to show that Jim Meadowcroft had smoked it, although he was a life long non smoker. In his defence, Demuir had suggested that whoever had buried her had left it and that the Marlboro stub suggested an American presence at the burial.

"Better and better" said the reporter to himself, "the case gets clearer and clearer by the minute".

He knew that he must begin investigations in the anglicised Americans living around Lakenheath and he had a fortunate contact there. That would be his first move when he got back home, those times were sufficiently turbulent to be memorable, so he was hoping that one of his contacts could give him a lead. First, he checked the funeral notices in both of the local newspapers that served the county border area of Cambridgeshire and Suffolk in the early 1980s'. Quite swiftly, in one he found the notice of John Bradleys death and the notice of his burial, so the plot could all have revolved around the date of Bradleys legal internment. Next, to try to find any connection between Jim and an American pilot, he contacted an ex-Lakenheath flier who had stayed on in Suffolk when his tour of duty ended.

Talking to the ex-flier, he found out that Caroline and her sister had been well known to the fliers in Lakenheath. Caroline was described as 'senior officers only' material and had had many liaisons with American fliers. When the reporter described, briefly, his theory, the American looked serious.

"You going about this the wrong way up" said the Pilot. "Look, had your friend come from 'stateside on one of our transport, no records would exist, it would have been done as a favour or to settle a debt".

"Are you saying that Jim Meadowcroft couldn't have come in via Lakenheath?" asked the reporter.

"No, I'm not. He could well have come back that way and then been taken back 'state side from Lakenheath. What I AM saying is that you'll never find any record of it, so you'll never prove it!" commented the pilot.

"How can I get any lead on this?" requested the reporter.

"Now hold hard, boy. When did all this happen?"

"July 1983, why?" said the reporter.

"Gimme a minute, I've gotta drag an old memory from outa my skull." answered the pilot. "I remember 'bout then that one of our finest and best put in a transfer request to return 'state side in a hurry. Senior Officer just had to get back home and took a demotion to do it. We all thought it was for personal reasons, but could have been anything".

"Who was he?"

"Can't remember now, so long ago. But he was a womaniser. Tall good-looking bastard who threw his money at any skirt he thought he could straddle" reminisced the pilot. "Enjoyed his drink and enjoyed his women in equal measure, but a mean tempered S.O.B." As the American pilot was drawn more deeply into the plot his neutral accent slowly slipped back towards that of his roots and slowly a Southern drawl became pronounced.

"Could he have known Jim Meadowcroft?" said the reporter.

"No reason why not" answered the pilot "but you inferring that Meadowcroft had a hold over the flier?" asked the pilot.

"That would explain a lot" said the reporter.

"Would have had to been something BIG, know what I mean? Otherwise, would have been Meadowcroft himself in that grave" commented the pilot.

"So, my scenario is possible?" asked the reporter.

"Yea, but not very likely" replied the pilot.

"Remember Sherlock Holmes's comment 'When all other possibilities have been discounted, the last remaining, however unlikely, must be true'" quoted the reporter.

"Who you saying did the killing?" asked the American.

"Either of them, but the way the flier left quickly does indicate he probably did it" commented the reporter.

"How she die?"

"Never established, except that it wasn't violent", the reporter told the American.

"Don't sound like our guy, he was physical, know what I mean?" replied the pilot "'cept he was supposed to have tried to smother a broad in California once when he was drunk. Is why he came to the old continent, in the first place".

"Did you ever operate British cars in Lakenheath? asked the reporter.

"No, always American, but plenty of the troops had their own Anglo cars, said they wus easier to drive around the lanes" commented the American. "Why?"

"A small van was seen in Chilham St. Margarets the night Caroline went missing" answered the reporter.

"Could have belonged to one of our boys. Easier, though, if it belonged to one of yours!" commented the pilot.

"It's all there, thin but continuous" commented the reporter "And it makes sense and could be done so easily through Lakenheath".

"What you doing this for, boy?" the Americans' Southern Charm accent now carrying a hint of hostility.

"Meadowcroft just got off the charge, so he's untouchable now, but the Police made an absolute pigs' ear of the case. There had to be a more logical explanation and I think I've just found it!" the reporter was triumphant.

"That all? Just curiosity?" asked the American pilot "'cos you've proved nothing to me".

"I've got the story, I've cracked the plot. I know how it was done!" the reporter was exuberant.

At his next meeting with Jim, the reporter laid out his case in great detail. He pointed out all his findings out and how Carolines' killing had been carried out. Jim asked a few questions and always received answers back quickly. When he could think of no further questions, the reporter puffed out his chest with pride. He told Jim that he was going to write a book about the murder of Caroline Meadowcroft and tell the truth as he knew it.

"Don't use my name, or I'll get the libel boys on you" said Jim easily.

"I won't. My problem is that I have to write a true story, but without using the actual characters." replied the reporter. "What can I do?"

Jim looked at him and replied quite simply "Call it fiction".

Chapter 17

Early summer 1982

"Mummy, he's doing it again ! He's going off to Brazil for the summer and he's not taking me with him!" Caroline cried tearfully to her mother.

"I don't know where he'll be, but he will be away for over a month and I'll be here with only work to go to. It isn't fair. He goes all over the world in his vacations and never takes me with him". Mrs. Ellis, Caroline's mother, spoke soothingly into the 'phone, attempting to calm her youngest daughters' ire, without loosing her neutrality, for she, at least, believed in letting married couples sort out their own problems without trying to attach blame. "Have you asked Jim why he's going off again ?", she enquired. "All he says is that it's the only way of getting known internationally and that is what the University wants him to do. He only took me with him that first time that he worked abroad and he's never THOUGHT about it ever since !" complained Caroline. "Why don't you go to Ginnys' cottage for a while, I know Ginny'd love you to be there and you wouldn't be too far away from Dick and Shirley, so you could see them, too" suggested her mother "That would be pleasant for them as well and you know how much you like Suffolk in the summer".

Jim had actually thought about taking Caroline a few times, but had not felt it worth the trouble to pursue further since Carolines' first & only visit a few years earlier. Jim had taken Caroline away with him when he had had that first contract in Jamaica, working with U.W.I. at Mona. Caroline had flounced around his work area all the time interrupting, demanding and unyielding. Her attitude had nearly lost Jim his contract, so snobbish was she to the locals. Early in the visit, Jim had asked Caroline to behave like the other academics' wives did and take advantage of the fact that she was in the Caribbean for free for a month and to go and tan on the beach or go shopping. This had not appealed to Caroline, who was too busy trying to play the role of the arch—colonist, much to everyones annoyance. Also, in the early years of the Thatcher attack on education, Jim would have had to pay for her ticket and that would have meant doing the contracts for nothing. That Caroline earned more than Jim did never seemed to enter the equation at all, Carolines money was for Caroline, whilst Jims' was for both of them.

Still angry that Jim had arranged a working month in Brazil for himself, Caroline decided to take her mothers advice and to go to stay for a while with Aunty Ginny, who had been her kind and generous God-Mother. Ginny (who had been christened Virginia, but had accepted the shortened version given her by Caroline when she began to talk) was really a substitute mother to Caroline and almost treated her as a younger sister and was always happy for Carolines visits, especially when her health deteriorated in the last few years. Caroline could wrap Ginny around her little finger, always could and always would, even more so after her return from Guildford University with her degree. From that day on, Ginny had treated Caroline as an equal and frequently deferred to her judgement. Whatever Caroline did was O.K. with Ginny, for wasn't Caroline the most intellectual and sophisticated member of her family ?

On the day that Jim gave her the final, fixed dates for his working visit, Caroline asked Ruth, her secretary, to come to the house for drinks. Ruth duly arrived, before Jim, who hadn't been told, had returned from the University, Caroline poured the drinks and she and Ruth sat down to begin to plot the next few weeks of liberated life. Ruth had a whole series of telephone numbers of men who were happy to spend an evening or a week or longer with her and some were specially selected as being suitable for Carolines more refined tastes. Luck was with Caroline, on the first call, she contacted a man she knew and he would be happy to come around and see her that very evening. Ruth was nearly as lucky, it took her three 'phone calls to make the same arrangements, but eventually she did. After the 'phone calls were over both of them sat and had a few more drinks, Jim arrived at this stage, asked what the party was and was curtly told by Caroline that Ruth and she were going out for the evening and their escorts were due at any time. Jim wasn't unduly perturbed, similar things happened before and it had always been work related, for both Caroline and Ruth acted as unpaid entertainments secretaries for their company. Jim went out to fetch a take away and when he came back there were two men in the house talking to Caroline and Ruth and two cars newer and bigger than his, parked in the street. Caroline cut him cold, on his return and neither introduced him to the men or even talk to him, both pairs (for that is what the four had become) swept out at about 7.30 totally ignoring Jim.

He knew Carolines moods and did not like it but thought it a passing phase, so he did not worry. When he went to work the next morning, Caroline had not returned, that was unpleasant, but not unprecedented, she would frequently stay over at an hotel after a company party and go straight into work the following day. Returning home at his usual time that evening, it was obvious that Caroline had returned and was 'at home'. She was 'at home' and so was Ruth and two other men, all dressed ready for another evening out. As he walked in, Caroline grabbed him by the upper arm and said "These are important company clients, Ruth and I have been asked to look after them for a while, so don't make a scene", once more a not unprecedented occurrence, so Jim sat down in the lounge and quite blatantly read a book. Nobody spoke to him, no-one acknowledged him & nobody noticed him. Once again, the house emptied at 7.30, so Jim went to the local Chinese restaurant for his 'whoopy' night out.

This pattern of company visitors repeated itself three times in the next week, then Jim was off to Brazil to work. As he left to climb into his taxi to go to Heathrow, Caroline told him that she was going to spend most of the time with Aunty Ginny. That fact actually pleased Jim, who thought that, at least, her life would settle down somewhat and he expected Aunty Ginny to be a moderating influence on Caroline. At Heathrow Terminal Three, Jim joined the Varig queue, a long, straggling line of people waiting patiently for the one Varig check-in desk to open. Moments after the desk opened, the airline announced a 90 minute delay in the flight due to late departure from Copenhagen, so Jim steeled himself to the wait. His turn at the check-in desk came surprisingly slowly, his reserved seat had not been reserved for him and he found the only remaining aisle seat to be in the smoking section. Quickly weighing up the options, Jim plumped for the aisle seat and hoped that he wouldn't be near a chain smoker.

As luck would have it, he found himself with a party of British electrical tool salesmen, all whose trip to Rio was their sales bonus for the previous year. They adopted him immediately and included him in their merry and friendly group, so it was quite light heartedly that the long flight to Brazil passed. Jim was standing waiting in the immigration line with his flight companions when Allen, the groups' 'Elder statesman' saw an attractive woman in a tight skirt and tiger skin jacket standing a few rows in front of their group. Immediately, Allen began taunting Jerry, the youngest of the sales group about this woman and telling him to go and talk to her and get a date. "You were trying to get into her nickers on the plane, go and get a date now" encouraged Allen, all the more to see Jerry squirm with embarrassment. Jim could understand Jerry' reluctance to talk to the woman and said so to Allen. Allen just told Jim to bide his time and he would find the reason for Jerry' discomforture. Eventually, the woman got to the front of the queue and presented her documentation to the Immigrations officer. He examined the documents carefully, looked at the woman and re-examined the documents, then he shook his head and pointed out something to the woman on her immigration form and sent her back to correct the error. She went to one of the writing tables at the back of the Immigration hall and completely filled in a new form then walked back to the front of the queue and to the same immigration officer, who looked at her form shook his head, tore up the form and sent her away to fill in another one. This performance happened twice more as the queue slowly snaked its' way through into Brazil. Just before the sales group advanced on the Immigration officers, back she came with her fifth form and went ahead of them. This time they could all hear the discussion of her immigration form and the Immigration officer was quite adamant that she would not be admitted to the country until the details of her sex agreed with the details on her passport. Voices were raised, soon the whole Immigration hall knew the problem, she was a he and his passport details did not agree with the completed immigration form details and until they did, the officer said, she would NOT be admitted to the country. Allen began to laugh at this and reminded Jerry that he had said that he wanted to get her alone, "Go on" taunted Allen "and see what you get !". Jim was taken aback by the performance between the immigrations officer and the 'woman' and asked Allen how he know that she was a bloke. "Simple" was the reply, "I came from Copenhagen as he did and he tried the same thing on there, but the Danes made him change into mens clothes so that he looked like his passport photograph before they allowed him through. Why do think that we were an hour and a half late ?". Jims' first few minutes in Brazil were certainly extending his education, he hoped that the remainder of his month there would not be so educational.

As he left the customs hall, Jim spotted a sign with his name on and walked towards it. Underneath the sign was a short and very attractive Brazilian woman (Jim had no doubts about her sex, as her neckline gave ample evidence that she was really female). "I am Sylvia" she said in reasonable English, "Professor Sergio De Laurencia d'Arbre welcomes you to his country and has asked me to take you to your hotel and then to meet him at the University". Mentally, Jim threw away his Portuguese phrase book and realised that there would be plenty of English speakers around and he wouldn't have to try any set phrases on unsuspecting locals.

At the University, Sergio greeted him warmly, giving Jim a bear hug and dancing him around in delight. Jim and Sergio had been students together in Britain and had a friendship that went back to days before either had married and both had chased the girls mercilessly. Jim was introduced around to other members of the team who would work this same month as he would, all the time Sergio kept up an endless flow of talk and questions about mutual friends. Drinks were served, then the project briefing began. Work tasks were given out and team leaders met their teams of Brazilian Postgraduate students and then all sat down to discuss detailed plans for their segment of the work. Sergio acted as a Master of Ceremonies, introducing people from various countries who had similar specializations and trying to establish international rapprochement. Jim was introduced to Prof. Abel Kingsman from Miami University, another environmental biologist, who was hoping to get a large contract 1 year hence for work in the southern 'states of the U.S.A. Jim and Abel would be working in neighbouring sectors and so would be able to meet and talk at intervals.

Sergio told Jim that the Research sponsors were having a symposium at Wayne State University in Detroit in September to discuss the result and implications of the work they were about to do, prior to drafting the final report for the U.N. Before Jim could say anything Sergio continued, "You don't have to say that you don't have the money to go to the U.S. in September, you're a Brit and your government doesn't believe in education. Leave it to me, I'm working on a plan to get you there, but it will take a few days. I'll tell you when I've got things organised, until then, don't worry !" With that, Jim turned his mind to the project before him, he had to control and direct the field studies that a number of Brazilian students had to do for their various degrees. Mans depredations of the rain forest was having a significant effect on both the flora and fauna whose habitat was that hot, humid and green organism. Typical of Sergio, many of the researchers were women and not one of them could be described as unattractive, Jim looked around at his team and thought that his group must have been hand picked by Sergio to test his resolve over what would prove to be a long and exacting month.

A week before the project month was over, Abel Kingsman walked into Jims' camp, he headed directly for Jim and said, directly, "I have to return to Miami immediately, that means my group will be without a leader for a week, will you take it over ?". Dumbstruck for a second, Jim looked flustered before he agreed. With his agreement given, Kingsman said "Good man, I was told that I could rely on you ! I want you to come and see me in Miami when you've finished here to talk about next year, shall we say Wednesday, the week after next ?" Still off balance, Jim agreed and Abel told him that he had arranged for all his researchers to come to Jims' camp at 8 a.m. the next morning, "so's you can get to know 'em and their programs and help 'em over their last week", at that he turned and walked back to his own dominion. "Great" thought Jim "I've got to pick up the reins of another ten students and do something sensible with them ! When I get to Miami, I'll bet all Kingsman'll do is to give me a good lunch and say thanks. Ah well, I agreed to do it ".

Despite the increase in student numbers, the last week passed uneventfully enough and they all climbed aboard the bus back to Rio for the farewell feast. Looking at Kingsmans' group convinced Jim that Sergio had organised the groups to put temptation in his way because all of Kingsmans' students were ordinary looking and there had been more men than women !

At the feast, Sergio asked Jim for his return air ticket, so that he could get it re-directed to allow Jim to go to Miami and depart back to the U.K. from Orlando. In answer to Jims' questions, all Segio would do was to hint that he had arranged it all and, "please to trust me". Jim surrendered his ticket, Sergio made a couple of 'phone calls, wrote a note to go with the ticket and sent it via the University courier back to Varig Head Office and then took Jim to lunch. On their return, a sealed letter carrying the Varig logo sat on Sergios desk, "Aha, your tickets. Open them and check the details, Jim". Jim did. He was dumbstruck. "How did you organise THIS ?" Jim asked incredulously. Sitting in his hands were Business class tickets from Rio to Orlando and Orlando to Heathrow, in place of the economy class ticket to Heathrow that had been sent. "My ex-students" was all that Sergio would say, so Jim had no excuse not to go to see Prof. Kingsman now, all he needed was to phone Caroline and tell her of the change in plans. In Chilham St. Marys', the ansaphone cut through the ringing tones and Carolines voice asked for messages, so Jim relayed the events and said that he would be home a week later than expected, but it would be the same flight, with the same arrival time at Heathrow Terminal Three and that he looked forward to meeting her there.

Chapter 18

Miami 1982

Hertz had a car immediately available for Jim after he arrived at Orlando and the Hertz lady gave him a map of the road system around the Orlando/Disney World complexes. All the routes were there and she marked the best route for Jim with an orange highlighter pen.

Jim asked her the most pressing question that he had "How do I get out of the airport to be facing the right direction on the right route. Do I turn left or right out of your compound?" she looked at him as if he were suddenly illiterate.

After negotiating the Hertz exit, Jim found himself looking for the sign to the Beeline freeway, he saw it and turned right onto the six-laner and headed south, all the while glancing at the map. As the complex intersection approached, Jim slowed down and pulled into the right hand lane in an attempt to spot the correct off ramp. West Landstreet Rd. came up and Jim primed himself to turn off on either Route 17 or Route 91, the Route 17 turn-off flashed past almost immediately, so he set himself to find Route 91. He saw Routes 4, 408, 423 pass in quick succession, but saw nothing of Route 91.

In desperation, he took the last junction of the complex, the one marked 'Florida Turnpike, South', reasoning that at least he would be heading in the right general direction. It took almost no time for the elation to pass, as the car seemed to be directed in the wrong direction. Desperately, he looked for some salvation, but could see none. Only a few miles down the turnpike, he saw an off-ramp, which he took in the hopes of finding some human contact that might tell him the correct direction. He sailed up the off ramp, seeing no-one outside of their car, turned right at the top and continued towards a small mall on the right hand side. Before he could enter the mall, he saw on the left a small motel complex and reasoning that the people in motels are used to directing people, he turned into 'Silvermans' Long Term Motel'. At first, it appeared that he had made a mistake, he saw no-one, but then he drew up to the ramshackled office and went inside. Within moments, Jim was experiencing the basic friendly—& helpful-ness of the average American, as the proprietor had him sit down, offered him coffee and cookies and pulled out some route maps. Sitting in that office every day and rarely seeing anyone caused Mr. Silverman to be loquacious, but he was kind and very helpful. After coffee and cookies, he traced out the correct route for Jim, which seemed that he had been on, but that a dearth of long range route signs had confused him.

"Remember", said the old man, "always learn the name of the NEXT town down the freeway, 'cos that is how our signs work".

Knowing this and the next few that the old man told him, meant that Jim could tackle the freeway with confidence. Just before he left, the old man gave him a motel card with his name and phone number and told Jim not to worry, but to 'phone if he had further problems. Jim, being British, had a great advantage, as the old man had been in Britain during the 'war and had grown to like the people, so with Mr. Silverman, the British had a head start.

Back on the 'turnpike, Jim felt confident enough to push his speed up to the 55 mph limit, set the cruise control and watch the miles go by. About 6 hours after leaving Silvermans', he saw the first sign to the University of Miami, so he started to look for a place to spend the night. He didn't think about a motel, after seeing Silvermans', but a Holiday Inn was perfect and the one near the Miami campus was exactly where he would have liked to find one.

It was after 5 p.m., so Jim didn't think about phoning Prof. Kingsman, expecting that he would have gone home. His appointment was not until the next day anyway, so he thought about some more relaxation before business put paid to his working vacation.

Jim had never been to Miami before and spent a couple of hours just observing the people around. It was unbelievable to him, but the people were really like he had seen them portrayed in T.V. programmes, so much so that he was forced to accept that they weren't caricatures, but that this was real life Miami style. He felt like an extra on a film set, only he didn't know what role he was supposed to play. Leather clad bikers from Daytona paraded up and down the main street, bikini clad girls roller skated around the streets and vacationing American students seemed to be everywhere. His accent caused a small stir and attracted some attention, but it was more as a curiosity rather than as a real constituent of the social and ethnic melange of Miami. He returned to his hotel to wash and change before he went out for dinner.

On attempting to leave the hotel the burly, black doorman put his arm across the door and barred his way.

"Where are you going, sir?" was the polite enquiry.

"Out to a restaurant" Jim replied.

"Sir, it is not safe for you as you don't know the area" said the doorman "What food do you like?"

"Oh, just normal food like a steak" answered Jim.

"O.K. sir, leave it to me", at which point the doorman stepped outside whistled up a cab and told the driver "to take my friend here to Barneys".

As Jim walked past him, the doorman said "Return by cab, too, sir, we want you to enjoy our town".

In the restaurant, the food was good, the prices reasonable and the atmosphere relaxed, but Jim still remembered the doormans' words. As he left, he asked the doorman there to get him a cab back to his hotel and in a few moments was back in the Holiday Inn. As he entered, he made a point of asking the doorman about the need for cabs and was told that, despite the outward appearance, Miami was violent and strangers were easy prey. Shaken, Jim went into the hotel bar for a beer before bed, where he was accosted by a hooker. In response Jim, complete with beer, fled to his room and security for the night.

Chapter 19

Identity Theft

All the time Jim was staying long hours at the University, his teaching wasn't ignored and the first term was running on swiftly indeed. By the time Christmas arrived, Jim had finished a whole string of research papers, all of which he sent off for refereeing and, hopefully, eventual publication. More importantly, he had his plan almost fully formed with a list of requirements that he had to acquire and test before finally putting the plan to the acid test. As the University began to run down for the Christmas vacation, Jim suddenly realised that he had nothing planned and that only a bleak Christmas faced him. He was sure that Caroline would have something organised and whatever that was, it wouldn't include him, so he walked into the nearest travel agent and took the first cheap holiday that covered both Christmas and New Year. Somewhat surprised, Jim found that he was booked in for two weeks to Istanbul, it was at least something different and got him away from the coldest weather.

On his return to the house, he found a letter from a solicitor requesting an urgent telephone call, which informed him that Aunty Ginny had died on the second of January 1983 and that he was the executor of her will and would he come to the solicitors office to undertake the duty. He managed to get the cemetery in Suffolk just before Aunty Ginny was buried, he was unsurprised not to find Caroline there, although her sister, Shirley and Dick, her husband, were there. Shirley wasted very little time telling him that Caroline was skiing in Switzerland with a group from work, but had been told about Aunty Ginny.

Immediately after the funeral, Jim went to the solicitors' office and find his role in fulfilling Aunty Ginnys last wishes. Both Caroline and Shirley were to take their pick of 1 piece each from Ginnys' jewellery box, Shirley the elder, to go first, Caroline second. Shirley and her husband were left a sum of money, but Caroline was given Aunty Ginnys' cottage in Chilham St. Margarets (Aunty Ginny inferring, rather than stating, that ownership was to be between Caroline and her partner). Ginnys' sister (Caroline and Shirley's mother) received the residual money from the bank and the remaining jewellery, not a stingy gift, by any measure. There were a few remaining discrete benevolences for Ginnys' old friends, but these did not take up much time or money. Carolines bequest of the cottage was conditional on her not selling the cottage unless Shirley had had first refusal and other family members had had second refusal. This was the solicitors work to draw up the actual details of the cottage bequest, so Jim left him to it whilst he thought about the £ 50 that he had been left to compensate for his duties as executor. Jim was in no doubt that the cottage would be used as frequently as Caroline could manage it, but 'as her official partner' he was entitled to a key and to use it himself. As executor of Aunty Ginnys' will, he was also supposed to check the property fully and have any defects corrected. His executorship gave him frequent access to the cottage and ensured that, at least, he learned the easiest route to the cottage and got to know the locality better.

All his reading of 'The AA Book of the home' had impressed on him were the importance of electrical safety. Older properties often had haphazard wiring, many with very aged, rubber coated wires and without the Faraday cage approach could easily become unsafe. Besides that, the rodent problem had to be faced. Rats and mice apparently like the taste of electrical coatings and, in older properties, could cause short-circuits and fires. He undertook to rewire the cottage to current standards, but Caroline was unhappy with Jims' free access to the cottage and so arranged for Dick, Shirleys' husband, to 'help' him. Dick readily agreed and Jim was happy, at least at the start, for the help. Dick proved to be a well meaning but cack-handed electrician who resorted to replacing fuses with four inch nails to prevent black-outs. Dick was happier doing bits and pieces of plumbing, so Jim had him do work in the upstairs bathroom, which he knew would become Carolines' regal suite.

It was after Dick re-plumbed the waste water pipe on the old cast-iron bath that the spark of genius lit in Jims' eyes. Dick had used a copper coloured plastic U bend, disconnecting the electrical earth, something that Jim spotted as soon as he looked underneath. Dick quickly re-attached the earth lead after Jim had mentioned it to him. What Jim didn't say was the earth was useless attached to a plastic pipe, whilst the whole system appeared safe, but the bath would be part of the whole Faraday cage.

That tiny idea in Jims mind was literally shocked into a full blown plan when he leaned against the radiator and re-adjusted Carolines' ancient transistor radio. As he touched the radiator, Jim saw a brief spark flash across from his hand to the radiator. He stepped back and contemplated what he had just observed. Quickly, he pulled the plug from the wall socket, that simple act revealing the cause. He could shake the plug and watch the two halves separate and could see that the plug had been very inexpertly connected. 'Ah, another of Carolines' nail file wire-ups' he thought, then wondered how often he had told her how to do it correctly. She still hadn't learned!

These two items connected in Jims' brain. All he had to do was to organize it so that Caroline touched the radio whilst in the bath and that proved easier than it seemed. Dick had put an old stool near the bath, so Jim put the radio on it and then slightly de-tuned it so that the Radio 4, Carolines' favourite, came through, but very crackly. Caroline, he knew, would lay in the bath and re-tune the radio and electrocute herself. Dicks' four-inch-nail-fuse would see that plenty of power flowed; the lack of earth on the bath should complete the process! However, Jim spotted an immediate problem. Should Carolines' body be found electrocuted in the bath, then his part in the re-wiring would mean that the initial finger of suspicion directly at him! Sure, he could CLAIM that Dick had re-earthed the bath, but Jim was in charge. Carolines' body had to vanish and with it her identity! Very easy to assert, but how could that be organized?

Jim thought long and hard about this problem before deciding to dump her body in one of the many overgrown pot holes near a fishing spot that Dick had taken him to. To ensure that identification of the body was delayed for as long as possible, it would best be found (if ever) as a skeleton. Jim knew that blow-fly maggots could rapidly de-flesh a corpse. And blow-fly maggots were available in all good fishing stores!

It would be a risk, that he knew, but the time of year should help, warm enough to keep the maggots happy, yet too cold to invite too many fishermen to that remote and windy spot.

He thought of the possibility that somehow she might still be alive when he went there and what to do about it. He knew enough not to use violence, that would almost certainly leave skeletal traces; long term poisons did enter the bones. If the body was found soon enough even quick acting poisons could be identified, but unusual compounds stood a good chance of being overlooked. His studies of 'The Herbal Pharmacopeia' had taught him that herbal products deteriorated quickly in the ground and by combining easily available products very effective poisons could be made as he had been warned when at Wayne State. Thinking back to his O.T.C. training and the maxim that 'no battle plan survives first contact with the enemy unchanged', he had to have a number of options. He decided to cover that possibility by having a poison as an final resort. Three routes to Carolines' death seemed good planning to ensure her demise, the weakness lay in having only two disposal options, but he couldn't think of a third. Simply leaving the body to be found wasn't an option, he needed Caroline to vanish completely and for he himself to be too remote for suspicion.

Back at the University, Jims' life settled into the somewhat strange but even tenor that he had established during the winter term. Bitchy secretaries still talked about his love life (or lack of it) and he knew these rumours circulated all around the campus. On the whole, most people treated him as they had before, but some women couldn't resist blaming him and extending this blame to anything else that he touched. Jim had become case-hardened to this treatment by then and didn't allow it to bother him.

In mid-February, he was slightly surprised to be asked to join one of the Departments' teams for a charity 'Dig-in' at the old folks home close to the University sports fields. It appeared that the students had offered to construct a pair of flower beds along the front of the old folks' home and had turned it into a charity dig-in to raise money for plants and other gardening equipment for the home. At the briefing, Jim was given his task, it was his job to dig out the earth from the flower bed site so that some-one else could lay up the compost, after which someone else finally completed the flower bed. It looked as though the students had thoroughly organised the scheme into individual units

and equally had organised it so that Jim did much of the horse work
on their behalf. Things had gone even further, all the work was to be
timed and a prize was to be given to the winning team. Actually, the
whole competition took on the air of a school sports day, but with a
very active and very unofficial 'book' running on the winners of each
particular work section. Jim was not pleased to see that the student
bookies had made him second favourite behind a University gardener,
who was lead off man for another team.

When the day of the 'Dig-In' came, the whole University seemed
to go to the old folks home to see the fun. Six large flower beds
had been marked out, each plot carrying a team number. As usual,
on such occasions, the manageress of the home and the University
Vice-Chancellor attended, each making a little speech for the occasion.
In her speech, the manageress made some joke about some of her
'guests', seeing the marked out digging areas, thought they were graves
and so rumours abounded about the extra facilities being made for
the nursing home. After polite laughter, the Vice-Chancellor made his
speech and extended the grave theme by saying that he hoped no-one
from his University would occupy them. Simultaneously, Jim hoped
that he wouldn't be digging his own 'grave'!

As start time approached, the first team of diggers went to collect
their tools and prepare for the hard work to come. Jim was dressed in a
dark blue boiler suit, with only underwear on beneath, as he expected
to get very warm, unlike some of the others who dressed as if for Arctic
climes. Jims' closest competitor, the gardener, was dressed in working
trousers and shirt and big Wellington boots, whereas Jim wore a pair
of old trainers. Both had elected to do the bulk of the earth breaking
with picks, using only spades to clear the earth once it was well broken.
It was obvious that some of the other teams were aiming to use spades
for the whole task. Jim had been advised by one of the older gardeners
to use a pick with one flattened end, a mattock, he had called it & Jim
had followed this advice.

When the starting signal went both Jim and the gardener started to
swing their picks and tear into the earth. Although Jim was striking at a
slightly slower rate than the gardener, he was burying the mattock end
deeper than his opponent at each stroke and pulling more earth out
with each stroke. As he settled to the work, Jim kept up a regular pace
and he could feel his latissimus muscles working hard each time that he

hauled the pick from the earth. Once he had broken up a depth of soil, Jim went to work with the spade to clear the space. It was a close run race, Jim beat the gardener by only a couple of minutes, but at a cost, his boiler suit was black with sweat, his shoes were split and torn and he was steaming like a horse finishing a race. He happily passed over to the next team member and left to go and shower in the sports hall, so at least he could feel part human again. He didn't wait around to see the completion of the competition, he drove home, but treated himself to a night out in an Indian restaurant after a long soak in a warm bath.

In the University the next day, he found out that his team had won, but, more importantly, his victory over the gardener had been worth a lot of money to some people, but not to him and he still had his sponsorship money to collect. For the next few evenings, his sport wasn't so pleasant, his body was sore and let him know it. What was pleasant was the knowledge of just how quickly a grave could be dug. Jims' mind swung once more to the location of Ginnys' cottage, in a quiet little village. Believing in hiding things in clear view suggested to Jim that her resting place, in one of the old local grave yards, would be appropriate. Even better if an already dug grave could be located, then Caroline could be interred in it underneath the legal occupant! A risky approach, but potentially very long term solution seemed available, but he decided to cover both Carolines' dumping and burying plans, best not to be caught out by equipment shortages!

Generally, life went on as before, he used the house in High Wycombe only as a dormitory, getting all his social life from the University environment. To extend his social circle within the University, Jim decided to join the Drama society, perhaps he could meet a few women there who hadn't heard the wild rumours circulating about him. His acting test proved to be a total flop and he knew he wouldn't be treading the boards, but there must be other things that he could do.

As a student, Jim had been a proficient photographer, having his own processing kit in his digs and becoming competent in dealing with black and white photography. He mentioned this one evening during rehearsals and Suzanna Crossley, the driving force of the Drama group, applauded the news. As Suzanna said, with good photographs on posters, the advertising would be much more powerful, but, she cautioned Jim, "you had better learn how to make up the actors, so that you can get the right look on the photographs". In all truth, Jim had not thought about this aspect and very nearly backed out of the photography as he couldn't see himself buying make-up in a shop. Suzanna soon disabused him of that notion, "Stage make up is not cosmetic make up, it's more powerful to look right on the stage and cannot be worn on the street".

Somewhat mollified, Jim swallowed his pride and began to learn the art of applying stage make up. As a small photographic studio had been organised, courtesy of one University department, Jim photographed the actors in various levels of make-up to learn how he could get the best results.

Jim attended the Drama group mainly over week-ends, when regular University life stood still for two days, but once a play was selected for the June performance, the rehearsals really began in earnest and began to happen during week-day evenings. As a make-up 'artiste' (how Jim hated that term), he tried to attend most rehearsals, so that he could experiment with stage make-up on the actors to get the correct 'look' for them and know what to photograph. Unfortunately, as part of his academic duties, Jim also had to visit students undertaking periods of training in Industry. Frequently these trips meant an overnight stay, which interrupted his attendances at the Drama group.

During one of these visits, he was at a company in North Yorkshire, visiting a student who had sent an emergency call to Jims' department. Such was the nature of the University/Industry relationship Jim had been dispatched at once to sort things out. After talking to the student for a while, Jim was of the belief that the company was willfully exploiting the student, but he decided to listen to the company's point of view before making any recommendations. A bluff, good natured man called Anthony Johnstone was the students' industrial mentor. Jim introduced himself and was immediately told to "call me Tony like everybody does' and then started to enquire about the problems with the student. Listening to Tony talk, he was impressed with the sincerity of the man and his obvious care for the students' education, but his approach was that he was trying to be too prescriptive. Tony, about Jims' age, had never been to University and didn't appreciate the independence and maturity that students felt and had taken the mentoring task too literally; the more he tried to mentor 'by the book' the more the student rebelled and became obstreperous. Neither Tony nor the student could see how they had reacted to each other, but Jim clearly did.

After a coffee break, Jim spent time with the student then with Tony laying out the problems as he had found them. Then he got together with both parties in the same room and repeated exactly what he had told each individually, after that he declared an end to the problems and told the student and Tony to co-operate and talk to each other, because each could learn from the other.

They all went to lunch together afterwards, a group at least working together in the same direction. During lunch, Tony proved to be as good humoured as he appeared, a bluff Yorkshire man who was proud of his county and who had rarely set foot out of it. Jim asked if Tony had ever been abroad, to which the answer was "No, don't see the need. It'll take me a lifetime to see all that this country has to offer." Talking further, Jim found that he and Tony shared the same birth year and was surprised when Tony told him his birthday and carried on with "that's what makes me such a bloody minded guy. Scorpio, you see!". He asked what Jims birthday was, was told and said "Gemini, doubled faced sign, you ought to be a diplomat", only to get Jim guffawing and saying he was nothing like a diplomat and would cause more trouble than he prevented.

"Well, you've done well enough here today" said Tony "I still think you're in the wrong career".

Driving back to Windsor University, Jim reflected how easy it would be to assume Tonys' identity for a short time during the coming summer and how Tony could unwittingly aid his plans. These thoughts occupied him for the whole of the drive back, so much so that he decided that it would be Tony identity that he assumed for the critical period. First, Jim had to get a legal passport in the name of Tony Johnstone, but with his face on it. He thought this no problem, he knew the passport requirements having signed so many applications for various students in the past, but he knew that the delay in getting a full, ten year British passport could upset his carefully worked out time plan, so he started on the job the next day. He had to go into London for a meeting, so he left the meeting as soon as possible and went to Somerset House. There he found the birth certificate of Tony Johnstone and bought a registered copy. He had a spare copy of the passport application sitting in his desk, so he began to fill it in, he needed a believable looking authenticator. What he did was to go to the University library and search through all the college prospectii until he found one of a college near to where Tony worked. From it he chose the name of an academic in the type of department that Tony would have attended (had he ever gone to that college) and signed the authentication sections in this mans name.

He still needed a photograph, there he was able to help himself, he stayed later one night after the drama group and made himself up to disguise his moustache and to use chalk dust to lighten his hair colour until it could almost pass as blond. He looked nothing like Tony Johnstone, but neither did he look too much like himself. When he was satisfied with his appearance, he sat in front of the camera and took a series of photographs at different exposures. When he developed them, two days later, he spent time deciding on the best negative, the one slightly over-lit had flattened out a lot of his features. During development, he deliberately marginally underdeveloped the prints (to lose more definition) and also under fixed them. Produced in that way, he knew that the print quality of the spare copy would soon deteriorate in storage and become useless for later identification purposes. Although poorly made, the photographs were no worse than some that the black and white photo booths produced, so he was sure that they would be accepted. After drying the prints, Jim carefully wrote on the back of one "I certify that this is a true likeness of Anthony Johnstone", signing it in the college lecturers name and title. He had manufactured, in his departments' laboratories, a rubber print baring the name of the north Yorkshire college and he used this stamp to endorse all the appropriate signatures on the application.

To make sure that nothing connected him to the passport, he bought postal orders in a number of different post offices, until he had the correct amount for the application cost. He then posted off the application using an address in Slough as the return address, knowing this address belonged to the uncle of one of his students and that the uncle charged five pounds for letting this service. This post box served as a 'dead-letter' drop for many of Sloughs residents, especially those having problems with the D.H.S.S. and other claim paying agencies. Uncle never telephoned anyone that there was a letter waiting for them, you just had to go into his shop to buy something and make an enquiry about post, pay the dues and collect your mail. Within four weeks, Jim had a completely legal British 10 year passport in the name of Anthony Johnstone, a passport that would stand any scrutiny and still prove genuine. Having acquired the new identity that he needed for his plan, he needed only a few other items and then it would be a matter of timing before the plan went operational.

Chapter 20

A cold, calculated insult on return (Sept. '82)

Jim stumbled through the formalities at Heathrow half asleep and walked through the green 'Nothing to Declare' gate of the customs area and then into the real life in Terminal Three. As he pushed his trolley past the faces waiting for other travelers, he scanned the crowds looking for Caroline, not really expecting to see her. He didn't find her, he had half expected her not to be there, so it was no surprise that she wasn't, although he was still saddened. Once he was sure that he had not missed Caroline, Jim pushed his trolley to the bus station to catch a bus to High Wycombe. From the bus station there he took a taxi back home.

At home, it was obvious that Caroline had been home, all the mail had been neatly divided, then piled tidily on the living room table. Jim decided to unpack and wash his dirty clothes, so he lugged his case up to their bed-room, only to find that the door was locked. Surprised, he tried a few keys from around the house, but the door remained steadfastly locked against him. Tired of trying and failing, Jim pulled the case down the corridor to the guest bed-room, where he unpacked the dirty clothes and hung up the clean ones. He went into the washing room, filled the machine and set it going. He had Carolines ear-rings in his pocket, so he took them out and put them on the table in the living room, where she was sure to see them when she came in. He pottered around the house a little more, making himself a cup of tea and a sandwich, before sitting in his old, comfortable leather chair and dozing off to sleep for a while.

Jim had just emptied the drying machine when he heard Carolines car drive onto their drive and as he made her a drink, she swept regally into the house and up the stairs.

"There's a drink here for you, Caroline", he called up the stairs and began to wonder how she had got into their bed room so easily. All riddles were solved moments later when Caroline came into the living room, picking up the drink that Jim had made for her & said, without preamble

"You've found your bedroom, stay in it ! I'm living my own life now !".

Jim looked startled, started to say something, but a glare of pure icy hatred from Caroline stopped him dead, instead, he pointed to the ear-rings and said "I've bought you these". Caroline barely glanced at the ear-rings and sneered "Trying to buy me, now, are you ? These aren't half expensive enough".

Thoroughly defeated, Jim stood open mouthed, whilst Caroline once more swept away and up the stairs. He decided to follow her, as he turned towards what had been their bedroom, Carolines glacial tones rang out again.

"Get away !", a simple, direct order, but with so much latent hatred that Jim did just what he was told to do and walked into what had become his bedroom and lay on the bed. He listened to Caroline energetically opening and closing wardrobe doors before she went to the bath room and noisily locked the door. He heard water running into the bath, Caroline climbing in and splashing water all around, then water emptied from the bath and a hair dryer started, still the lock had not been opened.

Jim was sitting in his chair again as Caroline came into the room preceded by the odour of hair spray and perfume. She had obviously gone to a lot of trouble, for she looked stunning, but she didn't acknowledge Jim, instead she put four champagne flutes on the table. From the kitchen she brought some small canapes on a plate and an ice-bucket containing a bottle of Champagne. "Expecting guests tonight, are we ?" asked Jim querulously, but he received no direct answer. Minutes later, the door bell rang, Caroline was obviously expecting it, the speed with which she answered it. A moment later Ruth and a man walked into the lounge, neither apparently seeing Jim, Caroline followed saying something about opening the champagne when Justin comes. Jim, feeling as transparent as the Invisible Man, just sat and watched, he had only a few minutes to wait before the door bell rang for the second time and Caroline admitted Justin. It was obvious that he and Caroline were known to each other and equally obvious that he knew to ignore Jim, he did know how to deal with champagne bottles and soon both pairs were drinking and chattering about 'Tonight'. Only a short while later, all four left together and Jim found himself once more master of an empty house.

Caroline had not returned by the time Jim went to his bed, neither had she returned when he got up to go to work, nor had she when he went to work. He returned from work that day after 6 p.m. Still no Caroline, although he noticed that the ear-rings were gone from the table. Curious about what she was doing and what she intended, he set to in the kitchen and made himself a quick salad. No sooner had he placed it on the table than he heard her car drive up.

"Hello", he shouted to her as she came through the front door. No answer, the only sound being Carolines' tread on the stairs as she went up stairs. Curious as to how long the snubbing would continue, Jim stayed in the living room. Nothing exciting seemed to be happening at the moment, so he went out to buy a take away Chinese meal. As he returned, he walked past the living room, it was obvious, even from outside, that the television was on, so someone must be watching it. In the living room, Jim found Caroline sitting deep within an armchair, looking incuriously at the television. He sat down in 'his' chair and ate his meal, Caroline never acknowledged his presence. He asked for the T.V. remote control to change the programme. No answer. He asked again, again no answer, so he stood up and began to look around, then he saw it, part hidden between Carolines leg and the chair arm, so went over to retrieve it. Caroline was as uncommunicative as the previous day, so he thought that he'd break the ice by tickling her and stealing the remote at the same time. He started to tickle her under her arm, he knew that it always caused her to collapse in laughter, so he felt confident of getting a friendly response. He didn't. Just as he touched her, grinning like a fool, she jerked her knee up, hard, into his groin and caused him to see stars and groan aloud.

"Don't touch me. Don't you every touch me again. I'm living my own life now, you live yours", she said, totally unfazed. Feeling sick, Jim crawled back to his seat, although it was some time before he could stand upright enough to be able to sit down, instead, in the immediate aftermath, he contented himself with kneeling on the floor, his elbows on the seat of the chair and his head in his hands.

She didn't go out that evening, although for the next four consecutive nights she did, not returning before Jim went to work the following days. Jim had thought that his marriage was maybe not the happiest before he went to Brazil, but he hadn't thought that Carolines' love had turned to the obvious loathing that it had. Always one for a quiet life, Jim decided that avoidance might be a profitable tactic. He thought he knew Caroline well enough to be sure that she would soon tire of the high living and come home, back to him, but he also covered his back by seeing a solicitor to get information about the possibility of divorce. Jim's solicitor, a partner in an old established practice near the University was older than Jim and an even bigger optimist. Heeding the advice he was given meant that Jim played an even lower profile role at home than even he had intended. He took to working much later into the evenings at the University and arriving there early each morning. This did not go unnoticed by the secretaries, who spent their break times poring over his 'case', totally uninformed, but totally sure of the problem and where the blame lay.

September came around with startling suddenness (or so it seemed to Jim) and he began chasing the tickets to take him to Detroit and the congress about the Brazilian work. Thanks to Abel Kingsman, Jim had only to dip into his savings temporarily, as the tutoring at Wayne State would cover all his costs, with, maybe, a small residual sum. Abel had pulled sufficient strings for Jim to do two weeks of work and attend the research congress, hopefully at no cost. On arrival in the Ecological Biology department at Wayne State, he was delighted to find that the efficient American machine had been at work and everything had been arranged. All Jim had to do was to attend the seminars each afternoon. Following the usual British criteria for visiting academics, Jim had been expecting to be accommodated within the student halls, but this was not so, he had been booked in to a cheap, but reasonable little hotel near campus and a cheap hire car was also awaiting him. Impressed, Jim intended to re-pay the trust by giving the students absolutely the most 'sharp edge' seminars that he could assemble. He need not have bothered overly much, the American Graduate students were very much like their British counterparts, not for them hours spend sitting in cavernous lecture halls, better a few hours more spent talking about the topic over a few beers.

Every afternoon, Jim walked off campus with his student group and down into the nearby locality that existed to service Wayne State students and staff. It very rapidly became apparent that the further you went off campus, the more specialist became the services offered. Jim and his group of six students used to go to the same beer hall each day, sometimes, in fact, they would lunch there on massive sandwiches and begin the seminar over food. This group consisted of four men and two women and seemed to be a fairly homogenous group except for Lori, a strawberry blond girl that seemed somewhat detached from the rest of the group. All the others called Lori 'Dreamer', an apt nick-name, for she constantly seemed to be looking at them from some remote distance. Occasionally, the seminars became free-ranging debates amongst equals which lasted long into an evening, at other times the seminars were truly seminal, intense, but short. Jim got to know all the students and to respect them and very quickly any barriers that had existed vanished. Jim enjoyed these talks, they kept him on his toes and the students liked them. Jim wasn't the stuffy Brit that all the students had expected and he demonstrated a remarkable ability (much admired by the students) to down large quantities of the chemical foam that was called 'beer' and still appear stone cold sober.

Of all the students, it was Lori who took to Jim the quickest. On the first day, she pressed up to him so closely that her breasts almost sat in his armpit. Slightly disconcerted, Jim asked Teddy, the obvious alpha-male and unofficial group leader, if this was normal behaviour for her. "Dreamer doesn't know that you've even noticed. She wouldn't care, even if you had. Don't let it worry you, she's like that".

It began one evening when Jim asked if anyone knew a good restaurant, after some suggestions Lori said she would show him one, but the better restaurants were across the river in Canada, in Windsor, Ontario. She had a neat way to get to Canada, so they could get in and out without a passport stamp. In a spirit of sheer devilry Jim said "Let's go for it and try Windsor for good food", so both he and Lori climbed into his rented Chrysler and drove away towards the Tunnel and Canada. As Lori predicted, a brief flash of the relevant number of documents looking like American passports sufficed and they were waved through by a bored looking Detroit policeman. Once out of the tunnel, they saw signs to Windsor International Airport, but drove in the opposite direction, towards town and the better food. That first night was one of exploration of more than food. After dinner in an Italian restaurant, they walked down to the river to look across at the lights of Detroit and by this time Lori was holding onto Jims arm tightly and rubbing her cheek against his shoulder. "Come on, let's get back. We've got work to do in the morning" said Jim somewhat huskily and together, they walked back to his Chrysler. Leaving Canada seemed as simple as leaving the U.S., the same trick sufficed, so Jim and Lori were soon back in Detroit and heading for Wayne State. Ever the gentleman, Jim offered to drive Lori home and was surprised when she said "Wisconsin" and she laughed at Jims' surprise.

"Where are you staying ?" she asked, Jim told her and she said that that was close by her flat, so to drive her to the hotel and she would walk the couple of blocks and not to worry because it was safe to walk at night in this part of town. Jim still persisted, wanting to take her to her door for safety, but Lori looked him straight in the eye and said

"Hey, Dr. Meadowcroft, sir, are you trying to get into my pants?".

Jim was startled and dumb struck, eventually stuttering that that was not his plan, he wanted her safely home.

"Pity" Lori said "I was hoping to get into yours tonight, when you get us back to the hotel".

Jim thought about Caroline, obviously enjoying herself with any man that took her out, then thought about looking gift horses in the mouth and said in an awful, fake American accent

"Why d'you wait so long to tell me, uh? I'd've driven faster !".

Lori became his regular dinner partner in Canada, staying with him, as she so calmly put it "For bed and breakfast". Neither made too much of the affair, undying love was declared by neither to the other, but both were comfortable with the impromptu arrangement. A few days after their first night together, Teddy said something about Jim succumbing to "The Dreamers" guile like many others. Jim said nothing, but noted this in his memory and thought nothing of it. That evening, Lori asked Jim what Teddy had told him and Jim told her in less graphic language than he'd been told.

"Sure, I like men" she said "but Teddy's jealous 'cos I won't boff him. He thinks he can have any woman he sees".

That said, neither referred to it again and it didn't affect their enjoyment of their 'bed and breakfast' routine.

At the end of Jims' tutorial employment, the research congress started. All the Eco-Biology staff and most of the graduate students attended along with the official delegates. Being a presenter to the conference, Jim had to remain at the front to be prepared for questions that fell within his area of expertise, Lori, like the rest of the Wayne State students, sat somewhere around the back, observing and learning. Tuesday evening of the congress week was the formal dinner and there was no way that Jim could get out of this being one of the programme research workers. Sergio lead the dinner, it had been his research programme anyway and afterwards walked around to meet as many people as possible. Jim had spotted Lori sitting on one of the tables at the far side of the dining room and after the food had finished began making his way towards her. En route, Jim met one of the other Wayne State students that he had tutored and together they made their way towards the back of the room where both the beer and Lori were.

Sergio, walking & talking with Abel Kingsman, joined the three of them just as all had started on bottles of beer, both were introduced by Jim to the students (both as 'one of my Wayne State tutor students') and Sergio commented that Jims' tutorials had been well received. At this, Abel Kingsman smiled and said that he hoped Jims tutorials would be appreciated as much next year as they had this year. Both students knew of Abel Kingsman and he was held in great esteem, almost awe, by them and Jim to be praised by Kingsman so openly was seen as a mark of distinction for Jim. After Sergio and Abel moved away, the male student made off towards the bar again, Jim looked at Lori and asked

"Bed and Breakfast, miss ?"

"Yea, this is too stiff for me !" she said "Let's go".

When Jim finally left Detroit to go back to Britain, Lori was sad, but not demonstrative, they knew that in the small world of eco-biology, both would easily be able to keep contact with the other, so the parting wasn't total, although it might be permanent.

Back at home, when he arrived, the situation with Caroline had not altered, he was still on his own in the marriage. Jim simply returned to using work as an escape until something should happen to change the situation permanently. He re-established his old work pattern, in early, work well into the evenings until it fitted him as comfortably as an old coat again. By this time, the winter term had started, Jim was into his lecture series and work regained an even tenor. Staying longer into each evening was actually proving to be very useful to Jim. He quickly re-established a routine of sport, dinner and writing, each evening either playing squash or circuit training, eating dinner in the refectory and then retiring to his carrel in the library to write papers for publication. This life was actually beneficial for Jim, he lost weight, shedding a few years with the pounds and boosted his publication record to boot. His squash was developing and he was becoming difficult even for some of the younger members of the University team to beat; circuit training, on the other hand, really allowed him prosper at the expense of the students. Jim always did the 'Army' circuit and got sufficiently proficient that he gave other people a start and could still complete three circuits at maximum level before the others. A big man he may be, but now he was a big, very fit man who could power his way easily around the circuit. His food intake had fallen, partly because he was paying attention to himself and partly because the University refectory produced typical Institution food, sufficient, but no more. He had acquired his own private little writing room within the library, where he could hide himself away amidst piles of text books and write until he could barely keep his eyes open.

If the Library staff had any surprises about the books that Jim ordered, they did not say so. All that bothered them was that he didn't exceed his annual allowance of Inter-Library loans for some of the rarer tomes, or retain the books beyond their return dates. Jims' requests were really catholic, from the current Pharmacopeia of drugs to the AA book of the House, with books on Herbalism and forensic science requested for good measure. No eyebrows were raised when Jim asked for, and received, the large scale atlas of the U.K., the southern and northern states of the U.S.A and the latest compendium of airline flights and costs. Had Jim worried that these books would cause him to be remembered by the Library staff (he wasn't), he had no worries. Government parsimony had forced academics in all Universities to make their international journeys by the absolutely cheapest way possible. So inventive were the academics that they pioneered many cheap routes and, in the process, taught many travel agents just how cheap air flight could be.

Jim could never remember whether it was whilst reading the 'airlines' book or examining the detailed road maps of the U.S.A. that the plan to get Caroline out of his life was first born. It certainly had been and slowly began to solidify in his mind and he found himself seriously examining its' possibilities and potentialities. Whenever it was born, it rapidly became more than simply an academic exercise to him and he began to weave the planning of his plot around his writing time.

Just before lunch the next day, Jim walked into Prof. Kingsmans' outer office and told the secretary there who he was and why he was there. Having his appointment immediately pre-lunch seemed to fulfill all Jims' worst fears of 'a good lunch and thanks' for supervising the extra Brazilian students.

"Professor Kingsman is engaged at the moment, but he has you in his diary and will be ready momentarily", said his secretary.

Jim hoped he would be ready for longer than that, but knew what the secretary was infering and in a few moments Abel Kingsman opened his office door and let a number of baffled looking students out, then greeted Jim very warmly.

"We'll go for lunch soon" said Abel, at which point Jims' stomach fell, so it WAS just a good lunch, "I have something of considerable interest to tell you in confidence, which involves you deeply" continued Abel.

Jim sat back, all his faculties were now on alert and his concentration was complete. "N.A.S.A. want me to do a research programme for them concerned with the environmental impact of their launchers. This programme will last at least three years and will be based in and around the coast-line of the state of Miami. I want you to lead a group next year" was what Abel said.

Jim was dumbfounded and really couldn't make sense of the offer, so Abel took Jim to the Senior Common Room for lunch and let him get his ideas back together again. Jim said that he would be delighted to be on the team for next years' program, for Jim that eased things considerably. That N.A.S.A. funding was guaranteed and would help eke out his salary, as all the summer work did, but he wouldn't have to compete to find the research funding himself. Life was definitely looking up! Then, like a blow in his stomach, he thought of Carolines' likely reaction.

She wouldn't like it, of course, but knowing about it 11 months in advance would surely give her enough time to accept it and may be even want to come and visit, although that would mean visiting the United States. Caroline had never been to the U.S., and seemed never to want to visit the country, inferring, somehow snobbishly, that America REALLY wasn't anything special and not worth visiting.

Jim couldn't rid himself entirely of the thoughts of Carolines' likely reactions, but he decided to enjoy himself until he told her the news. It would, at least, be about two days before he got back to the U.K. and into the trouble that his wife would cause, so best be hung for a sheep as a lamb thought Jim. He left Miami University in the early afternoon and decided to drive straight back to Orlando and spend the night there before going to the 'plane. Another steady six hours' drive brought him back to his starting point, but he continued to drive north for a short while until he was outside the immediate Orlando metropolitan area, where the hotel prices were significantly cheaper than a mile down the road. Jim found a hotel for the night and decided to eat in the hotel, rather than go out, so after a pleasant meal and a couple of beers he retired to his room, ready for sleep. After breakfast, he paid the bill and drove back towards Orlando, still far too early for his flight, but with sufficient time to look around the shopping malls for gifts. Eventually, Jim bought a pair of gold ear-rings for Caroline, discreet, but noticeable, just the type of jewellery that she liked. He turned the car back in to Hertz, caught the shuttle to the departure gate and was soon strapped into his seat as the 747 charged down the runway, before climbing like an elevator into the clear, blue sky.

Chapter 21

Into Action !

Jim invested a full week deliberately noticing the types of cars and small vans that inhabited the local roads, but that came and went completely anonymously. He also began to search out the buying places for small, anonymous vans. By paying attention to the cars and vans that passed him by in the street and made no impression on any one, Jim came up with a 'wish' list to try to buy. First and foremost came the Ford Transits, but they were too big for his purposes, so he looked at the smaller, car sized vans. After a week of careful noticing, he knew that there were three possibilities, a Ford Escort, a Vauxhall Chevanne or a Vauxhall Astravan. All he had to do was to buy a reliable old one, hide it away and use it for his plan and then sell it discreetly. Easily said & even easier thought !

He started to talk, generally, to the students about buying cheap cars and was soon fully informed of the local facts. What he had thought easy to think about but not to do, was actually very easily accomplished, but he would have to use one of the larger local car auctions. There were two suitable sales, one at Kempton Park race course and one in Slough, although other smaller, less frequent car auctions were scattered around throughout the region. Jim started by going first to the Kempton Park auction, simply to get a flavour of what cars were coming up for sale and in what condition and how the bidding process worked. This first trip told him that, although Astravans were on the market, they were highly valued, always attracting bidders and fetching high prices, so these he deleted from his list. His second trip was to Slough and he concentrated on his other two choices, both came up for sale and fetched prices that he could afford, many of both types were frequently sold after desultory bidding which attracted no attention whatsoever. Slough had other advantages, it was easily accessed from either work or home, but the major one was that if you paid cash, the registration papers were simply handed over to you with the car key and there were no identity checks of any sort. This was even better from Jims' point of view and placed Slough at the top of his list for auctions to use. On the other hand, Kempton Park had a 'drop-off' service, where the car could be parked outside the grounds and the papers pushed through the letter box into the auctioneers office for sale in the Sunday auction. Most of the 'drop-off' cars were cars at the end of their earthly existence and were bought cheaply and scrapped after being cannibalized for spare parts.

Now, he knew where he could buy a car, not register it in any name and where he could dispose of it anonymously, but he had not found a place where he could store it for a few weeks, without attracting any undue attention. On his way home one evening, he decided to have a drink at the Dedworth Arms, in Dedworth Road, in the centre of High Wycombe. As he drove there, he passed the towns' old car park, taken over by the students of the local college who parked their cars there. As he looked at it, he realised that he was seeing the solution to his long term parking problem. Some students lived in their vans and cars, so there was always some-one around, any car he bought would fit in very well with the general age and appearance of the cars and vans there and there were no parking permits needed, simply drive in and set up home ! His beer in the "Dedworth' went down very well that evening. Jim noted that a nagging thought had just vanished and in its' place he had a rosy glow of anticipation.

It was coming into June, Jim had finished his teaching duties and had only the examinations to mark, but he had to move swiftly on with his plans, as he was soon due to go to Florida and his summer research project with Abel Kingsman. Equally, in a few weeks time, term would end at the local college for the summer and his car hiding place would go, so he sat down and worked out a time table based on his U.S.A. visit. This done, he went to the Slough auction with cash in his pocket to buy a van. After an hour, the buyers were fewer in number as all the biggest bargains had gone when the cars at the bottom end of the market were sold. Within minutes, he had seen, bid for and bought a 1976 Chevanne, that had obviously been inexpertly repainted a matt dark blue colour. No-one else had bid for it, so he had had no opposition to remember him. He had liked the car as it driven in to the auction area, it seemed mechanically sound, even if it was unattractive. He paid in cash and the big Sikh salesman simply passed him a handful of papers with the comment that the car was taxed and M.O.T.'d for a few months. Better and better, thought Jim. He drove the Vauxhall back to High Wycombe and was pleased to find that it drove adequately well, a fact which gratified and slightly surprised him. Arriving in Wycombe centre, he parked it in the student car park amongst a crowd of similar aged vehicles where it did not look at all out of place. Walking to the bus station, he caught the first bus to Slough and picked up his own car and drove back to the University. He was sure that the car would be safe where it was for a few weeks.

A week later, dressed like a student, he parked his car on the far side of Wycombe market, bought a few things, then went to the old Vauxhall in the car park and started it up and drove out of town. Jim had thought that he would give the car a good drive to check it out thoroughly and also keep the battery fully charged. As he planned to use this car on both urban streets and motorways, he decided to drive up to Birmingham, the first part would be on the new M 40 to Oxford, the remainder on the normal roads, right into Birmingham. As he left Oxford, he filled up the car, so that he could check fuel consumption, it would be stupid to run out of fuel in the middle of nowhere when he had his plan part completed.

As he approached Birminghams' south-eastern suburbs, Jim saw the signs of urban decay all around. In Balshall Heath he saw just what he had been looking for, a run down shop selling ex-army clothing, he pulled in front of the shop and went inside. Five minutes later, he re-emerged with an old, but serviceable, dark blue boiler suit and a pair of Wellington boots, all of which he threw into the back of the Chevanne. Just up the road was a filling station where he filled up and noted the fuel consumption to be really quite good. As he was driving out, he saw another run down shop selling tools, so he went there and bought a pick—mattock in good condition quite cheaply. Driving back to High Wycombe, he pondered on what more he needed to bring his plan up to being fully operational and thought 'no more than a full tank of fuel'.

Within days, at work, he received confirmation of his working dates that in Florida and, to his surprise, saw that he had been assigned to an area near Orlando rather than in the Miami region. This confirmation came accompanied by a wad of briefing notes and detailed working instructions. All this still meant, however, that he would have to check in with Abel Kingsman when he got to the U.S.A. A few days before he left for Florida, Jim filled a shoulder flight bag with dirty clothes and threw the bag in the back of the Vauxhall. He drove the car down the M 40 to Uxbridge and then on to Heathrow long term parking, where he took a ticket, noting on the back where in the long term car park he had left the Vauxhall. He caught the courtesy bus to Terminal one, got off, walked into the building and out through another door. At the Heathrow bus terminal, he took the regular bus to Oxford, looking like a worker or a traveler returning home, climbed off the bus in High Wycombe bus station and walked home up the hill, still carrying the shoulder bag. He was alone at home, but he filled the washing machine with the dirty washing and set it on a long, warm washing programme.

On the day of his departure to Florida, he drove his own car to a commercial long term car park near Heathrow, took their courtesy bus to Terminal Three, unloaded his two suitcases onto a trolley and checked in on the Pan-Am flight to Orlando. His ticket, provided from University of Miami, was for coach class, one down from first, but Jim was already appreciating the American approach. This appreciation was heightened further when he found that each coach class passengers had virtually one stewardess each, there being so few coach class passengers. "Real Barby dolls" Jim thought, looking appreciatively at their long legs and short skirts and from then on he knew he was going to enjoy this trip. If the flight was anything to go by, the augurs were looking very good indeed.

Arrival in Orlando was as smooth as usual. At the immigration desk, Jims' life time American visa meant that formalities were routine and the immigration officer was at least minimally friendly. He had arranged a hire car from the U.K. before he left, so after collecting his bags, he loaded up the car and drove out of the airport looking for somewhere to stay for the duration of his project contract. That meant a long term hotel or motel to allow him to conserve enough money to operate his plan in an unrestricted manner and yet still retain options if he had to change details 'on the hoof'. After driving around aimlessly for a while, he remembered Silvermans' Motel, so he stopped at a bar, went in for a beer, found Silvermans' card and put a call through to the old man. Not only did Mr. Silverman remember Jim by his accent, he offered him a generous discount on a 1 month rental, an even bigger discount if he paid in cash and in advance. Jim, thinking that he would hardly see the motel after the first few days, accepted.

"I'll have the towels ready for you when you get here, young man" said Mr. Silverman "and coffee and cookies will be waiting, too".

Walking into the motel room as tired as he was, Jim noted that it was much as he'd imagined it to be, but it was clean, it had a big double bed which seemed to suck Jim deep into its' embrace. He woke up early in the morning aware that he was ravenously hungry, but also aware that he had to take the first steps in his plan, the timing would be tight and brooked no delay at this point. Jim drove his car to the nearby mall and went inside to find breakfast, which he did easily. Refreshed, he drove back to Silvermans, parked the car and then limped into the motel office. "Goddamn it, I've just turned my knee coming out of the room and I can't walk. Is there a doctor that I can see nearby?".

Mr. Silverman was concerned that Jim launch a legal action on him, but when assured that that wouldn't happen, he made an appointment with Dr. Levy for 9.30 a.m.

"Levy's the best doctor in these parts, but generally only the Jewish people go to him. I've told him you're from England and that you are Reform. He hummed and hawed a bit, but he'll see you at 9.30"

Mr. Silverman told Jim where to go and kept saying "Sure didn't mean you to hurt yourself, young man, like you'll be right as rain in a day I 'spect".

Jim tried to make Mr.Silverman feel less guilty, but to no avail and he was helped to his car by the motel owner, who was still discomforted by Jims' 'accident'. As before Mr. Silvermans directions were exact, he found the ground floor surgery where he was told it would be. Parking close by, he climbed out of the car as if in pain and limped into the surgery holding on to whatever came to hand. Jim reported to the receptionist, a dragon of an old woman, whom it was impossible to sweet-talk, but was Dr. Levys' mother. A typical American Jewish Momma, thought Jim, so protective of her son, yet so proud of him being a doctor. 'I wonder how many clients she loses for her son ?' Jim thought. He didn't have to endure her attention for long, the surgery door opened a woman left carrying a prescription and Dr. Levy himself came through the door to help Jim into his office.

"I hope mother didn't bite you too badly" said the doctor, "she's not too good with folks that she doesn't know".

Jim sat down and explained the 'symptoms' of his knee injury in detail, he know them well enough as he had had the problem he was describing. Jim briefly explained that he was supposed to start his project tomorrow and that it would involve a lot of standing and walking. Fortunately, Dr. Levy's advice was the same that he had from his British doctor, rest and regular mild anti-inflammatories and a prescription appeared for the pills.

"I'll phone Prof. Kingsman and explain your predicament and I'll tell him that you've damaged your synovial membrane in your knee and that I've laid you up for at least 1 week. Sort the bill out with my mother, or do you have an address that we can invoice you at ? Oh, and by the way, rest with your leg elevated to knee height and use an ice pack. See you in a week !" all from Dr. Levy as Jim limped into the waiting room and into the dragons' lair.

Back at Silvermans Motel, Jim told Mr. Silverman what he had been told, received condolences on meeting Mrs. Levy, and said that he would stay in the room for most of the time, but that he'd have to drive out to get food. Mr. Silverman was happy with this arrangement and told Jim to park his car around the back of his room and not on communal front car park, he could get to it easier and where it wouldn't be seen. Jim thanked him and limped to his car, parked it at the back of the room, entered through the back door, changed and left again. He parked the car in long term parking at Orlando airport, entered the domestic side and bought a single ticket in a false name to Detroit.

Chapter 22

Rent-A-Wreck (1983)

Getting from Detroit Metro Airport to the Middle Belt was no problem at all, after all the jets almost touched down on Middle Belt, even during the morning long rush hour. Ford World Headquarters at Dearborn, flags and banners flying proudly, dominated the first part of the ride from the airport. Here Jim had to leave the airport courtesy bus & take a fast city bus, which must have been new as it was graffiti-free and arrived at the appointed time. From F.W.H.Q. to the campus of Wayne State University the bus journey went via route 12, when he climbed off the bus it was opposite the central administration block. Walking through the small grassed area, he turned right opposite the door of the Ecological Biology department, then took the same route as the previous September towards the beer-hall and walking through the campus. Following that route from the campus presented possibilities of every sort, from the cultural to the carnal, exactly as Jim had discovered on his previous trip, but car hire was principally what brought Jim here. Directly across a side road from the central admin. block and the tired grey-green grass of its' sparse lawn was the area of town where students ate and drank in the many down at heel pubs and bars. This public facade of shabby gentility served well to hide the less genteel side of near campus culture. Here the street life contacted, and sometimes interacted with, academia as represented by the host of student enterprises cloaked by the eateries. All manner of things were possible here, but most were not why Jim was here this time so he walked confidently and directly two blocks down from the campus facade, passing seamlessly from bustling businesses to early urban decay and dereliction the further he walked.

Jim turned left at the end of the first block and walked straight into the first shop through the bead curtain hanging behind the open door. Directly facing him was an old style pharmacy display, complete with a row of enormous bottles full of garishly coloured liquids. Behind the mahogany counter stood someone who looked like a refugee from California and the late 1960's, complete with headband and chromatic spectacles. As Jim approached, the hippy stood like a wooden dummy, no sign of movement or life permeated the statue. Finally standing directly before the hippy, separated only by the counter Jim moved to prod the statue when finally it moved and a small smile crossed the previously immobile face.

"Welcome to Natures Miracles" said the statue in a surprisingly old voice "How can we permit Mother Nature to correct your problems?"

In a well practiced way Jim gave an order for small quantities of three tinctures, to be told that they would be made up freshly and would be ready in thirty minutes. Jim nodded, left the Herbalist, walked around the corner and went into the first bar, where he ordered a sub and a beer and remained until the half hour was up. He paid, left the bar and returned to the Herbalist to collect the medication. As he walked in, the aged hippy placed three small bottles on the counter and smiled his small smile again.

"You know your herbs, but do you know the dangers?" Jim was asked. "This smooth bottle is safe, safe, safe, but don't mix the other two!"

"It's O.K., I'm just re-stocking, I know what not to mix" was Jims' reply.

"Cool, then" the hippy replied, telling Jim the cost. Jim paid cash, from a fat money clip of dollars, waving away the few cents of change he was offered.

He turned right out of the shop and the right again on the second crossing, to find himself, as last year, walking down a deserted and grubby pavement. His knowledge, gained the previous September, was still sound. Mid-way down the block of derelict and semi-derelict shops and stores, on the left hand side, was a green painted door of rotting wood, hanging drunkenly from its' upper rail. An obviously hand painted sign (in beige paint) announced to the world the group headquarters of "Rent A Wreck Inc." car hire. This was exactly the place that Jim had been lead to by Lori after leaving a Wayne State students' party one mild September evening. It hadn't taken much finding, neither then nor now, neither had the name and back ground of the drop-out student owner of the enterprise.

Just seeing that hanging door again brought back the memories of that first party when the American Grad.students had taken the unstuffy and surprisingly approachable British visitor (they told him that after the fourth jug of beer) out to show him 'Campus life'. Images of dark wooden tables awash with beer and the feel and smell of beer soaked pretzels & nuts came back vividly. Of jeans and Tee shirt clad students, too, rowdily extolling the values of American student life and of Lori, the quiet, strawberry blond, nicknamed 'Dreamer' by the others, who hung onto his right arm and pressed her boobs into his shoulder all the time. Teddy, the group guru, had been praising the freedom of student life and available opportunities in the 'states when Rent-A-Wreck came up as a typical example of 'All American entrepreneurship'. A nearly destitute student had seen an opening, dropped out of the Wayne State basket-ball programme and set off to make his fortune in the car hire game. Destitution had posed a problem, overcome with 'All American Ingenuity', for how does anyone start a car hire business when they don't have money to buy their first decent car to rent on ? Thus, Rent-A-Wreck had been born in 'the Motor City' of U.S.A, where old cars could be had almost for free and a fleet of old 'clunkers' gathered only for the repair costs.

Being black and good at street basket-ball had helped Cecil acquire his early cars, in "Motor City U.S.A.". All of the junkiest cars were owned and kept in black neighbourhoods, so who thought anything of a tall Negro in a gas-guzzling mobile wreck being anything out of the ordinary in those districts? All the likely vehicular stock of "Rent-a-wreck" was spied out and sized up by the street basket-ball players who sold their information to Cecil for anything from him joining their team for a match to providing reciprocal services or information to his spies. Some cars were even legally purchased!

It was rumoured that organised crime used the services of Rent-A-Wreck when they wanted a nondescript car for a high visibility job & Cecils' particular brand of nondescript junkers were ideal. Rumour also had it that these cars were never rented out to ordinary customers, but received loving care in the Wrecks' mechanics shop until the time, after their second job, they provided a meal for an autocrusher somewhere in the state of Michigan. This invisibility was just what Jim wanted, to be an average guy in an average car doing average things and attracting no attention. 'Dreamer' had at least met Cecil and confided to Jim that cash money talked powerfully to Cecil. He preferred cash deals & all the cash was stashed in the butt pocket of his denims. It was that butt pocket stash that had entertained 'Dreamer' and her friends when Cecil had thrown a party in one of the seedier local bars.

Jim opened the wicket door, stuck his head inside and yelled "I want wheels!" loudly into the dim interior.

"Yessir, we got da wheels if you got da bread" came from deep shadows over at the far side. Cecil materialised out of the gloom, a huge black guy, dressed in the local uniform of jeans, Tee shirt and Lumberjack shirt. Jim was no small fry, but Cecil was a good 8 inches taller with hands and feet of exceptional size.

"I got cash money and I want a car nobody notices for a week, but one with some good miles in it".

"Sure thing, my customer. All our cars got good miles in, but you want something special ?"

"I want a car that I can park for a few days & be there when I get back and not be bust into either".

"Hokay, boy. You want Wrecks' built in anti-theft protection and invisibility deal!"

What emerged was a dull, matt grey Plymouth with light rusting on the wings & drivers' door & no hub caps, the tyres also having seen better days and the seats in need of a severe cleaning. Litter & wrapping paper, the debris of a young family, were strewn over the inside of the car. "*EVERYBODY* got one of dese" said Cecil, "Nobody sees a grey car & nobody goin' to pinch nuttin', 'cos there's nuttin' to pinch. The engin. is good, don't burn no oil & don't burn too much gas. Battery is noo and the body work'll last at least another week".

Cecil proved to be an astute business man, the cash deposit would have bought the car at least twice over. He did not demand insurance ("Who wants to get them jack-asses involved ? Don't do nuttin' anyhow") total loss was covered, generously, by the deposit. Any costs for damage were negotiable ("Might even be that I pay you, if it makes the car more average") & the rental costs of $10 per day would come from the deposit. Jim expected no return from his deposit. Approximate dates for the return were agreed and then Jim got the keys of the anonymous car. Sitting in the car, before he drove it from Cecils' garage, Jim slid his second passport, that for Anthony Johnson, under the front skirt of the drivers seat and set his own, brazenly, in his breast pocket, the blue back easily visible from outside the car. Jim Meadowcroft, soon to become Anthony Johnson, was now prepared for his mission, starting with an anonymous drive into Canada.

His first job was to gas the car up, then he wended his way through the Detroit traffic and into the tunnel to Windsor, Ontario. This under-ground border crossing was guarded both ways in respect of its' status; into Canada, a Detroit P.D. man watched out of a bullet-proof booth, from Canada a Canadian immigration officer performed the same function. Both had power over any suspicious car and, between both booths in international territory, was a pull-in for passport inspection & stamping. Dirt & the detritus of a million cars covered this pull-in; many years ago a mutual understanding between both gate keepers allowed cars of one nation to flow unhindered into the other and to return home, unhampered, at night fall. In theory, some identification was shown on passing the booth in either direction, normally this was just a quick flash of a passport. Lori had shown Jim in September how to fool the system using his U.K. passport when he took her for private dinners to Ontario, before taking her back to Detroit & his hotel on the Middle Belt for bed & breakfast. So regular had this become over that week in September that Jim just left the back of his passport visible in his shirt pocket. It always worked like a dream with no problem, but today Jim was doing it for real & alone. Traffic flowed into and out of the tunnel in a smooth, steady stream. Although traffic was always heavy and vehicles were rolling through all day and night, everyone diligently slowed down at the exit, on the Canadian side, to toss in the two quarters needed for the toll. Actually, metropolitan Windsor treated the tunnel as a source of some profit, because of the number of $1 coins in the blue collection baskets. Despite much of the television made in America, which seems to suggest that the 'States are wild and lawless, the average Americans' respect for rules & law and order were a tenet of Jims' plan.

Suddenly, Jim found himself back in Canada without a stamp on his passport & no record of him having been there. So far, so good!

He emerged into full Canadian sun-shine on Huron Drive, following the car in front through the traffic lights, to cross Riverside Drive, then University Avenue, followed by Wyandotte Street, before making a right turn onto the Row express way. From there, the trip to Windsor International Airport was a run of about 6 miles at a steady 50 M.P.H., no sense now in bringing himself to the attention of the Police by speeding. Cecils' old Plymouth really was unexceptional, nothing noticeable at all and ready to cruise all day at 50, if that was what he wanted. He didn't, but he felt that the heart of the car was strong and sound, which was reassuring. Less than twenty minutes after surfacing in Canada, Jim drove into the long-term parking lot at Windsor and parked the car in the middle of a row of other similar, non descript cars. Before leaving the car, Jim felt under the front edge of the drivers' seat squab and extracted the passport in the name of Anthony Johnson. James Meadowcroft's passport was put in the inside side of the seat squab and manipulated until it couldn't be felt from the seat. Before leaving Orlando, Jim had had his hair cut, shaped and blonded at a style clinic, so without his moustache, he actually looked like the photograph of Anthony Johnson in the passport. He took the car park bus to the European Terminal and got off at the British Airways sign and walked into the terminal building. Strolling through the active, but by no means crowded terminal he walked into a luggage shop and bought two nylon hand-grips with U.S. dollars. At another shop he bought a pair of jeans, a couple of dark, voluminous American sized Tee shirts and then went to the Pharmacy to buy tooth paste and a brush. The "Bookworms' Store' was next and, after a few moments' searching, purchased two large paperbacks, once more, weight fodder for the check-in bag. A few more minutes around other stores had produced other trivia, which gave his check-in bag sufficient weight to be un-noticeable.

A short stop in the Mens room to prepare saw Tony empty the bottle of harmless tincture down the drain. Using the empty bottle, he poured about half the contents of the other tinctures in and shook up the resulting mixture. An empty polythene bag carried the innocuous looking bottle, which was hidden deep within his hand luggage. After emptying the remaining tinctures down the toilet, he flushed away the chemicals, then unpacked the jeans, tee shirts and toiletries and put them into his on-board grip, only then did he feel safe to go and buy a return ticket to Heathrow. Leaving the mens room, he casually dropped one of the empty bottles in the trash can, the other he was going to drop into the waste system on board the plane. Before that was possible, he had to find a suitable ticket. Using a payphone in the hall, he 'phoned the ticket sales desks of B.A., United, Pan-Am and T.W.A., to find out who had the best price ticket. All quoted prices with and without an over Saturday night stay and were all sympathetic to the new immigrant who had to get home quickly to see his father before he died of the unexpected stroke he had suffered last night. United seemed not to be operating the cartel price of the other airlines, so Tony went over to their desk, repeated the story and the price he'd been quoted and found himself on the flight departing in two hours. The ticket selling lady could also check him in, if he had his baggage available, he had and he asked for and got, an isle seat, non smoking. All that was left was to walk through the passport check, be stamped out and then wait for the flight to be called. Before going through passport control, Tony looked around for a group to join, where he could be inconspicuous and just become 'one of the group' as far as the immigrations officer was concerned.

No such luck! Windsor International was not the heaving mass of Heathrow or Orlando, but a few small groups of holiday makers were about. Once more, Tony was visiting the shops, trying to find a way to tack onto one group and appear to be a member.

"Stop that thief, he's got my purse", the shout came from lower down the hallway.

"Attend, attend, voleur, attende cette homme !", now in a distressed soprano, just short of a scream.

Tony looked out of the shop door way in time to see a denim clad white youth come pelting around the corner with a womans' clutch bag under his right arm pit and his left hand catching the shop edge to pivot him around the corner at full speed. Without thinking, Tony shot out his left arm and braced himself for the stiff-arm tackle to come. It came and very nearly spun Tony around. It had the desired effect, the effect for which it had been banned from the Rugby field years ago. The thief momentarily hung horizontally by his chin from Tony's left upper arm, like washing on a line in a strong breeze, before dropping, quite gracelessly, onto the marble floor. In the cathedral silence in the shopping hall, the dull thud as his head bounced, almost blended in with the slap as his legs came to earth. Before Tony had time to react, they were upon him; at first it was the airport security personnel, college students all, working to pay their way through school, then it was the men from the woman's travel group. As the last of them slid up join to the stationary group, the first of the airport security people dropped on his knees to check over the prone youth, then bedlam erupted. Members of the travel group first recovered the womans' bag and started to pummel Tony with congratulatory back slaps. Airport security staff, however, called for the in-house medic to check the youth over before they moved him, then they called the airport police.

Tony was the focus of everyones attention & couldn't get away, indeed would not be left alone until after the Doctor had pronounced the youth 'alive, but he'll have one hell of a head-ache tomorrow'. Then the airport police called an ambulance to take the youth to the cells and proceeded to take statements of all concerned. So much for being inconspicuous thought Tony, they now have my new name and description, so someone is bound to remember me later. Only after half an hours' questioning by the hot, sweaty sergeant did silence begin to return to Tony's life. Convinced that Tonys' sudden appearance at the shop doorway had startled the youth and caused him to slip (despite him wearing trainers) and fall heavily that his injury was of his own making.

Finally, the sergeant closed his note book, said "Thank you, sir, we always get trouble like this at peak season.", then walked away.

The holiday group were not so easily placated, to them Tony had become an unlooked for "Sir Galahad". Try as he might, he could not return to anonymity. Eventually, Tony said that he had to go to the boarding gate and hurry to catch his plane. At this the crowd noticed, too, that they also had a plane to catch, so the whole group surrounded Tony and en-masse poured through Passport check and security. There were just enough people to saturate the system for a short time. A cheery group of that size, with an obviously popular group member in their midst, influenced the passport controller. Submerged by over fifteen passports, checks were perfunctory, all were stamped and returned.

Apart from the offers of wining and dining, Tony was in departure lounge, where he wanted to be, ready to fly back home in growing inconspicuousness. Looking at the departure board, he noticed his flight was from a gate just about as far as physically possible from the holiday group, so he walked to the gate and, to pass the time, submerged himself into a newspaper he found on the seat. Eventually, when the flight was called and the barely controlled bustle to get onto the plane started. When he approached the flight attendant with his passport and ticket, she did not look up, but muttered "Thank you, sir" and passed him back his passport and seat ticket stub. He walked down the loading tube, up the alleyway to his seat, sat down & strapped in, thankful for the next few hours of anonymity to come.

Chapter 23

The Mission

Piling off the plane at Heathrow meant the walk up the extended covered ramp tube and into Terminal 3 proper. Tony was at a loss to explain why flights always seemed to find a gate at the most remote end of the terminal, away from all the areas that the passengers had to use. Arriving on an American flight meant that the queue for re-entry into Britain was short. Most international travelers use their domestic airline, so coming from abroad on a foreign carrier meant that few other British passport holders were on the flight. There were sufficient U.K. passport holders coming from other flights to keep the immigration officer from boredom. Once through immigration (no problem, the official gave him a cursory glance, eyes then flicking to the passport photograph, before closing the passport, handing it back; all without a movement on his dead-pan face), Tony went down to the luggage reclaim area. As if wanting to reclaim his checked bags, he found the carousel for his flight & stood around looking as if he were waiting for his bags to appear. Once the luggage was in full spate at the carousel, he moved around to the far side, looking for all the world to be an anxious traveler searching for his bags. After a few minutes, he moved to another area around the carousel, still apparently seeking his luggage. A couple of minutes later he moved again, going in the direction of the baggage trollies, but this time he looped back around the other bank of carousels and walked directly through the green channel and out through customs with just his hand grip.

He walked out to the side of the building where the Long Term car park courtesy bus stopped, under the glare of the sodium lighting, hopelessly fighting hopelessly the rising dusk. After a few minutes wait, a yellow and black B.A.A. bus pulled in to take him to Heathrow Long Term parking to pick up his parked car. He shuffled through the five pound notes (and the one odd ten pounds note) in his British wallet to retrieve his parking ticket and read the ball-penned note of the section and row number where his old Vauxhall Chevanne waited for him. As the bus pulled up at the appropriate section letter, Tony started to scan the rows upon rows of parked cars hoping to locate the Vauxhall, so that he could walk towards it, but dusk was falling too rapidly now. He was forced to walk down the endless rows of cars until he found the correct row number, then start the daunting walk down the row scanning both the front and back car for one that he recognised. He felt stupid, but not obvious, as he undertook this 'find and match' task, plenty of other people, some complete families, were doing the same. At least he could look in peace for his car, unlike the man two rows away whose family dragged after him, the children transformed from eager searching to demanding whining in moments when Daddy did not produce the car like magic. As always, an A.A. van toured the area, ready to help members (or swiftly recruit new members) to start their cars and depart. Tonight, one newish looking executive size car was being pulled up onto the tow truck whilst the family climbed into the truck cab. 'Praise be for Relay' thought Tony, at least they'll get to their destination tonight, he might not.

Eventually, he recognised a re-sprayed car roof and pushing through the tight gap got onto the back row and so to his car. A fresh line of missing paint running from the drivers' door about a third of the way down the front wing, greeted him. 'Ah, a Heathrow kiss', he thought and immediately hoped that his new car, his principle car, also in a car park not far away, had not been similarly abused.

To his relief, the motor fired up at his first turn of the ignition key, lights on and carefully forwards to the exit lane. Here, as usual, small change seemed to be at a premium, the parking company even taking foreign cash to settle the bills. Tony could hear muted cursing from the car in front, which seemed to be the family with the petulant children. Father, it seems, had underestimated the parking bill and was raiding every pocket in the car to make up the cash. "You CAN pay by credit-card" said the attendant helpfully.

"I won't let him have one of them!" said the drivers' wife indignantly "they make money run away. HE is incapable of using something like that safely!".

"Well, missus, you would have been on your way home by now, IF you'd have had a card, instead of all this trouble" said the grinning attendant.

He, at least, was the only player in this mini-drama, getting pleasure from the obvious discomfort raging within the car. Tony sat back in his seat, slipped the gears into neutral and decided not to increase the pressure or embarrassment by blowing his horn. Of course, he wouldn't be paying by credit card, either. Credit card transactions were far too easily traced and for his plans, this visit to the U.K. had officially never to have happen.

Eventually the car in front cleared the pay booth and drove off, the occupants still fighting between themselves. Tony paid his bill, getting some silver small change, which he slipped into his shirt pocket before moving forward out of the parking ground and onto the partly illuminated Heathrow ring road. He exited Heathrow directly on to the A4 Bath Rd., turning towards Slough, passing through Colnebrook, then turning off the A4 through Langley and Iver and then to Denham to pick up the A 412 outer London ring road to carry him clockwise northwards around the great sprawl of London. Actually, to say this was an important route, it wasn't wide, but usually quite quiet. This night it was quiet, for which Tony gave thanks, he had a lot of driving to do tonight and plenty of physical work that must be finished well before dawn. Passing near Bushey, he was thankful that the Hertfordshire country side was calm and peaceful. At Hatfield, he turned north on the A 1 M, then Baldock—Royston road, passing the illuminated site of British Aerospace (Hatfield) as he turned. Miles rolled by, the countryside become quieter each minute.

In the small town of Royston, the roads were sparsely populated; even at the T junction, when he turned towards Duxford, there were few other vehicles moving. Out of the town, it really was countryside with no road lighting, but roads that were sometimes single carriageway, sometimes dual carriageway and all without kerbs on either side. Tony would have to remain alert from now on, it would be too easy to stray off the tarmac, onto the grass and lose control, he had seen the result of that the last time that he had returned back along this road at night-time. Passing the illuminated front fencing of the Imperial War Museum site on Duxford airfield, he glanced at his watch; good, just over the hour from leaving Heathrow. Soon afterwards came the junction with the A 11, where he turned left and began the long, curving run towards Ipswich, which turned into the A 14 just east of Cambridge. Tony would only just enter Suffolk to get to Chilham St. Margarets, the village that was the designated first stopping point for tonight. To get there required a further about a further 40 minutes driving at reasonable speed, which meant an E.T.A. at the cottage in Chilham about 10 p.m. Not too late, yet maybe too late as the brief spasm of action might have passed some time before, he was not sure.

He was sure of the general time table of Carolines' movements. She should have left work at about 5.30 and driven straight over to Chilham, which should have meant that she would have arrived at about 7.30 to 8 o'clock and it was at this point that her movements might become erratic. Normally, she would go straight to the cottage and establish her presence there, inevitably that would normally mean finishing at least one bottle of wine, bursting into copious floods of tears and then deciding which friend to telephone and invite to join her for the rest of the week-end. Even after a bottle of wine, she was alert enough not to invite the guest to arrive that evening, that would never do; in the morning (before lunch-time, at any rate) she would be sober and much more aware of her role. Tony contemplated her role for this week, what would it be? Would she be the seductress, would she be the seduced, would she be victor or victim ? Would she want to ravish or to be ravished? Depending upon the role that she had allotted herself would depend her movements and what they were really were crucial.

Really, all this could all be academic, she might have come to the cottage and gone to bed. That he didn't know and this was the weak spot of his plan, but, whichever variation she had chosen, the end game would ultimately be the same, because flexibility had been built into the plans. When he started planning for tonight' crucial phase, he had been able to rely on his Carolines' invariant reaction.

Always when he planned foreign business visits, she would throw a tantrum and accuse him of going to see girl friends and leaving her at home and bored. In Thatchers' Britain, family unity didn't seem to rate too highly. Financial accounting for trips was so tight that even the excuse of taking your wife at your own expense to get cheaper room rates created so many difficulties that living through a family crisis generally was an easier and a more pleasant experience. So, after the tantrums had finished and personal relations had moved from the fridge into the deep freeze, he just got on with planning his time-table in the cold vacuum of his marriage. She, on the other hand, would immediately move out, as always to the cottage and sometimes going as far as resigning her job, in an effort to pressurize him to 'come to heel', as she always said, like a trained dog. A routine had developed, she would, carefully, walk out and establish her self regally in the cottage, he would continue to work, this routine becoming less disruptive on each occurrence. This scenario had refined its' self over the years and certainly reached a new apogee when Aunty Ginny had died and left her cottage to them. Now Caroline could go to the cottage and be Queen of all she surveyed without having to ask Ginny's permission, so she would exploit this new freedom mercilessly.

Carolines' visits to the cottage were frequent, but not regular, and she had extended the range of her succor seeking, from the home town to using the cottage as a way station on her route to increasingly open affairs. One swift look at any of the cottage's telephone bills showed how far she had opened her wings, calls to Ipswich were predominantly to her sister, those to Gerrads Cross, Windsor, High Wycombe, Henley and many other Home Counties upper middle class towns reflected just how far and wide Caroline had scattered her charms in her search for comfort. That many of these calls were to single men had been easily verified by phoning the numbers, asking for a fictitious "Jim", then, embarrassedly pleading dialing errors, apologizing to the respondant (frequently the cleaning lady) saying "I'll just have to try Mr. Allots number again, sorry to disturb you". So fluid had become this approach that he often discovered the name of the telephone owner, when the answerer automatically said "No, Mr. Bloggs/Smith/Jones etc. lives here).

So, this month would see one, or more, men join his wife in the cottage to offer comfort whilst her careless husband gallivanted around the world seeking to do his job better (his opinion) or meet his multitudinous harem of women (her & her mothers opinion). Just thinking of this caused Tony to feel the anger rise again, but he forced himself to remain calm, remembering that this was what tonight was all about. At that point, a few minutes before 10 p.m., he entered the village of Chilham St. Margaret and slowed to a steady 20 m.p.h. Terraced houses down the length of the Main street were all neatly painted, in some lights burned, in others the night prevailed. At the far end of Main Street, the Maypole (the villages' sole pub) was a beacon of light and activity, a couple of cars were parked outside and Tony recognized them, so it appeared that no-one new was in the area. As he passed by, a young couple walked out of the door, glancing at the strange car cruising slowly out of the village. He knew that they would remember the car, indeed, it would be mentioned in the pub tomorrow lunch time. He drove on towards the cottage, seeing it a short time later. Approaching the cottage, he reversed the Chevanne up the stony drive until it was close to the garage, leaving just enough room to open the garage doors. He got out of the Chevanne, walked along the brick path to the front door and noisily rang the bell. Again, he was being obvious for the reason that he wanted anyone nearby to remember the caller and the lateness of the call. He could hear a radio playing music in the depths of the cottage, see lights on in the bedroom on the upper floor, but he couldn't get any answer. Silently, he inserted his key in the lock and opened the door and passed inside in a manner suitable for an obviously clandestine meeting. Turning on the hall light, he walked up the stairs towards the source of the music. At the top of the stairs, it was obvious that the radio was in the bathroom, that the light was on, playing radio 4 slightly off station and that the bathroom was occupied. That he could see from the shadow cast through the half open door.

Preparing for an unlikely confrontation, Tony walked into the bathroom, poison bottle held firmly in his hand. Caroline was in the bath, laying full length in the bath with one leg wantonly thrown over each side of the white enameled bath, defiantly displaying her pubic hair to any one who wished to look, but she lay still & unmoving. Pools of water lay around the bath and the radio lay on its' side on the linoleum flooring, next to the bath, but Caroline lay inert and unmoving in a strange atmosphere of bath scents and grilled bacon. That she was dead was immediately obvious, but Tony did not rush into the bath room, instead he leaned back against the door jamb and carefully examined the scene before he moved. He saw that Carolines' body had a few darkened marks on it that approximately co-incided with the water level and it was from these areas that the grilled bacon aroma emanated.

Carolines' sightless eyes continued to stare at the naked bulb hanging above the bath, her mouth still submerged beneath the water passing neither breath nor sound, the bath water lay still, bathfoam having deteriorated to a grey scum floating on the surface.

Coldly Tony surmised that Caroline had been electrocuted, as he planned, but not as she got into the bath (that would have thrown her away from the bath) but once she was immersed in the water, so she must have tried to re-tune the radio and, by that action, become her own executioner. Obviously the radio fitted the bill, connected to the mains to work without batteries, it lay OUTSIDE the bath, on the floor. Caroline must have spasmed as she touched the aluminium cased radio and knocked it to the floor. Tony could not reach the radio without stepping in a pool of water; he thought 'I haven't come THIS far to join her in eternity, so think out the moves'. Thinking his moves out, he walked down the stairs, turned left & switched off the hall lights, then continued through the hall and then open the linking door to the garage. Feeling on the back of the garage door, Tony found the emergency torch that they had put there so that they could find and fix any blown fuses. By the muffled light of the torch Tony saw the ancient fuse box on the wall, just inside the garage, he also noticed Carolines company car, with the boot part open. Looking back at the fuse-box, he saw that it was turned on, but not closed, a sure sign that there had been problems and that, almost certainly cured by Caroline, using the 'ultimate fuse' approach of Dick, her sisters' husband.

Looking in the fuse box showed that a fuse had been replaced with one of the nails that Dick had thoughtfully placed on top of the fuse box for emergencies. Tony turned off the power, pulled the nail from the fuse, tossing it randomly into the mess on the work bench, then replacing it by the spare ceramic fuse holder, which he held between the knuckles of his first and second fingers. He pushed the fuse fully home with the heel of his right hand & then closed the 'box, but did not turn the power on. Walking quickly up the stairs, he unplugged the radio and then turned off the bed-room light with his elbow. Back in the bath room, he laid Carolines' bath sheet on the floor and carefully laid her body on it. Rigor mortis was beginning, so Tony concentrated on lining up the body so that it lay 'to attention' with the legs together, arms by their sides, chin down and toes pointing downwards. By this time, the body was stiffening rapidly and he had to use force to point the feet, but very careful not to break any bones. This increasing rigor mortis meant that his wife had been dead for between one and two hours, this he knew; he also knew that the corpse would remain locked in the final position for only a few hours, until about dawn when everything had to be finished. Tony stood, pulled out the bath plug to let the water run away and then went back to the fuse-box & flipped on the power, knowing that no light would show outside as the bath-room had no external windows. His mind was racing with the implications of what he had found, Caroline must have bathed almost as her first act on arrival. Had she fully unpacked? Had she brought her usual comprehensive suitcases? Was she expecting anyone? Although he had visualised and trained himself for this eventuality, her electrocution left him breathless with the possibilities of the unknown. Rapidly he dried Carolines' body, then used the bath mat to mop up the spilled water, before rolling the corpse off the bath sheet and neatly folded both it and the mat and putting both over the heated towel rail.

Anyone examining the towel or the mat would soon not be able to tell how wet either had been, he was concerned about the radio, what would that tell anyone? Swiftly, he unscrewed the plug with Carolines nail file (her normal all purpose tool) and saw that the leads were all reversed and loose. A typical Caroline electrical job! How she had lasted so long was beyond him, but then, with a jolt, he realized that she had paid a heavy price for her inattention on matters electrical. He poured the contents of the poison bottle down the sink and flushed it away with running water. A quick squirt from her perfume spray would hide the meaty smell until it dispersed and by morning Caroline would have vanished without trace, or so Tony hoped.

A rapid, quiet search showed that she had opened, but not fully unpacked one case and that the other case still resided in the boot of her company Cortina. Tony repacked the one suitcase with the still folded clothes Caroline had taken out and then checked her hand-bag. Credit cards, cheque book and purse were still there, but no car keys. Tony stuffed the hand bag into the suit case and locked it, then carried it into the garage. Coming back for the body, he walked into the kitchen to get a couple of black rubbish bags to cover the body when he saw her car keys glinting in the feeble light of the torch, where she had obviously put them when she arrived and gone to make a cup of tea. He didn't touch them, but walked into the pantry to get the bags and saw, by the sink, her cup, neatly washed drying on the draining board. Tony metaphorically raised his hands to prevent touching anything and walked up the stairs to the bath-room. Council 'black' rubbish bags were actually 1 metre long & dull, dark, matt grey—ideal for his purpose. He carried his wifes' body into the hall near the garage door and then slid one rubbish bag over her feet and legs, up to her waist and the second over her head and down her body until it overlapped the lower bag.

It was now but a few minutes after 11 p.m. and Tony had only about 5 hours to complete the bulk of his plan before dawn revealed him to the awakening world. A last, careful look around the bed-room from the door showed nothing important to a woman had been left, then he moved onto the bath room. Already, the flooring was drying, the towel drying steadily, too, with no signs of his visit, but signs that Caroline had been there. He wrapped the dangling light pull around his first finger and then tugged the light off. Using the rapidly dying torch beam, Tony descended the stairs and entered the garage, where he carefully and silently opened one of the doors before stepping out and opening the back doors of his Chevanne. Stepping out of the garage once more he pushed the bagged corpse into the van, then followed it by both suitcases. He retrieved his clothing pile from the Chevanne and stepped back into the garage. He stripped naked except for his shoes before pulling on the dark blue boiler suit that he had left in the van a week earlier & bundling his clothes together with his belt, tossed them onto the passenger seat. A quick look around, then the torch was re-hung at the back of the house door and turned off before Tony closed the rear van doors followed by loudly closing the garage door. Although the cottage was somewhat remote, lying outside the village proper, Tony had always been surprised by the details in village gossip, which meant that people noticed and remembered everything. He had acknowledged this by the purchase of a nondescript van, his changed appearance and his assumed round-shouldered, height reducing posture when outside. In this vein, Tony had to assume that unseen eyes and ears would notice the external goings-on at the cottage. It was his plan that local gossip would report Caroline as sidling out of her marriage with her latest lover whilst Jim was abroad was what he wanted.

Her death, although he had planned for it, had occurred without any intervention from him, so it freed him from any feelings of being a killer. That a description of the van and the 'lover' would, almost certainly, be common knowledge by lunch-time, he relied on that innate conservativeness of the villagers not to interfere in other peoples' business to give him some further days grace.

Starting the car, he left, still driving at 20 m.p.h., by the same route that he entered the village. Some favoured locals would still be ensconced in the Maypole, enjoying after hours drinks, but his car passing through would, he knew, be noticed.

Chapter 24

Higham Green

Once clear of Chilham, Tony drove quickly back to the A 14, but turned eastwards traveling towards Ipswich. He continued until he saw the 'B' road leading through Needham Market to Barking. Soon after passing through the village of Barking rain started to fall and he slowed to find the right turn leading into the Tye group of villages, where he hoped to find a quiet church yard suitable to receive the corpse. This, he knew, was the weakest link in the whole plan, he had a weak fall-back position, which was to hide the body in any dense copse he could find and throw fishing maggots over it. Tony had read that, left undisturbed, the maggots would consume the flesh rapidly, the more so once decomposition began. By the end of summer, the skeleton would be stripped clean, but the skeleton would still not hidden from sight. If he had to employ this option, Tony would never be able to re-visit the copse and certainly never try to inter the skeleton. What better way of advertising guilt could be imagined? Guilty or not, he would have to become completely indifferent to the fate of his wifes body.

He wanted to use his preferred plan, the one he had practiced for and the one that he knew he could complete anonymously in the limited time available, despite the poor start in Windsor airport. Should the limited time be not too limited and were he to find a suitable resting place he could still be back in America before he had been missed. He knew that he probably had a few hours of driving ahead of him plus an unknown number of churchyard inspections to perform before the best location were found.

By now, the rain had become incessant and he had to limit his speed more than he would have liked, to stay on the narrow roads. Any mistake at this stage would put him into one of the steep ditches that lined the road on both sides and his well rehearsed cover plan would be blown away like cigarette smoke in a gale. So, Tony concentrated even harder on driving, the rain was hardly cleared by the jerky wipers of the old Chevanne and far too much time for comfort was being spent driving in a rain distorted haze.

At Battisford Tye, Tony slowed down near the small, local church, turned off the motor and cruised past the lych gate looking for the notice board before pulling off the road quietly under the dark shadow of an overhanging tree. 'Time to go looking for a site' he thought, but before he left the warm and dry Chevanne he changed his clean, dry shoes for a pair of builders Wellington boots, which he intended to wear for the rest of the night. He turned off the interior light, so that when he opened the door his presence wouldn't be accentuated, opened the door and slid off the seat. He didn't fully close the door, only onto the first catch of the lock so nothing broke the deep silence, then set off to do a high speed inspection of the graveyard. Despite the incessant rain, the moon was near full so Tony could see enough detail when the moon shone through a break in the rain clouds. It took no time at all to review the minute graveyard of 'Our Lady's' church and to see that it did not suit his plans. Back in the car, Tony re-started the engine and carried on through the village to his next target village, Charles Tye. He had a little more trouble here as there was a solitary street light almost opposite the church entrance, so he had to roll past the church and park in a cutting on the right hand side of the road before his car was hidden in shadow. 'Just what I need tonight, a walk in the pissing rain' thought Tony, but before he left the car he pulled a dark balaclava over his head so that he could more easily blend into any shadows. Neither the front nor the rear church yard proved to fit his requirements, although, he thought, the rear graveyard would have been ideal, IF . . . . , but it wasn't so he had to move on.

Driving back through the village the sign post to Ringshall said 2 miles, so he turned left and drove onwards to Ringshall village. Once more, he found the church easily and cut the engine to cruise quietly past and review the situation; on the notice board, he noticed two signs the first saying that services were held in rotation every four weeks, the second informed him that the graveyard was not by the church, but further on down the road. He immediately started to think that if church services were not daily or weekly then he might have problems easily finding the conditions he needed. In a spurt of urgency he turned the ignition on again, selected 4 th gear and dropped the clutch to bump start the motor.

His inattention was rewarded when the rear wheels locked momentarily and the van slewed to the left on the wet and greasy road at the precise moment that the engine caught and began to run. Engine power, though limited, proved to be sufficient to provoke a harsh skid to the left and the unyielding high grass bank. Reactively Tony de-clutched and steered into the skid, with the result that he did not hit the bank full on, but ran the near side front wheel half way up the bank. He knew that the underside of the van was taking a battering from both the noise and vibrations coming to him, the car ran off the bank quite suddenly with a thump that echoed through the still night and served to advertise his presence to every-one within hearing range. Tony performed a rapid about turn and left Ringshall rapidly. He didn't attempt to keep the noise down now, everybody with ears had heard him and his continued presence would only bring unwanted attention to him. As he passed the grass bank, he saw the deep scar that his car had carved and became aware of that a regular thump from the front near-side suspension might indicate suspension damage. He wasn't really surprised about the damage, just shocked that it had happened whilst simultaneously being grateful that the car continued running.

Down the road, to the right ran a small road, which a sign informed him that "Barkings Tye via ford" was yet another 2 miles away, so he continued. He was getting worried about both the time he had spent so far without result and the fact that he seemed to be getting deeper and deeper down minor roads which he didn't know and so wouldn't quickly find his way back down.

He saw the ford glinting in the intermittent moonlight in sufficient time to slow down so that he could crawl slowly through without raising a bow wave and drowning the ignition. Fortunately, the slow running ford proved to be less than a foot deep and only about ten feet wide, so just keeping the engine running in second gear got him across with no problem. Glancing to his left also showed him that the ford had removed much of the stray bits of the grass bank that had stuck to the bottom of his car in Ringshall. As the path (hardly a road) rose out of the ford, Tony saw with increasing disbelief the shape of a tower rising up on the left hand side. Hardly daring to hope, he continued and found himself approaching the small village of Higham Green. Really, it was a hamlet, with the tiny Holy Trinity Church between himself and the few houses that he could discern in the discontinuous moonlight. 'Nothing ventured' Tony thought, so he turned off the engine once more and drifted into the deep shadow that lay between him and the churchyard wall. He slid out of the car once more and walked up to the wall and scanned what turned out to be the graveyard. By this time the rain had become intermittent, although the clouds were still almost fully covering the sky. He had to wait for a while until a big enough gap in the clouds gave him sufficient light to scan the locality.

There it was! Perfect for his purposes, an open grave ready and waiting for a funeral service before it was quite legally closed. Tony easily crossed the low wall and headed towards the piles of earth which lay either side of the grave. Before he passed out of the darkest shadows, he crouched and flitted from head-stone to head-stone, pausing at each one and searching out the lie of the land. Three graves from the open grave, he found the sextons' ladder, so he remembered where it lay and continued to the newly dug barrow. Now, he lay full length at the head end and looked into the pit. Was it completed to full depth? Yes, to him it certainly appeared a good six feet deep, so the funeral must be in the next two days, probably tomorrow-today, he hastily corrected himself—as it was past midnight by then, perfect for his plans. Tony walked back to the car, whilst still remained bent over to hide his silhouette amongst the grave-stones and unlocked the back doors of the Chevanne, pulling out the mattock, before returning to the open grave. He dropped easily into the grave and carefully lifted the mattock in, using the four inch wide spade end he marked out a narrow oblong 56 inches long by 18 inches wide, with a further 10 inch by 6 inch box centrally positioned at one end. This he had to excavate to a depth of 24 inches to allow sufficient coverage and he had dig out two thirds of a ton of earth to make this shape. Training on digging such a shaped cavity earlier in the summer had shown that he could move the required amount of soil in just under the hour. He had trained on dry, loose earth in the old age home garden, not the rain soddened earth he faced tonight. On his training run, he had also used a mattock, so he was sure that he could complete the task well before dawn.

By 2 a.m. the mummy-like grave was ready, within the open barrow, earth was piled to either side and the cavity awaited its occupant. Tony was perspiring, his boiler suit (how appropriately named!) black with rain & sweat, steam rose from him in clouds, just as from a Grand National winner. Standing on the highest pile of earth at the bottom of the grave allowed Tony easily to vault out and onto the grass at one end. Without stopping, he walked-still in bent over mode—back to the 'vanne, opened the rear doors and pulled out Carolines' body. Still in deep shadow, he laid her along the top of the low wall whilst he climbed over, then taking the stiff corpse under one arm he walked as fast as possible with bent legs and bent back, back to the grave. Despite his fitness and strength, he could not complete the short journey without resting a couple of times. Back at the grave, he brought the sextons' ladders, laying them at an angle across the width of the grave, he slid the corpse part way across the grave opening, then jumped inside to pull the corpse fully into the grave. Heavy, continuous rain began to fall, big, heavy drops that hurt every time one landed on you. Tony stripped the body of its' covering and noticed how brightly white skin reflected even in the palest moonlight. Laying the body face down in the mummy shaped hole, he first bundled the plastic bags into his boiler suit pocket and then began covering the body with earth scraped from the internal banks until the corpse was covered.

To compact the soil, Tony decided to tread it down and during this process Carolines body emitted a load belch which echoed across the grave-yard and caused Tony to buckle at the knees. Despite his heart rate leaping to astronomical heights, Tony continued the process of scraping earth over the corpse and treading it down, although he was more cautious every time he put his foot down.

Eventually the bottom of the grave was level, not smooth though, the falling rain didn't allow that. Putting the mattock close by the ladder allowed Tony to reach it easily when he emerged from the grave, which he did by pulling himself up under the ladder, getting his right leg out and on to the grass between the ladder and the grave, then scrambling onto the ground by dint of a strong push with the left leg. On his knees, he looked into the grave to see if any obvious marks remained of his activities, but the rain seemed to sit in irregular shaped pools that identified nothing. Despite the rain, Tony removed his Wellington boots, he had no desire to leave muddy tracks back to the site of his car. Then carrying his mattock in one hand and his boots in the other he crouch-walked back to his car for the last time that evening.

By the time he arrived back at his car, what had seemed like solid shadows had moved and the front of the Chevanne was becoming visible, although barely visible, under the tree. In the half shadow, Tony didn't see that the plastic front number plate was missing, if he had, he would have looked briefly around where he was now parked &, not finding it, would have carried on. He was not to know that the front number plate lay on the scarred grass bank in Ringshall. Standing at the car Tony went into the deepest shadows and opened the rear doors. He tossed his Wellingtons inside, slid in the mattock and pulled his clothes bundle out, putting it on the roof of the car just above the open doors. He pulled down the boiler suit to his waist, holding it there by tying the muddy arms around his still clothed hips. For a few moments, he just sat on the open van floor resting and assessing his condition.

He had been flying on adrenaline for over 5 hours now and reaction in the form of fatigue was sure to set in soon, that he knew. To delay sleep as long as possible he slid his arms around the roof of the van trying to collect together all the remaining drops of rain water to splash over himself to refresh him and remove the odour of perspiration. He achieved little, other than a brief chill splash on his face, so he continued dressing. First, his shirt, then dropping his boiler suit and standing on it, he climbed into his trousers, finally sitting down again to put on his shoes. Once dressed, Tony carefully picked up the boiler suit and threw it on top of the Wellingtons before re-locking the rear doors and climbing into the drivers' seat. He started the engine and quietly reversed the car out of the shadows before heading back to the ford.

From the ford Tony retraced his tracks back to Needham Market and onto the A 14, turning east and following the great loop of road back towards east London, it was the best part of 60 miles, but Tony was in no mood for short cuts that could lead to delays.

Creaking and groaning, the little Vauxhall made good speed and it was only a few minutes before the A 14/ A 12 intersection arose and he continued straight on the A 12 direct towards Romford. Next stop, Docklands he thought, then he noticed the temperature gauge beginning to rise. Damn, that bump up the bank must have damaged the radiator, he thought, so slowing down to try and cool the engine he began to look out for an all night filling station. In the distance, he saw the neon glow of all night facilities and drove onto the fore-court. Rapidly, he assessed the situation, he was still out in the sticks and the cashier was bound to remember him, but he must keep the Vauxhall in running condition for the next couple of hours, at least. He pulled up by the fuel pumps and bought two gallons of petrol before walking into the interior to pay the cashier, once inside the shop he looked for radiator sealant, found some and walked up to pay.

"Had a rough night out with the Lads, then?" the bleached blonde cashier asked.

"Yes, an' now my rads.' leaking an' all. Is there any water outside?" asked Tony.

"You look as if you need more'n water, grab a coffee from the machine" said the blonde.

"O.K., but have you got a loo here? I need a leak, bad"

"Yes, go to mine through that door there, at least it's clean, so yer won't catch nuffink unless ya want to".

Thanking her, Tony made an urgent dive for the toilet and disappeared behind the door. She was right, her toilet was clean and neat, with the touches that showed that a woman had claimed it as her own. Taking advantage of the toilet was automatic, but he also used the wash basin to wash his hands and face and damp down his hair and finger rake it into some form of style. Carefully, he cleaned up the basin and folded the towel neatly before hanging it over the rail provided, it was obvious that the blonde cashier took some pride in her little facility and it was to him to respect it. Too much ruination lay outside and it was nice to see someone putting a bit of themselves into a sterile environment. He emerged, feeling much better and more respectable.

"I got yer a coffee while yes were in the loo. Hope yes don't mind. You DO take sugar don't you?"

Actually Tony hated sweet drinks, but he smiled at her and said "Thanks, this'll sober me up a bit".

After a few minutes of inconsequential chat Tony paid the bill, even offering to pay for her coffee from the machine ("Ooo, you aint 'arf a gent") & went outside to attend to the radiator. Opening the bonnet allowed Tony to see the damage, a radiator hose had been loosened, but he wasn't about to do a full repair, so taking off the thermostat, he poured the sealant in the radiator and filled up both the header tank and the radiator with cold water out of a yellow plastic watering can. Sealing everything up, he closed the bonnet than noticed the cashier waving him back inside.

"'Ere, go an wash yer hands again an' 'ave another coffee" she said, so he did both things.

He thought that the cashier was probably bored out of her mind and welcomed every little diversion that the night provided. Be nice, but not too nice, then, at least she would have no special reason for remembering you. As he emerged into the shop a large and dirty heavy goods vehicle whistled to a stop by the commercial diesel pump.

"Most o' them truckers think a woman like me are dying for their maulin', but that there is my Georgie Boy an' he's special "the cashier said to no-one in particular.

Tony picked up the coffee and left, with a bright "Thanks a million !" thrown back over his shoulder. He knew that from the look on the blondes' face he would be forgotten the moment Georgie Boy walked into the shop.

As he walked back to the Chevanne, Tony looked up to the sky, already lightening the false dawn was beginning and he knew that the real dawn was not too far behind. His heading still remained, ultimately, to Docklands and the construction sites there and he wanted to be there before dawn, if possible, but not too long afterwards, at the latest. Even on the periphery of London traffic was beginning to stir, some vans and lorries driving into town and a few private cars feeling their way into the traffic.

Despite the growing volume of traffic, the run towards Docklands was smooth and uneventful. In East Ham, Tony drove through a series of run-down terraced houses. Even in the pre-dawn breeze, newspaper pages and other litter skitted up and down the pavements, so Tony stopped and added the two black plastic bags to the medley of the other litter. Driving a mile further brought him to an area of obviously derelict buildings; a few minutes searching found a derelict factory where the basement level was visible from the roadway through an old iron fence. Looking down to the basement level, it was obvious that the kids had had a great time 'bombing' the basement floor with milk bottles. Tony dropped the empty poison bottle, which broke into disconnected shards of glass, joining all the other glass there. Other, unremarkable junk lay in piles on the lower floor, so Tony added the Wellingtons, discretely spaced apart, to the other shoes and clothes below ground level.

At the first construction site he found, he decided to dispose of the boiler suit. Virtually every construction site, in its' early stages seems to go through a stage where boiler suits and overalls exist with the rank weeds to be cleared away first before the real work begins. Where these odd bits of work clothing come from Tony didn't know, but he had seen enough sites to know that they were always there, like some sacrifice to the Gods of concrete and construction, so Tony added his boiler-suit as his votive offering for success. Now all he needed was a smaller building site, preferably where building were being built on one part whilst the ground was still being prepared on another part. He had to wait until he got closer to Docklands proper before anything suitable came to light. Dawn had broken a short time ago and the sparrows were already abroad, but not so the workmen in their Portacabins on the site. Looking around quickly Tony couldn't see a watchman, so he decided to get rid of the mattock. As events turned out, he should have survey the site better, for when he was close to the jumbled mound of mixed digging tools an Irish voice broke the early morning silence.

"You teeving bastid, put that fokkin' pick back".

Tony didn't wait to argue the toss with the man, he just dropped the mattock and run back to the car. Fortunately, he had left the engine running and as he drove away part of a house brick bounced on the road on his left. When he gone a safe distance, he slowed, looked in the rear mirror only to see the builder carrying the mattock onto site and throw it onto the pile with the other tools. His pulse still raced from the sudden challenge, but Tony drove away with a sense of achievement, his last personal link with Higham Green churchyard had just been absorbed into someone elses tool collection!

Next stop Kempton Park, unfortunately almost diametrically across an awakening London from where he was now. He had few options for his route, none better than to drive directly through the City and to turn off the A 4 near Hammersmith. That route, he knew would be the shortest and probably the quickest because he would be through the City before even the early risers arrived. In just over the half hour he was exiting South Kensington and minutes later turned off the A 4 at the Hogarth roundabout on the A 316 to Richmond. When the A

road changed to the M 3 motorway, Tony slid off on the left to get to
Kempton Park. As the signs for the race-track appeared he prepared to
turn left and stop at the entrance to the Grandstand car park, located at
the Sunbury end of the circuit. It was here that, most Sundays, a used
car auction was held and he knew that he could leave his car to be sold
anonymously.

He found the Grandstand car park entrance, it was far too early for
it to be open, but even closed other cars had been left there for the sale
waiting to be driven in and knocked down to some bidder. As he got
out of the Vauxhall, Tony looked around him at some of the cars left
the previous night by obviously unproud owners, most had been tarted
up by painting the tyres black and painting over rusty areas. He knew
that these cars, and his Vauxhall, would form the backbone of the cheap
and (maybe) cheerful cars sold without guarantee to the lads who just
wanted a set of wheels for a song. That thought did not offend him,
he had bought the car in the full knowledge that he would get nothing
back for it, all he hoped was that it would serve someone else well for
a short time. Tony pulled out his bags and opened one of Carolines
cases, he took the 'securities' bag containing Carolines valuables and
stowed it at the bottom of his nylon flight bag. He dug an envelope,
which contained the cars' papers and a written instruction to sell, out
of the glove box, locked up the car, put the keys in the envelope then
pushed the envelope through the letter box in the auction offices.

He picked up the suitcases and his bag and walked off, turning
left to the bus stop he knew was there. As he waited for the bus, Tony
reviewed the cut-off that he had just initiated, for that car could never
be traced to him. He had never registered the car to his address, the
log-book contained someones' name but whether it was the name of
the man who had sold it to him, he didn't know or care, it might
equally have been the name of the owner five sales ago. In any case, the
officially named owner would get a cheque through the post soon for
the sale of the Vauxhall. He had no doubts that the cheque would be
cashed and the proceeds treated as a windfall, he just hoped that the
money bought the 'official' owner something useful.

When the bus arrived, Tony pushed 50 pence towards the driver
to pay for the ticket to Kew underground station. Stopping frequently,
the bus took an hour to reach Kew, by which time Tony was having
difficulty staying awake. As he stumbled off the bus, he caught the

smell of strong, fresh coffee and decided to have a shot of caffeine to wake him up. A little Italian cafe in the station precinct had just opened and the smell of the first coffee of the day was magnetic, so he succumbed to the lure. An espresso that was thick, black and neat caffeine woke him up with a start, he felt a surge of energy run through him and the urge to sleep dissipated immediately.

A District line tube took him to Earls Court, where he changed to the Piccadilly line to take him to Heathrow, Tony being now just another anonymous traveler in the growing surge of humanity moved around by London Underground at the start of the working week.

At Heathrow, he made his way to terminal three and paid cash to Air Canada for an economy return fare to Halifax, Nova Scotia, from where he could get a feeder flight back to Windsor, Ontario. His flight was due out at lunch-time and that gave him four hours' to kill, so he claimed four seats in the departure lounge and, using his flight bag as his pillow, slept the time away until his flight was called and he could stumble down the loading ramp & into his seat to sleep his way back to Canada.

Chapter 25

Later that day

Ipswich.

"Dick, I'm going to 'phone Caroline to tell her about the arrangements for the party up at Lakenheath next weekend". Shirley telephoned, got the ansaphone and left a message. At the end of the message, a red light glowed on the machine, under the heading "new message"

"Oh damn!, I could only get the answer 'phone, so I've left a message for Caroline to call and tell us if she's coming or if her friend will be occupying her time. I also asked her to tell us how long she will be staying at the cottage & how long she'll be there."

"Dick, are you listening? We've got to get a car organised for Lakenheath and I was hoping that we could get Caroline to pick us up. 'Means you can have a few drinks and I can drive home if Caroline stays for the night".

Chilham St. Margarets.

"Can I have some of them brown eggs, Mrs. Reed? Our Max likes a coupla good eggs in the mornin'. Did you the car last night go old Ginny's cottage? Looks as if Lady Muck herself 'as got ANOTHER bloke on her string. Yes, was late last night, Mr. Webber an' me always got to bed early, him having to be up early for early duty and we were just dropping off when I hears a car go past and stop. Next, I hear her door being knocked, then closed. Wonder who this one is, this time?"

"Well Mrs. Webber, my John saw a car go past the pub last night an' it didn't go back while he were in the pub, so he stayed there for a bit"

"Our Max saw the car drive past the "Maypole" as he was taking Jilly home last night, you know how the Abbots like their Jilly to be home before 10, so our Max walks her home. Zoom, this little car goes passed them straight to the cottage and he heard him knocking, as well. After he'd taken Jilly home, our Max went near the cottage, told me he saw no lights on, but could hear something, so she must have been doing something depraved in there, like these townies do. Must be the country air or something!"

"Country air be blowed, it don't do nothin' for Mr. Reed, that I'll tell you for nothing. An' he be breathing it every blinkin' day !"

Ringshall.

Charlie Stubbs took Smiler, his old and arthritic mongrel for its' morning walk, as always, along the road through the village. From a distance away, he saw the scar carved out of the left hand side road banking, where the Chevanne had slid sideways when Tony had attempted to re-start the engine without stopping. Muttering curses under his breath, Charlie headed directly for the damaged area. He had seen, from a distance, something long and white & definitely out of place, which, on picking up, proved to be the plastic front number plate of the Vauxhall, torn off during the slide up the banking. Looking at it, Charlie knew what he had and knew that it was a direct link to the car that caused the damage. In righteous anger, Charlie strode off towards the part-time police box, where he suspected that he would find Constable Watson, the intermittent representative of Law & Order in Ringshall and the local Tye villages.

"Look'e 'ere, Constable Pete, I've found this thing in the middle of that new scar on the road bank near the church".

"Mornin' Charlie, ole Smiler there don't look too happy. You been causing her run with those arthriticy hips of hers?" Saying that the Constable bent over and chucked the dog under her chin and set her tail wagging in slow, laboured arcs.

stabling for the horses, but today wasn't a race day and she expected all to be quiet. She was mildly surprised, though not alarmed, to see a man with luggage waiting quietly at the bus stop. He looked neat and reasonably tidy, but there was something in the set of his shoulders that said he was tired, but had to push on. A second look showed a blondish haired man, above average size looking as if he had a train to catch, judging by the way he glanced at his watch, not excited, but resigned and waiting to move on. Immediately, she thought of those cold words of Norman Tebbits' "On yer bike" and thought that this youngish man was obeying that command and moving away to find work. Something indefinable about him told her he was off to start a new life. "Well good-luck to you", she thought just as the kettle whistled to her and she turned to begin the daily grind of victualing her brood.

Building site (Docklands).

Michael sat down at the crew table with his second brew of tea and looked at the sleepy, hung-over faces of his work-mates. He had been responsible for waking them all up in the crew hut and, besides threats of awful retribution, all his work-mates had somehow emerged into the light of the new day, still carrying the effects of last nights' drink. Everybody started the day with a mug of hot, sweet tea before dispersing to shave or make breakfast as fitted themselves.

"Wit, fer the luv of Riley, was that commotion dis mornin' Moike ?" asked the foreman brikkie.

"Oi came out de cabin to make moi tea an' Oi sees dis young bastid doin' a runner wid one of our picks. So's Oi shouted at him and lobbed a brick, but de bastid just ran to his van and fooked off. Oi put the pick back and made de tea".

"Prob'bly one of dem private boyhos, troyin' to get his tools on de cheap. Give us 'ere anither cup of tea, Moike, the Guiness's lying heavy dis mornin'.

Kemton Park Car Auctions.

Already the early cars left for the auction had been sorted out into price category, all were in the lowest band &, if not sold either today or tomorrow, would be knocked down to the breakers and stripped down for second hand spares. Each car was represented on the auctioneers' desk by a small pile of papers, ownership document, M.O.T. certificate and a letter of instruction to sell from the current owner, his secretary had been busy. That she had arrived before him was no surprise, she always did on auction day. As he walked to his office, the auctioneer looked the cars over and grimaced "Somebody's pride and joy, I'll bet," he thought to himself as he scanned the motley collection "but our 10 % commission won't be much on that lot !. Still, beats working for a living !".

As he sat in his desk, John the gofer, came in and took the keys to each car from the pile to get them off the public areas and to drive them inside the area set aside for the auction. Returning to the office, he made a small mark on the owners' document of each car. These marks represented his instant assessment of each vehicles road worthiness and driving qualities and would be referred to in the sale as "Our professionals' assessment" of each vehicle. Only one of this mornings' clutch of cars got the black cross, which signified 'not road worthy, probably dangerous'; despite the bank climbing of the previous night, it wasn't the Chevanne.

East Ham.

"Just look at all that shit down there ! That's all got to be moved before you start on the basement, so get the lads onto it and clear the area up. Burn all that bloody rubbish, then sort out the basement rooms for yourselves. This'll be the last bit to be demolished, so you and the lads can live here, free, 'til we get round to it. Just clear the place up first!".

This offer of free accommodation was sufficient to galvanized the team to attack the piles of rubbish and to make one big bonfire out of the lot, in a corner of the deep wall that when up to ground level. During the course of shoveling up the waste two Wellington boots were found, which seemed to be a pair. These were not burned, but taken away as a spare pair by one of the clean-up gang.

The Maypole, Chilham St. Margaret.

"Like I was saying, Jilly an' me be walking home last night, when this little blue van goes past, towards the cottage. Then I hears it stop and someone be knocking on the door, then the door opens and closes"

"Ah, Max, you be having good ears, you be. I ain't never heard a door open in all my life, but you be hearing it" said old Archie, the Farrier.

"I heard the door close, so it had to open afore it could close, couldn't it, eh Mr. Horseshoe ? As I was sayin', by the time I gets to see the cottage, proper like, there baint be a light burning in the whole place, but I's hears some sort o' moosic. Seems she had her lover boy in an' straight off to bed as quick as quick" continued Max, finishing off the story.

"She 'baint be there now, nor he, seems she done a moonlight flit with him" contributed the landlord to the debate about last nights' activities.

"How long'll it last, do you think ? Will 'er be back this week or next ?" asked Archie.

"Depends as who gets bored fust" said Max.

"Oh, 'er'll get *bored* fust, if you get my meanin', but it'll be who gets browned off fust as 'll decide how long it'll all last" said Joe, laughing into his pint.

Kemton Park Car Auctions.

"I have here a 1975 Vauxhall Chevanne, all the paperwork is complete & it's a good runner. In our professionals assessment, this is a good, tough little commercial that runs well, but needs a bit of T.L.C. What am I bid ?"

All the bids stopped at £ 55, however the auctioneer had a note from the owner saying 'No Reserve', so it was knocked down at that price. Both the buyer and the auctioneer were happy with the price, the buyer had just bought a little work-horse and the auctioneer had made 5 quid in less than a minute. Later that day, the Vauxhall was driven away to begin its' new life as service van for a cowboy gas-fitter.

Holy Trinity Church, Higham Green.

At the phrase 'Ashes to Ashes, Dust to Dust', the coffin containing the late James Bradley was lowered into the open grave. All the mourners, although there were not many of them, filed passed the grave and tossed either a hand full of soil or a flower onto the coffin.

Some said "Good-bye Jimmy, 'til we meet again", other simply said nothing & yet a few had tears in their eyes. Jimmys wife, Anne, was inconsolable, she had always loved the big man, despite his obesity and florid face.

When all the mourners had left and the vicar had gone back to the vestry old Josh and Darren, the Sexton and under-sexton, walked slowly back to the grave each carrying a spade. As they walked from the vestry, Josh begged 'one of his posh foreign cigarettes' from Darren. At the grave side they began to throw in spadefuls of earth, then taking a last drag Josh casually flipped the stub into the grave near the coffin.

"Try to throw in the dryer stuff first" Josh said "it'll be easier an' the wet stuff'll have a bit of time to dry out".

Darren did as he was bid, always in a rush to finish, because this "gave him the creeps" and he wanted to get away from the grave side. Occasionally, Josh stopped to roll & light a cigarette and, as was his habit, continued throwing the stubs into the grave to be buried under the spadefuls of earth that fell in. Darren always bridled at this, when he had done the same Josh had made him pick it out, saying "it's them filter things in new cigs. as never rots down like everything else. Be respectful, can't ya ?".

Eventually the grave was filled and the mound compacted by the blade of the spades.

"We'll have to keep a careful eye out on that one, all that rain water'll soon seep away and it'll need compactin' again, otherwise, one day, it'll all cave in. THEN you'll have to do the job all over again".

Darren had no intention of doing the job all over again. His flesh crawled just doing the job once and the stories Josh had told him about exhumations had persuaded him his long term future was definitely not as a Sexton, under or otherwise.

Chilam St. Margarets.

After 4 rings, the ansaphone began to play back Carolines recorded message requesting the caller to leave a message and she would return the call.

"Hello, Darling, Justin here, just confirming our arrangements after the weekend. I'll be round tonight at the usual time and I'll expect you to greet me wearing only that stuff I bought you last time. O.K. ?

I'm not due back in the City until Wednesday morning, so make sure you've got enough food and drink to last the pace because I'm only bringing 1 change of togs and they're for work on Wednesday ! Are we going for the weekday record, tonight ? Sounds good to me ! See you at about 5. Lovies, Justin".

As the phone line went dead, the ansaphone re-set its' self and the "New Message" light continued to glow.

Holy Trinity Church, Higham Green.

Josh left the vicars' office after completing the formal burial papers, where the vicar recorded that James Bradley, certified dead 1 week previously by Dr. Morgan, had been interred in plot E 5 12, meaning that the grave freshly closed was in the East quadrant of the church yard in row 5 and was plot number 12. As always at these times, Josh had put his horny finger on one area in the northern quadrant and said "That'uns mine ! Quiet and away from them trees, them trees ain't going to eat ME!".

There was never any doubt where Josh's chosen place was. So often had this ritual been undertaken that the map had the grubby imprint of Josh's finger right were he wanted to be put.

Windsor International Airport.

Arriving for duty, Sergeant Duchosny found a message to collect a letter from the lieutenants office. He presented himself at the office wondering if his little schemes with the duty free shop had been rumbled.

"Duchosny, it is my pleasure to hand you this letter of commendation from the Mayor for your arrest of that purse snatcher a coupla days ago. You sure don't look the part to be able to run down a young thief, but you sure got him, so ya must be able. Congratulations anyway, that will look good on your file !".

With that the lieutenant turned back to his desk load of paper and Duchosny was left to marvel at the power of the strictly accurate report. He hadn't said that he HAD run the thief down, just that he had CHASED him and arrested him in the International Lounge. Tony wasn't even mentioned and, anyway, was best forgotten. This was Duchosny's moment !

"The Maypole", Chilham St. Margarets.

"So, you say that Caroline had a late night visitor last night and that she's gone off with HIM ?" demanded Justin, becoming increasingly frustrated. He had driven all the way from his flat in central London in high expectations of a few days of unbridled sex and passion. Caroline had always been forthcoming to him, indeed, he had always thought himself her special lover and now, it was beginning to appear as if he had been cuckolded and betrayed by another man.

"Did you see either of them yourself ?" Justin demanded of The Maypoles' landlord.

"Oh deary me, No. I been in 'ere all night serving my customers. It's young Max Webber who as knows all about it an' he sittin' with his girl, Jilly, in the other lounge".

"Point him out to me, there's a pal, I'll talk to him myself".

"Well, see that young girl in the blue skirt ? That's Jilly and Max is in the toilet, so he'll be back quick, can't stand leaving a pretty little thing alone for a moment, he can't ".

Saying a brief "Thanks" to the landlord, Justin walked into the second bar, just as Max emerged from the heavy mock Oak door marked 'Gents' and once more sat on Jillys' right.

"Excuse me, but are you Max Webber, by any chance ?" asked Justin smoothly.

Slightly cautiously Max admitted that that was his name and enquired why Justin should want to know. Swiftly Justin told Max that he was there to stay with Caroline and to ask if the landlord was right to say that Max knew what was going on.

"All what I know is what I saw last night" said Max and continued to tell the tale which had become his and the pubs regulars' lunch-time supposition mixed with the unglazed truth of what little he actually knew.

"Did you recognize the man ?" demanded Justin.

"No. Didn't see clearly an' I ain't seen this car before, either" said Max "Me 'n Jilly was goin' home from here last night when this bluish estate came down the road"—at this Jilly nodded agreement—"but we didn't see the driver clearly"-more nods from Jilly-"but he stopped at ole Ginny's cottage. Next thing I knows, is that all the lights are out an' a bit later the pair of 'em drive off, that I DO know" continued Max, extemporising on the lunch time's conjecture.

For a policemans' son, Max's evidence was questionable, but delivered with an assurance that loaned it persuasion.

As Justin had arrived specially in his polished Porsche, at first he couldn't believe how Caroline ever deigning to climb into 'a bluish estate', she was far too much of a snob to do that. Soon, he began to accept the evidence that Caroline had seemingly picked up 'a piece of rough', as was the trend in London, but would soon tire and come back to him, of that he was sure.

"She'll get a shock, then" thought Justin to himself, but he couldn't stop a sardonic smile from forming on his face.

Chapter 26

In the U.S.A.

Tony arrived back at Windsor International Airport, almost at mid-night local time, too late to return the car that day, or even book into a near-by hotel without looking suspicious,. Both hotels at the airport were expensive & closely tied to the flight pattern, so that they might remember a non local arriving after mid-night from an international flight. He still needed sleep and some real food, plastic airline food and equally poor airport food and drink had left him needing some ballast of real food and drink. America was but a half hour away, the food would not be so good, but the hotels in the Middle Belt/ Metro Airport area of Detroit would not be surprised, as they would be more used to dealing with late arrivals, so he could buy food and a bed without arousing suspicion.

Within ten minutes Tony had retrieved his rented Plymouth from the long-term car parking and checked out and was soon on Huron Drive again on his way to the tunnel. Just before entering the tunnel, he tossed a dollar coin into the yellow 'Toll' basket and drove on, joining the cars on their way into Michigan. Suddenly he saw the passport booth in front of him as the car in front slowed and he began to scrabble in his shirt breast pocket for his passport, but he hadn't fully retrieved it as he came alongside of the booth. He couldn't afford to be stopped without either a Canadian or American visa & began to think wildly about gunning the engine and making a run for it & must have looked frantic. He must have exposed sufficient of his passport for the duty officer to see that it was dark blue and, with a grin and a sweep of his right hand, the officer directed him through.

By the time Tony had begun to breath again he was in Detroit, running on the road that could take him into the down town districts. He saw a sign for Dearborn and the Metro airport, so he followed it down a confusion of roads and directions. Just as he was beginning to think that he was spiraling around, he saw the glow of the airport lights ahead, and then immediately, he was in the hotel belt. A 'Holiday Inn' was the first that he saw that looked appealing, so he slowed down and turned left, across the main drag, and into the reception parking area. Walking into the reception area, he was pleased to note that he was not the only customer, he was certainly the most untidy customer, but not the only one. Checking in, Tony used his false passport and gave both this name and passport number and said that he would pay cash. Only this last comment caused any problem, the receptionist wanted a credit card number against which the room could be charged if he left unexpectedly or overstayed. It was only when he paid the room charge in full, that the receptionist relaxed, only when Tony reached the room did he realize that he had paid for the optional breakfast too. He picked up the phone and asked reception for a wake-up call at 10.00 a.m., only to distress the reception lady again.

"Ten a.m. is the check-out time, Mr. Johnson, sir" she said.

"O.K., make it 9.30 instead" said Tony "Oh, what time does breakfast finish, by the way?" "Well, sir, we have an all day breakfast service in the breakfast bar"

"Great, by the way, is there a 711 or K-Mart near here, I need to get some stuff?"

She told Mr. Johnson where to find the all night K-Mart (just around the corner) and reminded him that he must have cleared out of the by 10 a.m., or he must pay for another day. Tony elected to walk to the K-Mart and sauntered out of the Holiday Inn and round to the shop, where he bought tooth paste, tooth brush a comb and a bottle of Grecian 2000 hair darkening dye. As he walked back into the hotel, the receptionist reminded him once more about the check-out time and said for him, please to make the time, as her job was on the line not having obtained from Tony something that could cover further charges. Tony sympathized with her and told her he would be out by the check-out time and might even be on a plane by that time.

Tony surfaced from the type of dreamless sleep that only exhaustion can bring, well before his alarm call. He rolled from the bed and did his morning exercises in the narrow space between the bed and the wall, he went to wash and clean himself up for the new day. Under the shower, he first washed his hair with soap to reduce the blond dye on his hair, afterwards using the Grecian 2000 shampoo dye to begin to darken his hair a shade back towards its' natural colour. He choose a new pair of denims and one of the Tee shirts he had bought in Windsor airport, seemingly months ago. With clean clothes and washed hair, he felt fit to face up to the world, his unshaven face was not unusual, sporting three days growth of beard had become fashionable and thus, unremarkable.

In the breakfast bar, the coffee was hot and plentiful and a wide variety of food was there, from waffles and syrup through fried eggs & ham to health foods and yoghurt. Never one to dally in front of food, Tony decided on the fried breakfast on the grounds that he had a long way to go and couldn't be sure of when he would next eat.

He had just sat down in front of a steaming mug of coffee, after his food order had been taken when the night receptionist greeted him with a cheery "Good morning, enjoy your breakfast". Like all Europeans, unused to these apparently concerned comments, Tony responded politely, only to cause the receptionist to stop dead in her tracks and look at him once more.

She, in her turn, responded politely and then asked "May I share your table?"

"Please do" was his answer and he found himself looking into the grey eyes of the receptionist, seated across the table from him.

Damn, he thought, HOW could I not have noticed THOSE eyes last night ? Those eyes, he felt, he could drown in quite easily and happily. Obviously, the receptionist read his feelings and began to colour slightly at his direct gaze.

"I'm sorry, I guess I haven't woken up fully yet. Staring like that is rude of me."

Sophie, as her name badge proclaimed her to be, just sat back with a half smile on her lips, then said "you know, most clients never remember the check-in girl. We're faceless & don't exist apart from handing out room keys. At least you remember me".

In truth, Tony didn't remember her, like most clients he had been interested ONLY in acquiring the room key, but he wasn't going to

admit that now! Over coffee and food, Sophie and Tony exchanged
interested small talk, at the end of which Tony had found out that
Sophie worked permanent nights on the hotel reception, served in
a bar for two hours each evening immediately before coming to the
hotel, existed on about 6 hours sleep per day and had acquired this
round of jobs by leaving a day job as a secretary when her boss (Fiancé
at the time) went off one weekend end and came back married to a
'Southern Belle'. Reciprocally, Sophie had learned that Tony was Tony
(not Mr. Johnson), that he would be in the 'states for some weeks on
business, his marriage was rocky and that he had only once traveled on
business with his wife ('an absolute disaster' he had said). As careful
as Sophies' questioning had been, she still did not know the nature of
Tonys' business, just that, most summers, he went abroad to work for
some weeks. What he HAD said was that he was going 'down south'
for more than a month and might be back 'up north' for a while before
going home. What he had inferred was that he would be somewhere
hot and mainly outside doing something for his company with an
American petroleum company.

Tony looked at his watch and said that he must go to get his flight,
Sophie became a little flustered and started to gabble about just getting
to know him, when he leaned over the table, put his hands gently on
her shoulders and held her into her chair.

"Just because I have to go, you don't have to leave, too" he said. "Sit
down and take it easy. Give me that piece of paper that you've written
your telephone number on and I'll call you when I get organized down
south so we can arrange a night out when I've finished."

Sophie flushed once more and handed over the piece of hotel note
paper saying "I didn't think you'd noticed".

Glancing at the telephone number Tony asked if all the codes were
there and that this was not just a local Detroit number. Sophie assured
him that that number would find her telephone from anywhere in the
'States and that he could ring it anytime.

"If I'm not there, the ansaphone will pick up and you leave a
number where I can call you back" she said.

Tony held both the paper and Sophies' hand, then asked if Detroit
was on Central time, on being assured that it was Tony said that he
would be on hour different and what were the best times to call her. All
the time he looked deeply into those fantastic grey eyes, resisting the

temptation to dive in then and there. He was told the times that Sophie would definitely be in, her bed-times in fact, and told to ring her then as she wouldn't mind being woken up to talk to him.

"One last thing" said Tony "when you next see me, my hair will be brown and I'll have a full beard. This hair" he said touching the blonded strands "was done for a party near here, that's why I'm here, and I'm letting my natural colour grow back. We don't shave on site, so we all grow beards. So the next time you see me, I'll be brown haired and bearded, don't be surprised!" Having been through this change a number of times, Tony knew that few ordinary people were able to recognize even a close friend when the beard was missing or recognize a bearded man as an established friend. He had seen how the wives of some of his colleagues had stared straight past their husband even when the husband, who had come back with a beard, spoke to her, so he had no concerns that Sophie would remember him very much even if they did meet again.

Tony threw his flightbag onto the other luggage in the trunk of the grey Plymouth and apparently headed straight to the airport. At the first intersection he turned left and drove towards Wayne State again. Not only had he to return the car to Cecil before he went to the Metro airport to fly back to Orlando, he wanted to dispose of all Carolines clothes to a nearby charity shop. Once more, he went from the gentle affluence around Wayne State rapidly down the social ladder in a few blocks to the mean streets where charity was rare, to find the local project 'pre-worn' clothes shop. He stopped outside, went into the trunk and opened both of Carolines suitcases. One was filled with expensive dresses, neatly folded and packed, the other contained shoes, underwear, blouses and Carolines 'valuables' bag. All the other clothing he hastily piled on top of the dresses and forced the suitcase together and closed the latches. Carolines' bag of valuables were left in the second case, which was filled when he crunched his nylon flight bag into the case. Tony carried the suitcases full of dresses into the charity shop and handed it over saying "my wife has walked out on me, so you had better have her clothes, I don't want them!"

He was sure that similar scenes were played out often enough for the incident to be no more than vaguely memorable, but no more.

A block deeper into the run down area was where 'Rent A Wreck inc.' was situated. He found the green wooden door and pulled the car up in front of it. Once more, he eased the door open and shouted for someone, again Cecils' deep voice came from the gloom. Although he knew Cecil to be tall and broad, his size was still a shock close to when Cecil hove into view.

"One car returned, used and not seen" said Tony.

Cecil took a quick peek outside the big door, then came back inside. "Well, my man, I didn't expect to see you for a few more days, but you'se back now wid ma car. Everything go O.K.?" asked Cecil.

"Just like you said, no sweat and no tickets. I've been a good boy with your car, my man" said Tony "I've just got to get my things outa it and she's all yours".

"Where you be going now?" asked Cecil.

"To the airport to get a flight" said Tony.

"Weell now, you ain't got no wheels, but you got bags ! How's you gettin' there?"

Tony thought, then said that he'd catch the bus. Cecil was not impressed, saying that not only do Americans not walk if they can help it, they positively will not carry any luggage at all if they can avoid it, "otherwise you just be noticed". "Tell you what, call it part of the service, I'll get my grease monkey to go with you, then he can bring the Plymouth back home".

Tony agreed with rapidity, so Cecil walked off into the garage to get Tonys deposit money and find the grease-monkey to come to the car. Tony opened the drivers door and felt underneath the seat into the inner apron to retrieve his real passport and having found it, slid it into the suitcase. Moments later Cecil appeared with a hand-full of dollar bills, which he gave to Tony, then called out for 'Joe' to "come here".

Joe appeared, a mid twenties white man, who fully earned the title of 'Grease Monkey' and who was told by Cecil to "bring the car back here, when my man here (Tony) gets off".

At that, the grease-monkey got into the front passenger seat, lit a cigarette and put the earphones of his Walkman into his ears.

Cecil looked at him, shrugged his shoulders and said "Todays kids!".

Tony smiled, shook hands (once more Cecils' huge hand encased his), said 'thanks', climbed in the car and drove away following the signs to the Metro airport, much as he had done before. At the airport, Tony deliberately stopped at the door for west bound, internal flights, unloaded his suitcase onto a trolley and said to the grease-monkey "She's all yours".

"U-uh" muttered the grease-monkey and then drove away at high speed out of the airport. That single grunted acknowledgment was the only sign that 'grease-monkey' had ever noted Tony's presence. He walked directly into the terminal, the turned sharp left and walked on into the area dedicated to internal southern flights where he bought the cheapest ticket on the earliest flight to Orlando International. As he had plenty of time to spare before his flight, Jim walked into one of the hair salons in the airport and asked for his hair to be washed, trimmed and died back to its' normal colour with a permanent mid-brown dye. Jim found it an easy and pleasant way to pass an hour or so, whilst waiting for his flight and at the end of it was looking much more like his normal self.

'Peoples Flights' departed to Orlando at 2 p.m. local time and arrived at 4 p.m. Eastern Standard Time. By 4.15 James Meadowcroft (once more) was looking for his rental car in the car park. Eventually, he found his maroon Plymouth Reliant, seemingly hiding behind a large, multi-coloured Pontiac van. He unlocked the car and left the front door open whilst the hot plasticky smell of stewed car dissipated whilst he put the suitcase into the trunk with the rest of his luggage. Even though it was late afternoon, the sun beat down relentlessly and the steering wheel was too hot to touch, after cooling off for a few minutes Jim was able to bear to sit on the seat and he drove away holding the steering wheel on the cooler bottom half. Immediately after leaving the airport vicinity, Jim found himself on the network of freeways and had to pay attention to ensure that he traversed all the intersections correctly and found Route 1 southbound. His accommodation was just off slipway 7 on Route 1, the road to St. Augustine road. He needed to stop off and buy food for the next few days, so he eased gently up off-ramp 7 and into the local mall, where he bought barbeque steaks and vegetables. He had selected Silvermans, a cheap single storey, down at heel long stay, breeze block motel, as his rental accommodation, found during the previous years' visit to Orlando for a conference.

His selection had not disappointed him, the motel had mainly long stay, poor white family and the parking lot was half full of their rusting hulks of cars, half of which would only ever make 1 more journey, and that to the scrap pile. At any time of day, the smell of boiled vegetables was present somewhere close and in many units, the television replaced a baby-sitter for many of the younger children, whilst the parents (more usually THE parent) worked. These people kept themselves to themselves and were used to an ebb and flow of neighbours, so Jim knew his absences would not be remarkable, the only weakness was that the doors and window shutters were so badly warped that access to each unit was simple. So Jim had decided to keep all his valuables in the Reliants' trunk and only to transfer what he needed, when he needed it.

One big advantage of Silvermans' long stay motel was that each unit was equipped with a kitchen, refrigerator, barbeque facilities plus a phone and colour T.V. Jim decided to have a steak for dinner, so he prepared the barbeque out side and lit the fire. When the fire was started & the charcoal glowing, Jim opened Carolines remaining suitcase and took from it her credit cards, cheque book, building society pass book and all means of identification, then he took Anthony Johnsons passport and solemnly incinerated them all. Although he was hungry, he waited until all the paper and plastic had burned away to ashes before he lowered the grill and began cooking his steak.

Whilst the steak sizzled on the grill, he went through the pockets of all of his shirts and trousers to pull out all pieces of paper including Sophies' telephone number, all of which he burned on the charcoal. As things burned, Jim said "Goodbye Caroline, Goodbye Tony, thanks for everything!"

By the time the steak was ready Jim had completed his passage back to his old identity.

As soon as he had dressed on the following morning Jim phoned up Dr. Levy and asked for how much longer must he rest his leg, as he was going mad just staying around the motel room watching T.V. all day. Solicitously, Dr. Levy asked if the knee was still painful, which would mean that the lining membrane was still inflamed and tender, to which Jim answered that it was less so than four days ago, when he had first consulted the doctor.

"Try a little light exercise, get out into the sun for a while, but sit down frequently to rest that knee. Tomorrow, the same again, but try a little more without causing yourself pain. Your knee seems to be getting along just fine, don't do too much and hurt it again. And I'll see you again on . . . .", here there was a shuffling of paper on the other end of the 'phone "on Thursday. Can I make an appointment for 10.30 for you?"

Jim confirmed that 10.30 would be fine by him and that he looked forward to it. He made another call immediately, this time to the Department of Life Sciences at the University of Florida.

When he got through, he found himself talking to Professor Kingsmans' secretary, "Oh, hello, this is Dr. Meadowcroft from Windsor University. I have just spoken to the medic, and he expects that I'll be fit enough to join you after Thursday, so if Prof. Kingsman can tell me where he'd like me to go to start then, I'll make sure that I'm on time this time !"

"Oh, hi, Dr. Meadowcroft, Prof. Kingsman won't be here today, I'll get him to call you tomorrow and if he can't reach you, I'll have the details, so you can ring me again tomorrow and find out" she said.

At that Jim said "O.K., 'til tomorrow".

When, at last Jim found out what he was meant to do, it was basically to become a paid beach bum, examining the flora and fauna of the intertidal region around Cape Kennedy. NASA were concerned that residual solid fuel from the space shuttle boosters was coming ashore and that it could be interfering with the natural balance of plant and animal life.

Before he could go and begin his paid beach-combing, he had to get a clean bill of health for his knee from Dr. Levy. Promptly at 10.30 a.m. Jim entered Dr. Levys' office and told the new secretary who he was and that he had the 10.30 appointment. Before entering the consulting room, Jim asked the secretary if she were Levys' permanent secretary, as he hadn't seen her the previous week. She answered that she was, just, having got the job at the start of this week, having been interviewed by Dr. Levy and his mother (the secretary that Jim had seen previously) and been deemed suitable. Jim was called in for examination and told the secretary that he'd talk to her when he left the consulting room. Dr. Levy greeted Jim like a friend of long standing, then asked him to roll up his left trousers' leg so the knee could be examined.

Gently palpating around the patella and to both sides Dr. Levy said that he was pleased with the recovery, he could find no tender areas and, more importantly, no inflamed regions.

"Just take it steady and keep taking the anti-inflammatories to keep the internal swelling down. What you did was most unusual, damaging the synovial membrane inside your knee, it takes time to completely heal, so take the pills and take care. If there is a next time, it will not be quite so easily taken care of. Keep in touch, especially if the knee starts up again. Pay my secretary and she'll issue you with a receipt. Have a good holiday".

Jim stood in front of the secretary, whilst she made out his receipt and he took time to study her cleavage when she leaned forward to check details from her desk file. He wondered just what a Jewish mother was doing letting her son employ a secretary with such obvious charms as she had. Whilst he looked down, wondering how much further forward he would have to lean before he eventually saw her navel, she suddenly looked up, looking him straight in the eye and seemed to sense all that he thought.

"Just admiring the scenery" mumbled Jim sheepishly, "I'm in Florida to examine the native flora and fauna in its' natural habitat".

"All Floridian and proud of it" said the secretary "I'm Rebecca and my family are friends of the Levys from the schule, otherwise I wouldn't have been let in through the front door! I know that I'm not the usual type of secretary that a Jewish momma chooses for her son".

"Ah, so you are Dr. Levys' girl-friend, too, are you Rebecca?"

"No way! And it's Becky. Our families are friends and I needed the job".

"Oh, call me Jim, everybody else does. Have you been a secretary long?".

"No, not too long, I'm paying my way through law school, ever since that creep of a husband left me".

Jim said that it was still strange to him that people had to pay their own way through university and that it wasn't like that in the U.K. Becky said that when she had married, her parents had ceased their financial responsibilities towards her, her husband having bought them with the wedding ring, but that he had stopped supporting her in favour of her younger replacement. "Imagine it, traded in like an old car, for a lower mileage model" was how Becky expressed it. They talked on for a while, Jim told her he would be spending his summer vacation with three American graduate students, beach-combing for NASA, and that could be worse, at least he would get a decent tan whilst being paid for the privilege.

"Can I come and tan with you on my days off ?" asked Becky, innocently. "With you a doctor, my mother won't worry. Otherwise it's tanning in our back yard for me and, boy!, THAT is boring !"

Jim took her telephone number and promised to phone her when he saw what the organisation was. He might well be studying hermit crabs, but what the point of being a hermit himself?

For the next five weeks, Jim spent his time on the glaring, yellow sand beaches on the north east coast of Florida, peering into rock pools and counting species. All three Grad. students were extremely keen on the work, for them it was an integral part of their doctoral programme and they worked unceasingly hard. They did not, however, expect him to work so long or hard on the menial tasks, very soon they let it be known that they valued him more as a reference point and sounding board for their own ideas. Jim was happy to oblige, even if it meant spending some evenings discussing data until late in the night. There was always time for a beach meal and a few beers during these discussions, before he crawled into his tent to sleep. As there were four of them, they operated a rotating weekends schedule, which allowed both of the female students to see their boy friends and the young man his girl friend on a regular basis.

Jims' free time could have weighed heavy on him, but he phoned Becky, who was overjoyed to come to the coast each weekend and 'top up' her tan and talk with interesting people younger than herself. At the end of a tiring days' tanning, Becky would swim in the sea and then change into her street clothes in Jims' tent, before both of them took one of the cars and had a meal together somewhere. Neither of them drank much at these meals, but spent much of the time just talking quietly together. Becky had decided that she needed two full days per week on the beach, but she didn't stay over, she drove home each night, only leaving her bikini in Jims' tent and arrived early when the 'gang' was sitting around a camp fire having breakfast and deciding the days work pattern She claimed that these home visits were to mollify her mother, but she always brought back with her food that was something special for the 'gang'.

During the last week of work, Jim began to analyze the collected data, this was, after all, why NASA were paying him and he took to working very late hours. Early, on the morning of his last working Friday, Jim stayed longer under his bed covers trying to sleep and make up for sleeping time lost the previous night, the tent flap bulged inwards as Becky, talking to one of the students, backed into the tent to change into the tanning bikini. Jim didn't say a word until Becky had stripped off her clothes and was naked.

In retrospect, to say "A better specimen of the brown and white banded Floridian female, I haven't yet seen !" was, perhaps, not the most delicate thing to have said.

It was also said more than a little late. Becky screeched and found a towel from somewhere, covered herself and drove Jim out of the tent. As he emerged from his tent, the students looked at him and, as one, grinned. When Becky emerged, she pointedly ignored Jim and disappeared beyond the first dune. All the students had heard Jims' comment and the squeak that Becky made and when she walked away from all of them, all four researches looked at each other and shrugged their shoulders.

"Qui cera, cera" came from one of the girls, that said they all set to work on their own tasks.

So immersed was Jim in his work that the whole day passed without thought of Becky. Only when the sun was descending rapidly into the sea did Jim look up to see Becky walking back towards him, a stern look on her face.

As she passed him, she just said "Stay" and pushed into his tent to change. She came out of the tent a short while later fully clothed and walked off towards the main road and away from the group without a word to any of them. Once more they looked at each other again, shrugged their shoulders, but this time it was Jim that said "The end of a beautiful friendship".

None of the four had moved to follow Becky or to talk with her, for, although she had become part of the group, she was not a member of it.

Jim stayed talking to the students until late in the night, this part of the programme he had never regarded as work as he enjoyed it too much himself. After a last beer, he decided to forget work until the morning and took a walk up and down the length of beach that had become so familiar to him over the last weeks. As he walked he started to review the options before him. If Caroline had been missed and if her body had been found he would be the prime suspect, despite this

American vacation, on the grounds that the partner is always suspected and statistically always more likely to have done the deed or been involved in it. If she hadn't been missed, or missed and not found, then he would have to play a role of deserted husband and he didn't know how well, how long or how convincingly he could carry the part. How long he walked or how far he walked, he never knew, but it was with tears of regret in his eyes that he pushed through the tent flaps and passed into his tent.

He was still abed when Becky walked into the tent the next morning. She was earlier than normal, that Jim could see by the light of the new dawn outside. Being somewhat shorter than Jim, she could stand upright under the ridge of the tent, which she proceeded to do and she continued to stare down at Jim.

"Just what I want on the last day on site" thought Jim "a crazy scene with this woman in my tent and no witnesses", so he continued to look at her and she at him. It was Becky that broke the chill silence.

"Don't you have anything to say ?" she demanded "not even 'good morning'?".

"Good morning, you're early this morning and I'm in no mood for a fight, I've had too many with my wife back home to want another one here." said Jim dispiritedly. "Give me five minutes and I'll be out of here, then you can change".

"Who says that I'm changing? I've done enough tanning for a while".

At this, Jims' heart fell and inside his head he heard the word 'TROUBLE' rebound around in his head, a great summers' work about to be ruined and for what?.

"Do what you're going to do and then get out ! We've all got work to do" was what he heard himself say.

At that, Becky began to disrobe and Jim could see that see had nothing on under her summer dress. Two thoughts flashed through Jims head, the first was 'Oh no, she's setting up a 'Rape' scenario', the second seemed completely random about seeing her navel, at which Jim grinned. "Don't leer like that, it is NOT one of your most attractive features, although it is nice" and with those words she climbed into bed with Jim and pulled his hands down onto her white, untanned buttocks.

"You see, the brown and white banded Floridian female really missed the hairy, brown Brit last night. I hadn't realized just how deep you'd wormed yourself into my life".

Had he but thought, Jim would have realized that he had just spent a large part of his resources extracting himself from a similar situation at home, but he didn't. He took advantage of the free offer.

Chapter 27

Return to a lonely house.

Becky was happy to stay with Jim for the whole day and night in his unit at Silvermans motel, but the next day being Sunday, she had to leave for work at Dr. Levy's surgery. As she dressed, she told Jim that Benjamin Levy ran a very orthodox practice, respected the Sabbeth and closed for the traditional weekend of Friday and Saturday.

"You were lucky that you hurt your knee on a Thursday, a day later and Ben Levy's practice would have been closed, then we wouldn't have met. In fact you're doubly lucky, Ben normally only takes Jewish patents, you look Ashkinasim, but I know your not ! I've seen bits of you that PROVE you're not !".

"Look, Becky, come back here tonight."

"What? Back to this roach hole again? There is only so much that a girl can stand! Have you NO style Dr. Meadowcroft?"

"I was going to say 'Come back here tonight, I'll delay my flight home for a day, so we can check into one of the hotels in Orlando for tonight and then I can pat you on your butt as you go to work before I go home to sort my troubles out".

Becky agreed, but she was saddened at the thought of tomorrow. Once she had driven away, Jim picked up the phone and phoned home. He spoke to the ansaphone, leaving a message to Caroline to tell her he had had to delay for 1 day, but would be back, he hoped that she would get this message before he arrived home. Next, he phoned the cottage in Chilham and spoke to the ansaphone there, which cut him off before he had finished. Before he left Silvermans' Motel, he phoned the airline and requested a 1 day delay and a re-booking of his ticket. By using his formal title and saying that his work required him to stay an extra day, he manipulated the situation, got his 24 hour delay and was re-booked & his flight confirmed and even got the $ 5 change fee waived.

Once he told the motel management that he was leaving that evening, they charged him for Monday ("check out time is mid-day, if you stay longer, then it's charged as another 1 day. We've got to think of the cleaning staff, can't pull them in here every which hour of the day". 'WHAT cleaning staff' thought Jim). He didn't bother arguing about the extra charge, for an extra $ 10 it wasn't worth the trouble and paid the bill by credit card. He drove out around the area, feeling strangely free and detached from the people around him, he knew the feeling, he had felt this way before. With the imminent return to real life after an intensive work programme, this "return to the world" feeling came unasked. In central Orlando, he found a 'Hair Salon' open & went in, when he sat in front of the mirror he was startled as to how his hair and beard looked. His hair completely hid his ears and looked shaggy and unkempt, which it was, but was lighter than he remembered it. Not as blond as it had been, but shades lighter then he was used to. His beard was looking full and his mustache long enough to require trimming, so he discussed his hair colour with the stylist who recommended a light, but permanent, dye to overcome the sun bleaching, then almost reduced the stylist to tears when he insisted on his usual 'short back and sides & show the ears'. After a full service, he paid the bill and returned to Silvermans Motel, this time being more neat and tidy, looking so clean as to be out of place there. He worked in his unit for a while on the analysis of the research programme, before changing to his clean, neat 'return flight' clothes in preparation for Beckys' appearance.

Becky had taken the initiative whilst at work and booked a room in one of the hotels surrounding Disney World. She explained that she had never been there, but always wanted to go, never having been allowed by father or husband to waste money on such frivolity.

"We can drive round after we check in, so we'll see SOMETHING" Becky said.

Jim wasn't worried about Beckys' little girl syndrome, he thought it rather charming that she felt sufficiently free with him to indulge her desires like this. Without being asked, Becky had left her car on

Dr. Levys' property, so they could drive together to the hotel. Jim went back to the grandly titled 'Management Suite' of Silvermans Motel to pay the phone bill and return the keys and then drove the Reliant back towards the airport for a short way before following the signs to the Disney World hotels. All the hotels were the tall, impersonal buildings that comprise much of Americas' hotel 'Industry', places running on the production line principle, but with a customer sensitive interface.

In the morning, Jim took Becky down to the foyer to get a taxi to take her to work. Becky was tearful, but not clinging.

"Just write to me, or may be phone me sometime, PLEASE?" she pleaded.

"Once I'm back home, Dr. Levys' office is going to get sick of me calling & that's a promise!". With that Becky climbed in the taxi and was gone. Jim found his eyes prickling, 'must be the exhaust fumes' he thought and walked up to reception to settle the bill, once more by credit card, before he himself left.

Jim did not drive directly to the airport, he drove into the nearest shopping mall and walked into the first bank he found. His request for a safety deposit box caused no problems, he didn't even have show any identity papers, all he had to do was to register the box holders name and pay the first 5 years deposit charges. As he filled in the form, the bank teller said "You can use any name, but please NOT Mickey Mouse, or variants of it, we have too many of them!" Jim registered the account holder as Anthony Johnson (an ironic twist, he thought) and into the box he put all Carolines' jewellery and traceable valuables. He paid the box rental charge in cash, got the receipt and then drove to the airport.

Jim had no trouble with the flight back to Heathrow, the plane was not even half full, so there was plenty of room to stretch out and relax. At Heathrow, he passed through the U.K. citizens passport control quickly and easily, collected his luggage and then called the private long-term car parking company. As their advertisements promised, Jims' own car drove up within 20 minutes and the delivery driver climbed out without turning off the engine. Leaning on the front bonnet by the drivers door Jim examined the bill he had been given, he could see that the car had been valeted inside and out, but had to trust that the service had been equally well performed. Writing out a cheque and showing the cheque guarantee card freed his Ambassador back into his ownership, opening tail gate he put his suitcases in the back and then drove home.

It was faster for him to drive westwards on the M 4 to the Slough turn off, drive through Slough, Stoke Poges and the Farnhams to intersect the M 40 at Beaconsfield, then to drive westwards for 2 junctions before entering High Wycombe via Marlow Hill. Part way down Marlow Hill, Jim turned left into the quaintly named 'Poets Corner' estate, in which his house stood.

He pulled onto the concrete drive and then climbed the three steps and opened the porch door, waded through mounds of post on the floor, then opened the front door proper and entered the house. It was obvious that no-one had been in after he had left to go to the 'States, the house had that stale, sealed up smell and most of the plants were dead from lack of water. Fetching in arms full of post, Jim sat on the sofa and began to divide up the mail into 'hers' and 'mine', the next job was to check the messages on the ansaphone. Twelve messages were indicated, so Jim sat with paper and pen to hear the messages and write down the telephone numbers. Shirley, Carolines sister in Ipswich, had left a number of messages for Caroline, succeeding messages getting increasingly more worried. Jim even came across his own message of Sunday from Florida.

At the end of the telephone messages, Jim phoned Shirley and said "I've just got back and your messages sounded more & more urgent. What's the matter?"

"Thank God you're back, we haven't been able to get in touch with Caroline for weeks and weeks. Is she with you?"

"No, it looks as if she hasn't been here for weeks, either. There's a mound of post for her here, that I've just sorted. I thought that she'd gone to Aunty Ginny's cottage, as usual".

"Yes, she did, but she left there 4 or 5 weeks ago without telling anybody where she was off to. Dick & I went over there a few weeks ago and there was no sign of her, the cottage was totally deserted. Dick went to the pub and heard that she'd had a late night visitor in the first week and the next day one of her yuppy friends went to the pub to see if anyone had seen Caroline. Apparently, he was her, er, one of her friends from work"

"And he just HAPPENED to be passing, miles away from anywhere and decided to call and ask Caroline for a cup of coffee, I suppose ?" said Jim.

"Well, no, he said he had business with her" answered Shirley.

Jim was amazed how angry he felt at Carolines' behaviour and Shirleys' obvious unquestioning acceptance of it.

"Anyway, to cut a long story short, after we'd been to the cottage, we reported her to the local police as a missing person. I know Caroline and you were not on the best of terms when you went to the 'States and we are worried for her EVEN if you aren't!".

"O.K., I'll call the local cops and do the same thing here. Let's see if we can get something out of them".

That seemingly mollified Shirley and she hung up without even a 'good-bye'.

Chapter 28

Cometh the time, cometh the man

Jim called the local police station and they promised to send someone round 'straight away' to take a statement. Five minutes later, a white Panda car drew up outside the house and a middle aged policeman walked towards the door. Jim beat him to it, opening the door before the bell rang.

"Dr. Meadowcroft ?" the policeman asked.

"Come in, please" said Jim and lead the way into the lounge.

When both were seated, Jim told him the brief outlines as given to him by Shirley whilst the policeman listened quietly. He only stirred when Jim said that Shirley had reported Caroline missing some weeks ago. At this the policemen asked to use the phone and promptly phoned the local station to check the national missing persons list to see when Dick and Shirley had filed the report.

He walked back into the lounge, sat down and said "seems as if you wife has done a runner. "Have you had a letter, or a note from her?"

"I don't know, there" said Jim, pointing to the sorted mail pile "that is all the mail since I went away, I haven't had time to open it and read it yet".

"I think that it is best that you do that now" said the policeman "I think that she has walked out on you and she might have left a note for you".

Jim started to open all the mail addressed to him, briefly scanning each one before dropping it on the left hand side of his chair. Part way through this orgy of letter opening and scanning, the policemans' radio beeped and he answered it and listened to the information before answering tersely "Understood. Out".

He turned to Jim and said "Your sister in law reported your wife missing about 4 weeks ago. She made a full statement at the time and the local witnesses have been interviewed. Seems as though your wife was a popular lady, she had a number of male visitors and appears to have left with one of them one Friday night. Have you found anything from her, yet?".

"No, nothing at all, Just the usual letters from family and friends and bills, nothing from the wife, though" said Jim.

"Well, I have to ask you for a statement and if you have a recent photograph of your wife that I can get copied".

Jim went to an photograph album and removed a colour print, "Here you are. Where do you want me to start the statement?"

In his statement, Jim outlined the reasons for the many fights he and Caroline had and that she always went to Aunty Ginnys cottage, for as long as it took either him or her to swallow their pride and talk to the other. He had tried phoning from America, but it was the ansaphone that answered and he couldn't leave a full message. Most of his time he was spent working on the beaches around Cape Canaveral with three students, but he had had one week laid up with an injured knee. Then, he had returned today and listened to the phone messages and called the Police, that was the gist of Jims' statement

"Seems to me as if desertion is the likely reason" said the policeman. "You've had a number of fights over the years and it just seems as if your wife called it a day and discretely left!"

At that the policeman left, asking Jim to get in touch, if he should hear anything, otherwise the case would remain on 'the books' and he might be visited again.

Tuesday, the next day, Jim went into the University to work and bring the NASA report to fruition, so that he could claim the money due for his work. There was also a chance that parts of the work may be able to be re-written and published as research papers in one of the academic journals. Many of his colleagues had spent their summer writing up their research of the past year, vying for publications to demonstrate their scholarship. What a system, Jim thought, where the weight of paper written actually outweighed the scholarship value of the papers produced! This was, however, the 'measure of success' foistered upon the University community by the accountancy minded Conservative Government of the time. Everyone had been pulled into the same mad merry-go round, where success was measured by an arbitrary numerical scheme. He found a pile of telephone messages from Shirley and various police forces awaiting him. Because of police involvement, these messages had made Jim something of a source of curiosity and he soon knew that everybody in the department and beyond knew something of his predicament. Of course, the jury of the chattering classes had come out against him, in their eyes what he had done, by leaving Caroline alone so often when he went abroad, was unforgivable and he found himself branded as an unreconstructed chauvinist. Caroline, though no one knew her, was, by common consent, as pure and innocent as the driven snow; it was obvious that he was to blame for the whole thing.

Of course no-one knew what the WHOLE truth was, but that did not stop the secretarial parliament labeling him as being treated responsible for his wifes' desertion. There were a number of women, generally secretaries, who changed their attitude to Jim and became totally obstructive, so convinced were they of his chauvinism. Few people were even secretly on his side, some seemed helpful, but only to get more dirt with which to smear him still further. Jim was effectively isolated, it was more than simply being alone, it was total isolation, as effective as if he had plague. When he was visited at the University by the police, the whispering campaigns re-started in full. Any-one to whom he had spoken, or with whom he had worked was pilloried and deemed guilty by association.

Jim was able to immerse himself in his work and, once the students returned from their summer vacation, other issues became more important, the embargo against Jim easing somewhat.

Within the confines of the Thames Valley Police force, however, the disappearance of Mrs. Caroline Meadowcroft nee Ellis, was not forgotten. Fresh out of Detective Training, Detective Constable Rigby was assigned to the case. His superiors gave him this case, because, in the short term, it seemed a simple case of desertion, which may shortly come to completion with the re-appearance of Caroline.

Arriving at the house in 'Poets Corner', Rigby walked straight up to the door and rapped on it in a very professional and policeman-like way. Jim came to the door and invited Rigby in once he had seen Rigbys' warrant card.

"I'm here to follow up on the missing persons report" he said.

After talking to Jim for a while, covering the same ground as had been covered by the sergeant previously, Rigby asked if Jim had a photograph that he might borrow so that they could copy it, to help other people identify Caroline. Jim stood up and went to a drawer and took out a pile of photographs and began sorting through them, occasionally tossing one onto the table top.

"These are all of my wife, select whichever one you think best, none is more than two years old." he said.

Rigby stood up and began to spread the photos out on the table top, but caught his breath as he did so. "Sylvia", he thought to himself as he looked at the oval face regarding him steadily from the photographs, for what he saw was a woman so like his dead elder sister that, at first, he couldn't believe it wasn't her. Sylvia and he had been very close, in many ways Sylvia had been more like a mother to him than a big sister. She had always been on his side and always protective, giving to him freely the love and care that their mother did not. Her death, at the hands of a would-be rapist, had nearly unhinged him and had certainly been the cause of his joining the police force. Now, here he was holding photographs of a woman that could be her twin sister, his big sister, but she was missing.

"Would you mind if I borrow one or two of these photo's, please, so that we can copy them ?" asked D.C. Rigby.

"No, not at all, take as many as you need, I am interested in finding my wife back, though she may not be interested in coming back" said Jim.

Rigby shuffled the prints around selected six and wrote out a receipt for five, the sixth, he would keep to remember Sylvia. With that, Rigby left Jim alone and walked back, down the hill, to the Police Station, all the time vowing to himself to find Caroline and make Dr. Meadowcroft pay for whatever he had done to drive her away.

It had been drilled into all the trainees, during basic criminology lectures, that the report of a 'Missing Person' was the most frequent prelude to a murder investigation. Finding the corpse became the occasion to review the missing person file for clues. Rigby also remembered that, statistically, most murderers were either the partner, or a family member, of the victim. Thus, Rigby was certain that Caroline would be found and that, if it were the body that was found, Jim would be her murderer. That idea fixated itself in his mind and became his driving force of his investigation.

Thames Valley Detective School had not actually forged the connection quite so immutably. They had taught the accepted '4W' approach to murder (Who, Why, Where and When), Rigby had missed the last three lectures on Why, Where and When due to a bad hangover. He thus believed the close family member killer to be the only acceptable truth. He took over all the interviewing duties of this case, even convincing his superiors of Dr. Meadowcroft's unquestionable guilt. Rigby had his beliefs re-inforced when, on reviewing the file of Dr. James Meadowcroft, he found that Jim was known to the police and had actually assisted their investigations as a forensic biologist. Rigbys' distrust of science and scientists verged on the paranoid, he treated everything approach to investigative science as exercises in the paranormal, its' practitioners as magicians, never to be trusted by a 'down to earth' cop like himself. His suspicions thus strengthened, Rigby decided to examine every aspect of Jims' alibi in minute detail and find the loose end.

To start the investigation, Rigby began by visiting the University & asking people whom he judged should know something about Dr. Meadowcroft what they actually thought of Jim. Unfortunately, his research began before the students' returned from summer vacation, when the comments about Jim Meadowcroft were at their most acid. These comments served to enhance Rigbys' impressions of Jim as a man capable of anything and with cunning to match. What he didn't realize was that his own interest in Jim Meadowcroft served only to fuel the fires of the chattering class.

By the end of the first month, Rigby had assembled what he claimed to be a full dossier on Jim Meadowcroft, showing Jim, in his opinion, to be psychologically capable of any crime. He interviewed Jim relentlessly, catching him between classes, at coffee time and at home after work. Quite illegally, Rigby taped every interview, even when he was checking a small point for the fifth time. His reason, as he thought himself, was that he would soon reveal an error in Jims' alibi. Rigby was neither mature enough, nor sufficiently worldly wise to know that people forget things, or the order that things happened in, especially when in stressful work situations. Inevitably, Jim statements contained slight differences, some he corrected, some he wasn't aware of. Each minor variation from the initial statement was seen as a potential weakness for Rigby to try to exploit.

During the course of Rigbys' investigations, Jim was asked to undertake more forensic work for the police force, to which he readily agreed as he enjoyed the challenge and experience it provided. Rigby, on hearing of this, engineered a series of 'accidental' meetings which he used to quiz Jim about the work he was doing. In these investigations, Jim took extreme care with the obtaining & examination of samples and in the reporting of results. To Rigby, these precautions indicated the excessive compulsive behaviour (he didn't know what it meant, so it sounded suspicious) of someone trying to cover their tracks. Believing this to be the case, Rigby intended to catch his man by being even more careful of details and waiting for the error to be revealed like a stream bed during a drought. First, he removed Jims' passport and had it scrutinized first by the Passport office and then, via a friend in Special Branch, by the documents section of M.I.5. Both groups were looking for forged entry or exit passes or deletions and erasures. None were found, Jims' passport was what it was, a normal, part used 10 year U.K. passport, no more, no less.

It was M.I. 5, who raised the possibility of a second passport. This was their usual suspicion and would mean that the target had been helped by other people. Should that be the case then it would also mean that the crime totally premeditated, an important point should the case become one of murder. A one year British visitors passport was the easiest to get, they said, and defined the documents necessary to have to be able to demonstrate a second identity.

"Are you SURE that he went to the U.S. when he said he did? America does not allow immigration with a B.V.P. (British Visitors Passport), but it allows EMIGRATION with one. It's only Jamaica, in that region, that accepts the B.V.P. for immigration purposes. Jamaica is an hours' flight from Miami, so he could have come to the U.K. via Jamaica and returned the same way" said the faceless official from section 7 (documents) of M.I. 5.

At this, Rigby gave a start and said "That's it. This bastard thinks he's so clever, but I've got him now".

In a meeting with his controlling D.C.I. the next morning Rigby said that he, himself, was convinced that Jim Meadowcroft had traveled back to Britain on a false passport, killed his wife and disposed of the body then flown back to America via Jamaica to convince people that he had not left America. He needed more facilities and more officers and such was the enthusiasm and certainty portrayed by Rigby that his superior supported his case. To prove the connection there were three things that needed to be identified. These were the names of all U.K. male nationals who traveled from the U.K. to Jamaica over the weeks of Jims' visit, the passport details of each person and then a comprehensive cross referencing of the passport bearers name and death certificate of people with the same names and of approximately the same age, but who had died too young to have had their own passport. This was because the M.I. 5 officer had said that this was the known way of taking a second identity without risk of being revealed, as the real person (being dead) would never apply for a passport! Obviously, the place to start was to get all the airline passenger lists for that period and cross reference them with the nationality of the traveler. Once the U.K. citizens were identified, then finding out on which passport they traveled would be straightforward. This would rapidly yield a list of people traveling on BVP's, then that list could be checked against death certificates in Somerset House to identify holders of fraudulent passports, a review of the applicants photograph and there the net would begin to close tightly around Jim Meadowcroft.

Within a week, all the cross-referencing and sorting was finished and five names had been found to be obviously fraudulent. When the retained photographs of the applicants were examined four were immediately rejected, Jim Meadowcroft was not an Afro-Caribbean. One last subject remained, a white man that, in a bad light, COULD be Jim Meadowcroft and the address given was in north London. Rigby organized a raid on the north London address after taking the precaution of bringing Jim 'in' to the police station for an identity parade.

Briefing the officers before they raided in north London, Rigby told them that he expected them not to find anyone, as he had detained the suspect, but they might find accomplices who should be arrested. Giving out copies of the passport photo, Rigby told the raiding officers that that was the man he was interested in and to question accomplices on the spot and to show the photograph.

In the event, the raid was mounted, two officers were shot before, with the aid of fire-arms officers, the people at the address were arrested and later found to be drug smugglers, with a large cache of marijuana. Rigbys' stock in the Thames Valley Force rose, as a consequence of the result of the raid & his controlling D.C.I. was happy to live in the reflected glory of 'his lad'. Although Rigby displayed only frustration at the result, his controller, was well pleased with the result saying that Special Branch had had a fillip with the drugs discovery. Special Branch explained the raid as a Special Branch/T.V.P.F. co-operative project, which meant that Special Branch 'owed' the Thames Valley force a favour.

Rigby was allowed to continue his interest in the Meadowcroft disappearance case, but cautioned to take a different approach and to begin 'at the other end', in Florida. This suited Rigby, for it added to his lustre within the local police force, especially when Rigby started talking to Winter Park, Orlando County police officers in Miami. They checked the principal facts in the case and reported them all correct and verified Jims' statement. Rigby was surprised at the thoroughness of the American police, in a short time they had thoroughly checked Jims' statement with the proprietors & 'guests' of the Silverman Motel, Dr. Levy, all three students, Professor Kingsman, Becky, the airline, the Florida car hire company and the Disney world hotel. Their summary was that Dr. James Meadowcroft was where he said he was, when he said he was. This frustrated Rigby, whose thoughts were that they didn't know James Meadowcroft like he knew him. Rigby intensified his work, producing a table top sized time programme for Jims' actions during the vacation to try to spot the flaw in his alibi.

It was immediately apparent that the time that was 'available' for anything to have happened was during the week that Jim claimed to have been incapacitated with a knee injury. This being the only time period when he not been seen on at least a daily basis and this part of the alibi rested on three contacts with Dr. Levy, the first, the meeting on Thursday, the telephone call on Tuesday and the third on Thursday a week after the first. All three contacts had been confirmed by both Dr. Levy & Becky to the Winter Park police. Rigby highlighted the telephone conversation on the time plan in bright yellow marker.

"That's the one that is the weakness, of course, I should have seen it before! He could have made that call from anywhere, even Britain, just to create a better alibi" said Rigby to himself. "So he was probably in Britain or Jamaica then, so that is where we start and check out the flight plans".

It was during the course of these investigations, he found that it was possible to leave & re-enter the U.S. to & from Jamaica simply by showing a flight ticket to Montego Bay and a valid U.S. drivers licence. 'So, here was the route Meadowcroft used' Rigby immediatelt thought. International flights to and from the U.K. left from Kingston, but Mo' Bay to Kingston is an easy hour and a half drive over the Blue Mountains. Once more, Winter Park were asked to check out if a U.S. drivers' licence had ever been issued to James Meadowcroft and if a flight had been booked in that name to Montego Bay during the whole of the month of August. Winter Park responded that there had been, literally, hundreds of licences issued to James Meadowcrofts in the U.S.A., but no flights booked in that name. Rigby was impressed and believed that entry to and exit from Jamaica would be easy using a different name because the authorities there were not as rigorous as in the U.K.

Checking the story with his M.I. 5 contact, he was given a new possibility, that of travel to & from Jamaica by boat.

"In that case," Rigby was told, "the fastest would be with the drug runners".

Now, Rigby believed he had him. Rigby had found two routes into and out of Jamaica that left no official paper trail. All the other required pieces that could be put into place in the U.K. before going to Florida and could be activated at will, once in the U.K. Rigby felt confident enough to go and bring Jim to the station for a formal interview concerning the disappearance and probable murder of Caroline Meadowcroft. It was in Rigbys' mind to question Jim thoroughly, break him by confronting him with the truth and then arrest him.

For the first two hours of questioning, Rigby did not allow Jim Meadowcroft to call a lawyer, so confident was he that he would procure a confession in double quick time. Eventually, when he was allowed to call a lawyer, the working day had finished and his lawyer (who had done no more than house conveyancing for Jim) was no longer in the office, so Jim was allocated a young locum lawyer. Like most locums, this one was working on legal aid & was putting the hours in this way towards a practice certificate, so she did little other than go through the basic motions.

What was achieved was a half-hour break in the interrogation, whilst the lawyer and Jim talked over the charges and then questioning recommenced, but this time with the lawyer present and deflecting many questions by telling Jim 'don't answer this'. At one point the young lawyer actually confronted Rigby and asked him the grounds on which Jim was being investigated. Not being happy with the answer she received, she said that Rigby seemed to be operating from a basis of sheer malice, with no evidence. Frustrated by these blocking tactics, Rigby shouted at her that this was exactly what he was trying get. He shouldn't have shouted, the lawyers back went straight up and she openly accused Rigby of attempting to badger a witness into a false confession and attempted intimidation of herself. At this point, she asked to see Rigby's hand written notes to ascertain what had been said and to verify the start time of the interview. Her offensive gained strength when she saw that the reported timed start of the interview was some 2 hours later than Jim estimated. Jims' time estimate could be backed up by witnesses from the University who had seen Jim leave with Rigby, a canceled lecture being further mute testimony to the time Jim had left the building.

Much to Rigby's disgust, Jim was allowed to leave with the young lady lawyer, who advised him to contact his own lawyer in the morning and said that his lawyer could contact her to be up-dated on the back-ground. She asked Jim why Rigby had been as aggressive as he had, Jim could only say that he didn't know, but that Rigby had been virtually shadowing him for weeks. When, the next day, Jims' solicitor received all the information from the young lawyer, he began to seethe. When he checked Jims' story and then compared what the police believed they had, the lawyer asked to speak to the Chief Constable, pending the drafting of a formal letter of complaint. A copy of the complaint letter was to be immediately be faxed to the Ombudsman to bring before Parliament. At this point, the chief constable demurred and asked for some time to review the case, 'as he was not personally aware of the latest developments'. Within the day, the Chief Constable had reviewed the statements concerned with the case and then asked Rigby to explain his beliefs in light of the evidence. Rigby got as far as the first "I have my suspicions', when the Chief Constable stopped him and reminded him that he dealt with only with the facts and that there existed no evidence to support Rigby's case. Although this was a censure of Rigby, the Chief Constable believed it to be only an informal censure and advised Rigby to drop the case for the time being, but to keep the file open for any further developments.

In his eagerness, Rigby did exactly this and was to regard this case as his and stand guard over the files for many years. Everything that he could find out about James Meadowcroft found its' way into the file, generally with a negative translation concerning the happenings attached by Rigby.

Once he had been assured that his victimization at Rigbys' hands had finished, Jim began to try to re-build his life towards what it had been before the last visit to America. Carolines parents, who had never approved of their daughters' choice of husband, never communicated directly with Jim again. Two years after the apparent completion of the police investigations, Jim, at the suggestion of his lawyer, began divorce proceedings, citing the grounds as dissertation. As Caroline wasn't present, he had to apply for a court order, so that, in effect, the state represented Caroline in the divorce proceedings and settlement. Eventually, even legal tussles were settled and the divorce proceeded. Carolines' side was not contested, so the divorce proceeded almost automatically from the decree nisi to decree absolute once the division of the properties had been agreed upon. As two homes were involved, Jim suggested that he keep the house in Wycombe and that Caroline keep the cottage, as she always preferred it to the Wycombe house, which he keep and continue paying the mortgage, as he always had. A further part of the divorce proceedings were the division of the family property. He made no claim on Carolines' personal estate and left her bank & building society accounts untouched, although throughout their marriage they had lived exclusively on his earnings and she had saved hers in a personal building society account.

Suddenly, Jim found himself free and living as a divorced man. Behind his back, the chattering classes seemed to be, at last, mollified and Jim experienced true relief from their attentions.

Rigby, of course, noted all this, with the margin note that this attitude just proved Jims guilty conscience. Jim did not rush into marriage, either. He continued his summer working trips, NASA were so impressed that they happily extended the working arrangements for a further three years, until the whole project was completed. These three summers in Florida were actually quite therapeutic for Jim, as he was able to resume his beach bum activities with his established tanning partner, although the group of Graduate students changed each year. Just trying to maintain the large house in Wycombe, which was too large for one person took too much of Jims' attentions, so three years after the divorce, he sold it and moved into a smaller bungalow in the same area. He changed his car regularly, too, the unreliable, beige Austin Ambassador gave way to a steel-grey B.M.W. 520i and now, Jim seemed to be contented.

Rigby, of course, kept track of these changes, all of which were duly recorded and annotated with very negative comments. Eventually, Jim re-married, unsurprisingly his wife reflected all the time he had spent in Florida. Jim surprised himself by asking Becky to move to Britain with him and was astounded to find himself saying that marriage was, OF COURSE, the reason that he was asking her. Becky slid easily into the life of an academics' wife and showed only signs of complete contentment. Jim still kept his summer working visits alive, but, unlike previously, was always keen to get home.

Rigby duly noted all these domestic changes in his fattening file. When Becky became Mrs. Meadowcroft, his margin note was a blunt 'accomplice?'